By Bradley Lloyd

Shadow Fray

Published by DSP Publications
www.dsppublications.com

SHADOW FRAY

BRADLEY LLOYD

DSP PUBLICATIONS

Published by

DSP Publications

5032 Capital Circle SW, Suite 2, PMB# 279, Tallahassee, FL 32305-7886 USA
www.dsppublications.com

This is a work of fiction. Names, characters, places, and incidents either are the product of author imagination or are used fictitiously, and any resemblance to actual persons, living or dead, business establishments, events, or locales is entirely coincidental.

Shadow Fray
© 2017 Bradley Lloyd.

Cover Art
© 2017 Anna Sikorska.
Cover content is for illustrative purposes only and any person depicted on the cover is a model.

ISBN: 978-1-63533-359-6
Digital ISBN: 978-1-63533-360-2
Library of Congress Control Number: 2017900387
Published May 2017
v. 1.0

Printed in the United States of America
∞
This paper meets the requirements of
ANSI/NISO Z39.48-1992 (Permanence of Paper).

For Frank, Kristen, and Traci.

Acknowledgments

I WOULD like to thank and acknowledge all my early readers and supporters, including Catherine, Margaret, Rebecca, Dorothy, Katie, and many others. Mom and Dad, thank you for your support, and it's okay if you skim the sexy parts. It's also okay if you don't.

SHADOW FRAY

Chapter 1

First Fray. Arena: Mutual Conglomerate Building.

THE CONTESTANT peered at the faded "4" over the rusty door. He pulled out the small slip of paper from his leather armguard and read it again. *Mutual Conglomerate Building. Entrance 4. Visiting Team. 11:48 p.m. 9/08.* Justin hoped it was 11:46. He'd rehearsed the route, but if he was nervous and off by a minute or two, he could be penalized. He hadn't brought a watch or a phone. That had been his handler's job, and his handler was dead.

But he wouldn't think about that. Instead, Justin turned the paper over and read the note he'd copied there. They were his kid brother's words, and Justin mouthed them softly, like a mantra. *Justin does his best even when it's hard, even when he's tired and maybe hurting a little bit. He always shows courage. That's why he's the person I look up to the most.*

Tonight was for Charlie. Charlie was his reason to fight—his reason to win.

Justin tore up the note. The lake breeze slipped past him, carrying the bits of paper away—a prayer on the wind. It was cold for September. A thin layer of petroleum jelly covered his face, but his bare skin prickled along his arms. He turned to glance over his shoulder. Darkness and fog. He listened. Out over Lake Michigan, a distant foghorn sounded. Then silence. No drones buzzing, and no one was around.

He grabbed the leather mask he had hidden beneath his T-shirt and quickly tied it over his eyes, tightening the lacing. He removed the shirt and cast it to the side of the doorway, glancing one more time at the dim 4 overhead. He stepped forward, giving the metal door a shove inward.

It opened. He shouldn't be surprised. This was a Shadow Fray, and the doors to a Shadow Arena always opened, right on time. Justin stepped inside. No—not Justin. Someone anonymous. Someone who would win tonight. Someone who would finally earn a name.

The concrete corridor he entered was massive, supporting more than thirty floors and a cell phone tower. His mother once told him the building held the world record for the largest consecutive concrete pour. Cement trucks lined the streets for two days, stretching blocks back to their home. She hadn't been alive to see it; in fact, it was before the Thinning. How had she described the scene from the distant past so vividly? If it was even true.

No matter. She was gone, and he was here for his sister and brother. *My brother does his best even when it's hard, even when he's tired and maybe hurting a little bit. He always shows courage.* Justin took a step toward the one florescent lightbulb illuminating the long hall. Then another. Then another.

Boarded and reinforced doors lined the corridor, a few with the metal framing from years ago when they used to hold glass. It was clear this basement area hadn't been used in ages, yet he passed down the hall half expecting some random person to step out of a doorway.

His heart was pounding. Just nerves. He paused, bounced in place, and shook his arms out. He breathed deeply, slowly, and scanned above the doors, down the length of the hall, not spotting what he was looking for.

He walked to the first junction where the hall split left and right, then paused. To the left, three doors down, he saw it, almost in total darkness—the small green light above the doorway that signaled the show was on. He approached, saluting the camera.

Beneath the door, a dim sliver of light indicated the room ahead would at least be illuminated. He pushed the door open and stepped forward, already beginning to raise his arms.

"Hands above your head," said a voice to his right inside the door. He was shoved forward by a palm between his shoulder blades and assumed this was his opponent's handler.

Justin ignored the contact. In his periphery he saw his opponent, but his main focus was on the Arena itself, looking for any advantages. The walls around him were bare—just cement. The room was not overly large. The walls would be an issue, especially with someone stronger who could shove him around. Justin wouldn't hold up well if he was being driven into the concrete.

Not much to this Arena, so he shifted his focus to his opponent. The guy was bare-chested except for the leather harness crossing his upper body in an X. He was big—big arms, big chest. He had skinnier legs—

those would be a weak point. The center of his harness contained one pointed metal stud. Decorative, but also potentially very painful. Justin grit his teeth. It would have been Joe's job as handler to prohibit the stud. Justin would just have to avoid it.

Time to compare. Strategize. His opponent was several inches over six feet, a hair taller than Justin. Reach seemed about the same, though. Justin would be the fitter Brawler overall, but the other man looked to have more upper body strength. The plan would be to stay low, in the center, and go for the legs. He had to work at wearing the guy down—though in this small space that might be difficult.

Lastly he examined his opponent's face. The mask didn't hide the ugly. Eyes lidded with extra fat. Crooked front tooth protruding. Looked like a troll. He seemed familiar, but Justin didn't remember his name. Not memorable was good. For now Troll would do.

"Where's your handler?" said the voice behind him. The man's hands wandered down Justin's body, patting him down.

"I'm in the market for a new one."

"Fuck you!" Troll's words echoed on the cement walls. Since Justin was trying to steal Troll's handler, he understood the sentiment.

"What's your name?" said the man, stepping out from the shadows.

Justin hadn't earned a name—yet. "Whatever you want it to be."

"Tonight your name better be…." The raspy voice paused, and Justin turned to look at the handler. "Ruthless."

The man's bulging eyes peered at Justin from the holes in a sackcloth mask straight out of a *Batman* movie. Shit. Scarecrow. Justin's meager hopes sank, a weight in the pit of his stomach.

Any handler who wore that kind of mask to every Fray wanted a share of the spotlight. This fit with what Justin knew of the handler—he had more than one Brawler, but Justin couldn't name any of them. Scarecrow's image and reputation were as important as winning and money—and certainly more valuable than any Brawler he had.

Scarecrow didn't check Justin's armguards. That was on purpose, Justin was sure. Justin could be hiding a blade or something less conspicuous like powder, sand—anything to give him an advantage, but he wasn't. That Scarecrow didn't check indicated he liked to play dirty, and he wasn't attached to his current Brawler. A blessing and a curse. If Troll was expendable, then Justin would be too, someday. Scarecrow wanted this fight to be brutal. So after tonight he was likely only taking on one of them.

With that the man stepped back through the doorway into the dimness of the hall. Troll looked like he was about to explode with fury. Justin had only seconds more to evaluate.

"Do you forfeit your right to inspection?" Scarecrow asked from behind him, loudly so the mics would pick it up.

"Yes," Justin shouted, glancing around the room at the small green lights indicating the cameras. He tried to put some bass and confidence into his voice. More confidence than he—

"Ghaaa!" Troll bellowed and charged, looking like a barbarian from an old movie. Damn. No dancing around. Justin feinted right and dodged left to get out of his way. He could use another second, dammit.

He pivoted around, trying to stay low and keep his feet squarely under him while spotting Troll.

He never saw it coming. He only saw black and felt a fist like a brick on the left side of his face. Not a square hit, but not glancing either. The leather mask absorbed some, and he was low enough that Troll's height took off a little more. Troll had anticipated the move, and that meant he wasn't dumb.

Justin dipped his right arm back in the direction his head was going from the punch, using the momentum to dig low. He drove his right fist up into Troll's gut, aiming below the leather harness. Two of his knuckles hitched on Troll's bottom rib, and Justin screamed through with the uppercut as hard as he could. His knuckles slipped past the bone and into the softer tissue beneath Troll's ribcage. Cracked, he hoped.

He backed off. The move gave him at least a few seconds while Troll caught his breath. This was happening too fast, and with Troll's size, Justin needed speed to be his advantage. He needed to control the tempo.

And then he heard it—the blood dropping onto the cement floor with a thick splat, followed by another. He touched his face. Blood flowed freely down his chin from a gouge on his jaw beneath his mask line. He looked at Troll's knuckles, taped up like any Brawler. But no— Justin saw a fleshy smear on the tape, and beneath it a texture to the tape that shouldn't be there. Fucking sandpaper.

Troll had marked his face.

Troll let out a wheezing laugh as he stood, looking at his right fist. He brought his knuckles close, studying them. No way—

Troll grabbed a white spider web of Justin's discarded skin in his teeth and chewed it. "Tastes good."

Disgusting intimidation tactic. Justin couldn't let it deter him, so he compartmentalized, putting it away in a tiny box in the back of his mind to deal with later. Much later.

Behind Troll in the doorway, Scarecrow gave a laugh and clapped.

Screw that. Justin plowed forward with a yell, tossing his head before jabbing with his right and following with his left. Not full strength, not yet. He needed to see what damage he might have caused and get a taste for his opponent. Troll looked surprised, throwing up his arms to block, stepping backward once, twice, three times. This time Justin leaned into it, seizing on his advantage, driving his left fist forward straight toward Troll's face in a full-force power shot.

But Troll anticipated the strike. His fist glanced past Troll's ear, Justin's position now too far forward and open. Meanwhile, Troll countered with a right hook, direct and fast, like a turbine into Justin's chest. Justin swore his heart skipped a beat as white sparks flashed at the edges of his vision. He lost his breath, unable to inhale.

Stay calm. Power through. The breath always comes back. In the meantime he simply had to behave like oxygen didn't matter.

Troll lunged forward again with a right jab toward Justin's face, but Justin brought up both arms to block. Protecting his face from those sandpapered fists needed to be his priority.

With no choice but to try to create some space, he took a step back as Troll came through with another right, which Justin intercepted with his armguards. Another step back, and now Troll was battering forward with his fists, breathing out with each punch, increasing in momentum and power like a steam locomotive approaching full throttle. Scrambling backward, Justin could no longer keep on his feet. He was going down.

Don't fight it. Don't freak out. He used momentum and gravity, dropping backward onto his butt. This stopped him almost immediately. He used his abs to keep his body from continuing backward and kicked out fiercely with his left foot, driving it into Troll's shin. At the same time, he hooked his right foot behind Troll's opposite leg, pulling it forward. His abs clenched painfully with the strain of keeping himself centered.

With one foot forward and one foot back, Troll stumbled in place, dropping awkwardly to a crouch with an agonized cry. Justin quickly hopped back up on his feet, raised his hands high, and drove both of them down toward Troll's bowed head. He connected below the man's skull, feeling the push back of vertebrae like stones set into sponge. Troll's head snapped downward, bouncing off his knee. One more time, Justin hammer-fisted into the same spot, laying Troll flat on the cement. Now he had the advantage, and he leapt back, getting ready for the next move.

He took a second to breathe, happy to fill his lungs. The sensation of breathing and the effect of the oxygen was a heady kind of ecstasy. He easily could have lost this fight.

"What are you waiting for, Ruthless?" asked Scarecrow from the shadows behind him.

"Just takin' a minute to smile for the cameras." And he did, glancing around the room, making sure to look at each green flashing light in his field of vision. If this fight finished too quickly, Scarecrow would never pick him up. He needed Scarecrow to take him, even though the prospect of a handler like Scarecrow was far less than ideal. He was being tested. This had to be a good fight. It had to look good.

Troll was starting to rise as Justin rushed forward, grabbed him, and slammed his knee into Troll's face. It had to hurt, but at the same time, it had the effect of lifting Troll back to a standing position. Troll staggered backward, blood pouring out of his nose and over his mask. Justin ran his hand over his own face, collecting the blood from his chin and flinging it onto the cement. It would look good on camera, but he couldn't afford any more marks to his face. He was screwed with just the one.

"I'm gonna fuckin' kill you," Troll yelled, flecks of blood spraying out with the words.

Justin was never much of a talker, and he had no comeback. He kept his mouth shut. He looked Troll in the eyes as if to say, "Your turn."

He kept his arms high and purposefully left himself less guarded down below, where he could better afford to take some hits. He started circling, keeping himself ready. Troll took a few tentative swipes, and Justin let him graze his chest without taking any damage.

Justin spotted an opportunity and entered a rhythm. Troll was slowing down, and Justin turned from attacks just enough to never take a hit head-on—but it threw Troll off-balance, repeatedly. The guy was sloppy. Justin jabbed and hooked to Troll's head every time the man stumbled, which actually had the effect of keeping Troll on his feet. It was obvious Troll was hurting, and Justin was playing, practically teasing, but to put on a good show he had to make the Fray last a little longer.

He had to change it up, though. To risk such an obvious pattern was boring and amateurish. When Troll stumbled again, he punched to knock Troll down and at the same time kicked Troll's feet out from under him, bringing him to the ground. Justin danced backward, not quite ready to end it.

Troll got into a low crouch, half kneeling and appearing as though it might be difficult for him to stand up fully. He looked at Justin. Too bad for Troll, his mean look was stronger than his punch. Troll took in a long, struggling breath while slowly rising to his feet once more.

Time to end this. Justin closed the distance to attack. He was expecting the last-ditch yell that came from Troll, the bestial cry of the nearly defeated. He was not expecting the mass of blood and phlegm that hit him square in the eyes. Blinded but already committed, he tried to follow through with his punch but only grazed Troll. He expected a follow-up punch and tried to guard his face, but suddenly Troll's hands were on his chest. Troll yelled again, picking Justin up and driving him back into the wall.

Justin's head slammed into the cement, the impact so hard his ears popped.

Troll landed punch after punch along Justin's rib cage while Justin flailed, his hands high. He felt the skin tearing off his sides as if he were going through a cheese grater. Unable to see clearly, he punched back, hitting Troll on the sides of his head, but not from the best angle. He kicked out, aiming for Troll's groin, but barely made impact.

Fortunately it was enough. Already weak and unsteady, Troll lost his footing and dipped forward. His vision clearing, Justin advanced off the wall. Striving for balance, he put his right arm around Troll, driving forward with his more dominant left, striking again and again into Troll's chest while in the clinch. Troll tried to back away, at the same time punching at Justin with his right. The burning scrape along his chin let Justin know he had lost more skin. He tucked his chin and kept pounding into Troll. They had each other in a strange embrace, both trying to gain leverage, both landing one-handed blows.

Gradually, Troll took the advantage, pushing Justin back against the wall yet again. With his hands up to block, Justin was taking a beating on his ribs. He had to stay away from the damned walls.

He let gravity work, dropping down below the next punch. He threw his arms around Troll's waist, using the wall to push off with his feet and drive Troll backward. It wasn't easy, and something pulled in his calf as he pushed what felt like three hundred pounds of dead weight. Good thing his opponent had weak legs.

Troll flopped backward, knocking his head against the cement, and Justin fell on top of him. Quickly he climbed up Troll's prone body, staying low. Left, right, left, he drove his fists into Troll's jaw, Troll's head ricocheting off the pavement each time. This was the ground and pound. Justin felt Troll go limp but punched three more times before he stopped.

Stilling his clenched fists, he heard himself yelling—the bestial cry of the desperate turning into a howl of victory.

He stumbled backward. He had lost himself. He closed his eyes as his echoing scream died in the cement box.

Had he killed Troll? He saw his downed opponent move slightly on the ground, a few droplets of blood spraying into the air—a sputtering breath. Thank God.

Justin sank to his knees, landing too hard on the pavement. He was suddenly chilled, the gray stone leaching all the heat from his body.

From the doorway to his left, Justin heard a gradual clap. Scarecrow's steps on the pavement sounded slow and deliberate as he walked out of the hall's shadows and into the room.

"Impressive."

"Thanks." Justin still hadn't taken his eyes off the barely moving Troll. "Who is he?"

"Doesn't matter. You'll do from now on."

Justin finally looked at Scarecrow. From the gleam in the man's eye, Justin could see the grin hidden beneath the mask. His blood ran cold. Troll moaned, giving Justin the excuse he needed to turn away.

Attempting deep breaths, Justin stifled a wince. Breathing hurt. His ribs were throbbing, but he wasn't going to touch them to see if anything was broken. He couldn't show Scarecrow any weakness, not to mention the cameras, which were required to stay on until the victor left the Arena.

Glancing up, Justin saw Scarecrow was still looking at him. How much time had passed? Two minutes? Five? Shit, he was out of it. He noticed again the blood landing on the cement. It had dripped all the way down his body, off his thighs, and onto the floor.

Troll groaned again, a sound like he was trying to wake himself up from a dream but couldn't. Handlers didn't usually leave their Brawlers on the floor. Although Troll didn't have a handler anymore, did he?

Still acting on instinct, Justin got slowly to his feet and walked over to him. "Hey," he said, tapping him on the cheek. Weakly, Troll lifted an arm. Justin grabbed it, trying to pull him up.

"Let me help you with that." Scarecrow walked behind Troll, getting on his knees and lifting Troll from behind into a sitting position. Troll's body was as loose as a pile of rags. He had no muscle coordination, no way to sit up on his own yet.

"You all right?" Justin asked. What a stupid question. Troll was definitely not all right.

Scarecrow reached for something at his back. Suddenly this whole situation struck him as not right. He heard the blade snap out before he saw it in the light. He held his breath.

"Steady now," Scarecrow said, the words directed to Justin. Scarecrow held his gaze, the gleam in his eye matching the gleam on the blade. This was another test. Justin couldn't show weakness, but was Scarecrow really going to—

"I'd say you've earned this," Scarecrow said. He drove the blade in below Troll's ear and thrust it across his throat. In slow, jerking motions, the blade finally severed the windpipe with a crunch and a snap, blood spraying out with a choking sound. The sound only lasted seconds, but the blood kept spurting, each small gush one more beat of Troll's dying heart.

Scarecrow stood, letting Troll drop to the floor. Troll was no longer moving, not making any sounds. His half-lidded eyes were unseeing, while a pool of blood extended from his ruined neck. He never knew what happened. He hadn't been conscious. Probably. But it hadn't been quick.

"Get up. Let's go." Scarecrow's voice was level and calm. Justin wanted to move his legs, but he was kneeling on the floor. He felt unclean, as though he were a captive worshipper at an unholy altar of human sacrifice, bound by chains to that very spot.

C'mon. Move.

He felt detached. He was getting up but couldn't feel his legs. Was he going into shock? Unaware of any pain, he followed Scarecrow out into the hall.

Once out of sight of the last camera, Justin stopped. It was like he was no longer in control of his own body. Scarecrow paused after a few steps and turned around. "Leave the cameras," he said. "It's not worth it if we get stopped somewhere. Come on."

He forced his feet to move. What was wrong with him? He needed to pretend he was still fighting. He needed some drive to get through this.

He thought of his family—his twin sister, Ginny, and their little brother, Charlie. Charlie, who had written that note. Justin grit his teeth. He had to play this game. He had to fight.

Scarecrow stopped in front of the exit. He turned to Justin, pulling off the sackcloth mask. He was old. He had salt-and-pepper hair, thin wisps sticking up around his head like smoke. He was sharp in the face, with skin hanging off pointed bones. "Take off your mask," he said. "Let me see you."

It was easy to obey. It didn't require thought. Justin reached behind and loosened the lace, pulling his mask off.

"Look at me." Scarecrow put his hand under Justin's chin. The man was tall—and not gentle, though he kept his hand clear of any wounds. He surveyed Justin's face with a faint smile. "Yeah, not bad. How old are you?"

"Twenty-three."

"You're a good-lookin' kid. A lot better looking than that guy on the floor back there."

Justin didn't respond. "Here," said Scarecrow, reaching behind and pulling a brown bandana out of his back pocket. "You're still bleeding."

"Thanks." Justin took it and held it to the gouge in his jaw.

"Your DNA clean?"

"Of course."

"Good. What's your exit plan?"

"I don't live far from here. I walked." And then Justin winced. Shit. He passed it off as pain, but it was his stupid mental error. He'd just given away too much information. He couldn't have another Joe situation. This handler was dangerous enough. Not safe. Not for Gin. Not for Charlie. Fucking think.

"You able to get home?"

"Of course," Justin said emphatically. No way was this guy coming anywhere near his home. "I have a plan. I'm careful."

"You better be. I got my own plan, kid. I'll meet you in a couple days. I'm not local, so location will be the train station in Racine, early morning, 7:00 a.m. That'll be Tuesday. No—better make it Wednesday. Safer with that face. Best lay low, let it heal some, considering we just committed murder an' all, right?" Scarecrow smiled.

Justin had no words, wouldn't even nod. Scarecrow didn't look pleased, his smile fading. "C'mon, speak. Let me hear you say it, so I know you got it. This is your one chance. I ain't trying to find you."

"Wednesday morning, 7:00 a.m. Racine."

Scarecrow patted Justin's cheek. "Good boy." Justin wanted to recoil but stood his ground. Finally, Scarecrow turned and pushed through the exit. "Take care of that face now," Justin heard faintly.

The metal door slammed shut.

Chapter 2

"THIS CHANGES things," Hale told his handler as they discussed the Fray from last night. He pointed to the scene paused on his brand-new tablet. Super-high resolution, latest model, exorbitantly expensive. But if the image on it was any indication, he may soon have to switch to recycled tech like everyone else. Or maybe not. Maybe this was the beginning of something even larger, more lucrative. Judging from the number of views and comments on the web, the entire country was watching. Shadow Fray was exploding. Police and government authorities were still swarming the Arena at the Mutual Conglomerate Building in Milwaukee, adding to the show, increasing the hype.

Brilliant, really. All signs indicated this was planned—a strategy from the bosses. Surprising, really, that it hadn't happened before. But now….

"It's your call," Benz told him, standing in the middle of the spacious room. Benz would follow Hale's lead no matter what, but right now, Hale needed his handler to give him advice.

Hale took a sip of coffee as he looked out over the Chicago skyline from his window on the twenty-eighth floor of the Chixago Building. He'd hate to give up this gorgeous view, but maybe it was time to live smarter, save the money—while it lasted. "You have a say in this too," he said to Benz. "Honestly I don't know what to do. Let's talk it out. Be my brother, not my business partner."

"Things are getting real dangerous." Benz's cautionary tone had Hale wondering if Benz thought they should quit.

"It's always been dangerous." Hale gestured out over the horizon, sloshing his coffee. "This whole damn world is dangerous."

He shook stray droplets from his hand and leaned against the window to face Benz. Despite the early hour, Benz was in a black suit, having worked through the night. It was quite the contrast to Hale's jeans and T-shirt, not to mention the bare feet and dark scruff. He felt underdressed in his own home. "You got a kid to think about," Hale reminded him.

"Edna's your kid too," Benz insisted. The man's imposing mass gave anything he said greater gravity. No wonder he never had to raise his voice.

"Yeah, well, she doesn't know that." It was hardly a mumble, but then Hale cleared his throat and spoke up. "Besides, she doesn't need me like she needs you, and we both know it." He gestured toward Benz and spilled his coffee again. "Shit." The way he was behaving this morning, you'd think he was spiking the coffee again. He wasn't.

"Sit down before you make a mess." Benz was habitually calm and even-toned, but as Hale sat down, he wondered why Benz wasn't sitting down himself. Was he nervous? "We can give it up, quit the Fray," Benz continued. "I got a job; the club's not bad. We couldn't stay in this building, but there are other places we could go."

"What are the options?" Hale asked.

"There's a rise closer to the club." Hale knew Benz well enough to detect a half-truth and raised an eyebrow. Benz put up both hands to placate him. "Okay, not a rise exactly, but it's off the ground, starts at the fourth floor. A lot of the workers at the club are there. It's not bad."

"Just residences?"

"Not exactly." Benz sighed and finally took a seat on the other side of Hale's dining room table. "That's where the less official workers run their business."

"Uni business?"

"Uni business. Lady business. You name it—some real high-class people too—but don't do that stuff in my backyard. It's where I work." Even this warning was said without raising his voice a single decibel.

"I got no use for anything classy." He could give up this unit in the Chixago Building. Move. He looked away from Benz, trying to keep the frown off his face—but Benz wouldn't fall for it. Best to admit the crux. "I'd miss Eddie, but this place?" He gestured around again, losing more coffee. "Jesus Christ."

"You need a sippy cup?"

Hale slammed the near-empty mug on the table, the sound like a gavel. Screw this. He wouldn't give up the Fray. Fighting was in his blood. It had saved his life. He wanted to know where his brother-in-law stood, so talking it out was good, even as Hale became more certain of the outcome.

At the very least, it was comforting to have a backup plan. No matter where Eddie and Jess ended up, as long as his daughter and sister-in-law had Benz, they'd be okay. Benz was a monster, nearly a foot taller than Hale, and his shoulders were as wide as a refrigerator. People didn't fuck with him, especially not when he was in a suit, which was all the time. The man lived next door, and the only time Hale had seen him not in a suit was five years ago when Hale had accidentally passed out drunk on their bathroom floor. He honestly thought he was in his own bathroom until a naked Benz walked in to take a piss. At least he didn't sleep in a suit.

"Has Eddie seen you naked?" Hale asked suddenly.

"What? What the hell, Hale?" Benz actually did get a little louder on that one.

Hale put his hands on his face. "Sorry. My mind isn't here. It's jumping all over the place." Jumping to get away from the grim scene paused on his tablet, the scene that had his whole future in question. He'd taken a lot of punches to the gut, but that was a pain he could handle. This hole in his chest, this uncertainty about what he should do, was far worse.

"Maybe it's time to retire, man. Quit while you're ahead." Benz's tone was soothing. "Black Jim is just your persona. Let him go to rest. He's a legend. Quit at the top, and the legend will live on, man." Hale raised an eyebrow. This vibe from Benz didn't go with his suit.

"Be real. Black Jim is only a legend until the next one rises. If I fold, they'll have a new star by next Tuesday. Besides, I'm not sure I can separate myself from him. Whatever I was before, I am Black Jim now."

"You're getting old, Hale. This was never going to last forever."

"How old are you?"

"Forty-two."

"So watch who you're calling old." Hale was thirty-six.

"Aren't you touchy? Must mean you know I'm right." Benz leaned forward in his chair, bringing his tall frame down to look Hale in the eyes. "Shadow Fray is getting progressively more violent. You're king of the mountain. Most wins ever. You think they aren't already talking about who's gonna be the one to bring Black Jim down? Who's to say they aren't going to start gunning for you, and bring some hardware to do it?"

"That's where you come in."

"I don't know if I can keep protecting you, brother. This game is changing. It's dirty. The day might come when—"

"I know, I know," said Hale, waving him down to silence him. "Look. You've always had my back. You're the best man, the best. If something goes down, I would never blame you."

"We've made more than enough to get Edna started on a good life."

"That's a comfort," Hale said quietly. He could die knowing he was finally doing right by her, but he wanted more. "Truth is, even in Chicago money buys safety. And no matter where you are, the more money you got, the higher you live off the ground."

Benz nodded. Neither man spoke for several minutes. Hale looked at the tablet on the table, at the picture paused on his screen. It was a riveting tableau: the man in the scarecrow mask—Hale refused to call him Scarecrow—and the kid they called Dozer lying dead in a pool of blood. The other kid—the cunning Brawler with no name—kneeling. He had skills, whoever he was—a newbie Hale had only seen a few times. That kid sure was finding himself in some evil shit. By the hunched posture, Hale could see the kid knew he was in over his head. Hale felt bad for him.

He looked at his business partner, his brother-in-law, his oldest friend. It was settled, then, but Hale decided to say the words anyway. "We have to keep our little girl safe, Benz. We fight for what's important. We stay in the Fray."

Justin woke to little arms around his neck. The rest of his body hurt, but not that touch. He felt soft breath on his cheek and a kiss that was barely a whisper. He opened his eyes and looked at his little brother. The dim morning light filtered through closed blinds to show a boy only ten years old, with clipped hair hidden under a baseball cap. Charlie's eyes were so big, they reminded Justin of the big eyes behind the mask last night, but only for a second. Looking into his brother's pale blue eyes, Justin could chase that thought away. He leaned over and kissed Charlie's forehead, then pulled him in close. "Just watch the ribs, okay?" Charlie didn't talk, but he did communicate. He knew this was what Justin needed right now.

Ginny was standing in the doorway watching, a smile on her face. She was dressed for work, yes, but she also spent a lot more time on her hair and face than she normally would. Justin's twin didn't try to be beautiful. Not many women in this city did unless they were after something.

Justin frowned. "You're gonna fuck him, aren't you?"

Ginny breathed in through her nose—something their mother used to do before she would scold them. She lost her smile for a second but then put it back on her face. It wasn't the same smile, though.

"Justin, it's not so bad. Ray's not a bad guy, and I haven't had my daddy fix in a while." The way she smiled, Justin believed she didn't mind so much, but she was a fantastic actress.

Justin kissed his brother again on the forehead. "I need you to go in the other room for a little bit so I can talk to your sister." It wasn't so much that he was trying to hide what was going on—Charlie was way too observant for that. He just wanted the kid to feel like he was protected, that he had people looking out for him. His brother lifted his head and frowned, and Justin knew exactly what that frown said: "Your lack of trust is like a knife in my heart." Charlie got out of bed and left, closing the bedroom door none too softly.

"What time is it?" Justin asked, still sleepy. He couldn't believe he'd actually slept last night, but he had, at least for a few hours. He didn't even remember any nightmares.

"8:20. We have to figure out what we're going to tell Ray."

"You drugged me, didn't you?"

"Justin, focus."

"God dammit, Gin." He wanted to be angry with her, but did he have the energy? After he left that cement box of an Arena last night, she had fallen into step beside him. He'd nearly slugged her, someone coming up to him in the shadows like that. She'd had the gun leveled at him—not to shoot him, of course, but to say she had the situation under control and she didn't give a fuck what Justin said about it. He tried to tell her how stupid it was to leave Charlie home alone, how stupid it was to hang outside a building for an hour where she could show up on a drone feed. On the way home, they had stuck to cover, the trees and scrub along the lake, the shadows of the buildings, the parking garages. It hadn't taken long—their rise was literally a dozen buildings away from the Arena. They hadn't heard a single drone, and even if they had, the night imaging was imperfect at best, at least in Milwaukee. It wasn't like in Chicago, where drone feeds were used to prosecute even the smallest of crimes with hefty fines.

"Justin." Ginny snapped her fingers and frowned. She got down on the floor by his bedside and took hold of his hand. "What do we tell Ray?"

Justin was supposed to make a run down to Chicago today, but even in the safety of a truck, it was too easy for someone to spot his specific facial injury. It would be visible through the rig's windows—not to mention the people he may have to interact with at the different stops.

"How many views does it have?" Justin asked.

"It's pushing two hundred million."

"Jesus. In eight hours?" There were fifty million people left in the country. Two hundred million views this quick was unheard of. Those were Black Jim numbers. That meant repeat views and a whole lot of international attention. "What did I do?"

She squeezed his hand. "One thing at a time. The first thing we deal with is Ray. It won't be a problem, whatever we tell him, but we have to decide what's best."

Gin was right that Ray wasn't a bad guy, and he was a fantastic boss. Even if he knew, he probably wouldn't snitch. Ray was going to have to drive Justin's shipment today—a truck full of condoms. Gin had gotten Justin the job several years ago. She'd been in the business of condom-making and distribution since she turned sixteen. And the side businesses that went along with it.

"Do we say you got jumped, need some time off? Do we say you're sick? Charlie's sick?" Sickness wasn't something anyone took lightly, though everyone still got sick. Maybe if they blamed it on an STD, but in their business, that didn't go over well either. And he could only use the excuse of being jumped so many times.

Justin heard the softest shuffling sound from outside the door. He frowned. "Bro Bro, you might as well come in." The door slowly opened, and Charlie had his wide-eyed angel face on, with a smile at his lips. Jesus, what he wouldn't do for that kid. Justin held his arm out, wincing at the tightness in his ribs, and Charlie came right to him, thrilled to be in their exclusive powwow. Justin guessed he wasn't doing Charlie any favors by protecting him. The world was what it was. Better Charlie learn to deal with it.

"Char," Justin said, leveling his gaze and speaking low. "I have an idea, but we need your help. With my face like this, I can't be seen for a while. It's too dangerous." Charlie nodded, serious. "I think the best thing we can do is to use you as our excuse. Do you want to stay home with me for a few days? I mean, not go out, not at all?" Charlie smiled and nodded again. "I don't want to say I'm sick. I don't want to say you're sick, not exactly. But I do want to say you're having problems. That you're going through a… spell." Charlie frowned. It had been a couple years since his last spell. His whole life he'd never spoken except in his sleep, but he still communicated—save for a few stretches where he'd just sit vacantly. He wouldn't drink. He wouldn't eat. It would go on for days, and it was fucking scary. Justin hated bringing it up; it wasn't something they talked about, as if ignoring the problem would make it go away. Gin frowned at him now, like she didn't think this was such a good idea.

Justin spoke directly to her next. "This is the best idea. Ray knows Charlie. He'll buy this. And if it turns out I need more time, then we can say I got jumped. That I did something stupid because we were getting desperate." She nodded.

Justin wasn't comfortable with this either, but he did have to sell it. "Bro Bro," he said, looking again at Charlie. "We're including you in this. We're including you in all our plans from now on, okay?" Charlie got his smile back and nodded. "I need you to promise me something, though. If we need your help, like we do now, we need to be able to count on you. That means you need to be here for us. You can't go back to how you used to be, not ever again. This is pretend. Is that understood?" That's what his mother used to say when she was serious, although Charlie would have no recollection. Charlie nodded, and Justin saw the determination in his eyes. "Pinky swear."

Charlie clasped his little finger with Justin's.

"Whole family," Gin said and did the same. Then all three of them fist-bumped together.

"So," Gin said, putting on a patently false, cheerful voice. "Charlie is suicidal. Can't be left alone." She took off Charlie's hat and ruffled his buzz cut before putting it back on. "Thanks, Char." Her smile turned genuine, and Justin smiled in turn. He could always count on Gin. Even when he shouldn't have to.

"Charlie Bro, go find some cartoons. I need a distraction. We'll camp out on the couch."

Charlie lit up like Christmas and practically bounded out of the room.

Gin put her hand to Justin's cheek, the uninjured one. "You want me to send a girl over? You damn well earned it. Better than any painkiller."

Part of him welcomed the mind-numbing distraction of it. He could tune out the world for a few minutes. "No," he said. "Not this time. It's not worth the risk."

Gin nodded, though whoever she'd send would likely never talk. He grabbed her hand before she could get up, keeping it on his cheek. "Just promise me one thing."

"Anything."

"Promise me you'll never leave Charlie alone again." She certainly saw through his motive, knew it would effectively mean she could never follow him to another Shadow Fray again.

She nodded, kissed him on the forehead, and got up to go. He heard the TV in the other room, heard her saying good-bye to Charlie. Then he heard the front door shut.

Justin lay in bed for a few minutes with nothing but his pain.

Chapter 3

FACING A nearly empty gym in his building during his shift, Hale had been watching coverage of last night's Fray all morning on a computer from his desk station. The numbers it was racking up were beyond impressive and would no doubt surpass his own. The crime scene continued to be big news. Everyone knew about Shadow Fray, but this level of exposure was unprecedented. There had never been a death anyone knew about, let alone a murder. That's where the strategy came in. A death wouldn't be news, but a murder? The bosses were smart.

Or were they? Their anonymity was threatened by the coverage—unless they controlled the media. News was really just a composition, an orchestra, with the bosses the conductors. Speculation abounded about the sport—where it came from, its likely ties to organized crime, and what the police were going to do.

Of course the police would do very little, especially up in Milwaukee where law enforcement was lax. In fact, so many Frays were held there it had come to be known as Bruise City, a throwback to a long dead moniker about beer. Shadow Frays were always held in a different Shadow Arena—never the same one twice—and took place all over the country, but the vast majority were north of Chicago, with Bruise City a convenient trek. No Frays were ever held in the White Windy City, last bastion of the Old World. That whole notion of the White Windy City was, of course, bullshit. Chicago had more money, and therefore less violent crime, but it was far from civilized and far from what it was like in the Old World before the Thinning.

Anyway, the news reports didn't concern Hale. Mostly he had been watching the kid. He didn't have a name, so the media began referring to him as "the Visitor," and the name was probably going to stick.

From what Hale could see, the kid had earned a name.

Last night's fight wasn't the Visitor's first Fray, and Hale was now intimately familiar with all three of his matches. The first was a loss, and it was pathetic. Clearly the kid was so shit-scared that he didn't know how to handle himself. Decent skills but no clue about his environment, which in this case was an old abandoned factory. His opponent gave him the slip in the opening minutes only to drop on him from a catwalk. The Visitor fought well for a while, but then he got backed into machinery and cornered. The other guy used the surroundings to launch himself in the air and kick the kid in the face. The Visitor had finally been put in a choke hold when his opponent hung from a pipe and wrapped his legs around the kid's neck until he passed out. It was over way too quickly. At least he'd scared the other guy into not prolonging the fight, but it wasn't good for views.

After that the kid had been absent for almost a year, which wasn't surprising considering the beating he'd taken. However, about six months ago, someone had given him another chance.

Hale tapped his screen to run the second fight and tapped again to pull up a grid view on all twenty cameras to play simultaneously. This time the Arena was a drained pool, probably in an old high school. The Visitor fought desperately but much smarter, and Hale found himself mesmerized. The opponent was never really in the game. The Visitor used the sloping gradient of the pool to his advantage, incline and gravity adding power to his moves or quickness to his steps.

The twenty grid was too small, so Hale tapped his screen again to pull up a row of four. He loved being able to see the same move from so many different angles, to see how the Visitor's left bicep popped before a punch and at the same time watch how his back muscles corded through the blow.

The Visitor fought shirtless, and he was a thing of beauty.

He was big, but not overly so. Maybe six feet two. He was also broad—not as broad as Benz but broad like a swimmer. How had he achieved that? Good genes? Even Hale didn't have access to a pool large enough to train in. Maybe the kid had money—though Uppers didn't fight.

The rest of his body was clearly the result of a lot of hard work. He had a very distinguished V-shape on narrow but well-muscled hips. Hale paused the video as he got a good frontal view of the Visitor walking under a light, and was amazed that his abs actually cast little shadows. He had big thighs and bulging calves. God, those legs—this guy was strong.

Hale couldn't help but wonder how he'd compare. Pushing six feet, he would be on the shorter end of their matchup, but that often worked to his advantage. While the kid was fast, Hale knew he was faster, making Hale the harder target and a force to be reckoned with. He had spent a lot of time over the years fine-tuning every last muscle; he was balanced and evenly developed. Hale would probably have the kid beat if they got into a full-body flexing contest—except for the biceps, quads, and calves— all the important good-looking muscles. He frowned. That was probably why he was lusting over those areas.

Hale watched as the Visitor's numbers on the newest fight continued to go up. In fact, numbers were going up all over the system, Hale's included. Everyone was going to get a payout. Internationally this was an example of the new violent America, the Old West reborn. He had a feeling the real show was just beginning.

The Visitor was a great showman too. He'd clearly drawn out the fight. What did he look like without the mask? The leather fastened around his head, but his coffee-colored hair was free and his mouth and jawline exposed. The kid kept his mouth relaxed but his jaw forward and determined. In this game, Hale supposed most men ended up battered and grotesque—himself excluded, of course. Hopefully, under that mask the Visitor's unmarred face would look young yet roguish and innocent with a touch of danger. At least that's the impression Hale got from the way the guy fought—he totally wasn't fantasizing, not at all.

Hale flinched when his wife's sister sat down. He hadn't been paying attention.

"You can't stop watching it, can you?" Jess asked and smiled, nodding toward his computer. Why would she smile at that?

"No," Hale admitted, checking his emotions. They frequently butted heads, but that was to be expected, being that Hale was her husband's best friend and she was the only mother Hale's daughter had ever known. Considering that twisted mess, they did okay. Hale never argued with her, not outright, and they maintained a cordial coolness at all times. "Why'd you come down here, Jess?" She used the gym but never when Hale was working.

She sighed, glancing nervously over at the two men lifting weights. She spoke softly. "I guess I'm just checking up on you. Benz talked to me before he finally went to bed, and I wanted you to know I respect your decision to keep fighting."

Hale nodded. There wasn't much to say. They sat in silence for a time.

"What would you think if I moved out of here?" he asked at last.

"What?" Her tone was sharp. Often her first reaction to anything Hale had to say was to get offended. "What about your daughter?"

And now, Hale would have to talk her down. "I'd be doing it for her. I can slum it on the ground. This whole thing has made me realize this money isn't going to last forever. I'm not going to last forever. Any little bit I can save, you know?"

Jess nodded. The look in her eyes made it seem like she hadn't considered this scenario before. Impossible. Now he knew she was acting. They weren't rolling in money. Their money was new money, and living in relative luxury and safety in the exclusive Chixago Building came with a price—a high one. The pittance he made working in the gym was nothing. People didn't work in this building to make money. People with money worked to keep the building self-contained so they wouldn't have to go outside. From their own solar panels, their own water purification system, to their own gardens, their rise was as self-sufficient as possible. Jess knew they were Uppers in this city only as long as the real paychecks kept coming.

"Where would you go?" she asked at last.

"I have no idea. Could you keep your ears open in the market? Maybe ask around and see if anyone has connections somewhere?" She worked in the grocery on this same floor whenever she could, whenever Benz or Hale was around to watch Eddie.

"Where is Eddie, by the way?" Hale asked abruptly, realizing he'd skipped lunch entirely and it was already afternoon. How long had he been lost in those videos? Eddie should be done with school by now, just one floor above them.

"She's in the grocery. I left her with Sam for a minute. Said I wanted to stop in and drop off lunch for you." With this she picked up a cloth bag he hadn't seen on the floor and dropped it on his desk.

"Thanks."

"You know you can come see her any time if you decide to leave. You can stay over sometimes." They both knew that would be difficult. Building security kept tabs on everyone who came in and out and frowned on overnight guests. Owners didn't want it to become a slum. Hale guessed he would have some leeway since he had lived here and knew people, but how long would that last?

"Hale," Jess said, suddenly looking uncomfortable. "I want you to know…." She paused, struggling. "It's hard for me to say thank you—mostly because I don't owe you any fucking thanks." At this, Hale nodded. He agreed. "But I see you split fifty-fifty with Benz, though you don't have to. And I know you save for Edna. I know you love her." Hale nodded again. "You've cleaned up your act. I can never forgive you for Janie. I'm not going to say thank you for behaving like a man. But with how things are going, I wanted you to know what I see."

Wow. That's more than he'd ever gotten from Jess. Looking at her now, he saw Janie. The sisters shared the same blonde hair and blue eyes. Even the shape of Jess's face reminded him of Janie. He always consciously tried to shut that out, but maybe it was the little bit of sympathy she was showing him that triggered the association.

"But…." And now her features hardened up again. He should have seen this coming. "Things are getting dangerous. Deadly. After last night… if they found you, or if someone came after you, who's to say Edna wouldn't be a target?" In that moment, Hale knew this whole conversation had been a manipulation.

She looked him dead in the eyes, and all traces of Janie were gone. "I really do think it would be best if you left us. Best for Edna."

Hale swallowed his anger and nodded. "I agree with you." He wanted to think the small smile she gave him in response was one of compassion, but it could very well be relief.

She shifted in her seat. "I have to go get Edna."

"Thanks again for the lunch," Hale said, unable to keep an edge from his voice. She pursed her lips and got up to leave. "And Jess," he added before she could go, "Benz told me about a place this morning. It might just be for people at his club, but ask him for me, okay?"

She relaxed her expression and nodded before turning and walking away.

He left the bag sitting on his desk. He wasn't hungry. "Hey—Bobby, Trey!" he called to the two men currently lifting weights in the gym. "When you're done, could one of you give me a little break at the desk and one of you spot me?"

He closed the browser on the computer. It wasn't illegal to watch Shadow Fray, but it suddenly felt safer if no one saw him watching it. "Sure thing, Hale," said Bobby.

Hale made a conscious effort not to work out in the gym more than anyone else. He mostly did cardio and kept the weight training private, but he wanted the pain that came from lifting. "I got a little steam I need to blow off, if you know what I mean."

Bobby gave him a knowing nod. "Women," he said. "Sometimes I think it's better that there's fewer of them in the world now."

Trey laughed as he finished the rep and set the weight on the stand. "Yeah, you just keep telling yourself that every time you squeeze one off in your hand, right?"

Hale smiled, but the truth was it wasn't very funny, and he didn't feel like laughing.

JUSTIN UNWRAPPED himself from his sleeping little brother and turned off *My Little Pony*. He was constantly amazed by the number of shows from the Old World he hadn't seen yet. Professionally done media wasn't made as much anymore. Like technology, it had been frozen in time since the Thinning. Keeping power and communications had been a priority for a hundred years, but everything was reused and recycled—including television shows. When he was younger, he used to get worried that one day, the cartoons would all run out. That day never came, though.

He walked to the expansive floor-to-ceiling windows. Normally the blinds were kept up so the sun would heat the room, but not today. He peered through a slit to see a drone flying over the next building. The buzzing had been constant since sunrise, and while police drones didn't usually go spying in windows, he wasn't taking any chances. No doubt there were plenty of curiosity seekers flying their personal machines, but even those didn't usually get too close to their windows. As long as a drone didn't have the government logo, there was nothing to prevent someone from taking it out. Though in his condition, he wasn't about to step out onto the balcony with a salt-pellet pistol and risk being seen. Besides, he wasn't a great shot, not like Gin. Her reputation for dropping drones on the first shot pretty much made the whole fourteenth floor on the north side of the Lakeside Condominiums a virtual no-spy zone.

Another drone flew right down the center of the space between buildings, about two stories beneath him. He could easily make out the MPD logo, but he would have known it was MPD based on noise and size alone. This whole circus was stupid. All the police activity was likely for show, so the powers that be appeared to be doing something about last night. It looked good for the news cameras, but most wouldn't be fooled. This wasn't Chicago. The system there worked because people had money, and even civilians could earn a buck with a percentage cut of any video proof that led to a conviction for a crime as small as littering. But here? Fines weren't effective if citizens couldn't pay them. Weaponized police drones might stop a violent crime in progress, but those larger drones were easy to spot and not very quiet. Drones didn't even need to fly low; it just kept people in check to know they were being watched and recorded. That was the idea anyway. Drones must record plenty of crime, but unless something was actually done about it, what was the point?

Honestly he was more afraid of residents in neighboring buildings getting a look at him than the drones. All his life he'd lived in the Lakeside Condominiums rise, so the view he looked out on now was very familiar. The nearest building was small, not quite reaching up to their fourteenth-floor unit. Still, it was close enough that he had a clear view into someone's living space. A person probably wouldn't notice his facial injury even if they did look, but *probably* wasn't good enough. The next building over was taller, matching the twenty-eight floors of his own rise. Despite the greater distance, people could see into units clearly, especially at night.

Distance didn't necessarily mean protection from prying eyes. He sat at the window table and pushed the head of a telescope through the slits in the blinds. He zeroed in on the two officers strolling up the lake walk about two hundred yards away. Normally he never saw police about.

Looking beyond the officers to Lake Michigan, there were even police boats running surveillance. That was fine—clearly just for show. The mayor of Milwaukee—Mayor Cram—was all about appearances. Perhaps due to nearly nonexistent air travel, local city governments held most of the power, and while American government was supposedly still democratic, Mayor Cram had been in office for as long as he could remember. Rumor had it she was in the pocket of organized crime, and maybe under the thumb of the Shadow Fray bosses themselves. The Shadow Masters. Justin suspected Mayor Cram was the reason most Shadow Arenas were in and around Milwaukee. To many people it was known as Bruise City or Killwaukee. Like everywhere else in the country, the structures of government were in place, but crime was money, and money was the real government.

Right now the mayor and the police didn't concern him—but he kept checking again and again for an officer with a dog. He'd retrieved his shirt after the Fray, but that hardly mattered; his scent and his blood were everywhere in that Arena. They couldn't know he lived so close, and would hardly expect it, so they'd have no reason to bring a dog. That's what he kept telling himself. It was getting close to sunset, so if they hadn't brought one in by now, he was safe. Right?

He nearly fell out of the chair as the door opened and Gin walked in.

"Jesus Christ. Try knocking, why don't you?" he gasped, breathing deep to slow his heart.

"Knock on my own door?" Gin smiled and looked at him crookedly as she walked down the hall past the open kitchen into the living area. "Wouldn't that have scared you more?"

He removed the telescope and let the gap in the blinds fall closed. "Probably," he admitted. Ginny came and sat next to Charlie, who was blinking awake. Justin had thought many times during the day to call her, but he didn't like to think about what she might be doing. "How did it go?" he asked, dreading the answer.

"Totally fine. He wouldn't fuck me because he felt bad and was so concerned. Charlie, you gave us an excellent excuse," she said, turning to kiss him on his forehead. Charlie crinkled his nose, grabbed his fallen baseball hat, and shoved it back on his head. Justin smiled at the funny expression.

"He's gonna deliver the shipments, but he said some of it can sit until you get back," Gin added. "He'll just let them pile up and let you deal with all the cranky retailers." She smiled. "Of course, I got pretty affectionate and blew him eventually, so he might change his mind."

Justin lost his smile. He and Gin were frank about sex, and they often knew what the other one was doing… or who they were doing. She was the one who hooked him up. In fact, he had probably slept with most of her female friends. He was considered a friend-with-benefits by extension, safe for everyone involved. But he didn't like to think Gin didn't have a choice in her partners. He didn't want her to ever have to go back to that again.

Gin, of course, could read his mind. "You need to let this go. I *like* Ray. And he returned the favor. He got down under my desk as I was working the phone, kept trying to get me to mess up. Doubtful the people on the other line even care. I mean, we make condoms after all." She paused for a second, before continuing somewhat wistfully, "He's got that beard, and I really like—"

"All right, all right!" Justin said a little too loudly. Charlie blew a raspberry like he was trying to keep from laughing.

"And don't worry about driving your routes," she said. "Maybe somewhere a woman will get pregnant and give birth to a little girl all because you couldn't deliver the protection."

"Sure," he said. "Or die of the crank."

"No one dies from that anymore. How are you feeling?"

"Nothing worse than normal," he said, "except the scrapes and gouges feel different." He was bruised, but not terribly swollen. "Nothing broken, nothing cracked." Just a constant, sharper pain whenever he twisted his ribs. Or talked. Or turned to look at something. Or breathed.

"Good," she said. "I was worried. You didn't really talk last night. It was weird."

"Yeah, well...."

"You checked your numbers?"

"No." Previously he'd studied his film, but this one he hadn't watched once. He didn't want to think about it.

She looked excited but also tentative and nervous. She lowered her voice. "The numbers are through the roof."

"That's good, I guess?"

"It's going to be more money than we've had in a long time."

"Not necessarily," he said. "Scarecrow, he... I don't know. There's no telling what he'll do."

"They won't deliver to you? In your old pick-up location?"

"I doubt it, but maybe. It was through Joe before, so it was his location, not mine. I don't know if the money for this last Fray goes to me now or if Scarecrow gets it. Or we both do. I have no idea how this works. I don't think anyone does."

She frowned. "Oh."

"I'll have to go meet with Scarecrow on Wednesday. Maybe we'll find out then. But you can check Joe's location in the meantime, because I can't go outside. And we can always hope, I guess." He looked at his twin, wanting to hope. But their family had never known good fortune—if such a thing even existed anymore, for anyone.

Chapter 4

JUSTIN WAS having a hard time sleeping, and he missed Charlie. It was amazing how much more it hurt when he didn't have cartoons or siblings to distract him. The soreness and bruising he considered to be a good, clean hurt—like an ache after a hard workout. The skin he'd lost, though, that really hurt. It was a hot pain that kept him continually uncomfortable. Part of the misery came from the worry that it wouldn't heal soon enough for him to cover it somehow. Even worse, it was a perpetual reminder of the knuckles that had belonged to a guy who got his throat slit and died less than twenty-four hours ago.

No, he wouldn't think about that. Instead he reached under his pillow and pulled out the folded letter. The ambient light in the room was barely enough to read by, but he practically had it memorized anyway. He'd only had it for five days. He was going to have to tell Charlie about it, but not yet. Charlie's teacher, a nun named Sister Timothy, had given it to him. In a way it felt like she had betrayed Charlie's trust, but Justin was glad she had. He loved it. Without this letter, he might not have had the drive to win. It gave him the extra push he'd needed. He'd copied down the first few lines to read before he entered the Shadow Arena, but he took it out now to read the whole thing again. Unfolding it carefully, he handled it like a secret.

Handwriting Practice
The Person I Look Up to Most
To: Sister Tim
From: Charlie
Justin does his best even when it's hard, even when he's tired and maybe hurting a little bit. He always shows courage. That's why he's the person I look up to the most.

I think we all have secrets to keep. It's nice to have a little bit of privacy, like from the drones, and my brother tries to give us that. But we never hide. He wants me to have a normal life, whatever that is. My brother keeps secrets, but not from me. And he helps me keep my secrets too. Sometimes we hide from the drones like Shutters, but mostly we pretend like it's just us.

Justin always tries to do what's best for my sister and me. He raised me when my sister was at work. He always did lots of stuff with me. He read me books until I could read on my own. I didn't even need school for that, because he taught me. But our favorite thing to do is watch cartoons.

He tries to keep things from me, but not in a bad way. He puts his tablet down all the time, but I know he's reading. It's almost like he doesn't want anyone to know he reads, not even me. I think he doesn't want me to be too curious about things. It's another way he tries to protect me. So we just do kid stuff. But that's okay.

My brother is really strong. He works out and he lifts weights. He makes me come with him and read a book but I watch him too. I know he stays strong to protect me and my sister. My sister is fertile, and so he always feels like he has to protect her because she's in danger or something. My sister can take care of herself, but he does it anyway. I like that about him.

Justin's secret is that he's really smart. Like, really smart. Someday, my brother is going to figure out what is wrong with the world. He will figure out why all the people got sick and died so long ago, and what happened to poison the ground. Then he'll find out why there's not as many girls anymore, and why people can't have babies. Maybe he'll even find the cure for ground sickness, but that's probably asking too much. I mean, he can't do everything.

Here's a secret about him and me. He says there's two kinds of people—people who stay alive and people who go poking their noses where they don't belong. I don't say it (ha ha), but I know he's both, and I'm both too. So really, there's three kinds of people. But don't tell him I said that.

*He wants me to go to college at Exxon or DuPont
in Chicago. I like that idea. Because if my brother doesn't
find out what happened and how to fix it, I want to find
out for him. He'd like to take me out of Bruise City to
Chicago, but maybe someday I will do that for him
instead. Anyway, I like it here, because this is my home,
and this is where you are too. Thanks for being the best
teacher.*

*He would be so mad if he knew I wrote this. But I
know you keep secrets too. So please keep my secret. I know
you will, because you're the third person I most look up to,
and you always tell me I can do anything.*

My brother tells me that too.

From: Charlie

*P.S. My sister is the second person and I also have a
friend named Gristopher Mays and he's the fourth person.
He's really nice but I haven't known him as long as I've
known you.*

*P.P.S. I think you are that special third kind of
person too. Thanks for being the best teacher.*

Justin marveled at how neat Charlie's handwriting was—so much finer than his own boxy script. God, he could read and reread that note over and over again, but best not to overdo it. He'd save the assignment like a little treasure and bring it out when he really needed it. Which, granted, was quite a bit—but just one read-through at a time. He folded it up carefully and put it back under his pillow.

He couldn't quite bring himself to feel guilty about having it. He'd eventually tell Charlie his teacher had passed it on to him—after all, Charlie straight up said Justin didn't keep secrets from him, which was mostly true. Still, he'd hold on to this secret just a little bit longer.

He fluffed his pillow in an effort to make himself more comfortable but succeeded only in stretching the skin around his ribs while he turned. Christ, it burned with an almost physical heat. This sucked. He'd tried reading but words were unable to keep his mind from wandering. He needed to move, to *do* something.

Justin wasn't used to sleeping alone, but Gin had convinced Charlie to give him space. They didn't have assigned bedrooms per se.

Whoever went to bed first would take the larger master bedroom, and that's usually where Charlie ended up too, if he didn't fall asleep on the couch. Sometimes all three of them slept together in the large bedroom. That's what felt most comfortable.

Tonight, Justin was sleeping alone. Actually he was awake alone. He sighed and got out of bed, and the sigh turned into a groan. "Hurts," he admitted quietly to no one. He left the guest bedroom—so called because that's the bedroom he or Gin used if they brought over "guests"—and walked into the main living area. He hesitated.

"The hell with it," he mumbled, and walked over to the telescope for what seemed the ninetieth time that day. He didn't expect to see anything. This was more like an itch he needed to scratch. When the moon was out and large, it reflected off Lake Michigan and brightened the whole landscape, but that wasn't the case tonight. The water was a never-ending blackness, so he turned his attention to the neighboring rises and the units with lights on.

When it came to windows, there were two schools of thought. Some people liked to leave them uncovered, seemingly because they had absolutely nothing to hide, but more likely they wanted people to know who they were. It was no coincidence that the higher up you went on a rise, the more windows were uncovered at night. Justin imagined that displaying your home was a lot like how driving a fancy car used to be. These people were the upper class, or the Uppers.

Others kept their windows covered all the time, even during the day. The Shutters. These were the people who longed for the Old World, though they hadn't been alive back then, not unless they were very old like his friend Mr. Mays. A world of less violence, before the epidemics. No drones. No spying. No coastal flooding, no contaminated ground. A world you didn't feel the *need* to shut out. A world from which you didn't need to be protected. A world now limited to four corners and four walls to maintain a false sense of control.

Many Shutters witnessed the world only through the feeds of their personal drones. Ironic, considering most of them were afraid of drones. Shutters were afraid of everything, even walking on the ground, though twelve hours on the ground was deemed perfectly safe, even for pregnant women. Basically as long as you didn't live on the ground, you were fine. It took prolonged exposure, and Mr. Mays's ripe old age was a testament to that.

Unlike Shutters, Justin didn't long for the past. He made a conscious effort to be neither Upper nor Shutter and live naturally. But living naturally wasn't what he was doing if he had to make a conscious effort to do it, was it? That was one of his philosophical questions he could bring up with Mr. Mays the next time he and Charlie went upstairs for a visit.

Justin left the telescope and gave his attention to what he was trying to avoid—the computer.

He moved from the window table to the nearby minidesk where the computer was located. It was a pieced-together machine that took its own sweet time to wake up. He could watch this on a larger screen, but the smaller screen might be easier to bear and give him more privacy should Gin or Charlie wake. After the screen came to life, he took a deep breath and pulled up his Fray from last night.

He saw himself walk into the room looking confident. Prepared.

Then Scarecrow stepped away from the wall and into the frame to pat him down. Justin's stomach roiled, the room seeming to cant. He was going to be sick. He got up quickly and ran into the bathroom. He splashed cool water on his face—and was immediately shocked out of his nausea. He had totally forgotten about his facial injuries until they sang with pain. Antiseptic from the nearby skin must have washed back into the wounds. He stared at himself in the mirror, willing the pain to subside.

The bandages were soaked and seeping with red. He gingerly pulled them off, first from his chin, then his jaw. The one on his chin was minor—a scrape. But his jaw had three gouges where knuckles had connected. Two of them weren't terrible, but the third was deep. The shallower injuries appeared pinkish around the edges and had the yellowish fluid that came from covering a wound with a bandage, not allowing a scab to form. But the one deep knuckle mark was red and bleeding.

Crap. No way was this going to heal enough by Wednesday. Looking at his face now, he knew makeup wasn't going to be an option. He'd have to come up with something else, but he had no idea what the hell that would be. It was late Monday night, so he only had a day and a half to figure it out. "Next time, don't get hit so hard," he said quietly to his reflection.

He used a small cloth to clean the leaking blood from the deep gash and applied more of the stinging antiseptic gel, hoping that would help. The others he left naked and open to the air so they would start to scab over. He was still bandaged up along both sides of his ribs, but he didn't want to think about that mess.

He walked out of the bathroom and back into the living area, purposefully sliding sideways so he wouldn't have to look at the fight looping on the computer screen. Upon sitting back in the chair, he used his periphery vision to scroll to where his numbers were. Over five hundred million.

He suddenly became very aware of his heartbeat. Over half of the world population. No Shadow Fray had gotten anywhere close to that number, not even Black Jim's. In twenty-four hours. Damn.

He closed the browser and stood again. What the hell was he going to do? This was so beyond him. With views like this, everyone in Shadow Fray would start killing each other. Or maybe he'd be found out. And then what about Charlie and Gin? Shit.

Compartmentalize.

He took the panic and confusion and visualized putting it away in one of the little boxes he kept in the back of his mind. He took the smallest hope that this could be a big payday and brought it to the front.

He knew of one more thing to help clear his mind.

He snuck quietly into the master bedroom. He could hear Gin and Charlie breathing heavily. It was pitch-black, but he grew up in this unit and he knew every inch of the twelve hundred square feet. He took a few steps in the darkness before quietly pushing open the door to the walk-in closet. He got down on his knees and found the box in the corner hidden beneath his hanging clothes. Not really hidden, of course, because undoubtedly Gin and Charlie knew it was there. He reached in, felt the soft cloth on the top, and grabbed onto it. He rose and left the room silently, carefully closing the door.

He walked back to the glow of the computer and as he sat down, examined what he had in his hands. It was a white cloth, smeared and stained heavily by an oily black paint. It had a medicinal odor to it, as well as a musky scent within the soft cloth itself. This was his most prized souvenir.

He went into the computer files and scanned his saved list until he found BlkJmMcDonalds. He had watched this Fray well over a hundred times. It was one of his favorites. The Arena was a McDonald's.

The video file started out as Black Jim's matches always did. He would enter with his head slightly lowered, appearing almost reverent. He would go into position and raise his head and eyes slowly to the camera.

His eyes were vividly white amidst the black. Rather than masked, his face and hair were slicked with black grease paint.

Black Jim was the only one in Shadow Fray who didn't wear a mask. He was the only one who didn't have to.

The makeup covering his face and hair offered him enough of a disguise but little protection. The slick paint probably resulted in more glancing blows, but you couldn't play this game without a mask unless you were as good as he was—not without being found out.

It wasn't just about the disguise; too many injuries, too often, and they could easily be matched up with the video. Anonymity was a necessity but also part of the appeal. In a society where the watchers required watchers, to the point everyone was droned up and watching everyone else, anonymity was an alluring mystery. No matter what, once you were found out, your games were over. There were stories about losing a lot more than just your chance to play. People disappeared, permanently. No one had ever talked. No ex-Shadow Fray Brawler had ever come forward. Not one.

Black Jim's pose went on for long minutes. He was the only Brawler who had extended segments of video before his Fray even began, because people wanted to see it. He'd stand still as stone, with his arms spread at his sides, like a black specter from a nightmare. The theatrics of it all….

Sometimes, Justin would dream about Black Jim standing like that at the foot of his bed while he slept. He'd seen posters and printouts of this stance of Black Jim's. Nothing in their home had changed much since Mom died, or he might like one himself. He was a fanboy without the poster.

He didn't fast-forward the video. You would think Black Jim was in a trance or some type of meditation, but his face looked nothing like calm. In his too-white eyes, he had the look of a man familiar with violence. He had the look of a man who knew he was going to win, like once you walked into that room, you were screwed, because he already saw in his head every move you could possibly make.

You walked into that room, and you were his plaything.

This was what Justin brought to the front of his mind, to help him block out all the other noise of the last twenty-four hours. He had studied this man. Idolized him. He both feared and dreamed of fighting him. Justin wasn't excited for much, but this—

What would it be like to walk into an Arena and suddenly see this man staring him down? He rehearsed it mentally so when it did happen, he wouldn't crumble. He'd be able to look back into those eyes without fear.

He visualized walking in. He didn't look at an opponent directly during pat-down. He'd analyze the physical space of the Arena and indirectly study the other Brawler's body for advantages and threats. That would allow him to then raise his eyes and stare right back at the man with his full attention. Black Jim's eyes were actually blue. Justin had spent hours magnifying the video to find his true eye color so he would know Black Jim was just another man, a man who could be beaten. He wasn't some white-eyed black demon.

Black Jim always looked and dressed the same. His face was, of course, black. The paint disguised the true color of his hair, which was not quite shoulder-length. It looked like it might curl slightly when it wasn't slicked back. The paler skin of his arms and hands was overlaid with dark hair. He looked rugged, so he was likely one of those guys who had a permanent five-o'clock shadow.

He wore a sleeveless black shirt, one that clung tightly to him and moved with him. His arms could be carved from marble. He appeared to be all muscle and 0 percent body fat. His veins stood out along his arms and on his hands, but he wasn't huge. He didn't look like a bouncer like so many other Brawlers did. He looked like an athlete.

This was why Justin swam in the lake from June through October. No one swam in Lake Michigan. People were afraid of chemicals and said the whole water supply had been poisoned along with the ground years and years ago, either in an effort to combat the flu, or from the floods and industrialization, or some kind of terrorism. People said that's why there weren't so many girls born anymore. Everyone boiled and filtered their water, as if that would help. The truth was, it was no one thing that did the world in—it was all the little things people kept ignoring, a confluence of events people should have seen coming.

At the very least, the water wasn't any more dangerous than the ground. Don't live there, and you'd be okay. Plus the Great Lakes were supposedly one of the freshest sources of water remaining—but he had still been scared to swim. Facing the fear had been as valuable to him as the exercise. Now he knew how far he had to quietly breaststroke out, keeping his head down, until he couldn't be visible from shore in the darkness. Only then would he swim. The whole process would take at least two hours, and swimming through the currents and large waves could be dangerous, especially at night. But that was what gave him an edge. Gave him breath control. Kept his whole body fit, like Black Jim's. Or at least as close to it as he could get on a budget.

He even saw fish sometimes, and if fish could live in the lake, he supposed it wouldn't hurt him much.

Justin watched as the visitor walked on-screen, a Brawler named Lynx. The man was African-American, very large with leonine features. Standing across from Black Jim, though, he certainly looked more like prey than predator.

The one good thing this guy did was charge out of the gate. Black Jim usually had an opening advantage, knew the visitor would likely be a little shocked to see him, a little slow. Justin gave this guy credit for taking action and not hesitating, but he didn't have a backup plan. Black Jim wasn't surprised by the move even though it didn't often happen. He took advantage of the charging stance of Lynx and planted a jump kick into his face.

The man was pretty much done after that. His nose was broken and bleeding freely, and he looked stunned. The fight lasted for a long time, though. One of the reasons Black Jim was so popular was because he was quite the showman. Had there been a literal spotlight in that McDonald's, Black Jim would have completely absorbed it.

In this one he looked to be having particular fun. He slammed the guy's face into one of the old registers on the counter, knocking it to the floor. It was the only register on the counter, and Justin firmly believed Black Jim had planned this move and had removed the other registers in the Arena prior to the cameras going up. Showing up first was one of the advantages of being the home team, and as the top Brawler in Shadow Fray, he was always the home team, until someone took him down.

Then he did Justin's favorite move, grabbing the guy and standing him up to punch him backward onto the counter. Like the boss he was, Black Jim gripped the guy's neck and slid him along the countertop. It was a scene right out of an old Western. This was showmanship.

As the man fell to the floor at the end of the counter, he did something out of desperation. He grabbed for Black Jim but only managed to get the bottom of his shirt. As he fell, he didn't let go, and Black Jim was forced to bend over partially, the man pulling his shirt before hitting the ground hard and releasing it. With his shirt bunched up on his chest, Black Jim stood up smiling, as if he knew he was giving people a real show. It was one of the only times you got to see the magnificence of his upper body.

Justin paused it and replayed the move, watching it again and again, for two reasons.

First, it showed a potential weakness. If Justin ever fought Black Jim, he could use that shirt. Clothing was fair game. He could get it up, maybe entangle him somehow. While watching, he thought of the different moves he could use to accomplish this, planning scenarios to give him an advantage.

The second reason he watched this portion repeatedly was because, as an admirer of Black Jim's fitness, this allowed a rare glimpse at parts of his body that were otherwise covered. Justin loved the trimness of the man—everything was corded and tight. He had narrow hips and a V-line, with stomach muscles that popped. He had to be flexing for the camera as he lowered his shirt. Justin replayed it again, this time focusing on the flash of pec he could see, circular and very well defined. Both nipples were visible, taut and tight on his hard body. His chest was covered in dark hair, prevalent but not overly long—not something a Brawler could grab and hold on to for any kind of advantage. The hair on his chest narrowed and trailed down between his flexing abs and over his navel, disappearing beneath the waistband of his black pants.

Justin marveled at that body. For the physique, of course. Purely professional.

Sitting back in his chair, he lowered his hand to where he was tenting in his sleep pants. Through the material, he fingered the head of his cock lightly, circling it. He could feel a small bead of moisture soaking through the pants. Gin was right—this was a good pain reliever and a good way to forget. He dipped his hand beneath his waistband and grabbed on to his stiff cock. His eyes zeroed in on the screen, the heat he felt looking at Black Jim practically burning the image onto his corneas. He played with himself a bit, several long, very enjoyable strokes before stopping to squeeze himself—hard. He should stop this. He paused the video.

Black Jim froze on the screen, a statue of perfection. Apparently most men felt this attraction for other men at some point, but it wasn't a natural urge—just like the shrinking birthrate wasn't natural. The infertility wasn't natural. The ever-lower percentage of girls being born wasn't natural. Something had happened, something that changed the natural order of things, and these urges for other men were part of it. They had to be.

Justin didn't judge men who did this. There weren't enough women to go around. Most men used Unis, and Unis were technically part male. Many Unis chose to have an operation to become one gender, usually female, but as far as he knew, he'd never been with one. He didn't even completely understand how it worked. Unis were the product of fertility treatments designed to produce females, but unlike more sophisticated interventions, the fertility treatments that produced Unis were free—corporate sponsored and constantly evolving. To date none had created a viable fertile female. Most treatments didn't even result in pregnancy, so if you were successful in becoming a parent, in creating a new life, it could hardly be called a failure. On the contrary, Unis were a miracle. But a man having sex with another man? That was considered the opposite of a miracle. An antibreeder.

Justin's hand hovered over the keyboard. At one point, back in the Old World, it hadn't mattered. Men could be with other men if that's what they wanted, and no one cared. Some still lived that way, though not openly and never safely. Not in a rise where a building association could cast a single man out on the street based on what kind of porn was in his Internet history cache—let alone what some conniving resident using their personal drone spied you doing with your "roommate." Money might be tight, but there was always someone under you with just enough to move up a floor and steal your unit right out from under you.

A stupid prejudice led to so much paranoia, but he supposed for most men, to give in to these baser urges was like giving up the fight—the fight against the world, the way it was today, and the fight to continue on the planet by having a family. It was fear, plain and simple.

Justin refused to live in fear. He already had a family. And he would always continue to fight. His fight was just a bit different than most.

After tapping the screen to get rid of the visual, he leaned back and closed his eyes. If he wasn't looking at anything, then he wasn't giving up the fight, right? He'd just keep his eyes closed and enjoy the feelings he could give himself.

He fingered the cloth by the computer, the cloth he had searched thirteen different McDonald's to find.

He had so many fantasies of Black Jim. Which one would it be tonight? No matter how it started, Justin was always drawn to the counter in the video, but there were a hundred different ways to get there.

First he and Black Jim would fight close, grappling on the floor, trading submission holds as they struggled for dominance. Justin imagined being pinned to the floor facedown, Black Jim's arm around his throat so he could barely breathe. He'd revel in the man's tight grip, feeling surrounded and controlled. He'd give in to the feeling briefly, even enjoy it.

Unexpectedly he'd find a way to turn the tables. He'd lift his ass up, pushing back into Black Jim, and the man would become distracted. Loosen his hold. Push back. Justin would hear him groan in his ear with pleasure and permission.

Swiftly taking advantage, Justin would turn and flip the man over. Now they would be face-to-face, Justin looking into those blue eyes, the man looking back at him. An unmasked passion would burn between them, unmistakable. The fight disappearing to the background, Justin would begin to move his hips. He would feel the hardness of Black Jim's cock through the material, a hardness that matched the marble-like perfection of his body. Black Jim would welcome the feel of Justin's erection, asking for it in his gaze. Those blue eyes would tell Justin to keep going. To take him.

The emotions that had been building in Justin for years, the impossible yearning, would finally have release.

With surprising speed, Justin would pick Black Jim up off the floor and shove him back into the counter. Justin would continue rutting against him, listening to him groan. Justin's gaze would move from the man's blue eyes down to his lips. He'd feel Black Jim's hand stroke his bulging cock through the material.

"That's right, stroke it," Justin would tell him, and the man would be eager for more. Hungry for it.

Black Jim would notice Justin studying his lips and take it for an invitation. He'd lean forward, wanting the kiss. But no, Justin wouldn't kiss those lips.

He'd punch his face, knocking him back onto the counter. Stunned and surprised by Justin's power, Black Jim would lie helplessly as Justin jumped on top of him. Body to body, he would grab Black Jim's hair in his fists, using it to hold his head down. After that he would bury his face in Black Jim's neck, inhaling deeply. Would the man smell the same as the cloth souvenir, of oil and musk? Justin's breaths quickened.

Black Jim would reach down again, freeing their cocks between them, holding them together as though they were joined there.

Justin's cock flexed in his hand, the pressure building, the hardness straining in his grip.

Black Jim would have the firm grip of a fighter. Justin would increase the pace, his hips arching, grinding, pushing into Black Jim's hands. Black Jim would shout, unable to hold back the tide of absolute lust. In firm control, Justin would bring him to release. He would feel Black Jim coming between them, the hot jets of semen a testament to Justin's dominance and prowess. Justin would look back into those blue eyes, now full of submission and satiation, Jim's hand working Justin's cock with the wet semen slicking him, making his thrusts slide faster and faster….

Justin bit back any kind of sound as he climaxed, catching as much of his come as he could with his free hand, his rapid breathing beginning to slow, his eyes becoming aware of his surroundings in the darkness.

Damn. He needed that. Deserved it, after what his body had been through. The rationale didn't completely alleviate the twinge of guilt, though. This was a forbidden fantasy, one he shouldn't be having.

But the guilt wasn't strong enough to hold back the exciting and impossible thought. One day, maybe….

Chapter 5

JUSTIN PULLED off the freeway at the Racine exit that led to the train station, Charlie barely fitting on his left knee and Ginny in the passenger seat. The rising sun actually made the fields of barbed wire pretty, the points glinting, coiling around like an iron briar patch into the distance. Scenes like this were plentiful around the Great Lakes, particularly in the semipopulated areas. Racine had many raised farms, and the farms required workers. While people out here lived closer to the ground, they at least lived in fenced communities with a level of protection.

Women were even more outnumbered outside of the largest cities.

"Makes me nervous bringing you out here." Justin kept his eyes on the road, unable to see her because his hoodie was pulled so far forward.

"Phht." She had this way of popping air out of her mouth whenever she thought someone was acting foolish. He felt a blast of air on his cheek from Charlie, who was obviously mimicking her. Apparently they both thought he was being stupid.

"It's not cute when you act like the oldest," she said. "Besides, I can shoot straighter than you." He heard her cock the gun but knew she wasn't pointing it at him. "A lot straighter."

Probably wasn't pointing it at him.

"Justin, if you want to worry about me, then worry that I might fall into a puddle facedown, break my arms and legs, and the only way to save myself from drowning would be to drink all the contaminated water. That's ovarian cancer for sure."

"You're definitely staying in the truck."

"Can't shoot a puddle, so fine."

Oncoming traffic thickened, and Justin scooted Charlie forward on his knee. Good thing the kid was small for his age or he might not fit. Justin had makeup on his healing skin, but his injuries were still obvious. The gash on his jaw was open and red in the center, though puckered and healing from the sides. He'd decided a bandage would be too conspicuous, and the hoodie hid most of it. Taking the train would have been too risky. So they had the semi, or as Gin liked to call it, the Fully Erect Penis, because calling it a semi when you delivered condoms wasn't exactly good for business.

They'd told Ray that Gin would be at home with Charlie today, so Justin had picked up the truck early to supposedly catch up on his routes. They could have taken their small family car, but the truck kept him high and less visible to traffic. In the unlikely event someone looked up at him, Charlie on his knee blocked the window on the driver's side, and Gin was the focus on the passenger side. So far no one had paid Justin any mind. He'd just have to make it mostly unseen from the truck into the station where he hoped the meeting would be out of the way. Why the hell had Scarecrow wanted to meet at the train station anyway?

"I just want this to be over," Justin said.

Gin squeezed his leg. "I'm nervous too. Scared as hell, actually." She said it like it was a fact, not an emotion.

She had checked their communication point twice since the Fray. It was at a half-burned house in the central city. Nothing. No cash. No new arrangements. It could be the wrong location. They'd found the communication point only because Gin had kept an eye on Joe. She'd weaseled her way into his complex, into a neighbor's place for a couple nights. Gin knew a lot of people, had even gotten friendly with the doorman—which had come in very useful the night Joe died, but Justin wouldn't think about that night, and didn't want to think about what she had to do to spend any of the other nights there. She said she cashed in a couple favors owed to her, and Justin could usually tell when she was lying. It was one of their twin superpowers or something. Even though she'd been in a good position to follow Joe, maybe he had known she was running surveillance. Maybe he had deliberately led her to the wrong place.

Probably not, though. It was the right house. The people behind Shadow Fray—the Shadow Masters—they didn't deal with Brawlers. They had their own men. Men like Joe. Men like Scarecrow.

Fucking rat bastards.

Closer to the city of Racine, the sky filled with drones. Justin wasn't worried about these drones, though. Racine was barely big enough to have its own drones. No—these would be corporate drones guarding the farms, and they were thick as flies on a corpse. Talk about overkill. A starving Groundling would have to be out of his mind to attempt to steal.

Corporate drones didn't even shoot bullets, but a powerful tase could easily kill someone who wasn't healthy to begin with. It must happen frequently enough for the Corporates to go through all the trouble.

"Whose fields are these?" Justin asked Gin.

"I don't know. Exxon, I think. Why?"

"Maybe we should be more concerned about which company we get our food from."

Gin shrugged. "You know what they say. If it's green, it's clean. And anything is better than powdered bug protein." He glanced at her as she made a face, though decent powder was mostly flavorless. "Why do you suddenly care? Are you worried about the money?"

True, they always went with food that was in season, and whatever was closest was usually the cheapest. Where it came from was never their concern. Dow, Exxon, DuPont—they were all the same. Really, though, he was thinking about Charlie's letter and figuring this shit out so people could actually grow food on the ground again. But who was he kidding? Justin punched stuff. He was no farmer, no scientist. But maybe it was time to start thinking about which company was better, for Charlie's sake.

"Charlie's going to be going to one of those corporate colleges someday. Maybe we should start paying better attention. Do a little research."

Justin glanced down to see Charlie smile at him. Gin reached over to pull Charlie's cap down over his eyes, teasing. "True enough," she said, "but research is your department. You do books, I do people. I'll just put my stamp of approval on whatever you two decide. And remember—I have total veto power. I'm the oldest."

"But I'm commanding officer," Justin said, smiling. "My muscles are bigger."

"My boobs are bigger. They are far more powerful a weapon than your mere muscles."

Charlie snorted, but Justin couldn't hold his own smile long. As the train station came into view, the pleasurable conversational diversion gave way to a sinking feeling in his gut, fanciful dreams replaced by the reality of the world outside the windshield.

They all became silent.

After pulling into the train station, he parked the rig in one of the loading zones. With no air travel, trains were heavily used for passengers as well as goods and produce. Plenty of other trucks were pulling in, pulling out, or parked. Justin tried to tell himself it was good for the place to be busy. He'd be able to blend in more easily.

He left the truck running and took a deep breath. Charlie turned and put his arms around Justin's neck, pressing his forehead and nose against him. So soft. So delicate. It was soothing.

"Thanks, Bro Bro."

He looked at Gin and could see fear only in the clench of her jaw, her eyes showing nothing but resolution and support. "Hold your hood getting out of the truck," she said. "Might be windy."

"Thanks, Gin."

"And remember—no matter what, we can always bail."

He nodded, and with that pushed out from under Charlie, opened the door, and exited the truck. He wouldn't count on being able to bail, not anymore. He was in too deep, had too many views.

He was stuck, so this better go well. It had to.

HALE TOOK a breath, put his game face on, and rapped hard on the door three times.

Jess answered almost immediately, in a red dress and light makeup. She looked remarkably well put together for 7:00 a.m., but then she always did. She and Benz both—him with his suits and her with her dresses. After all this time, he honestly didn't know if it was part of who they were or if they were dressing like Uppers.

"Hi, Hale, come on in."

"Thanks," he said, deciding to take his hands out of his pockets. It was the only formality he could offer. He was wearing jeans with a black T-shirt under his vintage leather jacket. He wasn't going to dress up or anything, but her opinion of him did matter.

"Edna's in the kitchen. If you want eggs and toast, feel free to make yourself some breakfast."

"Maybe some coffee."

"There's that too."

She was making more direct eye contact than usual. Something was up. "Everything okay?" he asked.

"More or less. When Benz came in, he said you've been assigned a new Fray. The order came in last night."

It was strange Benz hadn't given him a heads-up with a text. "Did he say how long?"

"Two weeks."

"And the Arena?"

"He doesn't usually tell me where—the less I know and all that. But he didn't seem concerned or anything."

Hale nodded. He and Benz would talk when Benz woke up. Benz typically didn't get home until sometime after 4:00 a.m. The guy must have been exhausted, maybe had a rough night. This didn't explain the weird vibe Hale was getting from Jess, though. He sensed she had more to say, so he waited.

"He also said something else," she said, shifting her tone.

"Oh?"

"He said they have a place opening up by the club. That building he talked to you about."

"Oh."

"You'd have to move on it quick. I just wanted to let you know."

"Okay. Thanks."

She smiled at him, a closed-mouth smile that he thought showed a measure of sympathy. "Benz will tell you more later. That's all I know. We don't talk too much when he comes home."

"Okay."

"I'll see you, Hale."

She left in a hurry.

Hale just stood there. The excitement he had over seeing his daughter, as he did every Wednesday at this time, was invaded by reality. He saw Eddie plenty, but this was the only day he had her for breakfast and took her to school. If he left the Chixago Building, would he have any more breakfasts? Would he still be able to take her to school and for a span of minutes pretend he was her real father, doing real father things?

Moving was a good thing, though. It's what he wanted. It was better for Eddie. So why did he feel so shitty?

He shrugged it off. The present moment was too precious, and it was no use wasting it feeling bad. He put on a smile as he walked down the hall to the kitchen.

Eddie stared at him, half hiding behind the table with a sly grin on her face.

"You look like the cat that ate the canary, Baby Doll!"

"No! I'm eating eggs, not canaries!" He laughed at how she stretched out the last word.

He walked up and kissed her on the head, through her beautiful blonde hair. "I'd love you even if you did eat canaries for breakfast," he said, sitting down.

"No, Hale. That's so silly." She giggled, again drawing out the "silly."

"How's that tooth?"

"It's still loose, see," she said, opening her mouth to wiggle it.

"Oh gross!" he yelled, putting his hands up in front of his face. "Finish chewing first!"

She thought this was hilarious and started laughing hysterically. A little piece of egg flew out of her mouth in Hale's direction.

"Ah! Now you're attacking me!"

She started the kind of full-body laughing where there's not enough air going in but the laughs keep coming out. Just like that, Hale was laughing too.

Her blue eyes glistened as she fought to gain control of herself. Unable to resist the childlike impulse, Hale flicked the little piece of egg right back at her. It stuck to her cheek.

She snorted, a barrage of soft yellow projectiles flying from her mouth.

Now he'd done it. She truly lost it, and Hale laughed loudly with her. They were probably waking Benz up, but he honestly couldn't control himself. Eddie flopped on the edge of the table with her head on her arm like she couldn't hold herself up any longer. "I can't stop attacking you!" she cried finally, gasping.

Hale got up to grab a towel, dabbed it in her glass of water, and then rubbed her mouth off with it. Just like a real father would do.

As JUSTIN walked into the station, he immediately spotted Scarecrow in the corner off to the left. The shady man embodied every element the word *lurking* brought to mind—black trench coat, hands in the pockets, piercing stare. Justin steadied his nerves by observing, just like he would going into a fight. Scarecrow was taller than Justin remembered, taller than himself. His black-and-gray hair was thicker on the sides, but he was balding on top. The giant brown eyes were the one thing he distinctly remembered, although in his memory from that night they were darker. Scarecrow was old, but he looked hard too. Grizzled. He was leaning back against the wall in a blatantly relaxed pose. As Justin approached, the man straightened.

Scarecrow looked him up and down. "Seems like you're healing pretty well."

No thanks to you, asshole. The words went unsaid as Justin stopped several feet away. "Care to explain that—the sandpaper, or whatever it was?"

"No." Scarecrow's tone was level but authoritative. "It's not my job to explain things to you. It's my job to tell you what to do. It's your job to listen."

Justin nodded, never breaking eye contact. Not for a second.

"What's your name?" the man asked after a pause.

"Justin."

"Justin, call me Vaughn."

No thanks. He'd stick with Scarecrow.

"What happened to your old handler?" Scarecrow asked.

Justin tried to sound casual to avoid any follow-up questions. "He died."

"How?"

Damn.

Justin hesitated. He'd expected this, but when he said it in his head, it never came out smoothly. He returned his gaze to Scarecrow—and shit, when had he broken eye contact? "I killed him," he said, trying to reveal no emotion in his voice.

"Murdered your handler, eh?" Scarecrow laughed. "I guess I better watch my back with you, Justin." But in no way did this man look scared. In his eyes he looked amused.

"It wasn't like that," Justin said.

"What was it like, then?"

"He went crazy. He was sick."

"Ground sickness?"

Justin kept his gaze steady and nodded. "He became delirious. Paranoid. He wasn't making any sense. He was in a lot of pain. His body was wasting away. I don't know for sure what was wrong with him but probably ground sickness in the brain."

"Why didn't you find him a doctor?"

"Not my job."

"The pills always help, at least for a while."

He needed this line of questioning to be over. "Maybe he couldn't afford them. I don't know. He was my handler, not my friend."

"So you killed him."

No. Gin did. But without hesitation, Justin said the rehearsed words. "He was becoming a danger to other people. In the end he couldn't take care of himself. I put a pillow over his face. Drugs and liquor—he passed out and never woke up."

"So you're a killer. Can't say I mind. In fact, I think it's to your advantage."

Even though Scarecrow seemed to believe him, Justin's body went all tingly, like every part of him was falling asleep, starved of blood.

"The games are changing, Justin. And I think they might be perfect for you."

"I don't...." He wanted to say *I don't kill people*, but stopped himself. He couldn't show weakness, and proclaiming his limits wasn't going to accomplish anything. Besides, hadn't he just told Scarecrow the opposite? The lie was important, for Gin's sake. No one could know she was involved. "I don't understand," he finished.

"The grit that sliced your face wasn't my idea. It was in the instructions. Do you know what else was in the instructions? I was supposed to take you on all along, at least if you survived in any sort of shape to continue in Shadow Fray." His tone was so casual it was unnerving. "For the most part, you came through with flying colors."

"So they knew—?"

"About Joe, your dead handler? Of course they knew," he said in a tone where the *dumbass* was implied.

"Joe. You said his name. You knew him?"

"'Course I knew him. Can't say I liked him or that I'm sorry he's dead. Ain't no one sorry about that." Scarecrow raised an eyebrow, his large eyes looking at Justin appraisingly. "You know what they don't know, though? They don't know you did it. I think that will stay our little secret." Scarecrow winked.

Who are *they*? Justin wanted to ask, but he didn't dare. "So it was they, uh, them, that told you to kill... to cut his throat."

Scarecrow laughed. "Oh no. I was to take only the winner, but the grand finale was my idea. And what a damn good one. You've seen the hits? That's all money, baby."

Justin nodded. "About that...."

"Yeah, about that," Scarecrow imitated. He reached into his pocket and pulled out a wad of cash, glancing around the station as he handed it to Justin.

Justin wanted to count it. Paused, then thought better of it, but it didn't go unnoticed.

"Don't count it, fuckwad. Not here. It's the same you got for the last Fray with Joe."

"The same," Justin said, voice flat.

"That's right. The same. Because all those hits, all that dough? That's because of me. Not you. Me. Because I slit a kid's throat after you beat him to a bloody pulp." He got in Justin's face as he spoke. "After this, though, you do right by me, and you'll get a square cut. We split fifty-fifty. But you do what you're told, no questions asked."

Justin had no response. No nod. No words. Scarecrow's breath smelled of mildew. Justin clenched his jaw, silently grinding his teeth together.

"Your next Fray is in two weeks," Scarecrow said, backing up a step and once again taking a casual tone. "The Basilica of St. Josaphat, south side of Milwaukee. You know it?"

"Two weeks," Justin said. "That's...." Too soon. It was too soon.

"Here's the info, direct from the source." Scarecrow passed him a small slip of paper. Justin took a breath to steady himself, making sure his hand didn't shake before he reached out to grab it. He slid it in the pocket with the cash.

"There's something else too," Scarecrow said, reaching once again into his trench coat. "They want you to use a ringer. They want you to use these."

Scarecrow handed him a pair of black leather gloves. Not full gloves—his fingers would be free. Gloves like these were common in Shadow Fray, though the leather was rarely genuine.

Scarecrow glanced around the station again. "Go ahead, put 'em on."

Justin slid them on as Scarecrow kept his eyes on their surroundings. Justin's back was to the rest of the station, but he kept his hands in as a precaution, shielding them with his body.

"Now flex. Make a fist."

Justin did. Four small metal claws revealed themselves on his knuckles, peeking out from the leather only when he was making a full hard fist, and only on the right hand. The fact that they were only a quarter of an inch long did not make him feel better about this.

Scarecrow looked at him sideways. "Don't pussy out on me, killer. You look like you're gonna cry." Justin forced himself to stop looking at the claws and make eye contact with the man in front of him. "Don't worry so much. They aren't gonna kill him. Just hurt him a little bit."

"They want this next guy out, then?"

"Not necessarily. But the bar has been raised, and you're gonna command attention. Gotta give 'em something good to watch." Scarecrow's smile revealed yellow-stained teeth. "Now this is important. When the other handler checks you before the fight, clench your left fist, leave your right one flat. The left fist is the decoy. Understand?"

Justin nodded. He removed the gloves and stuffed them in the pocket of his hoodie. He and Scarecrow stared at each other for a moment. "Is that all?" Justin asked when the silence grew too long.

"Give 'em something good to watch, killer." With that, Scarecrow began walking toward the trains.

Justin stood there a moment. A bead of sweat dripped down the back of his neck under his hood. Except he wasn't hot. His hands were cold. He stuck them in his pockets but felt the gloves and stopped.

He didn't sign up for weapons, or for this level of violence. But he was stuck—and now everyone would be watching.

Chapter 6

UNABLE TO take the isolating blackness any longer, Hale opened his eyes.

He lay on his bed, staring up at the ceiling. Why wasn't he sleeping? It wasn't like there was noise keeping him awake. He hadn't even heard a person yet, but it was only his first night here. The move had happened fast, in just a matter of days, but that was for the best. He hadn't had time to change his mind.

The place was nice enough, he supposed. Clean. His bed was in the main living area, having set up the bedroom as a kind of gym with his weights and a punching bag. He hadn't used the bag yet, though he wanted to. It was like a craving. The activity was what he needed to let out some frustration so he could fall asleep, but he wanted to make good and sure the noise wouldn't carry. The middle of the night wasn't the best time to put it to the test.

Hale looked across the dark room to his Harley Iron. It wasn't big or flashy, but it was his baby. It had cost a small fortune. The complex didn't have a garage, but he didn't mind having it in the room. In fact, he kind of liked it. Maybe he should get up and ride. Drive a couple hours north in the middle of the night. Check out the Arena in Milwaukee for the Fray that was just over a week away. The church might be locked up, but he could peek in a couple windows. Maybe he could plan out a strategy. He could use an advantage, because he sure felt off his game.

He needed to work out. He missed the gym.

But if he were being honest with himself, it wasn't the gym he was missing. It was Eddie.

He wanted to fill that emptiness with a drink, or the sharp chemical smoke of a hit. Maybe some of those little blue pills to take the edge off this feeling. It didn't help knowing all he had to do is go up a few floors and he'd be able to find whatever he wanted. So easy.

Instead he closed his eyes. Benz had taught him a trick that helped when he had these cravings. Hale took himself out of the moment and imagined what it would be like if he did have a drink. If he did have a hit. And it was weeks or years from now.

He pictured himself losing a Fray, his body no longer able to maintain its high level of performance. His eyes swollen shut, nose broken. Missing teeth. He pictured Jess's eyes on him, disapproving. She'd be fearful and disgusted enough to keep Eddie away from him. He pictured Benz having to pick him up off the floor as he sat in his own vomit or piss. Benz taking him to the bathroom and cleaning him up like he was a baby. He pictured Eddie with a mouth full of big-kid teeth and a beautiful smile he would never get to see.

No high was worth missing that.

Relief from this single moment of loneliness wasn't worth trading down for a lifetime of regret. Because that's what it came down to, didn't it? He was fucking lonely.

But perhaps there was a different fix for that.

Benz might not like it, though. "Don't do that stuff in my backyard," he remembered Benz saying. But maybe Benz wouldn't mind, not if he knew how hard up Hale was right now. Hale threw the sheet off his naked body and got out of bed. He grabbed his jeans from the floor and walked over to the window, where he put them on.

He was on the sixth floor, and from the window he looked across the street to Excalibur, a forty-story playhouse for the rich and the superrich. Uppers. Business deals, dining, shopping, pool, gym, spa, but mostly a lot of games for throwing money away. He glanced down below the neon sign and saw Benz. The front man. The man everyone needed to see before they got in. He saw a man speak in Benz's ear, and Benz pointed across the street to Hale's building, officially called "The Lady of the Lake," but everyone referred to it as "The Lady."

It was really an extension of Excalibur for the less official side of business, which meant alcohol that flowed a little more freely, drugs that were overpriced, and whores that were clean. Probably. The apartments came in handy for the people who worked there but also served as a cover that allowed the police to look the other way. It was a residential building, after all, one even the police would visit when not wearing a uniform. Chicago's finest needed a place to blow off some steam.

Hale understood the need. He pulled on a black T-shirt, stepped into his boots, and left before he could change his mind.

The building had a functioning elevator, but he decided to take the stairs. He'd been avoiding the rest of the building and had yet to see anything of the upper floors.

He went to the top, where he exited on ten and walked right into a bar. The walls were painted black, the bar accented with red velvet chairs. The lighting came from behind red sconces. Red velvet couches bordered the bar. In the couch nearest him, a lady in a flowing dress reclined, reminding him of a goddess. She was tall and slender, and one of her long hands was on the thigh of the man sitting next to her. The man had been wearing a suit, but the jacket and tie were draped over the back of the couch. The bar was long and had few empty seats. Music played from speakers he couldn't see.

The bartender gave him a strange glance, as though recognizing that Hale was out of place. Hale didn't spend much time looking around, and as he walked past, he pointedly did not look at the bar or bartender. To his left, opposite the bar, were rooms with black-painted doors outlined in red borders. All the doors were closed, but he could smell the very pungent odor of pot, and behind it the more soothing and spicy aroma of opium. It looked like people could sit at the bar until a room opened up and then go inside to sample and purchase a product. This wasn't what he came for, though.

Past the bar, he approached the opposite stairwell. In his periphery he saw someone flag him to stop, but he didn't feel like answering any questions, so he kept walking through the exit like he knew where he was going. He went down the next set of stairs, relieved that the door he'd come through didn't open. No one was following him.

Walking onto the ninth floor, he saw that while the décor was the same, the floor had a very different layout. Where the bar had been were more rooms. Gone was the music, and as he walked down the hall, he could hear grunting behind one door. Past another door, he heard moaning. Down the hall a man opened a door and walked out, never glancing back. His jacket was over his arm and he was using one hand to close the last button under his collar.

Jacket. Collar. Well shit. Hale didn't get embarrassed, but he was supremely underdressed, wasn't he? No wonder he'd gotten strange looks up above.

A brighter light suddenly illuminated him from the front, making him feel like he'd been caught. But that wasn't it. He blinked. Ahead of him another door had opened, casting a whiter brightness into the darker red-lit hall.

He was drawn toward the light like a moth to a flame. He didn't care one lick if he got burned. Hell, he could use the warmth.

He slowed and stopped as he walked by the doorway. Inside on a couch facing the door sat a woman. She had a flowing robe that was nearly sheer. She didn't see him. She sat rubbing lotion on her long legs. Her skin was a dark ebony, her hair coiled high on her head in braids. Her legs glistened in the white lamplight, and her breasts dipped down as she bent over, showing a perfect line of cleavage.

As she rose up to a full sitting position, her movement fluid and graceful, she looked at Hale.

In her hand was an AMT .380 caliber semiautomatic pistol.

Her large brown eyes studied Hale's face. After a moment she spoke.

"Honey, I don't like surprises."

Hale smiled and put his hands up. "Maybe you'll like this one."

She raised her chin, squinting her eyes slightly. "Where'd you come from?" She didn't sound the least bit intimidated if he had surprised her. Her voice was feminine but deep, her tone curious and playful.

"I came from downstairs. Couldn't sleep."

She slid the gun back under the couch cushion from where she'd so expertly raised it.

"You're him, aren't you? The new guy. Benz's brother."

"Not by blood."

"Does that make a difference?"

"Only if it does to you."

"What I'm saying is will he care that you're here?"

Hale shrugged.

"Sure, honey. That's what I thought."

Just then the door at the end of the hall opened. A suited man, hefty and very much out of breath, walked quickly in his direction. He had a firearm at his hip but hadn't drawn it yet. His words were pointed. "Sir, you can't be here."

"Sure I can. I live here," Hale drawled.

"It's all right, Raul," she said, leaning forward to be heard into the hall. "I got this one."

Raul slowed his quick pace, appearing grateful that he didn't have to hurry.

"Step inside, honey, before we really get an audience."

Hale smiled at Raul, who was still coming toward him. He stepped inside the apartment and closed the door just as Raul neared.

An abrupt knock immediately followed. "You sure you're all right?"

"I'm peachy, but thanks for checking, Raul. You always got my back."

Hale could hear the muttered "asshole" from the other side of the door, and he was pretty sure Raul wasn't talking about the lady in front of him.

She reached up and flipped a switch on the wall. It looked like a light switch.

"Now, that means I'm busy, so we shouldn't be disturbed, but it also means you just started paying. Come sit down by me, honey," she said, patting the couch beside her. She didn't move over, even though she was sitting in the middle.

As Hale sat, he could smell incense, or perhaps opium, but it was overpowered by the smell of cocoa butter the woman had been rubbing on her legs.

She produced a card, holding it up between two long fingers, the nails painted red like the velvet accents in the room. "Next time call first if you don't want to go downstairs to the visitors' entrance. I'll come to you. That way you'll be safe from prying eyes."

Hale took the card from her and leaned forward to put it in his back pocket. As he did, he could feel the warmth of her exhale. Her breath smelled faintly of citrus, which was very rare in this region.

"You're not gonna look at it?" she breathed.

"I thought I'd ask your name the old-fashioned way," Hale whispered in her ear.

"Of course Benz's brother would be a real gentleman." She traced her hand along his arm. "You can call me Wilma."

That was an odd name and one Hale didn't immediately find sexy. He cast the thought aside. "Pleased to meet you, Wilma," he said, raising her hand and kissing it. He usually was nothing close to this chivalrous, but she was beautiful. Maybe this would be a long-standing relationship, one Benz didn't have to know about if she didn't decide to tell him.

"It's on account of my hair, see? Like the lady in the old cartoons."

Hale noticed she had streaks of red braided into her hair. He didn't watch television shows, though, so he had no idea who she was talking about. But no matter. He leaned forward to kiss her softly.

Her lips were like velvet. It felt like years since he'd kissed someone. Was it? It was after Janie, for sure, but part of a drug-fueled fuck-a-thon he didn't care to remember. He wasn't sure why he kissed her now, except he found Wilma charming. In a way, she sounded like any whore, but for some reason her *honey*s and *darlin'*s (and no doubt he'd soon get some *sugar*s) rang true. He could almost believe she was attracted to him.

"God, I hope you have a dick," he said. His tastes had been fairly singular for quite a while, and Benz had said women worked here.

She laughed, throwing her head back and opening her mouth to show big pearly teeth. She certainly was high class. He wasn't used to this.

"But of course, sugar!" she said.

Hale smiled genuinely. "Uni or trans?"

"Baby, I was born this way… more or less, anyhow. Now, what's your pleasure?" she asked, sitting with her legs crossed.

"I want you to get down on your knees and suck me hard. I want your dress open on top so I get flashes of those gorgeous breasts and your dark nipples. Then I want you to stand up, turn around, and face the wall. Drop the dress. Drop it slowly. And then I want to take you from behind."

"Can I touch myself when you're fucking me?" Hale assumed she meant the male part of her.

"No. That's my job."

She looked surprised at that. Could be most of her clients didn't like that part of her. If her voice was any indication, she went from surprised to very pleased, as she practically purred her next words. "Why do I get the feeling you're the wrong man saying all the right things?" She ran a finger down his chest, toward his jeans. "I haven't come all day, you see. I like to wait for the right man, and the right man is always the last one of the night. But you, you're not the right man at all. You're different. Just showed up at my door. And I really shouldn't be doing this." She smiled. With the lamplight behind her, her eyes were nearly black.

"You and me both," Hale said, placing a hand on her cheek and leaning back, signaling that she could get on the floor. Relaxing, he closed his eyes. It would be better to watch, to know someone was there in front of him. And yet….

Despite all her charm, Wilma had never even asked him his name.

He left his eyes closed. He should get used to the blackness.

Chapter 7

JUSTIN OFTEN worked out first thing in the morning, but not like this. Walking up fourteen flights of stairs, from their unit to the twenty-eighth floor, it became obvious that he wasn't in peak condition. He hadn't been swimming since the Fray; going into lake water wasn't especially wise when one had open wounds. In fact, he likely wouldn't be swimming any more this year. In a month the water would be far too cold.

Charlie was handling the stairs fine. Maybe smaller legs and a lower center of gravity were good for stairs—or just the fact that he was a kid. Char was so small and skinny he could practically have flown up given a feather.

Once at the top, they opened the stairwell door and walked all the way down the long hall, past all of the doors, to the end. The prime penthouse suite in the Lakeside Condominiums, where Gristopher Mays lived.

Charlie knocked on the door, having run ahead of Justin. What was it that compelled kids to run down long hallways? And who would run after fourteen flights of stairs?

Justin caught up as Charlie waited. Inside they could hear noises. A dull metallic bang, footsteps, the hum of voices. Justin considered knocking again as Charlie looked up at him anxiously, but eventually they could hear someone walking toward the door.

Devin, a light-skinned black man with meticulously close-shaved hair, answered the door. Immediately, Justin caught the rank smell of shit. Faint, but unmistakable.

Devin smiled at them with genuine delight, though their timing was clearly not the best. "Justin. And Charlie! Come in, come in."

"Are you sure? We can come back another time."

"Yes, I'm very sure. He insists you stay. It's been too long. He's…." Devin turned to glance down the hall, and when he looked back, his sincere brown eyes were apologetic. "We're cleaning up a little accident. If you'll wait here a few minutes, I'll get you when he's ready." The tall man then bent down to Charlie. "It's especially good to see you, Charlie. We were worried about you. Give me a hug."

Charlie readily went into his arms, and the man gave him a deep embrace, holding him close. "It's so good to see you, kid." Devin seemed sincere, and it was a long moment before he let go. "I wanted to come down, you know, but I thought it best to give you some privacy. I hope that was the right decision." As he rose, he took a good look at Justin's face and frowned. "The nurse quit rather suddenly this morning, and I'm not so good at this, so it'll be a minute."

"I can help," Justin offered.

"No, no. He would be mortified. It's bad enough I'm doing it. Just have a seat in the living room. I'll get you when we're ready."

He hurried off as Justin and Charlie sat on the couch facing the large windows and the expansive view looking out onto the lake. The bright morning sun was low on the horizon, and the light shone directly into the unit, almost blinding in its intensity. Behind them a door opened and closed, and Justin heard muffled voices before music started playing through the unit. Otis Redding. Nice. Justin always liked Mr. Mays's taste in music. New music was not popular; most people preferred music from before the Thinning.

Mr. Mays liked the really old music. Justin remembered sitting with him as a child, and their eyes would both be closed, listening to whatever Mr. Mays wanted him to hear. Justin would peek every once in a while to make sure Mr. Mays's eyes were closed, and Mr. Mays would do the same. Occasionally they'd both peek at the same time and have a laugh about it. They wouldn't talk. Just listen. That was one of the things Justin liked best about Mr. Mays: they could be in each other's company, and silence was okay.

Justin put his arm around Charlie, leaned back, and closed his eyes. He loved the music, but the lyrics to "Just One More Day" were almost too much. The notes, that voice—it resonated in his chest, cut to his heart. He swallowed, with effort. At ninety-one, Gristopher Mays wouldn't be around much longer. Justin wanted more time, time to learn to finally call him "Griz" to his face. Gin always had, but he found himself unable to break from the "Mr. Mays" that he'd called him consistently as a child, though everyone else referred to him as Griz. Justin was caught somewhere between child and adult. Mr. Mays was his authority figure and mentor; Griz was his friend.

Six more songs passed before Devin told them they could come in to see Griz. By this time the washing machine was running and the unit smelled like bleach.

Paraffin candles lent a warmth to Mr. Mays's room, and walking in felt like coming home. The rest of the unit was changed and not what Justin remembered as a kid, but Griz's bedroom had pictures of his family, black-and-white shots of his favorite singers, and colorful music album reproductions. Wall space was at a minimum, and the room was cluttered but comfy. The items in this bedroom had previously hung on all the walls in the suite before Mr. Mays moved to Denver seven years ago. He'd just come back this year. He wanted to die where he felt at home, surrounded by the things he loved.

Devin sat down in a wooden chair in the far corner, using a phone to turn down the music. He'd come with Griz from Denver, and Justin wouldn't call him a friend yet. He didn't look forty, and Justin wasn't sure if he was Griz's true blood grandson or not. Family lines were often tangled and didn't always follow blood. Griz had said many times that his second cousin was Justin and Gin's blood granddad, and they were all family. Justin doubted that was true, though their mama had said they definitely had African-American heritage in their bloodline. In the end it didn't matter if genes were involved or not; Griz was family.

Griz lay in his bed, the covers up to his chest and his thin veined hands at his sides. It was a hospital bed, so he was propped up. He had an IV connected to the back of one hand. Justin had seen the saline bags in the room before, but never attached. Perhaps Griz was suffering from diarrhea or dehydration. Mr. Mays's dark skin was covered in white stubble from his chin to the top of his head. His brown eyes were determined. Actually he looked pissed.

Justin sat down on the small futon along the wall, but Charlie walked right up and kissed Griz lightly on the cheek. Then he walked down and grabbed his hand with both of his small ones, hooking around a couple fingers. Charlie blinked and smiled up at Griz brightly. The joy on his face was more powerful than any spoken hello and softened Griz's expression.

"Hi, Mr. Mays," said Justin, the greeting feeling very impersonal in comparison.

Griz looked skeptically at Charlie. "You don't look none too sick to me, Charlie boy." Griz's voice was dry and not as deep as usual, but it was still strong. "Not nearly as sick as your brother over there."

Charlie smiled and shrugged, his expression saying, "Yeah, that's about right. Funny, huh?" The little traitor.

They all three turned to look at Justin, but only Griz spoke. "Nice face, Just."

Justin felt himself getting hot. He gave Charlie a glare, but Charlie didn't waver.

"Whatchu mean-muggin' Charlie for?" Griz scolded. Had Justin really been looking forward to this visit? "Simmer down now. We need to talk. For real. I don't know how much time I got left, and things look pretty serious from where I'm layin'."

Justin wanted to hide under his hoodie. His face wasn't *that* bad. Well, it didn't hurt anymore, anyway, and at least it was scabbed over. Justin raised his chin determinedly. "Yes, sir."

Griz's eyes lost some of their hardness. Charlie looked at Justin hopefully, and Devin started staring at the floor.

"Don't worry none," Griz added. "When I say talk, I mean you just have to listen." Justin nodded, and Griz took a deep breath. "I was three years old when the world really started goin' to shit, so I don't remember nothin' except what we have here. Even in my earliest memories, the virus that started killing people had already seeped into the ground. Not many people get to be as old as me, and the ones that do, well, they've done plenty in their life to make it this far, plenty they ain't proud of. So I ain't judgin' you none. Not at all." As he talked, the power behind his voice remained strong, but he started growing hoarse. "I'm proud of you, son. Always have been. And your sister and Charlie too. I wish Devin here had a bit more of your blood than mine."

Devin didn't glance up, but Justin could see his frown.

"I know a whole lot more than you think I do," Griz said, meeting his eyes. "A whole lot more than I ever let on." Griz paused, taking a few breaths. Regrouping.

When he continued, there was a distinct sadness to his voice. "I had to go to Denver. Things weren't safe for me here anymore. The only reason I came back was because the folks that wanted me finally decided it was crueler to let me suffer by allowing me to live. I paid a price so I could come back here. Come home. I always had friends here, though. I always had eyes on you. I wish I coulda made it easier for you, but I did what I could."

"I know, Mr. Mays," Justin said. He and Gin and Charlie had a lot to be thankful for. For the unit fees Griz had paid for two years after their mother died. For getting Ray to give Gin and him a job. For getting Charlie into the Catholic school down the street. But he simply said, "Thanks."

"Some say I'm lucky to have such a big family. And I feel it. But I'm only one man, and nothin's been harder than some of the choices I've had to make. With a big family, you can't help everyone." His eyes glistened. "With a big family, you have to do some stuff. But I know you know how that goes."

Justin was calm. All along, his whole life maybe, Griz had known more than he let on. Justin hadn't given it much thought before. Whether he had been in denial until now, or just preoccupied, he wasn't sure. He had never asked Mr. Mays for help, but he had taken the help he could get. Justin didn't have friends—except for Griz. So it made sense his one friend saw more than Justin thought he did.

"So you know about Shadow Fray," Justin said finally. He glanced nervously at Devin, who met his eyes briefly before returning his gaze to the floor. He supposed if Griz trusted him, he would try to as well.

Griz nodded. "I know more than that. I know about what Gin's had to do. I know about the man she killed. I know more than I can say." He paused, his eyes watering. "I know more than to tell you to get out, because you can't get out no more, but I'm thinkin' you know that. There's big money on those fights, and when they look at you, they see dollar signs, and you're not out until they bleed you dry. I can't tell you what to do, because I don't know. I'll just… I'll do what I can. And you'll be smart. Careful. I needed to tell you. You can do this, Just."

It would be appropriate to match his friend's emotion, to have a tear drop down his cheek, or at the very least be concerned that someone knew his secrets. But in place of emotion were the simple facts. He had a job to do. He would do it. They would survive.

"Where is Gin, anyway?" Griz asked.

"She's with friends."

"Good for her. You send her up to talk to me, first chance you get."

"I will."

"I'm almost done talkin' now. Just a few things left to say. Just gotta give me a minute to remember what they are…."

Griz closed his eyes. Justin thought he might be asleep until he spoke again abruptly, eyes still closed. "Devin, here… I know you don't trust folk easy, and that's all right. But when I'm gone, Devin will be here. If he decides it's safe, he'll bring his family here. You can trust Devin, Just." Justin looked at Devin, who returned his gaze and nodded briefly before looking away.

"I feel like there was something else too, but I've forgotten…."

Charlie patted Griz's hand reassuringly. The gesture seemed to shake the memory loose, and Griz's eyes shot open, alert. "It's Gin and Charlie. You feel like you have to protect them. And you do. But remember too, they have to protect you. You gotta mind them."

The different ways "mind them" could be interpreted set Justin's mind spinning. Once again he started to get uncomfortable, like this talk about his brother and sister was more personal than any of the secrets he thought he had been hiding.

"And this one here," Griz said, smiling at Charlie. "You gotta remember that I was there when Charlie was born. I knew your mama, loved her even. And I know Charlie."

Justin's gut dropped. Where was this going? Because there were some things he didn't want to think about right now, not with everything else going on.

Griz reached to Charlie with both arms, pulling him closer but looking at Justin as Charlie hugged him.

"You done your best with Charlie. I don't question none of your choices, not at all. I know you promised your mama. All I ask is you remember that as people get older, they change. Charlie's changin' and changin' fast. And maybe you don't see it. All I ask is that you be open to it. You let Charlie be who Charlie's gotta be. That's all."

Justin nodded as fear crept in like something solid from the sides of the room.

"Now," Griz breathed, sounding much relieved and releasing Charlie. "Go sit by your brother, Char, and let's listen to a little music. I know you might have more questions, but I'm tired. Not feelin' so well today. I got out the stuff in my head, and the rest will have to wait for another time, God willing. You all can go once I fall asleep. It's nice to be in some company. Real nice."

Devin turned up the music once again, and Charlie snuggled into Justin's side. Comforting. Sam Cooke sang "Bring It on Home to Me."

Justin tried to relax and leaned back, closing his eyes. His heart was drumming.

Let Charlie be who Charlie's gotta be. He didn't like to think about Charlie's secrets, but Justin would keep them to his grave, keep his promise to his mama. And the best way to do that was to keep on like he always had. Best not to think about it. That's what kept trouble away….

He kept Charlie tucked close with a protective arm. Justin emptied his mind as best he could and tried to let himself get carried away by the music.

Chapter 8

Hale hated churches, and this one was awful nice, which made him hate it more.

Walking into the Basilica of St. Josaphat, he'd scoffed at the two marble angels holding the bowls of holy water. He'd wanted to spit in them. Come the dark of Wednesday when it wasn't packed with people, he promised himself it was the first thing he was gonna do. If the church would sell those pretty angels, they could feed all the meth heads in this atrocious city for a month. Come to think of it, meth heads didn't eat much, so it'd probably feed them for six.

When he sat down, he'd looked up and cursed the holy God in heaven—the one painted right there on the dome well over a hundred feet up. He could tell from the outside the church was big, but he didn't expect the inside to look like a damn palace. The outside was gray stone, but the inside may as well have been layered in gold. Much of it actually was. All these domes and arches, murals and curlicues. Gold crosses, gold leaf—the whole thing glowed with excess.

Sitting here now, he didn't know why people filled a church that looked so pretty when half of them were probably hungry. It was like putting a steak outside the cage of a starving dog, just so it could smell the meat.

Hale glanced at Benz, sitting in the wooden pew next to him. Benz's head was facing the priest like he was listening, but his eyes were looking everywhere else. Good thing someone was getting the lay of the land, because Hale couldn't think straight. Benz met Hale's glance and gave him a slight nod. Hale nodded back.

Benz knew him well, knew churches made him crazy and brought out the worst in him. Mostly they didn't talk about why—hadn't in years. When it came to Hale's history, there were only a few painful specifics he left out. Benz had never pressed, but the man could probably fill in the blanks. Most of them anyway.

Hale's own church—practically his home—hadn't been near this nice. That simple country church was far, far away from here. He'd grown up living on the land, such as it was. Nothing much grew in the poisoned ground, or maybe because they were deep under the dark shadow of the Bible, which was another poison entirely—and perhaps a far worse one. The same good Christian people day in and day out, their numbers dwindling over time. They thought God was gonna save them. Things changed as their settlement's situation got bleaker. They wouldn't be saved, but if they met their end, it would be God's will.

Then a funny thing happened. People took greater notice that Hale had three older sisters, none of whom were getting pregnant. Yet three girls was so unusual, all signs pointed to Hale's family being blessed. Maybe it was in their genes. Maybe it was in Hale's genes. When faced with dying out, those good church-going people suddenly said it was God's will for Hale to procreate with his own sisters. Considering Hale's daddy was the preacher, the Father's will and his father's will were often indistinguishable.

So right before Hale walked out on them, he beat his father to a bloody pulp. He clenched his fist, remembering how his father's blood had stained his knuckles, how he hadn't washed his hands for days. He'd never had a more satisfying fight in all his life.

Hale glanced around the church, keeping his eyes off the priest. Some of the people around him were skinny, dirty, and desperate-looking, some looking like they were making a decent time of it, but none as well off as the paying customers up in the balcony. Isn't that how it always was? The Catholic Church wasn't even the worst of them, not by a long shot.

The people around him were fools. Hale couldn't wait to fuck this place up.

JUSTIN LOVED churches. When he was younger, he used to dream of living in one. That was one of the things he loved about Milwaukee. Looking out from their rise at home, he could see the church steeples peeking up for miles around, their crosses on top marking them like an X on a treasure map. Even in the burned-out parts of town, the churches remained, their stone walls standing like they'd been blessed by God Himself.

He didn't put much stock in any of the words he was hearing per say, but the building sure was magnificent. The Catholic church a few blocks from their rise was nowhere near this ornate. They didn't go to a mass often; they just used the school for Charlie. The nuns accepted Charlie and kept the other kids from bothering him, especially Sister Tim. Justin would have to thank her for sharing Charlie's letter. Anyway, the Catholic Church seemed to do right by Charlie, and that was all that really mattered. There was truth in this religion, and beauty. It was going to be a shame to have to mess this place up. He hoped they wouldn't break anything too important, but come Wednesday that couldn't be his concern.

He felt out of place sitting up in the balcony, but since he was with Mr. Mays, he'd been ushered right up along with Devin, Ginny, and Charlie. They'd had to carry Griz up in his wheelchair, and Justin was going to suggest sitting down below, but this gave him a better vantage point to scope the place out. That wasn't typically something that could be done before a Fray.

He tried to get a strategy while he was there, but it was hard for him to focus. He made a mental map of the pillars. How could he use the pews? Which area would be the most advantageous for him? The front was the most open. Safest. But there were plenty of obstacles. He'd have to watch the metal candleholders.

That all had been thought out in five minutes. The problem now was that Jesus wouldn't stop staring at him. Jesus was on the wall wearing a crown of thorns, the blood running down his face. Funny how the blood didn't run into his eyes, because in Justin's experience that was the first place it always seemed to go. Maybe with blood in his eyes, Jesus wouldn't keep looking at him.

Every time Justin felt the eyes of Jesus, his thoughts went back to that glove.

It was playing dirty, using that glove. It gave him an unfair advantage. But that was life, right? All the people around him up there in the balcony had been born with an unfair advantage. Uppers. They wore the golden glove. They got the best doctors. The cleanest food. The most extensive fertility treatments. They got the places off the ground and the longer lives that went with them.

Besides, who was to say his opponent wouldn't have an advantage of his or her own? Justin had four quarter-inch pieces of metal. One inch total. Maybe the other Brawler would have a boot with a three-inch blade. He hoped he could trust Scarecrow to find it, whatever it was.

He couldn't help picturing what that glove could do to a person. Not kill, but it would certainly mark and draw blood. Or would it sever veins and arteries? He'd be the crucifier. If he didn't kill his opponent, he'd leave scars that could end their career. It was pretty much the same thing.

What if his opponent was someone like him, with a brother and sister, a son, or even a daughter?

But he had no choice, right? Griz said he couldn't get out.

And how did Griz know it was Ginny who killed Joe? Justin had been so overwhelmed, he hadn't even asked about that particular revelation. Scarecrow didn't know the truth, but who else might? Who the hell were these people running the show, these Shadow Masters?

He tried to tell himself it didn't matter. None of it mattered. All that mattered was winning this Fray, in this Arena.

Chapter 9

JUSTIN HELD Charlie's hand tightly. The air was cool but dry, new sunlight brightening the street. The sky was nearly white, caught in the transition between the golden hues of sunrise and the blue sky of day. A blank slate. Anything was possible.

The six-block walk to St. Hedwig's where Charlie went to school was relatively safe this time of day. Justin loved the morning walks, and he tried to love it today, making every effort to be in the here and now. He didn't want to be all doom and gloom, but he tended to take these moments more seriously before a Fray.

So just enjoy the walk. Don't think about the Fray tonight. Most of all don't think about the glove.

Charlie squeezed his hand, and Justin looked down at him. The kid clearly knew the Fray was on Justin's mind. His blue eyes showed concern—but they also sparkled with hope. Charlie believed in him. Looking into those eyes, he could almost forget about everything else.

"I know," Justin said. "It's hard for me not to overthink. But you're right. I'll win tonight."

Charlie nodded once and then swung Justin's hand playfully as they walked.

He better win. Thankfully, Justin had a little cushion in his record, so even if he dropped down to two and two, he'd still get another Fray eventually. Probably. With the number of views the last one got—

Charlie tugged on his hand.

"Sorry! Sorry," Justin said. He smiled down at Charlie apologetically. "No more thinking for the rest of the walk. I'm here with you." Charlie squeezed his hand in agreement.

Justin looked around the deserted street, taking in the sights. This area had once been a business district, but none of the buildings were high enough for residences or businesses today. Instead they'd been cleared out and fitted with cell phone and Internet receptors, solar panels, and rooftop gardens. This time of year, the gardens were empty, their meager harvests long since collected.

Electrified barbed wire enclosed some of the rooftops, though with no crops to guard the current would be cut. The protected gardens were owned by various residents in the rises along the lake. Justin could never afford a garden, but several people in the Lakeside Condominiums building owned plots. Truth be told, it almost wasn't worth it. These gardens got scavenged frequently, despite best efforts to keep Groundlings out. That's why most of the rooftop gardens were managed by the nuns of St. Hedwig's. It was charity work. The only reason these other gardens lasted to harvest before being scavenged was that each plot was adopted by a group of Groundlings who'd stand guard over it in exchange for produce.

The nuns also got a level of respect that Uppers didn't. That probably helped.

Justin's thoughts were broken by a loud hacking cough nearby. Charlie pulled on his hand to get him to stop and tugged again. Justin understood the signal, though part of him wanted to keep walking.

"You okay, Levi?" he called loudly, his volume just shy of a shout.

There were no windows in the nearby building, which honestly looked like it might fall over any day now. The angled roof had been removed to accommodate a garden, overseen by a shiny government-installed communications antenna, which looked severely out of place on the old, crumbling building. The walls and ceiling had been reinforced by the man living inside, and new timber supported the corners as well as the center. Levi sat up, his head and shoulders poking above the large space where the front window used to be.

"Fine, fine," Levi said between coughs. Of all the Groundlings on the street, Levi had lasted the longest. Almost eight years now, but from the looks of him, he wasn't going to last much longer. He'd held a job for much of those eight years, forced onto the street to pay for the meds that kept him alive. Meds he couldn't afford anymore now that he couldn't work.

As Levi turned to face them, Justin could tell from the bloodshot eyes that he had been using. Normally drugs made his skin crawl, but in the case of Levi—why not? Levi was a decent man, and at this point, whatever comfort he could get he was entitled to.

"Hi there, Charlie. Get your homework done?" the man asked hoarsely.

Charlie nodded and smiled at Levi. Levi smiled back, showing more gap than teeth.

"Good, good." Levi barely got the words out before another coughing fit overtook him. Charlie walked up to him, reached into his backpack, and removed a book. *Watership Down.* That one wasn't familiar. Justin frequently got Charlie books on his wanderings about town. Old books weren't hard to come by if you weren't picky about the condition, but Charlie also traded with kids at school to get them. He must have done just that in order to get this one.

Charlie had to hold the book for a minute before Levi could take it. The man nodded and held up a hand in thanks, unable to get words out. He wheezed, his eyes fixed on Charlie, the look between a silenced dying man and mute child conveying more than Justin could guess at, but something passed between them.

Justin put a hand on Charlie's shoulder. Levi's eyes were watering, and he didn't look to recover anytime soon. Levi motioned for them to continue on, and Justin understood this took the place of what the man would usually say: "Go on now. Don't be late for school."

Justin gave him a smile, though it seemed out of place. Levi needed to find a place indoors and off the ground, but they'd already had this conversation. The man refused. He wouldn't even go to the old stadium, which didn't offer much in the way of shelter, but it did keep the homeless off the ground. In squalor, perhaps, but off the ground. Instead, Levi would stay the remainder of his days under the garden, now just a rooftop covered in two feet of dry clarified dirt. The choice meant he'd be dead in a couple months. If the sickness didn't take him, he'd end up freezing to death. But that was his choice. He wasn't the first Groundling they'd said good-bye to, and he wouldn't be the last. Someone new would take his place, and Justin and Charlie would be friendly to him too. Just as they were friendly to all the Groundlings on this street.

Charlie gravitated to them—all of them—having no fear of interacting with others. What could have been a danger had grown into an asset. While Justin would never let Charlie walk to school alone, he had no doubt Charlie could do it and be relatively safe.

Men like Levi would see to it.

"See you on the way back, Levi," Justin said. He and Charlie turned away, hand in hand, and walked on. The wheezing sounds faded with the distance, and Justin was grateful not to hear any more coughing.

"HALE, WHAT are you making?" Eddie asked, swinging her legs at the table.

She knew what he was making, had seen it before, but she was in one of her talking moods. "Protein shake," he said, adding bottled water to the green powder. Hale screwed the cap on the canister and inverted it onto the blender's base. He watched the water thicken and turn green while the noise of the blender filled the kitchen.

"Eww, gross!" Eddie screamed over the din, smiling. Hale had to admit, it was gross-looking, but at least it was green.

And what was with Eddie putting on such a production? There was no need for the theatrics. It seemed she was starting to take after him. He smiled back at her. "Eat your toast, darlin'. Enjoy the jam for me too."

God, those preserves looked delicious, all shiny and red with visible bits of strawberry. Hale was fine with carbs on a Fray day, but he tried to stay away from sugar. It was more a mental thing than a necessity. Probably. He unfixed the canister from the blender and unscrewed the cap.

"Can I have some?" Eddie asked in the sudden quiet. Hale raised his eyebrows. She'd never asked that before.

"Protein shake? You just said it was gross."

"I'm a lady. I can change my mind."

Hale burst out laughing. "My thoughts exactly. Who told you that?"

"You did, silly."

"Well, if I said it, then it must be true, 'cause I'm the smartest guy alive. Of course you can have some."

"Why is it all green?" she asked as he swirled the contents around for good measure.

"It's green because it's made of seaweed. That's what gives it all the vitamins."

"Seaweed like in the lake?"

"Kind of. This comes all the way from the ocean, where it's cleaner. And it cost way more than your strawberry jam."

"That's 'spensive," Eddie said, reaching for the glass. "Mom said this is the only jar of jam we get." Eddie set her toast down, a strawberry glob dripping off onto the plate. The preserves must have come from the Chixago Building's gardens. Hale had fixed her a pretty generous helping too. Oh well.

He held the large glass down to her and helped her take a sip. Eddie had a silent look of deliberation on her face.

"Well?" he asked.

She stiffened her lower lip. "It's good," she decided at last. "I'm gonna eat my toast now."

Hale laughed again. She was totally trying to save face and act tough for him. He was proud of that. "Hold on. You got a green mustache." He brushed her upper lip with his thumb. "Gotta wipe the fly guts off."

"Fly guts?" Her eyes got wide.

"Just teasing, Baby Doll," Hale said quickly. "No flies in this one." Although there were crickets.

"Why do you always tease me?"

Hale paused in his motions, caught off guard. The question seemed an accusation. "Well, I suppose it's because I love you so much." Shit. Now he felt bad. He stared down into the green gloop.

He did tease her a lot. Maybe it was because she reminded him more of Janie every day. He'd loved teasing Janie. Not in mean ways, he hoped. In fun ways, like with fly guts, and Janie could stand toe to toe with him, giving as good as she got. But Eddie was just a kid. "I'm sorry, Eddie. I'll try not to tease you anymore. I didn't...." Here he was trying to spend some time with her on the day of the Fray, and he was making her feel bad. It seemed like he hardly even saw her anymore, and—

"No, it's okay. I like it," Eddie said, her legs swinging again. Her blue eyes sparkled as she took a bite of toast. She had to bite carefully, her mouth a beautiful assortment of mostly baby teeth, with a brand-new space in the front where she'd recently lost one. "You're funny. Mama and Daddy are always so serious."

Hale smiled and knelt down close to her. He kissed her on the temple. "Well, I'm gonna be serious too for a second. I love you so, so much, and I'd do anything for you. Never forget that."

"Would you eat a million flies?"

"I would eat a billion flies."

"Would you eat a million grasshoppers?"

Hale took a big sip of his shake, making sure to leave behind his own sloppy green mustache. He put a hand to his mouth and belched audibly. "I think I just did," he said.

And Eddie laughed and laughed, all beautiful baby teeth and toast crumbs.

CHARLIE'S ARMS released their grip on his neck, and Justin felt the chill air in the absence. He and Charlie always shared a hug at the drop-off point, but today it had been extra long. He smiled at his brother.

"Have a good day, Bro Bro. I'll try to be here to walk you home." Unfortunately it might have to be Gin. Justin still had to work today, though hopefully not another long day catching up from when he'd been laid up. At least work would keep his mind centered. He already had a playlist picked out.

Charlie took an extra second to lean forward and put his forehead against Justin's. Justin closed his eyes, then felt a pat on his shoulder. He opened his eyes as Charlie turned to go into the double doors of the school building.

Charlie waved a hello to Sister Timothy, who was standing in the doorway. Several other children were arriving, stepping out of vehicles, but Sister Tim's eyes were on Justin.

She was beautiful, even in her nun's habit. Her beauty was in her eyes, in her thick, dark eyebrows that arched almost severely. She was clearly well into middle age and projected a wisdom that must have come with her years and her experience. Should she purse her lips or show any sort of tension in her face, she might look frightening, but she always appeared relaxed and in control, as though she could handle anything. The relaxed facial expression softened her look and made her appear kind, though Justin had no doubt she could, indeed, handle anything.

She caught him looking at her and smiled. She wasn't shy about looking at him. It might have unnerved him, but for some reason her gaze was allowable. Trustworthy. He could almost mistake it for interest of a more carnal type, but nuns were bound to celibacy.

Across from her another nun welcomed the children. She was new and much younger. Justin had no idea who she was, but he noticed she was pregnant. Good for her. Many nuns chose to be surrogates, or to have children and give them up for adoption. This was one of the reasons the sisters demanded such respect. The difficulty of the responsibility struck him as saintly. It was almost supernatural, how nuns had a higher birthrate than other people. There had to be a scientific reason behind it, but no one had figured it out yet. Maybe something with the celibacy. Even the percentage of girls born to nuns was slightly higher than in the general population. It almost made one believe in miracles. Almost.

Looking back at Sister Timothy, he wondered if she had ever had children. Of course, he would never ask that question, just like it wasn't appropriate to ask a nun about her biological sex. Within the church it was forbidden to ask by order of the Pope, though clearly the pregnant nun was biologically female and not Uni. Unis were infertile.

Was Sister Timothy Uni? Justin shook his head to dispel the thought. It didn't matter, not in the least, and—

"Everything all right?"

Surprised, Justin saw Sister Tim approaching, just a few steps away. Damn—he'd been inside his own head again.

"Yeah, just…." Just what? Fuck. He didn't know what to say. And he should probably keep the *fuck*s on the down low since he was talking to a nun. He could feel his cheeks heating. "Um…."

"I saw the extended hug. It looked like you and Charlie were sharing a moment. You don't have to explain. When I saw you standing here, I thought I'd check in. That's all."

"Ah, yeah. Sure, everything is fine."

"Good." She arched an eyebrow at him, not unkindly, but in a way, that seemed almost inviting, like that eyebrow had the power to pull words from his mouth. It made him want to confess… something.

And then he remembered. "Actually I wanted to thank you. For sharing Charlie's assignment with me. You have no idea what it meant to me, and it came at just the right time, so yeah…."

She smiled. "Then I'm glad I got to share it with you."

Justin brought a hand to the back of his head, running it through his hair. He looked away from her for a moment and lowered his voice. "I just… it almost makes me feel guilty. Him not knowing that I've seen what he wrote. I've been meaning to tell him and maybe this morning would have been a perfect opportunity—"

Her laugh cut him off. She reached over and touched his arm lightly. Looking back at her face, he noticed how white her teeth were, in contrast to her dark eyebrows. "Justin, Charlie told me to share it with you. I'm sorry if I gave you the wrong impression."

"What?"

"Yes. I gave it to you with Charlie's permission. I assumed he didn't want you to be mad about his being so revealing in the essay, and he thought if it came from me, you would be more likely to accept it with an open heart."

"Oh."

"You aren't upset I hope."

"Oh—no. Not at all." Justin smiled nervously and knew he was blushing. He looked away again. "God. I'm sorry. I mean—no, no. Of course. That makes sense." How could he have thought a nun would go behind the back of a ten-year-old? No, on second thought a nun would definitely go behind the back of a ten-year-old. It was Sister Tim he shouldn't have doubted.

He felt a light squeeze on his arm. "You two share a very special bond."

Her sincere tone put him at ease, made him want to be sincere in return. "Yeah. We do."

"It makes me glad to see it. He's a very special boy."

"Thank you, Sister."

She didn't reply but smiled again, this time with closed lips. It was a warm smile, one of closure meant to spare him any more words. He smiled his own good-bye in return and watched her walk back into the school building.

Justin turned as well, moving at a brisk pace back down the street. He had a mission. He'd check on Levi. In fact, maybe he'd buy the guy some beer while running deliveries today. This Fray would be a payoff, especially since he was going to win, so he could afford it.

He felt like doing a good deed, and Charlie would definitely approve.

Chapter 10

JUSTIN PARKED his semielectric car several blocks from the church. An amalgamation of replaced and reprinted parts, the vehicle was nothing to look at, and no one should pay much mind to it, even at night.

Looking around, he saw only one residence close by. It was a brick four-story complex a block from where he parked. Several other buildings surrounded the Basilica, but these were not more than two stories and showed no evidence of life. If people were in them, they would be focused on whatever they were snorting, shooting, drinking, or fucking, not tonight's Fray.

As he knew from his visit Sunday, the street was pretty well taken care of, and that made him nervous. Most of the city streets had only a minimum level of maintenance and were largely gravel, but this one had asphalt, indicating this Arena was another high-profile building. It wasn't unheard of to have an Arena that was in-use as opposed to remote or abandoned, but this was the most prominent one to date. Thankfully the road looked deserted right now.

A sudden rap on his car window startled him, but he immediately recognized the trench coat. Scarecrow walked around the car, opened the door, and sat down in the passenger seat. Justin gripped the wheel and tried to slow his breathing.

"You look a little jumpy, kid. That's all right, though. Nothing wrong with a little extra adrenaline before a fight."

Justin nodded.

"You don't talk much, do you? Can't say I mind. You greased up?"

Justin nodded again.

"Good. Put the gloves on."

Justin reached to the right of the seat, picked up the cold leather gloves, and slid them on.

"Remember, keep the left hand in a fist, and keep the right one relaxed when you walk in."

Justin nodded once. He couldn't wait for this fight to be over, to not have these gloves constantly on his mind.

"One more thing I didn't tell you last time. This is important. They want you to go for the face."

Justin clenched his jaw. Swallowed.

"Don't pussy out on me, killer. This is big time for you. Everyone is gonna be watching you, especially the people in charge. Don't piss them off, and most of all, don't piss me off."

"Why go for the face?"

"Don't fuckin' ask why. It's not healthy. Question these things and you'll be on the wrong end of one of these arrangements."

"Wasn't I already?"

"There you go, then. Either this guy tonight is a nobody like you and they want to make it more interesting, or…." Justin turned to look at Scarecrow as the man rubbed his hands together. "Or it's someone so good people have stopped betting against him."

Justin went cold. He could only think of one person people wouldn't bet against. But that made no sense. They wouldn't want Black Jim out of the game. He brought in more views to Shadow Fray than anyone else, by far.

It couldn't be Black Jim. It must be some poor schmuck they wanted out. But that still wasn't okay. Could Justin somehow hold back and get away with it? He'd never envisioned clawing someone's face apart. He couldn't do that. Could he?

"Ready?" Scarecrow asked. "It's time."

Justin had to make this look good. He had to make everyone watching believe. "I'm ready."

He was not ready for this. Not at all.

HALE WASN'T ready for this.

He stood at the front of the church a few yards from the altar. Moonlight entered the glass at the center of the dome far above his head and cast a silver glow to his shadowed form. He stood in pose with his arms slightly away from his body, palms facing back. Behind him on the altar, a much smaller crucifix looked down. The outspread hands and upturned palms on this ivory Christ were a stark contrast to the demon standing before it. Looking at the tiny lights of about thirty different cameras around the church, he knew he cast an imposing figure in this holiest of places. He loved the theatrics. He should feel like a god awakened from the underworld.

Instead he felt like a puppet hanging on strings.

He'd seen his little girl every day this week, and yet he was still lost. When he'd lived next door and all that separated them was a wall, he could at least pretend he was living with her. She was in the next room. Now that he'd moved, he felt every single foot of the distance between them.

Here in the Arena, he felt that distance more keenly. He had a bad feeling about tonight. Whether from the lack of sleep or the disruption in his life, he was nervous like he hadn't been in years, with a gnawing thought that he might not see his baby girl again. Maybe he should get out of the games after all.

But those were ridiculous thoughts. Benz would catch any questionable shit someone might try to sneak by. Everyone in Shadow Fray was on alert, and nothing like what had happened in the Mutual Conglomerate Arena had happened since. No one had died. Besides, he was doing this for Eddie. He couldn't back out. Why was he thinking about this at all? This had been settled with Benz weeks ago.

He needed to get his mind on the fight. Be Black Jim.

He heard the large front doors of the church open. Benz stood three-quarters of the way down the center aisle, careful not to block his view, but it was too dark for Hale to see clearly. Whoever it was, they weren't making a subtle entrance. Of course, this was hardly the Arena for subtlety.

It had been a long time since he didn't have to consciously drag out a fight. He'd be fine. Everything would be fine.

And then he saw the brown-hood mask of the man walking toward him, the man everyone called Scarecrow. That meant—

Shit. He never should have spit in that holy water. But Scarecrow had other Brawlers, right? It might not be him. It might not be the Visitor. Hale tried to look down the aisle, but now Scarecrow was in the way, and Benz was getting ready to inspect whoever was behind him.

Scarecrow took the long walk down the aisle and knelt before Hale. The freak began inspecting Hale's boots, pressing the thin soles to find any irregularities. Scarecrow's hands wandered up, patting Hale down so thoroughly that by the time he was done, Scarecrow knew exactly how big Hale's dick was. Hale didn't even glance at him.

Scarecrow walked back down the aisle. Hale's mind was frozen.

As Benz lowered himself to the floor to begin his inspection, Hale finally got a look at his opponent. Lit only by the candles along the sides of the church, he was just a shadow, but Hale recognized him immediately. Those broad shoulders were unmistakable.

The Visitor.

The kid could easily wrap a man in his arms and fold in on him, like a mousetrap. The flickering light gave a hint of his bare chest, and Hale pictured the sparse dusting of hair. He could see the outline of the guy's hip bones and was familiar with the ridges of stomach muscle between them. The kid didn't appear to be returning his gaze, though. Odd. Usually his foes stared like an animal caught in headlights.

Hale started to tremble slightly, thankful for the darkness so no one would notice. Was he scared? This poor kid, the one he had spent weeks watching, was going to fight Black Jim. Why should Hale be scared? Because he felt bad for the kid? Was there a part of him that didn't want to hit him? No, that wouldn't explain the bad feeling he had, the feeling that something was wrong.

Hale spent the remaining seconds trying to put his poisoned thoughts aside and focus on that other feeling he had. The feeling that he was going to put his hands all over the Visitor.

The feeling of excitement.

Chapter 11

Second Fray. Arena: Basilica of St. Josaphat.

JUSTIN HAD to consciously keep his feet planted to the ground because his whole body was telling him to run. Run before he got caught. Run before he had to face this man who stared him down now like an unholy beast. Run before he had to tear the flesh off that pitch-covered face.

No.

He wouldn't go for the face. Decision number one.

I need a plan and fast. Was that a line from cartoons he watched with Charlie or some old movie? Seconds. He had seconds.

The church was dark. Candles lit the side walls, but not the altar or the front of the church. It would be darker there. Could he find a way to let Black Jim know he had a weapon? Without anyone knowing? And how? Whisper in his ear like they were kids with a goddamn secret? With fifty cameras recording their every move?

The hulk of a handler before him was moving his hands up Justin's body. Justin clenched his left fist. Could he signal Black Jim's handler somehow? Give himself away? Scarecrow was standing about a foot behind him, watching. It would be difficult but his best shot.

The man brought Justin's arms out and forced him to put both his hands flat, palms down. He sandwiched Justin's left hand, kneading the underside with upturned fingers. He might feel it. He might find it. *Please find it.*

The man moved on to Justin's right hand. All Justin needed to do was make a fist. The man's fingers probed the palm-side of the glove, his other hand running across the top. Justin's hand twitched. The man didn't even notice. Instead his fingers trailed over Justin's fingertips, missing the small pieces of metal hidden at his knuckles.

He didn't find it. A cold sweat broke across Justin's bare back.

Fight one-handed? He was screwed. He had to find a way to disable the glove or remove it. Maybe he could get Black Jim to remove it. Best bet.

It was time to meet those eyes. Justin looked up, focusing on his target. The shadowy specter might look like the angel of death, but he was just a man—a man with blue eyes.

Justin counted down in his head.

Three. He squared himself. He could feel the handler in front of him finishing up. Every muscle tensed, preparing.

Two. He took a deep breath. This was the moment he had dreamed about. He was facing Black Jim. Terror.

One. Anger. This moment was stolen from him. He should have a measure of excitement. He should be admiring the figure standing in front of the altar, muscled and unmoving like a black marble sculpture. But no, just terror and anger.

Zero. The handler stepped aside. Anger. Now there was only anger.

Justin tore off down the center aisle with a guttural yell. Tonight he would be the demon.

THIS WAS interesting.

Hale could count on one hand the number of men who had tried to rush him. Speed was Black Jim's advantage, and such a move reeked of desperation.

Hale got lower in a ready stance, watching the kid's midsection as he neared. While the direction of the legs, hands, and head could be misleading, the navel didn't lie.

As the kid approached, Hale actually relaxed. He needed to be loose. Dodge low, punch to the groin. That'd slow the guy down.

Hale could see the windup. The kid was telegraphing his punch—a nervous and hasty mistake. Hale prepared to hit where he anticipated an opening in the kid's side. He'd go easy on the nuts for now.

And then the kid fell. No, not fell—it was on purpose. The kid slid on the marble floor full tilt into Hale's legs. Hale tried to sidestep, but it was too late. His balance gone, Hale fell awkwardly on top of the Visitor and felt the kid's fingers grasping for purchase, trying to roll him and gain the top position.

Shit. Smart move, that. Using the aisle and the slick surface of the marble showed an awareness of the environment Hale should have anticipated. No matter. He closed his arms around the kid, feeling the tight muscles compress against his own. They clutched each other as though in a face-to-face hug.

Hale went with the direction the kid was trying to roll him, allowing himself to be on the bottom. But this was a bluff, as Hale continued the roll, flipping the kid back over, using the momentum to disorient and assume the top position.

On top, Hale used his knees in a crushing grip. The kid couldn't throw a good punch lying on his back. Hale used one hand to brace the kid's shoulder while he slammed into the kid's face, striking right three times in succession—bam, bam, bam. Dark blood squirted out from under the leather mask.

The kid returned the punch as best he could with his left, but it was weak. Then he tried to squirm out, but Hale held him with his knees. Hale felt the kid's legs wrap around his trunk, looking to gain leverage. Hale gave him another two punches, this time to his jaw, because c'mon—he didn't want to ruin the pretty face he hoped was under that mask.

The kid managed to shift his shoulder, and Hale's grasp fell to the inside. The kid immediately wrapped his arm around Hale's hand, pinning it in his armpit. Now he had a grip on Hale, and between the kid's legs wrapped around him and his trapped arm, the tables turned as the kid rolled him over.

Without warning his shoulder hit the wooden pew at his side. Shit—out of space. He was not only on the bottom but cornered, one side effectively eliminated. He wrapped his legs around the kid as the kid connected with three hits to Hale's ribcage. Bam, bam, bam.

He knew after the first punch, but he could do nothing to stop the second and third. This hit bone. He could see the small metal spikes poking out, metal spikes that were digging into his skin and scraping against his ribs.

The pain was not as keen as the panic. He couldn't escape. This fucking kid had a weapon. He instinctively brought his hands up to his face as the kid wound up for another punch.

But then the kid was on his feet, bouncing back away from Hale, slipping into the shadowed chancel. Hale was free. The kid had let him up. But why?

Hale kicked up, going from his back to his feet in one fluid motion. The kid seemed to be taking a moment to recover from Hale's assault, clearing his throat and coughing something thick and bloody onto the marble floor.

Hale winced, clutching his side. How had Benz missed it?

Hale's only chance to get out of this was to negate the glove. The best way to do that would be to remove it. The best way to remove it would be to try to take the kid down, fast, into a submission hold, preferably one that restricted the airway. Fast, fast, fast; the longer this went on, the more likely Hale was to be torn up.

He was on his feet for less than a second, and like a bolt he was off, closing the distance between him and the kid.

He faked a left but didn't intend to drive it home. He wanted to get the kid's right fist up where he could see it, and punching with his left would force the kid to block with his right and keep that glove high. It worked, and he danced around the kid, tempting punches with his left, looking for an opening.

Despite the advantage the kid had with a weaponed right, he seemed in no hurry to use it. They circled each other. Hale took a moment to look into the kid's eyes, to peer behind the mask. He'd looked into a lot of eyes in his career. He knew determination when he saw it. He knew confidence. But the look he saw now was far more familiar: fear.

The kid took the moment's pause to attack hard with his right, driving toward Hale's face. Too slow. Hale bobbed backward, the punch doing nothing but giving off a stiff breeze.

Seeing his opening, Hale swung his left foot, high. He heard the smack as his foot connected, not from the sole, but from the top, like one would kick a ball or a pigeon. The connection was solid and fast like a snakebite, the foot impacting around the ninth and tenth ribs, the toes angled back toward the kid's spine.

The kid bounced back. One step. Two steps. In his third step back, he clutched his side and went down. Hale had hit his liver.

When delivered correctly, a liver shot can completely incapacitate an opponent, interrupting their circulation and causing excruciating pain, often effectively ending the fight. But Hale wasn't taking any chances that this fight was already over.

He punched the kid on the raw side of his face, landing him flat on the ground. He got on top of him, completely stretched out, using his whole body to hold the kid down. He could feel the soft groaning of his prey. He wrapped his arms around the kid's shoulders and neck and heard a muffled choking.

Pressed body to body, Hale could feel the taut muscles under him struggling weakly for release. He still wasn't in a good position to remove the glove, but he wouldn't have to if the fight was over. He stayed on top of the kid, their groins pressed together, the kid's head in the nook of Hale's neck as his arms worked to squeeze the air from him. The kid's arms were out, flailing more than punching, nothing connecting. "Shhhh," Hale whispered in his ear, smelling the kid's sweat mingled with the rusty scent of blood. "Just relax. It'll be over soon."

He took a second to revel in the kid's body, to feel it writhe underneath him. In a flash, Hale knew he wanted the chance to do this again, to have the Visitor under him, to have this man at his mercy. Hale was like a god, in complete control, able to do anything he wished. It was a feeling better than any drug, a feeling he hadn't had in his other fights, at least not this intimately. As the kid struggled, Hale felt their legs slip, interlocking side by side like teeth in a zipper, his groin pressed to the kid's upper thigh, rubbing as he struggled.

But Hale's mind wasn't in the fight, and the second cost him. The kid used the leverage in his legs to roll onto his stomach. Shit. But Hale still had him contained. The Visitor was still Black Jim's bitch.

Then the kid arched his broad back, bringing his knees under him and tipping his head down.

Hale was falling.

Gravity forced him forward and down, his arms slipping as his head got closer to the floor. In an instant the kid had Hale's left leg, grabbing him above the knee. Hale tried to use his other leg to hook around the kid's neck and force a different hold, but he didn't have the correct position. His body was collapsing, curling in. Only mere seconds, and all advantage was lost.

Now mostly on top of him, the kid wrapped his arms around him, folding Hale's bent body inward. The pressure in his chest and pain in his ribs made it difficult to breathe. The kid tried to get a better grip, pushing Hale upside down along the slick marble surface inch by inch.

His foot was by the kid's neck, and that was his best shot for an escape. He managed to hook his other leg to the opposite side of the kid's body, bracing his foot against the kid's torso. With his legs in a scissor position, Hale twisted his body around, using his core, straining with the effort. The kid's grip faltered. Creating space for himself, Hale was able to swiftly unscissor his legs, sliding into a better position where he quickly wrapped his legs around his opponent's waist. Now he had the Visitor in his guard, had some control. Better, even if he was still on the bottom.

The kid was crouched over now, Hale's gravity pulling him down so that he had to put both hands on the marble to keep himself from falling forward. Quickly, Hale shot his hands upward, grabbing the kid's arms and forcing them up into the air. Hale let the kid struggle for a moment as he tightened his grip. It felt painstakingly gradual but only took seconds. Hale inched his left leg up toward the kid's neck until he was able to reach his right arm over and grab that ankle. Now he had the kid around the shoulders, arms, and neck.

This left one hand free to grab that Mother. Fucking. Glove.

With a furious yell, Hale reached up, unclasping the glove strap and removing the glove. He flung the glove back among the pews where it would be difficult to find, his yell echoing off the stained glass and marble.

It happened so smoothly. The kid hadn't tried to make a fist, or Hale wouldn't have been able to rip the glove off so easily. The kid had left his hand open. On purpose?

His position now too high on the kid, Hale released him, scuttling backward none too gracefully, his boots squeaking on the marble from all the sweat and blood.

Ready to bounce back onto his feet once clear, Hale saw the kid wasn't getting up very quickly. That's fine. Good. Hale could use a breather. The kid could stay on the ground for a second, give or take thirty. Longer would be fine too.

Hale took his bearings and scooted back slowly, taking his time until he was on one side of the aisle and the kid was on the other, both of them now just outside the deeper darkness of the chancel, away from the pews.

With about ten feet between them, he and the kid both rose slowly to standing. Their heavy breathing was impossibly loud in the empty caverns of the Basilica.

He looked the kid right in the eyes as they panted like animals. The fear he'd seen earlier was gone. Staring, he saw in the kid's unwavering gaze that the real battle for dominance was about to begin.

Enough of this rolling around. He spat on the floor, his fury rising. He lifted his shirt to look at the bleeding on his side and ribs. Twelve wounds, individual punctures and gashes indiscernible through the blood.

Hale growled, "Kid, you got me fucked up."

Hale strode forward quickly before the kid could recover, feinting with his left as he closed, bobbing his head, then another tentative left before preparing to drive hard with his right where the kid was already hurt.

Lightning fast the kid pounded forward with his left arm, using anticipation and his longer arms to glide under Hale's punch, slamming into his ear.

Damn good striker. Hale was driven backward, his head snapping to the side, but already the kid's right fist was bearing down. Hale put up a block, but the kid managed to power inside, smashing into Hale's jaw.

His face felt like it was coming apart.

The momentum of his own head was killing him, snapping from left to right as the kid landed two additional punches.

Each punch seemed to have an echo, a sound he could feel first inside his head before he heard it on the outside. He was stumbling backward. Off-balance. Unable to throw an effective block. Head pounding.

Two more punches landed.

Then two more.

The next thing Hale knew he was on the ground, on his back, the kid closing quickly.

Fear. Pain. Hale wasn't used to these feelings, not in a Fray.

The emotions gave him an uncommon surge of adrenaline. He kicked out, more in desperation than anything. His foot connected with the kid's shin, causing him to stumble, giving Hale one extra second to get his feet under him.

In the span of two heartbeats, he sprang up, his vision blurry. Backing away. Dizzy. The kid had driven him to the side of the church, and Hale was now retreating down the candlelit wall.

Black Jim was retreating.

Wet blood ran down his face and over his swelling lips.

He was really off his game. Good thing he had more than one game. He just hadn't had to use it in a while.

He started moving forward, closing the distance. He mustered up a hard strike on the right, but his real motivation was to completely swallow up the distance between him and the kid as the punch was blocked. He kept moving forward, directly into his opponent.

As Hale pushed him backward, the kid grabbed him, and they were back to the clinch—body against body, skin on skin. He could feel the black grease from his face and hair rubbing off onto the kid's chest, mingling with their sweat and blood.

Hale was stronger. Smaller. Slicker. Slippery. If he had to fight like a snake to win, he would.

As they battled for position, the kid thrust his knee up, aiming for Hale's groin. Hale stepped back and clear but maintained contact, keeping the kid in his grasp, staying close. He closed the distance, and the kid tried again, but this time Hale stepped to the side of the knee, using it as an opening to swing behind the kid, keeping his arms around the kid's waist.

Now he had the kid from behind, clasping his hands together, squeezing, pressing their bodies close. The kid struggled to break the hold, but Hale jerked back, lifting him and driving forward with his hips. Once more the Visitor tried to free himself, but Hale jerked back again, each time tightening his grip further and closing his arms around the Visitor like a boa constrictor.

Time for the takedown.

With his feet centered and a solid grip, Hale picked the kid up entirely off the ground, clearing him by at least a foot. At the same time, Hale twisted his body toward the pews to his left, driving the kid into the wood. The kid went down, his head cracking against the wooden edge. The sound rang through the church like a bell.

The kid got his feet under him quickly, but Hale still had him from behind. Trying to retreat, the kid used his strength to power between the pews back toward the center aisle. Hale's grip loosened in the close quarters as arms, elbows, and legs bumped against the pews on either side.

The kid seized the moment to turn to face Hale, backing up as Hale lost his grip completely.

Shit.

Hale jumped to the side, landing on the pew bench with both feet. He sprang off his left foot, swinging his right around. He was fully airborne for only a brief moment before the top of his foot sank into the kid's neck, the airy sound very similar to landing a punch on a bag.

The kid went flying to Hale's left. Hale heard the pew crashing but didn't see it, as he himself was off-balance and falling, landing on the right pew bench more or less on his back, cracking his own head in the process.

Despite the white flash of pain on the back of his head, Hale knew this fight was over. A kick like that to the side of the neck could interrupt the flow of blood to the brain, rendering someone unconscious or worse.

He breathed in, sitting up to spot the kid. Several pews were down. He'd managed to get a little church destruction in after all. Bonus.

But then he saw the kid moving. Twisting. Heard him retching. Damn. Kid was tough.

Hale didn't feel up to bounding over the pew just now, but that was okay. The victory was close. He could feel it.

He got to his feet as the kid did the same. Hale walked around the pew as the kid stumbled toward the center aisle, Hale following. He was in no rush. Now free of the pews, the kid backed down the aisle, his back toward the chancel. He kept backing up until he was inside the moonlight under the dome, where Hale had begun the night.

The kid had a nasty cut and goose egg forming at the edge of his mask toward his temple. He looked like he was struggling to breathe. He eyed Hale, but his gaze was not as sharp as before. Still determined, though.

The kid put his arms up in a ready stance. Hale obliged and moved toward him, taking the offensive.

They traded punches and blocks for some time, neither of them as strong as they used to be. Hale was having difficulty landing any power shots, and the kid just wouldn't go down.

His arms began to feel like jelly, his head pounding with his pulse, the pressure building behind his eyes. Hale was moving in slow motion, punching through cotton.

This couldn't go on. It was time to make a different move.

Hale kept up the dance a little longer, waiting for the kid to bob down, waiting for him to drop his taller body into a low enough crouch for him to deliver the final blow.

And then he saw his opening as the kid bent his knees and brought himself down to Hale's level.

Once more Hale flew forward, leg extended, aiming again for a kick to the neck.

But the Visitor was more alert than he seemed. He was ready for it. Had planned for it.

The kid sidestepped the kick and dove into Hale before he could rebalance, knocking him onto his back.

With amazing speed the kid was on him, driving punch after punch into his face. A ground and pound. Dimly, Hale could feel the cut of the kid's knuckles from that naked right fist—bone on bone, no barrier but for the thinnest layers of skin.

Hale sputtered. Blackness was closing in. Amidst the punching frenzy, Hale finally managed to flip over onto his stomach. The kid dropped into a rear choke hold around Hale's neck. But Hale was expecting this. He was able to get one final breath.

He struggled to get free but to no avail. So this is what losing felt like. It had been a long time. His struggles became weaker, the darkness more complete. He was losing consciousness. No—his eyes were closed. But he didn't have much longer. Only one chance left.

He ceased struggling completely.

Without resistance the kid's grip tightened around him like a vise.

Hale tried to count but got his seconds mixed up with his rapidly pounding heart before he remembered to say banana.

One banana.

Two banana.

Three banana....

If he had to fight like a snake to win, he would.

At ten banana the kid's grip loosened.

Hale's lungs were ready to explode. He forced himself not to gasp. He tried to breathe through his nose, but there was too much blood. He let air slide between his teeth and tried not to vomit.

The kid promptly fell on top of him. Hale, crushed, had a moment of panic. He forced quiet, slow, painful breaths. On top of him, the kid was probably just exhausted. Could be he wasn't able to get on his feet yet.

The kid stretched out, his face in Hale's hair. Hale could feel him gasping against his neck. The weight was strangely comfortable—except for the stinging pressure in his bruised ribs and the throbbing in his face.

Suddenly the Visitor's hot breath was on his cheek.

Was the kid going to kiss him? No—just checking to make sure Hale was breathing. How fucking nice of the guy. Hale made sure to let an audible whistle escape.

Still the kid lay on top of him. Minutes must have passed. Finally he felt the kid get up, the heavy weight lifting.

Hale sensed one of the kid's feet step between his own, toward his ankles. This was his chance.

Hale snapped around, his legs spinning and bringing the unsuspecting kid down. Hard.

Hale pounced over, never really getting off the ground, but he was quick enough. He slammed the back of the kid's head into the marble floor, then drove a snapping right punch into his face for good measure, the kid's head once again rebounding off the marble.

He sat gasping over the Visitor's limp form for a few seconds, shaking out his stinging hand. Punch of his motherfucking life. Had to be out cold. Hale moved to the side, out of any damageable range.

He grabbed the kid's legs and dragged him toward the front of the church. Next he spun him around and lifted him from behind. From the looseness of the kid's body, Hale was pretty positive he was unconscious, but he was still cautious.

He propped the kid against the altar under the ivory Jesus. He slapped his cheek a few times and could see that he was breathing.

Finally, Hale stepped to the side. He turned to face the church. He surveyed the ghosts of the congregation, knowing his real audience was watching behind the cameras. Those viewers, millions of them, were his church and his congregation.

He raised his hands as though for benediction and said in a loud voice mimicking his father's brimstone sermons: "Opponents. If any of you ever bring a weapon to one of my Frays, to any of my Arenas, I swear to fucking God I will kill you."

He turned and spat on the kid, then strode down the center aisle. He kicked an angel in the face on the way out. He heard it crash behind him but didn't turn back to see what he'd broken.

Chapter 12

WAKING WAS like trying to crawl through a thousand heavy mattresses. Justin couldn't do it. He couldn't make it through the crushing weight.

And then he threw up and was forced out of the blackness into what little light was in the church.

The fight. What happened? But it was over. Thank God, it was over.

He spit. Tried to take a deep breath. What hurt? Everything, but it was like all his body parts existed in their own separate space and none of them were connected with each other. He couldn't get a read on anything except the awful taste of acid and iron.

Couldn't think.

His pulse pounded in his head like a hammer. That was what hurt most of all—his head.

It was hard to see with so much blood in his eyes. He wiped the vomit and blood from his face, feeling flashes of pain as he ran his hands over his mask and skin.

His mouth was sticky and vile. He spit again. Blood. He needed water.

Looking up, he could see Black Jim's hulk of a handler removing the last of the cameras. He couldn't have been out too long.

He couldn't remember clearly if he won or lost. Considering he was the one struggling to remain conscious, he supposed he lost. But at least it was over. He almost smiled in relief.

He wanted to curl up. Not move. But the need for water drove him unsteadily to his feet. He wobbled, nearly losing his legs until he braced himself on the first of the pews. If only the floor would stop shifting.

He could see Scarecrow's blurry figure at the end of the aisle, standing in the doorway of the church. Arms crossed. Not moving a muscle to help him.

He moved up the aisle from pew to pew, bracing and pausing at every opportunity.

Then a steadying arm fell around him, and someone was helping to support all the extra weight he seemed to be carrying. Confused but too grateful to care, Justin took several stumbling steps with the assistance. Gradually the church stopped rocking, and he turned a stiff neck to glance to his side. Black Jim's handler. The man had a simple black mask covering his eyes. Funny, Justin hadn't noticed that before.

"You'll be all right, kid," the large man said.

Justin tried to point to the stone angel, but his arm was so heavy. "Water," he said weakly.

The man helped him to the water, transferring Justin's weight onto the remaining stone angel. It was more delicate than it looked and not fixed to the floor, but sturdy enough. He didn't remember breaking the other one. God, what had happened?

Justin palmed water into his mouth and splashed it over his face. His jaw and temple ached with a singing pain, and even in the scant light, he could see the water in the font run red. He put his damaged jaw against the cool marble of the angel's face and closed his eyes.

He became dimly aware of low, angry voices a few yards away. Scarecrow and Black Jim's handler were having an argument. Maybe he was too far gone to grasp it, but the exchange seemed odd. There were rules about this stuff—not removing your masks, not speaking to the opponent. His own mask felt terribly constraining, like the casing on a sausage. It needed to come off.

"You losing piece of shit." Justin opened his eyes. Scarecrow, of course. Black Jim's handler was nowhere to be seen. "If you weren't half-dead already…."

What? Then what? No words came out, but Justin didn't care anymore. Not at all.

Scarecrow got in his face. "What do you say I cut your throat like the last one?"

Justin managed a sound of some sort, but he could barely keep his eyes open.

"You didn't follow the fucking instructions!" Scarecrow bellowed.

"I tried," Justin said weakly.

"Tried. You tried." Scarecrow's words were a sneer. Fine, let him sneer. Justin didn't remember everything, but he knew he put up a good fight. Hadn't he been winning? Even with the glove, he put on a decent enough show. No one watching could prove a damn thing.

He saw Scarecrow kick at him but had no energy to stop it. At once, Justin was falling backward, the angel toppling over with him, by some miracle not crushing his legs as it crashed on the floor. The world spun for a moment, but he'd managed to land mostly on his ass. The holy water splashed cool against his skin, soaking into his clothes, further mixing with his blood.

That brown mask loomed over him as Justin looked up. He looked away because he wasn't afraid of Scarecrow anymore. This bully was pathetic.

The next instant, pain. The cold press of a gun against his injured temple. Shit.

"Give me one good reason why I shouldn't," Scarecrow said, driving the gun painfully into the knot on Justin's head.

"There's two reasons right behind you, asshole. One of them is cocked." The click of a gun's hammer filled the church. "The other one is me."

Oh God. The voice. It was Gin.

Justin was paralyzed. He saw Gin standing with her gun leveled at Scarecrow. Scarecrow turned to look but kept his gun hard against Justin's skull.

"I'm guessing from the striking family resemblance, this must be your sister," he said, looking back down to Justin.

"Fuck off," Justin rasped. In no position to make demands, the words were unfortunately feeble—a cliché for the powerless.

Scarecrow's eyes showed the smile under his mask. He didn't appear afraid. He'd even taken his eyes off Gin. "Your brother here is the one in the habit of killing his handlers," Scarecrow continued. "To be quite honest with you, I don't think you have the balls to pull the trigger."

"That's where you're wrong. Justin's never killed anyone in his life." It was her turn to smile, while Scarecrow's smile appeared to be fading. Perhaps he read in Justin's look that she would do this. Had done it before. Even through the mask, Justin saw the dawning of fear.

"Gin—" Justin said. Just the warning, pleading, in saying her name. This situation was insane, and he couldn't think it through. But he needed her safe. Would do anything.

"If I don't kill him now," Scarecrow spoke in a more pacified voice, "he still belongs to me. It can happen another time. You can't always protect your brother. So why don't you just shoot me now?"

The silence stretched. The smile never left Gin's face, but she also didn't have anything to say. She didn't make a move. So Justin did. Scarecrow had to be bluffing. He shifted to stand, but Scarecrow jammed the gun into his temple, forcing him to stay put.

"You stay," Scarecrow said and then turned to Gin. She wasn't smiling anymore. "Your brother needs me. Without me he's out of the game. Not to mention they'd come after him if I disappeared. Handlers can't keep showing up dead. I can always get other fighters. The truth is, you need me a whole lot more than I need you."

"I know," Gin said. Her tone of voice was unwavering, like she wasn't intimidated by this revelation at all—like she had planned for it. "That's why I have a proposal for you."

"Oh?"

"Every time my brother loses a Fray, you get to fuck me."

Justin felt as still as the statue at his feet, feeling broken into just as many pieces.

Scarecrow laughed as though truly amused. "What makes you think I'd wanna? As beautiful as you are, I can buy beauty, and the kind I buy won't have a cunt like a steel trap. You're a fuckin' psycho bitch if you think I'd get near you."

Gin raised an eyebrow. "I didn't finish," she said. "Every time my brother loses, you get to fuck me… without a condom."

"Gin—don't." Justin pushed the words through gritted teeth. But she wouldn't look at him, keeping her eyes on Scarecrow. Determined.

"I menstruate," she said, "so I'm fertile. I'm guessing whatever you buy won't let you put it in 'em like that. Ever thought of being a father? Ever want some part of you to live on when your miserable little life is snuffed off the face of the dying planet?"

She paused, her words like gravity, before going on. "What I'm offering you isn't just a fuck. It's a chance for immortality. Men kill for it."

Scarecrow paused a long minute, considering. Why would he of all people even think about—

"Gin, stop!" Justin said, desperation helping him find his true voice. "He's not gonna fuckin' kill me. I had Black Jim. I had him. You don't need to do this."

Scarecrow finally removed his mask. He put away the gun, and Justin saw a smile spread across his face. No.

He'd pushed Scarecrow over the edge. Scarecrow would agree. Justin should have kept his damn mouth shut.

Justin looked away to the floor, the broken stone angel, the puddle of holy water.

"How do I know you're not on the pill?" Scarecrow asked Gin.

"They make blood tests. I'll take one."

"And how do I know you're clean?"

"You don't, except that I have never had unprotected sex in my life. I don't care to get sick. And honestly, between the two of us, I'd say you're far more likely to be a carrier."

"I don't want to raise a baby with you."

"You think I want to raise one with you? Hell no. If I get pregnant, it's yours."

"Starting tonight."

"Starting tonight." Her voice was steady and strong.

Justin looked up at his sister, pleading with his eyes. *Don't do this. It's not too late.* But she'd put her gun away and wasn't looking at him.

Scarecrow returned her gaze, their eyes locked. "You'll meet me four days after sex at the train station in Racine for a follow-up test. I don't want you taking an after pill."

Gin frowned. "Fine."

"And you expect me to do all this for the chance at having a kid?"

"Do what you want. I won't be crying any tears if I don't have to fuck you. I'll just collect my brother and go."

In his frozen mind, a glimmer of hope. This was crazy. It wasn't going to happen. It couldn't happen.

But then Scarecrow flashed his yellowed teeth in a smile, his wide eyes like a predator's. "Your place or mine, sweetheart?"

"I'm not going anywhere with you. We do it right here, in the church, but first we get my brother to the car."

Justin tried not to drag his feet as they carried him out. Time and distance couldn't be measured in steps. All the pain and fog were back, but he didn't care. He willed his body to shut down, to stop feeling, but crouching into the car was still an exercise in agony.

"I'll be back in five minutes," Gin said to him as she closed the passenger door. With numb fingers Justin finally removed his mask.

Black Jim may have beaten him, but this was far worse. Now he had truly lost.

LEANING BACK against his bike, Hale bent forward just far enough to pour another bottle of water over his head. He reveled in the shocking coolness of the water as it ran across his aching face, but in a few seconds, the pain was back full force. He threw the bottle aside, hearing it rebound against the cement foundation to settle with the other debris. He was under a roof in an old garage, away from any drones that might be making low patrols in the darkness. He hadn't heard any, but his attention was not on his surroundings.

He gingerly pressed a fresh white cloth to his face. The black makeup was only a good idea if he could make it through a fight relatively unscathed. The rubbing was agonizing. The cloth came away more red than black. Damn. He was probably going to need a couple stitches.

Christ, that kid had done a number on him. The Visitor's hands were like pistons, landing punch after punch in dizzying succession. Hale had to admit the kid's hands were faster than his own, at least tonight. He had underestimated him. He grabbed another bottle of water from his saddlebag and wet another cloth, which he put around his neck. He'd be surprised if he had any range of motion at all tomorrow. As it was he could barely look from side to side.

His ribs ached with every breath he took, his wounds still leaking with the unavoidable rise and fall of his chest. He forced himself to carefully drink the remainder of the water in the bottle before tossing it aside. He took out two more cloths—his last two. He held one to his face and one at his side to stanch the flow of blood.

Shouldn't he be pissed? Scared? Someone had come after him with a weapon. It was difficult to work things out when he'd taken so thorough of a beating. Maybe a punch had broken his brain muscles.

The truth was, though, he couldn't help feeling a little grateful.

The Visitor could have hurt him a lot more than he had. The guy could have gone for Hale's face but went for his ribs instead. He'd tipped his hand, so to speak. Hale's disarming moves had been pretty genius, but removing the glove could have been a lot more difficult. The kid hadn't fought it.

So Hale wasn't furious—he was intrigued. No, he was fucking exhilarated. He felt like he was coming down from a high, and he missed the pull of adrenaline, the way it had made him feel hypervigilant, the sudden bursts of energy like a stimulant in his veins.

But it wasn't just the adrenaline that had been stimulating. He thought of the kid struggling against him, on top of him, underneath him. Even now it had his blood rushing.

The real drug had been the closeness of the kid's body to his own. Images of the fight came back to him, their bodies wrapped together, pressed together, bleeding, sweating, and intermingling.

His skin prickled, a pleasing sensation that penetrated the pain, as he pictured the kid's body marked with streaks of black paint. The Visitor would bear a lot of other marks tomorrow too, no doubt, but Hale owed him. The kid had left claw marks on his ribs, probably on his bone. For that, Hale owed him teeth.

He had the urge to bite him. Lick him. Taste him.

Fuck him.

He jumped as he heard heavy footsteps to his side and winced as he turned his head too quickly.

"Easy man, it's just me." Benz. "Cameras are all down. I kept an eye on the kid like you said."

"Did he wake up?"

"Yeah, he's awake."

"Will he be okay?"

"Well…."

Hale's pulse quickened. He felt sick. "I don't know what came over me. It was like I couldn't stop. I should have backed off at the end—"

"No, no, no, Hale. The kid'll be all right. You had to. You had to make a point. I meant he'd be better off without that hooded prick for a handler. Guy's a real piece of work."

That was an understatement. Was the kid in trouble? But Hale rephrased his question for Benz. "What happened?"

"I don't know. I didn't stick around for the whole thing, but I saw them leave. Why all the interest? And God, you look like shit." The large man looked at the ground. "I'm sorry. I should have found it."

"Shut up, Benz. It's not your fault. I was pissed at you for all of one second, and then I got over it." Damn, talking was difficult. Hale's lips were swollen and his speech was slurred. He'd need to speak in shorter sentences.

Benz raised his gaze from the floor to look Hale in the eyes. "It won't happen again."

Hale tried to look up at the man, but the twinge of pain in his neck put a grimace on his face that probably matched Benz's sorry expression. "I know it won't, man. I trust you."

Hale rubbed his neck, examining Benz. Benz wouldn't let this go. Dammit. Here Hale was the one who could barely stand and probably looked like he had gone through a meat grinder, and yet he was going to be the one to offer Benz comfort. Even having that thought made him a real asshole, he supposed.

"Benz, seriously. You saved my life. You've had my back more times than I can count, and not just in Shadow Fray. I wouldn't be here if it weren't for you. So do me a big favor and let it go. Please." So much for shorter sentences.

Benz nodded slowly. "I'll try."

"I wanna get back to the kid. Tell me about what happened after I left."

The pained expression left Benz's face. He cocked his head and stared at Hale quizzically, like he was working something out. "The kid's a piece of shit for what he did," he said at last.

"Maybe. I'm not so sure."

Benz snorted. He reached in his back pocket, drew something out, and tossed it to Hale. It landed in his lap. The glove.

"Thought you might want a souvenir. I was gonna keep it as a reminder, but maybe you need the reminder more than I do."

Hale picked it up. He bent the leather to expose the short metal spikes. He wasn't sure what he expected to see—his own blood, perhaps? But they looked clean. He stuffed the glove in his saddlebag.

"Tell me about the kid," Hale insisted again. Why was Benz being so tight-lipped?

"I watched for a while. Scarecrow and a girl took him to a car. Then they went back inside the church."

"He's in the car now? Alone?"

"As far as I know."

"Close?"

"Just a few blocks."

Could he go talk to him? But as if Benz sensed the thought, he warned, "Don't even think about it. It's against the rules."

That didn't stop Hale from feeling an almost magnetic pull to find him. "Maybe rules don't exist anymore."

"Funny. That's what I told Scarecrow before I told him to watch his back."

Hale snorted. Painfully. "Is that all you said?"

"Nope."

"Shame on you, Benz. That's breaking the rules."

"Yep."

"Tell me more about the kid."

"Jesus. What do you want to hear? That he could barely stand? He looked like you do—beat to hell."

Hale winced at the rise in volume. "No. I want your read on the fight. He could have hurt me a lot worse than he did."

"You played that smart, brother. You got it off quick. If you hadn't, then—"

"No. He didn't want to hurt me like that. I looked in his eyes. He was scared."

"If he didn't want to hurt you, why wear it? If he was forced, punch a damn pillar. The glove ain't that sturdy."

"And break his hand? You ever punched marble before?"

Benz sighed. "Could be you're right. I don't know. Ask me tomorrow. This is all too… fresh. I feel like punching some marble, you know? Like maybe it'd be a good idea."

"I want you to follow him."

"What?" The man raised his voice for the second time.

"If you really feel bad about tonight, then follow him." Hale was being a manipulative bastard, but he didn't care. He wanted this. Badly.

"Why?"

"I don't know. Ask me tomorrow."

Benz glared at Hale, silent.

"It's a feeling I have, man. Please."

After a pause, Benz nodded once, turned his back on Hale, and left.

Hale got ready to ease his helmet on and attempt the drive home. No, not home, to the place he slept. Or tried to sleep.

Everything was so screwed up. So depressing. But this feeling he had about the Visitor—that feeling was something he could hold on to.

Hale had to find out who he was.

Chapter 13

"TALK TO me, Justin. Don't go to sleep yet."

But it hurt to talk. It hurt to think. He held his T-shirt against the right side of his face where the blood still flowed. He'd either opened old wounds or received plenty of new ones. Probably both. "Why'd you do it?" he asked hoarsely.

"Because I love you." Gin's face was blank, but her eyes were alive. Her short black hair was pushed behind her ears as she drove, her hands at ten and two on the wheel. She looked fierce and wary, but not sad. Not hurt.

"You didn't have to do it."

"I wanted to. You don't have to be my savior. This chivalry thing you're doing isn't cute. You watch too many movies. Women rule this world. I might occasionally use sex to get what I want, but that's my choice. I have a thousand other capabilities. This choice was just a little less bloody than my other 999 would have been." She paused for a few seconds and then added, "I'm not Mom, you know."

Justin avoided looking in her direction. He kept his eyes straight ahead as they passed through mostly deserted streets. Buildings out here were left to fire, rats, and drugs, but every few blocks were signs of a living civilization, usually in clusters of buildings about four stories off the ground. Some subdivisions displayed barbed wire, particularly those in ancient, shorter buildings that housed gardens on upper floors and rooftops.

"Did he hurt you?" Justin asked.

"Phht. Says the boy bleeding in the passenger seat. No, I'm not hurt. I'm fine."

"But what if—"

"What if I get pregnant? Chances are it's not going to happen, and if it does, we'll deal with it then. I'm not going to spend time worrying until I have to. But it wouldn't be the worst thing in the world, and there's always options. Maybe some will even work to our benefit." Her voice was steady. Justin wasn't sure he agreed with her logic, but the way she said it deterred any disagreement.

He sat in silence for a while as the car bounced over potholes in the rough road. With every bump, he felt as though his brains were rebounding off the sides of his skull.

"I just don't like it," he said. "I don't like any of this."

"We don't have to like it. But we do have to survive. I'm not going to spend time feeling bad about what I do for people I love."

Shit. Charlie. "Where is Charlie?"

"I told you I wouldn't leave him home alone, and I didn't. He's with Devin and Griz." So she hadn't lied. She just escaped on a technicality.

He closed his eyes. He was so tired, but he forced them open again. "How did Griz know you killed Joe?"

"I asked him that." Gin pursed her lips, like she was deciding how much to reveal. She took her eyes off the road to look at him. "He said he knew you wouldn't kill anybody. That's how he knew."

"He knows I'm weak." The words were hard to get out. The admission felt like gravel in his throat. "He knows you're strong."

"No. He knows you're stronger than any of us, and that's why you wouldn't do it."

Bullshit. That wasn't strength. "Yeah, well, I'm thinking I could do it. Right now I'm thinking about all the different ways I could kill Scarecrow."

"Don't worry about him. He's nothing. What about you? Is anything broken? You gonna be all right?"

"Nothing's broken. My head hurts. My face. Eyeballs too. Is that weird?"

"Not with the way you look."

"Is it that bad?"

"It's pretty bad. But at least it looks like what happened. It looks like you got beat up, got your ass handed to you."

"Gee, thanks."

Gin's eyes got wide as she realized what she had said. "Shit. That's not what I meant. You were brilliant tonight."

"I don't even remember. Where were you? How'd you get there?"

"I have friends. I was in the balcony. I only saw the last part, but I thought you had him. I really did."

"You gotta be careful. If they knew you were there, after what happened with Joe, if you showed up on camera—"

"I thought you wanted to know what happened."

Justin groaned in response. You didn't fuck with the Shadow Masters, and you didn't break their rules. But that was going to have to be a conversation for another time. He didn't have the energy. And he did want to know what happened. "Fine. Tell me."

"Black Jim played dead. He came back alive like some creep in a horror movie. Tripped you up, smashed your head on the floor. Twice."

"I guess that explains the headache."

"You nearly had him, you know. You nearly beat Black Jim. The bastard kind of cheated."

Her comment was a small comfort, but it helped. He relaxed back into the seat, the sense of relief physical, the pain ebbing. He'd almost done it. Hell, he had done well considering everything, especially that shitty glove. Well enough to come through this, maybe.

The car bounced over a pothole and the pain returned—a jolt back to reality. Black Jim would never know. He'd feel nothing but hatred toward Justin. Justin had tried to do right by him, and he'd never know.

But why should that matter? The hatred was deserved, after all. He better never see Black Jim again—wasn't sure he could face him.

There were moments in that fight, though, flashes that came to him now. The look in those blue eyes. He'd made sure to look, and what had stared back at him was… interest? Excitement? Something. Something that wasn't hatred at all.

He remembered the weight of Black Jim's body, his amazing strength as they rolled around, the heat of their blood and sweat against the cold marble floor.

It was still somewhat foggy, but more might come back to him when he watched the video.

Recollection was like a craving. He desperately wanted to remember. Everything.

"Justin." Gin's voice rose, her tone producing an immediate panic just from saying his name. "We're being followed."

"What?"

Her eyes were trained on the rearview mirror. "There's a car a few blocks behind. I've seen headlights from time to time, but they're also driving dark, like they're trying not to be noticed or want us to think there's more than one car."

Shit. Had someone seen Gin at the church? "Who the hell—" He turned to look back, but the shooting pain made him realize the effort was futile at the same time it halted his words.

"I don't know if I want to find out. Do you?"

"Yes, but not if it gets us killed. And we can't go home. We can't lead them to Charlie."

"I'll double back around. See if I can pull off somewhere."

"Loop back and head west. We can hide in the old fire station on Burnham. It's just a shell."

"Good idea."

Justin was almost too tired to panic, which was probably good. Panic was futile. Looking behind was futile. But one thought stayed at the forefront of his mind, a premonition he'd had only minutes ago: you don't fuck with the Shadow Masters, and you don't break their rules.

HALE COULDN'T believe he'd actually fallen asleep, with the lights on no less. He didn't remember sleeping, but he must have been, because he was hard as a rock upon waking. Had he been dreaming?

He recognized the pounding knock on the door as one belonging to Benz. He wearily rose from the bed, taking care to keep his head centered on his shoulders and not turn his neck. Naked, he bent down to pick up a sizable handful of old clothes from the floor. He didn't put them on, just held them in front of his crotch as he went to the door.

He undid two chains and two deadbolts before opening the door to let Benz in.

The guy looked tired. His suit couldn't counter the shadows under his eyes or the sheen of dried sweat on his face. Hale would feel bad for him if he wasn't sure he looked a hell of a lot worse. "Hey, Benz," he said, turning and walking back to bed, still holding the clothes in front of him.

Benz made no comment as Hale sat down on the bed. He stepped inside the door and closed it but didn't come in any farther.

"Did you find him?"

"No, sorry. They must have spotted me, gave me the slip."

"Fuck."

"They were definitely driving north on city roads. My guess would be they live in Bruise City."

That didn't narrow it down nearly enough, but it was something.

The two men were silent. Hale's mind was trying to work, and Benz looked as sad as the lake on a sunless day. Maybe....

"Benz, do you think… could you talk to some of the higher-ups?"

"Please don't ask me to do that."

Hale looked back at Benz. Naked. Afraid. He put on his best puppy-dog face, realizing it probably wasn't going to be as effective when his eyes were swollen half-shut.

"Hale, I'm a bouncer. I'm security. It's safe. It's safe for my family. If I start asking around, if I start calling in favors, they're gonna bring me back in. No more desk job, you know? I'm gonna have to get my hands dirty again." Benz started removing the tie from his neck. For Benz, it was the equivalent of a fighter taking off the gloves, but still Hale pressed.

"No good friends? No one to keep it on the down low?"

"There's no such thing as the down low. Privacy has long been a thing of the past."

"No one you trust? No one to keep your name out of it? This Fray is going to be all anyone is talking about for a while. Someone can't feign curiosity? It doesn't have to come back to you, does it?"

"You know what they say about curiosity."

"Well, shit."

Benz shoved his tie in his pocket and walked away from the door. He leaned back against Hale's bike, crossing his arms in front of him and looking down at Hale, who now stared at the floor, more or less.

"What's up with this kid? Why do you care so much?"

If it was hard for him to explain to himself, how could he explain it to Benz? "I feel… I don't know… protective?"

"Protective about a kid who could have clawed your face off? Ended your career?"

"But he didn't. Don't you see? I don't know. Call it fighter's instinct or something. I just get the feeling this kid could be in a lot of trouble. I know it's fucked-up. I know it's probably misplaced fatherly bullshit. I been missing Eddie, you know?"

Now he was using his daughter to get his way. He was being a scheming son of a bitch, but that was putting it in terms Benz could understand, wasn't it? Besides, it was all true. There was more to it, but everything he was saying was true.

Benz sighed. "I agree with you on one point. That kid is in trouble. I don't like how things went down after you left the church. That girl showing up, that's reportable. I saw her come out, but I never saw her go in."

"What happened to her?"

"She drove the car."

"Girlfriend, maybe?" Hale frowned, and Benz examined him a little more closely, perhaps gauging Hale's reaction to his own thought.

"Could be." Benz took a long breath, and Hale held his. Was Benz considering helping him after all? "Let's say you do find this guy," Benz continued. "What then?"

"Then we talk. Ask him what his story is." Hale prepared his most convincing voice, both pleading and authoritative. "This could help us. If we found out what the plan was tonight, why he did it, where the weapon came from, who it came from—that's important to us. Then we know what game we're really playing."

From the look on Benz's face, this was the line of reasoning Hale should have been using all along. Talking to the Visitor would help them. That, Benz could understand.

It looked like Benz had come to a decision, but the next instant he threw Hale for a loop. "Did you partake of some lady company the other night, Hale?"

"That narc bitch—"

"Don't call her that. You walked right through the bar from upstairs, jackass. You alerted every security gorilla in the place."

"Oh." Hale glanced up and gave a sheepish look. "Whoops?"

"Hale, if I do this, we can't be making waves. You gotta play it cool, man. If you need to let off some steam, do it elsewhere. Everyone in this building has the same boss, and the employees are paid to be observant. This needs to be under the radar. Way under. It can't get back to anyone. I mean, look at you. You can't risk someone seeing the wrong bruise. You know what happens to people that aren't discreet?"

He should have known Benz was no moral compass, that his partner's warnings had been for his protection. "I'm sorry," Hale said. "Maybe Wilma was a mistake."

"I'm not too worried about that one, but you got lucky. Next time you might not be so lucky, understand?"

Good thing Hale had only interacted with Wilma. He gave a very shallow nod. "I understand."

Benz came to him and bent down, putting a gentle hand on Hale's chin. He examined Hale's face, his ribs. Hale found the gaze rather comforting. It was nice to be taken care of.

"You'll live," Benz said at last. "You need any painkillers?"

"No. That's probably not a good idea." Besides, Hale wanted to feel the pain. It was the mark of the Visitor, a constant reminder.

"I'll see what I can do about finding the guy. It might not be anything, but… I'll try."

"Thanks, man."

Benz stood up. "I want to hug you, but you're pretty naked."

Hale stood up, still holding the pile of clothes in front of his crotch. "Hug me, then. Just go easy on the ribs."

Benz put his big arms around Hale, firm but gentle. Hale didn't return the embrace, but he did lean into the larger man. "I'm so sorry," Benz said quietly.

"No more of that now."

"I love you like a brother."

"I love you too, man."

"I'll do what I can. I promise."

That promise made for Hale's second dirty victory of the night.

But dirty victories were victories just the same.

As Justin stood under a stream of hot water, he tried to figure out what it all meant.

After pulling off the road, the car following them had driven by, headlights off. Despite the darkness, the shape of the man behind the wheel had been unmistakable. He was a big hulking beast—Black Jim's handler.

The most likely explanation was revenge. Justin had brought a weapon to the Fray on that man's watch. But it didn't quite make sense. The man had seemed sympathetic, helping Justin off the floor of the church while his own handler did nothing. He wished he had been paying better attention to the words the man had exchanged with Scarecrow. Had Scarecrow said something to make him go after Justin—or Gin?

It could be Gin. To anyone sticking around and observing, she would have been very visible. No one, absolutely no one, was supposed to know about a Shadow Fray except for the two handlers and the two Brawlers. Gin's presence was akin to a security breach. For all Justin knew, maybe handlers were supposed to dispatch anyone who wandered onto the scene. Might be the guy was tying up a loose end, that being Gin. A chill went through him, even under the hot water of the shower.

But everything would be okay. The danger was over—they'd never meet again. Rematches were exceedingly rare. So Justin would never know why he followed them, never know what he was after.

Who knows? Maybe Justin had somehow earned Black Jim's respect and the man had been trying to find out where he lived. Justin had nearly beaten him. But so what? Was the handler going to deliver flowers with a little note that said how much of an honor it was to fight against someone so worthy? Of course not. Totally dumb. Or maybe the note would say how sexy it had been rolling around on the hard marble floor of the church, and would he like to do it again sometime? His head said it was ridiculous, but his dick twitched at the idea.

Justin gave a couple playful tugs but quickly shut off the water. It was best not to let the fantasy continue, best not to think about how close he and Black Jim had gotten tonight. It had been crazily primal. The soreness of his fists attested to how much of a surge he'd gotten from the other man. Fighting Black Jim had brought out Justin's best. As sore as he was, Justin would fight him again in a heartbeat, despite the dangers.

God, he had thought about that fight for so long. Now it had happened. It was over. He kept fluctuating between a warm afterglow and depression.

Justin toweled off gently. He was starting to bruise along his side where he'd been kicked. That one would be a beaut. He wiped the steam from the mirror and surveyed the damage. He'd have another large bruise on his neck. He'd definitely have a black eye on his right side. He had quite a bump on his left side, but it was higher up at the hairline. His lip was fat. He had opened up the deepest slash from his fight two weeks prior, but it no longer bled. This was going to be hard to explain to Ray. He frowned at his reflection—and even the small movement hurt. He could not work in his normal capacity for a while. He was in the same shitty position he was two weeks ago.

Justin put on a loose pair of shorts and headed out into the main living area. It was still dark, but it would be getting light soon. He'd only taken a couple steps when Charlie threw himself around his waist, hugging him tight. He stood for a few moments as Charlie breathed deeply against him. Heaved would be a better description. The poor kid was emotional.

"He wasn't too happy being left upstairs," Gin said.

"Of course not." Justin picked Charlie up carefully, so small for ten, and held him close. "Hey, Char." He walked to the couch and sat next to Gin. He positioned Charlie carefully on his knee, which was unscathed and largely pain-free.

Charlie turned to look at him from under the brim of his baseball cap. His eyes weren't wet, but his expression was strained. He put a gentle hand on Justin's cheek. Justin could see his eyes taking in every injury, starting with his face and traveling the rest of his body.

Determined, Charlie got up and walked to the open kitchen. Justin and Gin didn't speak but watched as he grabbed four towels from a cupboard and laid them out neatly on the counter—four perfect squares of cloth. Next he went into the freezer and took out two handfuls of ice. He put exactly three cubes on every cloth, having to make a couple return trips since his hands were small. He wrapped up the first cloth carefully as though it were a little present, and then the second one, folding the corners in and twisting it off. With both hands full, he walked over to Justin. He put one of the little ice presents in Justin's hand and lifted Justin's hand to his jaw. He put the second one in the opposite hand, lifting it to Justin's neck. Then he went to retrieve the last two, taking the same care he had with the first. He carried them back to Justin, facing him. He reached one of his hands up to Justin's temple where he pressed the ice, and the other to Justin's side. Finally he ducked under Justin's arms and settled against his shoulder. He was so gentle, making sure he had a light touch.

Justin's eyes began to water. "Thanks, Bro Bro," he said softly.

Their family sat quietly for a few moments, and Justin was sure they were all thinking the same thing. They would do whatever they had to in order to stay together. Anything.

Gin broke the spell. "I have to go to work soon. We need to tell Ray."

"I agree," Justin said. At this point it was inevitable. Inevitable, but not safe. "Carefully, though. It could put him in danger." And us. Those last words went unsaid, as if not saying them would somehow make him less afraid.

"Yeah, I get that." Gin nodded as she spoke. "I'll figure out a way."

"No. We'll all go. If he sees me, maybe we won't have to use so many words. Just let him put it together, and he can deny we ever told him anything."

"Are you sure you're up for that? What if somebody else sees you?"

No, he wasn't up for it. His sides ached, his face pounded, his eyes wanted to shut. "We'll go now, while it's still dark. Charlie too. I think that will have the most impact."

"I think we can trust him."

"I hope so," Justin said, but his gut was clenched so hard it felt like he'd eaten stones.

And that didn't feel like hope.

Chapter 14

The LIGHT entering his window did nothing to lighten Hale's mood. He'd been unable to sleep after Benz left. His emotions were as multihued as his bruises. Relief. Excitement. Guilt.

But mostly loneliness.

Emotions didn't feel right to him. Growing up in his small community, he hadn't had many friends, no boys exactly his age. He got along fine with his sisters, but he wasn't working side by side with them. He'd gotten attention from some older boys, one in particular, but that relationship certainly couldn't be called emotional.

And he didn't miss his parents. The only ones he gave a thought to were his sisters, but it wasn't so much missing an emotional connection as the guilt of leaving them behind. They were victims as much as he had been.

The first person he'd had an emotional connection with had been Janie. Even then, he hadn't fallen in love with her as much as succumbed to her attentions. He'd been like an injured wild animal to her, one she couldn't help but want to heal and tame. He wasn't used to anyone's care or affection, not until she offered him hers.

Hale didn't miss her as much as miss the idea of her. Perhaps the man he was now could love her better. At the time, he never opened himself up, never really gave himself to her. He'd simply taken what she'd offered. He was a real prick for doing it too.

Now, Hale only loved two people in his life. One was the brother he'd seen a couple hours earlier.

He picked up his phone. Dialed the number. It only rang three times.

"Hale." Her voice sounded a little desperate but not upset that he had called.

"Morning, Jess."

She sighed loudly. Maybe he didn't love this woman, but as Benz's wife and Eddie's stand-in mother, he would take a bullet for her. He owed it to Janie too. All right, maybe Jess made it three people he loved, but he wasn't about to admit it. "How are you?" she asked.

He almost smiled. "A lot better now that I know you actually care."

"God, Hale. Don't be an asshole. Of course I care."

"She must not be up yet if you're cussing."

"She's just getting up now."

"Can I talk to her?"

"Yeah. Yeah, of course." It was like she added that last bit to talk herself into it. "She'll be a few minutes. How are you holding up?"

"I've been better, but I could be worse. You watch it?"

"No. I don't usually watch that stuff, not much anyway."

"The numbers are unbelievable. You must be the only one who doesn't want to see me get punched in the face and get my ass handed to me for once."

She laughed softly. "Well, I didn't say I wouldn't watch it. I said I don't usually. Benz told me everything, though. That bad, huh?"

"Afraid so."

He heard her sigh again and breathe in like she was going to say something. Part of him wanted to make her say it first, but he caved.

"I guess it'll be a while before I can see Eddie." He could feel his swollen face tightening up and hear the gruffness in his voice. "Can't really have her see me like this."

Her slight nod and pursed lips would make no sound, yet he knew that's what she was doing.

In the uncomfortable silence that followed, Hale considered not telling her the next part, but he kept going.

"Look," he began, "I'm sure you heard the fight last night had… irregularities. Benz and I talked, and he's gonna make a few subtle inquiries."

Silence.

He kept going. "We need to know more about what's going on. He's concerned if he asks for any favors, he's gonna have to… that he's gonna get sucked back in. They're gonna want him to take up some of his old duties."

"I'd say that's a damn valid concern for him to have."

"Yeah." Hale had a moment of panic that Benz had already talked to his wife about this. Had he told her that Hale had a weird fascination with the kid? Did she figure Hale may have manipulated Benz into this situation? Could she see that this wasn't about Shadow Fray at all?

"Why are you telling me this?"

"I want you to know what's what, and I want you to hear it from me, since I'm the one who asked him to do it."

"Consider me informed."

"And Jess… I don't want anything bad to happen. Tell him to be careful. If he can't do it without going in deeper, tell him not to do it."

"You think he'll listen to me?"

"He always listens to you."

The breathy grunt he heard over the phone let Hale know clearly that she didn't agree. "Not where you're concerned, Hale. He doesn't listen to me then."

Silence.

This time it was Jess who continued. "If you don't want him in any danger, you need to call him off. Don't put this on me." He could hear the anger building in her voice. "How in the world you managed to get your hooks so far into everyone I love, I have no idea."

"If I wasn't in Shadow Fray, who knows what Benz would be doing right now? He could still be offing people in dark alleys, if he didn't get a bullet to the head himself."

"Don't, Hale. You don't know that."

"Don't know nothin'. All I'm saying is that I'd rather be on your team than against you. We're all in this together, like it or not." Why did things always go to hell when he talked to this woman?

"All right." He could tell the "all right" didn't necessarily mean agreement. "Here's Edna."

He took in a big breath while Eddie accepted the phone. He could hear Jess indistinctly in the background saying something. He wanted to be in the moment with Eddie, and he needed to put all those other emotions with Jess aside. Transition.

"Hi, Hale!"

"Hey there, Baby Doll."

"Mama says you're sick."

"Yeah. Yeah, that's right. I'm real sick."

"Why? What's wrong?" He could hear the fear in her voice and realized *sick* could mean a lot worse than sick. Even at her young age, the Thinning had apparently been ingrained in her. Puzzling, because Benz or Jess wouldn't have talked to her about the epidemics that had a hand in wiping out so many people so long ago, not yet, and he knew for damned sure he didn't talk to her about so dark a topic. She was too young. Must be that fucking Chixago Building school. What other horrors had they taught her? Theories on the poisoned ground? The coastal flooding? Jesus, she was only six....

He swallowed his anger, making sure his voice was calm. "Oh no, no, no. I'm not sick like that. Nothing serious. I got body aches is all. I'm sore. Can't move around real good. I suppose I'll have to stay in bed for a while."

"Can you come over tomorrow?"

"No, I'm afraid not," he said sadly. "I just love you so much that I can't get you sick, and I don't wanna get your mama or daddy sick either. So I better stay away for a while until I feel better, but I'd sure like to talk to you every day."

"Mama says I can play online with you after school. We can video too."

"Oh, I'd really like to play games with you. That's a great idea. I don't think I can video yet, though. This new place I got, they're real strict about that."

"That's so silly. Everyone can video, you know. Just use your phone!"

His kid was too damn smart for her own good.

"It's not that I can't do it; it's that they don't like it here. But you know what? I'll ask 'em. Maybe they can bend the rules for me a little bit when I tell them how pretty you are and that I just can't not look at my beautiful Baby Doll." Parenting Strategy 101, there. When you don't have an answer, put it off.

"Okay. Mama says I gotta eat breakfast."

"I sure will miss my breakfast with you."

"Me too. Breakfast is no fun. It's so *boring*." In that moment he could picture her expression. She'd open her mouth and get this look and sigh. She hadn't picked up the eye roll yet that would one day replace it, so it was still cute.

"Tell you what. I haven't been sleeping so good, so you'd be doing me a real favor if you let me call and read you a story at night before you go to bed." He immediately felt guilty for mentioning his troubles. She didn't need to know about his problems. He should be protecting her from that, not making her a part of it. "Maybe you're too big for stories, though."

"Mmmmm… well I could read *you* a story."

"Could you? Wow, I sure am gonna look forward to that." He was certain she could hear the joy in his voice. He was smiling as big as he could with hurt lips and a sore jaw. It felt like the biggest smile he'd ever had. "You have a good day at school, Baby Doll. I sure do love you lots and lots."

"Love you too. Take lots of naps."

"I'll do that. Bye-bye now."

"Bye."

He put aside the phone and closed his eyes. At least for a little while, he'd be able to sleep.

JUSTIN, GIN, and Charlie sat waiting in their small car as the dim light of dawn turned into the full light of day. They were parked next to the semi in the garage. Other workers were beginning to show up, but the only one who would notice their car was Ray. He'd go right by as he went into the adjacent manager's office.

As exhausted as Justin was, his nerves kept him semialert. He needed this job. Badly.

The complex not only manufactured condoms but also handled sales and distribution for lube and other accessories. Most of Justin's deliveries were to retailers along the 90/94 freeway corridors, but he occasionally made special deliveries to large rises in Chicago and rarely trips to the north or farther south around Lake Michigan. Now it would be a while before he could do that, and Ray would have to cover for him.

Gin worked with Ray in the office handling sales and shipments, although she was quite capable of working the factory line as well. While they owned their condo and it had been in the family for generations, ever-expanding fees ate up the majority of both of their paychecks. It was a good job. It was just enough to maintain their level of comfort. They were very lucky in that regard, but they hadn't always been so.

Barely maintaining was fine, but Justin and Gin both wanted a future for Charlie. With his disability it might be difficult, but they wanted Charlie to have options. Ideally he'd go to Chicago and train with the big scientists. If money was to be made, that's how it was made. With brains. Otherwise the Uppers kept circulating the money amongst themselves. Unless you had something they wanted, like treatments in genetics, fertility, or medicine, you were continually looking up at them from the street level.

That's why Justin needed this job. Gin should be okay—Ray was more than a boss to her; he was a friend. Justin, however, knew him only as a boss. A decent enough man, sure, but if Justin couldn't do his job, why wouldn't Ray throw him out on his ass?

That's why this face-to-face meeting would be their best hope.

He'd spent the last hour sitting in the car trying not to think about the other possibilities. Those darker outcomes began with the words, "Reward leading to the arrest and conviction of...."

Ray could report him. The weird thing was, Justin was pretty sure the police didn't care. It was the people who controlled the police and controlled the money—perhaps the mayor or the same people running Shadow Fray—that's who cared. The Shadow Masters. Information was their safety net. If someone was careless enough to be reported, it was a sign that the rotten fruit needed to be cut off the tree. Disposed of.

Justin did not want to be disposed of. It was common knowledge that people disappeared all the time. Running across a corpse was a regular occurrence, and no one would think twice about finding one wearing his shoes and hoodie out in the wastelands of the city, even if it was a little fresher than most.

Such cheery thoughts. Justin's eyes were heavy, but he was unable to doze. In the distance he saw a drone on the skyline, like a bird that flew in an unbelievably straight line.

"He's here," Gin said. Suddenly alert, Justin looked to see Ray coming toward them. Finally.

Ray was generally a friendly looking guy. He was slightly overweight, a dark-skinned black man with a round belly, black beard, and kind eyes, solidly middle-aged. Justin tensed as he saw that his boss looked troubled, his brow creased. Uh-oh. But of course he was troubled. Seeing them all here was a little out of the ordinary.

Ray came walking up to the car in jeans and a red jacket, always casual. Ray was a casual kind of guy. Justin had never seen him look upset.

This was it. The moment of truth.

He opened the passenger door where Justin was sitting.

"What the hell are you all doing here?" Shit.

"Hi, Ray. Nice to see you too." Gin waved. "I take it those just look like jeans, but they're really your cranky pants."

Ray glared at her. "I'm not cranky. I just have a violent reaction to stupid people."

Ray looked angry, but not exactly surprised. In fact, Justin was pretty taken aback that Ray didn't look at all shocked, despite Justin's bruised and battered state. It was Justin who was suddenly feeling surprised.

"You all are gonna have to get in the truck and let me drive you home. Leave your car here. I don't want you driving around in broad daylight with this one looking like my mama caught his dumb bum broke ass with his hand in her cookie jar."

"Cookie Jar. Is that your sister's name?" Gin asked.

"You shut up. I ain't in the mood for your jokes. Now move before anyone else sees you."

"You're always in the mood for me, Ray," Gin said with a smile.

Justin sat with his mouth open for a moment. "I don't…."

"We can talk in the truck," Ray said. "Now c'mon."

Charlie opened the back door and hopped out. He went up to Ray and gave him a fierce hug, wrapping his arms around the thick waist.

Ray's expression immediately softened, a smile on his face and a twinkle in his eyes. "This one's my favorite out of all of you. You gotta keep a tighter leash on these two, Charlie. If only your brother had your brains and your sister knew how to keep her mouth shut. You work on that for me." Charlie nodded into his belly enthusiastically, Ray patting him on the back.

Even the usually quick-witted Gin only gave Ray a smirk as she got out of the car. They piled into the truck, Justin and Charlie in the back, Gin and Ray up front with Ray driving. He started up the engine. It gave off quite a racket in the enclosed garage, but he didn't go anywhere.

Time for Justin to explain, then. He took a deep breath. "Ray—"

"Whoa now," Ray said, holding up his hand. "I don't want you sayin' too much. There ain't no need. I got a call from the boss man this morning sayin' you'd be out for a while."

"Boss man?" Justin asked.

"Yeah, that's right," Ray said. "He's an old friend of yours. Bought the place sometime after Gin started working here, then put me in charge. You didn't think this was my operation, did you?"

Justin felt stupid for not putting two and two together. That's how he'd gotten the job there, then. "Did you know about this?" he asked Gin. "Why didn't Griz say anything?"

Gin shrugged. "The old man was asleep when I got Charlie."

"No, not just today," Justin insisted. "Ever. He never said anything, ever."

"One thing you two oughta have down by now: sometimes saying less is better." Ray's tone was scolding. "Isn't that right, Charlie?"

Charlie nodded with a thumbs-up.

"Damn, but you guys got yourselves mixed up in some shit, though. That old man leaving town was one of the worst things that could've happened. Seems he came back at exactly the right time."

"I'm starting to think that was a lot more than coincidence," Justin said. "It's not just him wanting to die at home."

"Best not to think too deeply about stuff," Ray warned.

"Tell that to his brain," said Gin. "I have a feeling Justin doesn't talk much only because too many thoughts are trying to escape at once. He suffers from mental traffic jams."

"Surprised he can do much thinking at all with the knockabout he's had."

"I thought we weren't supposed to talk about that," Justin said sourly. All these attempts at humor were making his head hurt.

"Nah. I said that to you. I can say stuff, especially when it's as plain as the bloody nose on your face."

Justin needed this conversation to take a detour. "I'm really sorry about the job."

"Justin, boy—you deliver condoms, not antibiotics. It'll be fine."

"I don't mean to make more work for you, though."

Ray shrugged. "Work is work. I put in the same amount of time regardless. It's just a little less time I'll be sittin' on my ass in the office. Bein' up and moving around'll be good for me. Maybe I'll even lose a few pounds, make your sister take notice. Hell, if I'd known lifting boxes of rubbers would give you muscles like that, I'd'a switched places with you long ago."

Gin gave Ray a coy smile. "How long you known about all this, Ray?" Gin asked, tipping her head in Justin's direction.

"Not long at all, or you better believe I would have tried to talk you out of it." Ray sighed, his hands on the wheel, still not driving. "Truth is,

Gin, you know I been keen on you for a long time. I ain't got no family of my own, so sometimes in my head, I start thinking of you all as my family. God knows you talk about these two enough. I feel like I know 'em better than I do." Justin could swear he saw a blush on Ray's dark cheeks.

"You sure are sweet, Ray." Gin smiled.

"You all need anything, all you gotta do is ask." Ray pressed on the gas, and they finally started moving. "Now let's take you all on home. I can tell none of you got any sleep. You look like the walking dead."

Gin reached over and put her hand on Ray's shoulder. "I'll be comin' back with you. I'm fine to work."

Ray looked like he was about to argue, but then he nodded, a smile on his lips.

True exhaustion settled over Justin. He couldn't possibly keep his eyes open another second. As he drifted off, he thought about how funny it was, the way his mind worked. An hour ago he never would have expected this could go so well.

Sleep overtook him.

Chapter 15

FOR THE first time in five days, Justin's head didn't hurt, but he couldn't imagine feeling shittier. The bruising on his face wasn't as incriminating as the marks he'd gotten last time, but he wouldn't be getting out of the truck. Unfortunately this meeting with Scarecrow was for Gin.

She looked so normal sitting in the passenger seat staring out the window. Her face was free of worry lines. Her honey-colored skin was smooth and unmarred, a rarity for someone who got her hands dirty from time to time. Joe hadn't been her first, not if you counted self-defense.

Mom had taught Gin to shoot at a very young age, and she'd practiced religiously ever since. Any woman walking on the street had at least one gun. Gin never wore hers in the same spot. If he had to guess, from the way her chest was flattened and a little less shapely, today she was carrying in a holster attached at the front of her bra. She liked to call it a bolster.

Generally women could walk around in the populated areas unmolested, at least in big cities. If assaulted, a woman could shoot to kill. After questioning, the cops called in the body, and depending on the perp, it often ended there.

Only men not in their right mind would try to touch a woman. Like with Gin's first kill. They were twelve years old, Justin remembered. The man had been skinny and malnourished, terrible teeth, dirty. He'd bounded out from behind a wall. The guy was on top of her before Justin could do anything. Gin had her gun up immediately. A shot to the gut to get herself out from under him, and then a shot to the side of his head. Easy as one, two, and you could spare the three. She never hesitated.

She was briefly questioned on scene, and that was all. Police didn't ask many questions over a guy like that, someone who clearly lived on the ground. Justin had learned two things that day. The first was that he would kill someone who threatened his sister. The second, that he would never have to.

"What are you thinking about?" Gin asked him.

"Villains," Justin said.

"Villains?"

"Yeah. I was thinking about how all the villains in our life had a pretty short time of it. Hopefully the same applies to Scarecrow."

"In terms of villains, I'm not sure Scarecrow qualifies," Gin said. "He's just an asshole."

"Gin, he slit a guy's throat right in front of me. On camera."

"Oh yeah," she admitted. "I guess that does put him in the villain category, doesn't it?"

"You've never thought of offing him?"

"No, not really. He's playing along. And we need him, at least for now."

He kept his eyes glued to the road. He was terrified of Scarecrow on some level, whereas Gin wasn't scared of him at all. Why the difference? He was under Scarecrow's thumb and hated it, but Gin acted like she had Scarecrow right where she wanted him.

The whole situation was as tangled and sharp as the barbed wire he saw coming into view. They were nearly there.

At the train station, they pulled into one of the loading zone spots. It was exactly 7:00 a.m. The morning sun had risen only ten minutes ago, but to Justin the light was too glaring. As Gin opened the door, he could feel a chill in the air and was reminded it was the last day of September.

"I'll bring him back to the truck," Gin said, "You should probably get in back."

"What if he doesn't want to come?"

"He'll come."

Justin moved to the back where Charlie would normally sit. His brother wasn't too happy with him right now. They'd left him with Mr. Mays and Devin, because no way in hell would Scarecrow ever know he existed, not after what happened with Joe. Devin would be taking Charlie to school, and that made Justin slightly nervous. For the first time ever, neither he nor Gin would be able to do it. The six-block walk to the school at the Catholic church was something he held dear. Plus he didn't know Devin very well, though he seemed trustworthy.

Before he could dwell on it too long, Gin was walking out of the train station with Scarecrow a few steps behind. His thinning smoke-colored hair stuck up in the breeze. With his hands in the pockets of his trench coat, the man looked crazed.

Gin opened the passenger-side door for Scarecrow like they were on some twisted date. It was a subtle control move on her part. She was the one in charge.

"Justin," Scarecrow said as Gin went around to the driver's side and got in. "How are you feeling?"

"A little more bruised but less flayed than last time, thanks."

Scarecrow smiled. "You know, Justin, I actually like you."

Justin just eyed him.

"First things first," Scarecrow said, pulling out a wrapped packet from his coat and handing it to Gin. "I need a blood sample."

"Got my own needle," Gin said, reaching across him and opening the glove hatch. She pulled out a similar packet. Where the hell had she gotten that? "If you think I'm sticking a needle in my arm coming from you, you're crazier than you look."

"Ah, ah, ah," Scarecrow said, extending his packet. "How do I know yours isn't contaminated with something that'll fuck up the results? You use my packet. And before you disagree, look at it. It's completely sealed. And know this: there's no way in hell I'd give you a dirty needle when you have something I want. That would defeat the whole purpose, wouldn't it?"

Gin examined the packet before nodding. "I'll consent to this." She made it sound like a contractual agreement.

"Need any help?" Scarecrow asked.

"I can manage." As though she knew exactly what she was doing, she tied off her arm with a small band that came in the packet. Without flinching, she inserted the needle. Justin watched as dark blood bubbled up inside the vial. "Little help with the band, Justin," she said.

Justin leaned forward and unwrapped her arm as more blood pulsed into the vial. It was over quickly. She removed the needle, handing the whole contraption over to Scarecrow as one dark bead of blood surfaced on her skin. She picked up a small piece of gauze and wiped it away as Scarecrow bagged the blood sample and stuck it in his coat.

"Fingers crossed, I'm sure," Scarecrow said with a smile. Gin just crossed her arms and looked at him, returning the smile.

Justin did not smile.

He tensed, the physical effects of the anger rising in him, Scarecrow's glibness compounding his frustration. He wanted to explode. "Why the hell do you even want this?"

Scarecrow looked him in the eyes, serious now.

"Redemption," he said simply. As Justin tried to make sense of the response, the man's expression softened.

"You'll also be wanting this," Scarecrow said, reaching into his pocket. He pulled out a very significant wad of cash. "I owe you some props, Justin. Our invisible bosses didn't see the fight the way I did— they said nothing about the glove, only that they were impressed. You brought Black Jim to the brink of defeat. This is nowhere near what we would have gotten if you'd won, but it's a very sizable amount. Half of it is yours. This half."

Scarecrow handed the roll of cash over to him. "Don't count it now. It's ten times what you got last time. Make sure you take good care of your sister for me."

Justin felt like his heart had fallen though his chest. With everything that happened, he'd half forgotten about the money and half didn't put any stock in it amounting to anything.

"Don't get me wrong, kid. I still think you got a soft spot, and I know there was something janky with that fight, but people aren't seeing it that way, and I guess that's all that matters. You know how to perform for the cameras. And with this new arrangement we three have, I gotta believe you won't be throwing any more fights."

"I didn't…." But Justin trailed off, stuck between denial and thinking of the unfortunate "arrangement" that would now have him winning every Fray. No matter the cost. He had to.

Scarecrow raised an eyebrow, eyes glinting. "I take it you've seen the views?"

"I'm aware, yeah." He'd only watched the fight at least a hundred times. It had already become the most widely viewed Fray of all time.

"Turns out you are the new number one. Not in terms of rank, but in terms of views. The St. Josaphat Arena and the Mutual Conglomerate Arena sit at number one and number two. Top two Shadow Frays. Not even Black Jim can say that, can he? Of course, I give myself some of the credit, but I'll give you credit where it's due too."

"Thanks," Justin said quietly. Had he just thanked Scarecrow? He really must not be thinking straight.

"You also have a name."

"A name?" Justin asked. This he didn't know.

"They've taken to calling you the Night Visitor. 'The Visitor' was too plain, apparently. I tend to agree. This one has a nice ring to it. Anyway, it's got the seal of approval from the Shadow Masters, bless their anonymous asses. It's going up on the pages and promos soon. You've hit the big time, kid."

Gin smiled at him, proud.

"You don't have another fight scheduled yet. I think they want to make sure their new star is camera ready before they stick you back in a Fray. Take your hoodie down for a second." Justin complied and Scarecrow eyed him, seeming to study his injuries for the first time. "Even with all those bruises, you are a good-looking man, aren't you? No homo, 'cause I'm not bent. I prefer your sister's pussy, but those genes practically have me creaming in my pants." Scarecrow turned to Gin. "I don't suppose you'd want to go another round quick, would you? I can make it fast."

Gin seemed to think about it. "Tempting."

Scarecrow laughed loudly, opening his mouth to reveal smoke-stained teeth. "I could throw in another 10 percent."

"Don't," Justin practically growled to Scarecrow as he flipped his hood back up.

Scarecrow laughed again. "Only kidding, only kidding. Mostly, anyway."

Scarecrow was looking between Justin and Gin. Justin was sure his face looked as pissed as he felt, but Gin sat with her arms crossed, a slight smile on her face.

"One final thing," Scarecrow said, reaching again in his pocket. "Take this phone." He handed a plain-looking phone to Justin. "It's untraceable, a burner, but don't try to call me or anyone else on it. I have my own. I will only turn it on when I get the info on the Arena for your next Fray. My guess is it will be weeks, not months. I will only turn it on to send you a message to meet here again, same time. After that it will be off. I suggest you turn yours on only once a day to check for a message. Turn it off before sixty seconds pass and don't check it again until the following day."

"I don't understand," Justin said. "Why so secret?"

"Kid, you've got millions of people watching you. You just rocketed up to the top. This is a big money business, and you're the hot new commodity. People will be gunning for you, looking to find out any information they can. If either one of us is compromised somehow, I don't want info to spread. I don't need to remind you that your sister being here right now as we talk is really fucking dangerous for all of us. Don't take any chances. Don't speak about it at home; don't speak about it on the phone or in any electronic communication. You never know who out there might be listening, and that includes our bosses. We can never meet inside this truck again. For all we know, this truck is bugged and we're already fucked. Keep that in mind."

With that, and without waiting for any response, Scarecrow opened the door and was gone.

Gin turned slightly pale. Her strong façade had finally broken. She may not be afraid of Scarecrow, but his parting words had rattled her.

Hale was going crazy, and it was only Monday. Thank God the day was nearly over. Or was it? He supposed not if he'd be awake half the night again. The sun would soon set, but it didn't matter. He had no view to appreciate the dying light. He'd never been able to see the sunset from his old place, but he had watched it reflect off the tall buildings of Chicago. Why was he missing something he never really had? Stupid, insipid thoughts wiggled through his brain like worms. Truly this was insanity. He wanted to pound his head against the wall.

Why not? Hale beat a steady rhythm on the wall with his forehead. He needed to get out of here. He hadn't left these four walls since returning from the Arena. Tonight, he vowed, he'd wait until it was good and dark and take his bike out. He'd be fine under the safety of his helmet. He'd wear all black and scream through the night on his Harley, ride her dark and go as fast as he possibly could. The moon had been half-full the night of the Fray. It should be approaching full now. That should be plenty of light to see by once he got out of the city.

Maybe then he could get the Visitor out of his head too. Every time Hale closed his eyes, he thought back to the fight. He got images like flashes of film in his head. He'd watched the video plenty, watched all of the kid's videos. There was something about him….

Hale paced to his bed, then back to the window. He was obsessed, and it wasn't just the kid's skills, although no one had given Black Jim a match like that in ages. No, it was more than that. The kid's body, that broad chest, those stacked shoulders, his dark hair and eyes, his tanned skin, even the scent of his sweat—the kid himself excited Hale, had Hale wanting to taste him, run his tongue along the lines of his muscles, every single one. Could be he was projecting, but Hale also perceived a mysterious kindness. This guy wasn't like other fighters—

Someone knocked on his door, startling him. That was weird. Benz had a very distinctive knock, a hard four-beat rap that only his big hands could make. Whoever knocked was not Benz, and it made no sense for anyone else to visit. Hale couldn't show his face right now. He walked as silently as he could from the window, knowing very well he might have to pretend no one was home. What if they heard him? Saw his shadow? He paused. Maybe he shouldn't approach the door to see who it was. Maybe he should wait—

"Hale, it's me." Benz. Good. But what the hell? He looked though the peephole, confirmed Benz was alone, and quickly undid the two chains and two dead bolts.

Hale saw that Benz was holding a dish of something, something that smelled fantastic. Venison? "God, man, am I glad to see you. I'm going insane here."

"Jess made you food. Figured you could use it."

He was starving. "I've been living off protein powder for the last two days. Tell her thanks."

As Hale reached for the covered dish, he noticed the fingers on Benz's right hand were wrapped up thickly. "That explains the knock," he said, nodding toward the hand. "What did you do?"

"Yeah, had my hands full and then this…." He waved his hand in the air. "This is what I came to talk to you about."

"Uh-oh. Why do I suddenly have a bad feeling?"

"Must be psychic. Put that away, okay? We need to talk."

As Benz locked the door, Hale quickly went to put the dish in the fridge. Despite the savory aroma, he suddenly had no appetite. What the hell was this all about?

Back in the main room, Benz was leaning on the bike. Hale sat down on the bed across from him. It made him feel small, sitting on the bed with the large man mostly standing, looking down at him. "So, you gonna tell me what happened?" Hale asked.

"A friend happened."

"Some friend."

"It's a dead end, man. I'm sorry."

"What do you mean?" Hale spoke slowly, like time was standing still.

"I tried to make inquiries about the kid, find out who he is, but I didn't get very far."

"Shit." Hale rested his arms on his knees, deflating. "Someone did that to you, just for asking? Makes no sense."

"Like I said, it was a friend. When she saw that I was going to keep asking around despite her warning, she decided to let me know how serious she was."

"She broke your finger?"

"Two of them. With a paperweight."

"Who uses a fucking paperweight?"

"Someone who wants a weapon close by."

"You okay?"

"Could be worse. Had to bust a hole through my nails to relieve some of the pressure. They're swelled up pretty good."

"Jesus." Hale exhaled like he had been holding his breath. "I'm really sorry."

"She said it was better to break my fingers now than someone break my skull later if I was gonna keep it up."

"Are you… safe? Are you in danger?"

"Nah. She was the first person I asked."

Hale hung his head, staring at a spot on the floor. He closed his eyes and the spot turned black, a spiral, like his hope was being sucked down a drain. "So we'll never find him, then?"

"Afraid not."

The two men were silent. Hale opened his eyes but couldn't bring himself to look at Benz.

Finally, Benz stirred, shifting position to settle next to Hale on the bed. "What's going through your head?"

Hale looked at his feet. "Honestly, nothing. The last few days I've been going crazy, couldn't turn off my thoughts for the life of me. But now there's nothing."

"Sorry, brother. I tried."

"Thanks for trying."

"Welcome." They sat in silence, for how long, Hale couldn't say.

"I gotta get to work, man," Benz finally said. "I'm sorry to leave you like this. I'll stop by again soon. You know, Edna's getting a real kick out of reading to you."

Hale lifted the corner of his mouth in a weak attempt to smile. "Highlight of my day, man."

Benz chuckled, his eyes lighting up. "She's familiar with those stories and can read parts of them, but when she gets going, it's all coming out of her own head. The stuff she comes up with cracks me up."

"Yeah. The way I remember it, Goldilocks didn't tame the bears and ride them into the forest looking for the Big Bad Wolf. Smart idea, though. Better than the original."

"You should give her a call once I leave."

"Maybe I will. Might take the bike out later."

"That'd be good. Just be careful."

"I'll be careful enough."

"And Hale? Clean up in here. It smells like spunk."

Hale shrugged. "That would be all the jerking off you smell. Bored off my ass. And protein powder makes it really potent." And he also couldn't stop thinking about the kid—or the Night Visitor, as they were calling him now. Hale would never know his real name.

"Glad you haven't lost your sense of humor."

"Yeah. Night, Benz."

And then Benz was gone. The man could probably sense that Hale wanted to be alone. The last four days he would have killed for company, and now he couldn't manage it at all.

He picked up his phone and texted Jess: *Can't do a story tonight. Tell Eddie I love her.*

Hale would feel better with a phone call, but he didn't want to talk to her like this. He couldn't let her know anything was wrong.

After sending the message, he sent another, adding: *I called off Benz. You were right.*

As soon as he sent it, he wondered if it was a mistake. Would Benz tell her the real reason his fingers were broken? He doubted it. Benz didn't want any more tension between his wife and Hale. Their tenuous hold on courtesy made Benz's life a whole lot easier. As a rule, Benz didn't lie to his wife, but little white lies went with the territory. In his line of work, an injury could have a hundred causes. That wasn't to say she couldn't put two and two together, though. Knowing Jess, she probably would. Hale probably deserved her anger. It was his fault, wasn't it? He lay back on the bed, arm under his head, and stared at the ceiling.

What did it mean that a simple inquiry was shut down so completely? Through all his victories, he'd never thought much about how Shadow Fray was run. He collected his paycheck and never really had to worry. Now it was time to start asking questions. Follow the money back to the source, and you'd find the Fray bosses—the game masters who organized the rankings, set up the matches, collected the money.

Where did the money come from? Advertising revenues were minimal because economies were far more localized than they used to be. Hale wasn't sure how overseas distribution was handled. Could be they charged money, or were looking to start charging, and set it up as pay-per-view entertainment. In the Old World, people used to pay for entertainment. He knew Hollywood had once been a huge city in the industry—long before climate change, floods, and all that other shit had decimated the coasts. Shadow Fray was certainly growing in popularity. This could be the new form of entertainment, cheaply made and seen by millions. Maybe Chicago would be the new Hollywood.

It had to be Chicago money. While Frays took place all over the country, the vast majority of Arenas were here—never in the city itself, but in the area. Chicago was the largest city in America by far, so it made sense. They would have a larger pool of people to draw from but maintain the mythical image of luxury and safety within the city limits.

So the *where* was pretty clear. The bosses were in Chicago. But back to the money—just how lucrative were the games? And why the need for secrecy? Though even Hale had to admit he benefited from getting paid under-the-table. It was difficult enough to stay off the grid. Nigh on impossible. He supposed the secrecy was understandable— though the secret was so closely guarded that people had most certainly been killed to protect it. Nothing proven, of course, but rumors had to be true. No one had ever come forward who'd left the games. Brawlers just disappeared, perhaps into obscurity—as long as they stayed quiet. That was what he'd always assumed.

He brought his other arm up to clasp his fingers behind his head, still staring at the ceiling. He'd been so naïve. Part of him always thought the secrecy was just for the theatrics of it all—a way to bring in views.

He'd found his way in on the ground floor of this business, before it really took off. Maybe that's why he'd turned a blind eye for far too long. But now there was no doubt the secrecy was more than a mere ploy. It had to be big money to go through all the effort. A lot of money.

The most likely source was the most obvious: gambling. A prime example would be directly across the street in Excalibur. Whether on the web or in-house, they had to make a killing. Create something that people like to watch, that gets a wide audience, and as the audience grows, there's no limit to how much the house could make.

Trace the money back, and that's where it had to lead. Shadow Fray was just another casino game. The bosses could even start to manipulate the outcomes to their advantage. Say, give one of the contestants a weapon. Not only would it feed the bloodlust and increase views, but it could be tied into strategy. The house would always have the advantage because they knew how the game was to be played.

Go behind the curtains at these Chicago gaming palaces, and you'd find the Fray bosses. The Shadow Masters.

It was a scary thought. Maybe it was time to quit. Could be this last Fray was a fluke—that bastard Scarecrow wanted more attention, more blood. Or… maybe someone on the inside wanted him out, had decided to give the last guy who faced him a weapon. Would the bosses even let him walk away? Or would he have to go down on camera? Hale might be in as much danger as the kid was.

He unclasped his hands, brought his fists to his sides. His pillow felt hard beneath his head. He closed his eyes. Blackness. He'd been through worse times, sure, but lately he'd been living under a shadow of doubt. He needed to get away from this melancholy, this loss, and find some light. If only he could locate the kid, he'd have someone else to talk to. Benz was a good friend and protector, but it wasn't enough. When the Fray started, Hale was out there alone. He wanted an ally who knew what that felt like.

He was so fucking tired of being alone.

Hale got off the bed and shucked his jeans and T-shirt, exchanging them for black versions of the same, and threw on his jacket. It was time to ride.

Putting on the helmet limited his vision indoors, but it couldn't be helped. He easily found the balance point of the bike, walking it through the hall and into the elevator. His all-black Harley Iron was compact compared to other models. It was vintage, and he'd had to pay a pretty penny to print and mold parts that needed replacing. It had all been worth it.

It didn't take him long to get outside. He recognized the man at the front door as the man who had chased him into Wilma's room. What was his name again? The man opened the door for him, and Hale smiled and gave him a knowing smirk before realizing the guy wouldn't see it through his helmet. That was all right, though. From the sideways glance the guy gave him, Hale was sure he was recognized.

It was fully dark now. People filled the street, just arriving to Excalibur, a few passing Hale to enter the Lady. He decided to walk his bike out away from the crowds. From overhead came the steady hum of a nearby CPD drone.

He'd taken about ten steps when a man walked directly into him, hard. It was more than a brush by. Hale's immediate instinct was to fight, but he didn't want to let go of the bike. Instead he let go of all the negativity he'd been bottling up over the last miserable days, along with all sense of discretion. "Watch where you're going, asshole!" he yelled, turning toward the man who was already behind him. The man, tall and African-American, dressed in a suit, didn't turn around—just kept walking into the club like he was on a mission.

Fuck the crowds. Hale got on the bike and started it up, the loud rumble of the engine drawing the gazes of all those around him.

"Y'all better get the hell out of my way," he yelled, clearing out none too slowly as people scattered.

Tonight he would ride fast until all the anger, sadness, and frustration were blown away by the wind.

He had no doubt it would be a very long ride.

Chapter 16

Every time Justin used the elevator, he was reminded how their building had no thirteenth floor. The buttons went from twelve to fourteen. Of course that was bullshit—they lived on the thirteenth floor, were on the thirteenth floor right now, but it was numbered fourteen in order to skip the unlucky number. Stupid, really.

Charlie hit the button for twenty-eight. Even though Charlie was ten, Justin let him push the buttons like he was a little kid. The elevator shuddered as it began its ascent. At least it was working this time, but who knew how long that would last?

Arriving on the top floor, Charlie took off down the hall again. Kids and long hallways—but Charlie really wasn't that young, so when would he start growing out of these cute yet juvenile behaviors? Though he didn't look ten. He was very, very different from Justin and Gin at that age, more slight of bone and light of skin. But how much of that could be chalked up to Charlie's father, whoever he was? Justin's mom had never said, if she had known.

Charlie didn't wait for Justin to catch up and knocked eagerly on Griz's door while Justin was only halfway down the hall. The door opened immediately, and Charlie stepped back in surprise. A burly man stepped out, glaring down at Charlie. Justin saw fear in Charlie's eyes and quickened his pace.

The man didn't spend much time looking at Charlie, walking right past toward Justin. He was moving quickly. The man had thick red hair and was slightly shorter than Justin. He did not look friendly, and Justin gave him a threatening look. The other man was clearly street, returning Justin's stare. Not an outright challenge but a sign that neither of them would admit weakness. Justin couldn't help the mean mug. The flame-haired guy had scared Charlie.

Justin turned his head as the man passed, seemingly eye-to-eye despite the height difference. Justin was close enough to notice the man's green eyes were spotted with brown.

Justin's pulse was up, his heart thudding. Out on the street, this would be a fight.

The moment passed. He didn't turn around to look at the man. He continued walking, acting as if the stranger was no threat. Charlie watched from the end of the hall, and Justin looked him in the eyes, wary for any sign that the man behind him posed any further danger. Charlie was holding Mr. Mays's door open, a scared expression on his pale face, but he wasn't panicked.

At last, Justin was able to put his hand on Charlie, possessively pulling him close. They stepped inside and Justin closed the door. He immediately turned and engaged the locks before peering through the peephole. The hallway was empty.

"Who's there?" Griz called from inside his bedroom.

"It's Justin and Charlie, Mr. Mays." Justin was pleased his voice sounded so strong even though his heart was still pounding. This whole situation was off. Where was Devin? Or the nurse?

Justin still held Charlie tight to him, and they walked down the hall to Griz's open bedroom door.

"Didn't mean to scare you," Justin said. "Someone was leaving just as we were coming in." Griz was sitting up in his bed, a phone in his hand. The crease of his brow and set of his jaw told Justin he was troubled. Was he shaking?

"I'm glad you're here." Griz sounded truly relieved. "It was good timing, or I'm not sure I would have been able to get out of bed to open the door for you."

"Where's Devin? Or your nurse?"

Griz closed his eyes for a moment, breathing deeply. "Devin is working. The nurse… was sent home."

Justin had to take a deep breath himself. The man leaving the unit had not been the nurse. But best not to agitate Griz. Only easy questions. "Are you okay? Can I get you anything?"

"Yeah," Griz said, sounding stronger. "You can help me get out of bed. Let's go sit in the living room. My walker's against the wall. I'll need help standing up."

As Justin aided in getting him out of bed, he took note of Mr. Mays's legs, looking bony through the material of his sweatpants. He seemed so frail. Charlie was quickly on the floor, slipping Griz's loafers on his feet.

Griz smiled down at him. "Thanks, Charlie. That's the hardest part for me. Can't do it myself anymore." Justin positioned the walker in front of the old man and helped ease him off the bed into a standing position. "Feels good to stand up," he said. "Grab my phone, would you, Charlie?"

"Do you need to use the bathroom?" Justin asked.

"No, I'm fine. Been up already before you came over. Had breakfast and everything. I was expecting you, lookin' forward to the visit. Just didn't expect… no matter, anyhow. You're here, everything is fine." The old man's smile was strained, but his brown eyes turned bright.

In the living room, getting Mr. Mays seated was a much easier job. He had an elevated electric recliner and used a switch to lower himself. Charlie handed him his phone, and Mr. Mays looked at it.

"Now let's see what we can do about some music," he said. He scrolled through his phone with a contemplative look on his face as Charlie and Justin sat on the couch. Outside, Justin could see the endless blue of the lake stretching off into the distance. It hadn't been overcast in ages.

"Here we are," Griz said after a minute. "A good album for a Saturday. Let's see if you can guess it, Justin."

Justin heard a lively piano. As soon as the distinctive voice joined in, he knew immediately. "Tom Waits," he said.

Mr. Mays laughed. "Took you long enough. That was near on fifteen seconds. Thought I had you. Get yourself some coffee in the kitchen if you like. I already had mine, but there's some in the pot yet."

Justin got up, grateful for the opportunity. Coffee wasn't common or cheap.

"Feeling a mite better than when you were here last time," Griz said upon his return. "Some days are better than others."

"You look good," Justin said, though it was partly a lie. Griz hadn't been back from Denver more than six months, and it was a shock to see how he'd deteriorated over the seven years he'd been gone.

They listened to the music for a while, looking out over the lake. The trees on the lakeshore were a mix of green, red, and yellow, while the lake met the sky in a contrast of dueling blue. The summer had been wet and hot, but the fall was very dry and cool. From one extreme to the other, but that's how things were more often than not. Looking at Griz,

Justin wondered once again about the timing of his return. No way it was coincidence.

"Go ahead and ask your questions, boy," Griz said, returning his look. "I know you got 'em. Can't say as I'll answer 'em all, but you can go ahead and ask."

Justin nodded. It wasn't like he and Griz had been in constant company before he left, but he did know Justin pretty well in his first sixteen years. And Justin cared for him, if not as a father, then like a grandfather. "Who was that guy leaving your apartment?" Justin asked.

"That's my business. Different question."

Okay, then…. "Why'd you come back now, Mr. Mays? Was it for me?"

"Took more than one reason to bring me back, but you were one of 'em. I promised your mama before she passed that I'd do what I could. For a time that meant I had to move to Denver. Wouldn't have been no help to you here if I'd ended up dead. Can't say as I was much help to you over there either, but I did what I could."

"Mr. Mays, you don't have anything to feel bad about."

"I feel bad about plenty. You and Gin droppin' out of school at sixteen to take care of your brother here, that wasn't an ideal situation."

"Plenty of people have had it a lot worse."

"That's true enough, isn't it? Still, it's not wrong to wish for more for you."

"You came back because I was in… because of what I was involved in?"

Griz paused. Thought. "Partly," he said at last. "Maybe even mostly. I'm an old man, Justin. I know people. Once upon a time, I was people. By virtue of my age, I'm the last of that group left. I'm all alone now, but I know more than I should. I have limited influence, so of course I'm going to look out for my own. It's to be expected."

"Are you putting yourself in danger?"

Griz waved his hand as if to banish the thought. "What harm am I gonna do to anyone anymore?" But Griz hadn't answered the question.

"My handler," Justin pressed, "he was spooked. Thought people might be listening last time we met, or that it was a possibility. Are we safe to talk about this here?" It would have been real easy for the man who walked out of the apartment to plant a listening device.

"Whoever has an interest knows I know, knows I tried to look out for you, knows it's personal. That's not a secret. Us talkin' ain't gonna come as a surprise to no one. I can support you, but I can't… *interfere*."

Mr. Mays had always done plenty to support them. "When I was younger, those trainers I had. I thought that was normal at the time. Mom took Gin out shooting; I learned to fight. I thought Mama arranged that, but it was you, wasn't it? You paid for it too, I'm guessing."

Griz nodded.

"Did you have this in mind for me all the time?"

"No!" Griz was emphatic. "I had no designs on you that way. I knew you were a boy that liked to keep to himself. You didn't have no friends 'cept your family and me. You were always so serious. Fierce. Quiet. At the heart of it, I knew the fierceness was love, not nothin' vicious. When we'd listen to music, I saw… your soul. I knew you'd get yourself killed trying to protect them. Couldn't have that."

Justin nodded and put his arm around Charlie. He looked the old man in his eyes. "Thanks for that, Mr. Mays."

Mr. Mays smiled fondly. "You're welcome."

Justin smiled back. Words didn't do the exchange justice, but he and Mr. Mays understood each other.

With someone possibly listening in since Griz hadn't denied it, what more could he ask? He certainly couldn't bring up anything about Gin. He wanted to ask about the people behind Shadow Fray—the Shadow Masters—but wasn't sure it was wise.

Perhaps it was safe enough to ask about one individual in particular. "This handler I have. I'm not sure I trust him. Can I?"

"Absolutely not," Griz said. "Wish I coulda done more about that. Wasn't s'posed to happen this way. You get a chance… let's just say, you're popular enough now that if he's not in the picture, they're gonna find you someone else. It's worth the risk, 'cause not too many are worse than him."

"You sayin' to…." Justin made a cutting motion with his finger across his throat, unwilling to say *kill him* out loud. He was just being cautious, but part of him was relieved not to have say it out loud—and yet he also had to acknowledge that another small part of him was very eager for something else entirely.

"Look to get away from him. As long as you're valuable, you have more power than you think. Not many will miss him, but best if it doesn't come to that." Griz turned the music up and lowered his voice. "And best not for you to do it."

"Why?" Justin asked. "If you don't think—"

"Got nothing to do with your ability. Anyone can kill a man. I'm sure you could, no doubt about it. I know there's people you'd kill for." Griz sighed. "Don't want it to change you, though. It's too easy to become vicious, for it to become part of the game. Killin' ain't something you do unless you gotta. Take it from someone who knows." Griz got quiet, a distant look in his eyes. The silence was deep, had weight.

So he'd killed people. What stories lurked behind that gaze? What memories haunted him? And did Justin really want to know? If it was a matter of survival—

But then the old man shook his head, as if to snap himself out of it, and continued, "Besides, from a professional standpoint, it's best not to go up against your boss, not directly anyway. That kind of challenge isn't appreciated, because the next person down the chain wonders if he'll be next. Guys in power like to be in power; they'll hold on to it no matter what. If you gotta challenge 'em, best to work indirectly. It's no less effective, and it's a hell of a lot smarter."

Justin nodded.

"And remember this too: no matter how awful a man is, he's always got someone else on his team. No one gets to be where they are all alone, even if they *are* just using each other as stepping stones. Don't give nobody cause to come after you to save face or get revenge. Keep your hands as clean as possible, and when it's not possible, get someone else to do the dirty work and do it quiet like."

What he said made sense. Already, Justin's mind started churning, trying to come up with ways to do Scarecrow in "quiet like." As if to let him think, Griz turned the music down.

"Hey, Charlie," Griz began in a lighter tone. "You know what I need your help in doing? We gotta get your brother someone. A friend."

Wait. What?

Charlie raised his eyebrows as if considering. Then, agreeing, he nodded emphatically.

"You need someone, Just. You got us, but you deserve more. You need someone who's yours and yours alone."

"You trying to play matchmaker now, Mr. Mays?" Justin shook his head, not believing what they were trying to pull. "You got someone in mind?"

Mr. Mays laughed, that spark returning to his eyes. "I didn't say that. I didn't say it had to be a woman. Just a friend. A man's gotta have friends. And that goes for you too, Charlie. Do me a favor and before I die, let someone else in, the each of ya."

"Ain't that easy, Mr. Mays."

Griz shook his head. "Certainly not. Sometimes lettin' people in hurts an awful lot. But it sure is worth it. Take your mama for instance. If I didn't come to love her, look at all I woulda missed out on. You remember her at all, Charlie?"

Charlie frowned and shook his head but then thought. He gave a hand signal that meant "Sort of." Justin slept next to Charlie enough to know that he dreamed of their mother sometimes, enough to know that Charlie *could* talk.

"Your mama, she was way too young for me, but I loved her nonetheless. You know why? Because she loved. She loved people something fierce. Her patients, myself included, but you especially, of course. That can be a rare quality today. Too many people in it for themselves. I was in that bad way for a long time. Hard. But that's survival for you, isn't it? My own mama died when I was young, but I remember her enough to know that's not how she raised me. She didn't go until after the third flu came around, and after that, that's when I got hard. And they used me like a tool, used that hard edge. Hungry for food. Hungry for blood. But it was people like your mama helped me come back to myself again. Best for you both if you never lose yourself to begin with. Life's too short to lose all them years."

Silence fell over them again for a minute. Justin was almost relieved. He forgot how much Mr. Mays liked to talk, and this was plenty to think about.

"Take Gin, for instance," Griz continued his last thought, though minutes had elapsed. "She been through a lot, but she's got friends. Lots of 'em. In addition to the two of you. She's tough, but she ain't hard. She's still got a heart. A big one."

Griz's eyelids drooped. Finally the guy was exhausted. Justin supposed he and Charlie would just hang out, listening to music. He wasn't willing to leave the old man alone until Devin came back.

"Best to find someone," Mr. Mays mumbled. A few moments later, he began a soft snore that let Justin know he truly was asleep.

Sure. Best to find someone. But easier said than done.

Best to find someone. But who?

HALE GRUNTED. One more chin-up, and one more day. He needed to make it through one more day. He could do both.

It had been ten days since the Fray in the church, and Hale had a breakfast date on Monday he was really looking forward to. He dropped from the chin-up bar he had installed, his arms feeling rubbery and his muscles bulging. He'd been surprisingly active since his late-night ride, at least as active as one could be in a small apartment. He'd reminded himself that every push-up, chin-up, or sit-up was one closer to seeing his baby girl; at this point, he hoped any exercise would get the circulation going and help the bruising fade away so it would be safe for him to go to her.

After showering, he walked through his now clean apartment, a towel around his waist. Beyond the window the night was clear, the moon bright, a mite past the full stage. Looking down at the street, Hale was amazed at the amount of slow-moving traffic. Chauffeurs helped Uppers out of shiny cars, and Benz had a line of people waiting to get into Excalibur. Hale had come to realize this was normal for a Saturday night. He turned from the window. He should make the call. He'd been thinking on it for days, and soon it would be too late.

But could he trust Wilma? He was mostly healed. It was safer for him to stay in, and Benz had said she was okay. Wilma would be his one. His only one. And he'd let Benz know too. Later.

Better to ask forgiveness than permission.

He picked up the card from where he'd placed it on his recently made bed. Dialing the number, he noticed for the first time the card smelled faintly of citrus. The phone rang five times, and Hale began to wonder if she was already busy. On the sixth ring, she picked up.

"Hello?" Her voice was warm but uncertain.

"Hello, Wilma. This is…." Hale suddenly remembered he'd never told her his name. "The man from upstairs," he finished awkwardly.

Her laugh was warm and not at all insulting. "Well, my my my. I'm happy to hear from you, Hale."

He paused a beat, taken aback. "I didn't know you knew my name."

"Oh, honey, I know everybody's name here. I knew who you were when you walked in my door. Remember, I don't like surprises, and the best way to not be surprised is to make sure you know *everything*."

"So you're not surprised to hear from me, I take it."

"Not at all. I'm quite pleased, in fact."

"You busy?"

"Not just yet."

"Last time you said… I was wondering if you might be able to come up, pay me a little visit."

"Trying to avoid big brother's prying eyes, I take it."

"Guilty."

"You caught me at just the right time. Give me ten minutes."

"See you soon."

Hale ended the call and sat on the edge of the bed. He hadn't jerked off in days, hadn't even wanted to. If he was being honest with himself, he felt heartbroken. He'd never find the Night Visitor—but it was time to get over that.

It didn't take long for his visitor to knock. Three soft raps.

He opened the door, ushering her inside with a slight bow. She smelled clean and rich, like soap and cocoa butter. She was wearing a red dress that could open from the front if it became unbelted, and it accentuated her perfect bosom—ample but not too large.

She looked at him as he closed the door behind her, eyeing the towel around his waist. "Leave it to you to be underdressed yet again, and in your own house." From her smile, he could tell she liked what she saw.

He leaned into her, putting his hands on her hips. He kissed her softly on the lips, inhaling the savory aroma of her skin and the hint of citrus on her breath.

As she looked at his face more closely, he saw her expression change, and he took a step back. She frowned at him, putting a hand on his cheek and turning his head.

"You been through something," she said, obviously noting the faded bruises and tiny, white scars from where he'd required a stitch or two.

"Yes," Hale acknowledged, but he didn't offer any more. This was a moment of truth. He wouldn't lie, not right away, but at this point, his faded injuries could easily be explained away by a fall from his bike.

Her expression showed only a soft concern, but if she started asking questions, he'd have to reconsider this arrangement.

"Did it hurt?" she asked. True, that was a question, but a reasonable one.

Hale shrugged. "Not really."

She smiled slyly. "Liar." She leaned forward slowly, her lips tickling his ear, her words only a breath he struggled to hear. "Benz and I go way back. Your secret's safe with me."

Hale froze. She knew. He was certain she knew. Part of him wanted to run. A bigger part of him wanted to trust her, needed to trust her, in order to not spend one more fucking night alone.

Wilma made the choice for him. "Lie down on the bed, honey. I got the best hands in this joint, and I'm gonna rub that black and blue right out of you. Make you feel real good." She gestured to the bed, and for the first time, he noticed a small red clutch hanging from her wrist.

All right, then. In for a penny, in for a pound. Hale stretched out on his stomach, leaving Wilma enough room to sit on the bed by his side. "Is there anywhere you don't want me to touch?" she asked, removing the clutch and opening it.

This wasn't what he'd had in mind when he invited her up, but a massage might be a better idea. His skin practically itched. He craved someone's touch, much like his occasional cravings for other things. "No," Hale decided. He glanced back at her. "You can touch me anywhere."

"Good," Wilma said with a smile and a hungry look in her eyes. He couldn't imagine how many men she saw, but he wanted to believe she didn't have that look for everyone. That somehow he was special.

She reached around to his side where his towel was tucked in, releasing the bind. She brought it back toward her, exposing his rear end. The towel was half-under him, and she rose a little bit to sit on the other half, tucking it underneath her where she sat at his waist.

He heard the click of a bottle cap, heard her rub her hands together, and then felt her warm touch on his back. She was both strong and gentle as she kneaded his muscles. Occasionally he would feel the scrape of one of her long fingernails against his skin, and it would send a shiver through his body.

She worked his neck and shoulders, moving down his back. When she finished with his lower back, she switched positions and began at his feet, working up his legs. As her hands got higher, pressing into his upper thighs, he could feel her fingers lightly touching his balls and the head of his cock where it was pressed down beneath him, slightly exposed. Nothing too blatant or direct, just teasing.

It felt good. He felt himself melting like butter. But he wasn't aroused.

She began massaging his buttocks, pressing into the thick muscles with firm fingers. She separated his cheeks occasionally as she worked him. Her hands would dip down into his crease, her lubricated fingers grazing across his hole. The soft scrape of a fingernail caused him to inhale sharply.

It felt so good, but something was off. Her hands were too gentle, too soft. He found himself craving a rougher touch and harder hands. What would the scrape of a callous feel like, rather than the scrape of a fingernail? Or the strong grip of a fighter as hands spread his ass apart, teasing and touching him?

"Turn over now, honey," she said. Her voice was rich with desire, the air full of the heady scent of cocoa butter. Hale did as she said.

She began at his neck, massaging down his chest and working his pecs. "Hmmm…." was all she said as she got down toward his ribs where the glove had scraped and punctured. She traced the healing scars gently, not pressing. She moved lower, but stopped just when her touch was delving into the sensitive regions around his groin—those encroaching areas that tickled his reflexes. Instead she went down to his feet again, going slowly up his legs, pressing into his calves and his thighs, his muscles releasing all of the stress he had accumulated over the last weeks.

Finally she was at his cock. She went around it first, her hands running through his body hair and along and below his balls. Hale sighed as she began to knead his balls very gently with one hand. The other hand moved to his flaccid cock. She stretched it in her hand, touching the underside, stroking the head.

He wasn't aroused. "I'm sorry," he said, meeting her eyes.

"Nothing to be sorry about, honey. I've seen it before, and this look you have, this sadness about you, I know you're thinking about someone else. You're a million miles away from me right now, and you know what? That's okay."

"Thanks," Hale said. "Your touch feels so good. I really wanted to come."

She nodded. "Then I'll tell you what. Instead of tryin' to be here with me, you just close your eyes. Whoever's on your mind, that's where I want you to be."

Hale swallowed, nodded, and closed his eyes.

He thought of the Night Visitor sitting next to him, looking down at him. In his mind the guy was wearing his leather mask. It covered his forehead, leaving the shock of disheveled dark hair on top, where Hale could run his hands through it. Grab it. Hale would lower the Night Visitor's head, pull him down. The mask left his mouth uncovered, free to kiss. Hale would stroke the leather under his thumbs; he'd dip his fingers lower and take hold of that strong jaw, pulling him closer. He'd force his way in and hungrily take that first kiss….

Hale reveled in his arousal, in the heated swelling of his cock. A soft groan left his lips, his hips curling slightly.

Spontaneously he opened his eyes, grabbing Wilma's hands, stopping her.

He was a little breathless, his heart beating fast at this new idea that had sprung to mind. He reached with an arm beneath his mattress where he'd hidden it.

He pulled out the glove.

"Can you put this on? Please?" he asked. He knew his eyes were hungry, knew she must see it plainly on his face, see it in the twitch of his cock at the very thought.

She smiled. She wiped her hand on the towel, then slipped the glove on. Hale thought it might be too big, but Wilma's hand filled it well.

He reached out with both of his hands, grabbing her gloved hand, and pressed her fingers down, exposing the metal spikes.

"I want you to use your hands on my chest," he said. "I want you to use these claws on my chest. I want to feel them biting into my skin. Don't worry, you won't hurt me."

She nodded, silent. Maybe she didn't speak on purpose, didn't want to break the spell he was under.

Hale grabbed his cock and closed his eyes. He began stroking as he felt hands press across his chest, palms open. Rubbing up and down, the leathered hand was soft but also textured in a way that was rougher than skin. The hand closed into a fist, and the cool metal scraped across his skin.

One hand grabbed his pec, squeezing it. He felt the sharp bite of metal as the gloved hand cut through the oil on his chest with a pleasant sting.

God, yes. He was breathing heavily. He was close already. The claws continued scraping, starting high and going lower, grazing his sternum, his belly. He could feel them cutting over his abs as he curled into himself, his hand pumping.

The glove lifted, was gone, and he moaned at the absence. The next moment one claw followed the curve of his pec, under his nipple. Just one claw, pushing lower into the soft flesh. With a little *snick*, it dug in, puncturing his flesh, surely drawing blood.

Hale bellowed once and felt his come shoot high, spilling up his chest and landing below his chin. Another *snick* and his body was rocking, his heavy breaths emphasizing the continued spurts.

Finally it passed, his body uncoiling, his muscles relaxing.

He heard a whispered "shhhh." Before he opened his eyes, the soft leather of the empty glove covered his eyelids. He felt the body rise from the bed beside him. A moment later he heard the door open and close softly.

He breathed in through his nose, inhaling the scent of leather. Behind it, if it wasn't his imagination, he inhaled the musk of sweat and blood—the smell of the Night Visitor.

Chapter 17

"Mama, he's here!"

Hale could hear her voice before the door opened, as though Eddie had been waiting for his knock. She probably had been, and damn if that didn't make him feel good.

When the door opened, the blonde-haired angel practically flew into his arms, throwing herself against him hard enough to knock off her halo if she'd had one. In his mind, of course, she did. "Hey, Baby Doll. I missed you so much!"

"Welcome back," Jess said from behind the door. She sounded sincere, with no awkwardness to her voice. In fact, she was smiling brightly. Damn if that didn't make him feel good too.

"Are you all better now?" Eddie asked, releasing him from her tight hug and looking at him.

"I'm all better. Promise."

"Oh good. Because I was running out of stories."

He laughed easily. "I loved your stories so much. They were like my medicine." He meant it figuratively, but after he said it, he realized how true it was.

She was breathless with talk, and he could tell breakfast would be full of everything she'd missed saying over the last couple weeks. "And there were pictures in the stories too, and I drawed some pictures, but we couldn't even do video on your phone because you're so old-fashioned." The way she smiled, he could tell she had learned a new phrase and was pretty proud of it.

"Old-fashioned? Where are you learning those big words?"

"Mama says princesses are so old-fashioned because they don't know how to shoot and fight, and if there was a princess today she would just have to rescue herself."

"Your mama is smart like that. She's absolutely right. So, what does old-fashioned mean?"

"It means that you can't use things that you can fit in your hand like phones and weapons and things."

Hale and Jess shared a stifled laugh as he picked up Eddie and walked inside. Jess looked positively statuesque in a thin pencil skirt, lengthening her moderate frame. She was the same height as Janie.

"Help yourself to the coffee or anything else in the kitchen," she said, a slight smile still on her face as she kept the door open. "Hope we'll be seeing you more often." She wasn't sticking around, apparently. She left the apartment, and Hale locked the door behind her.

"How about breakfast? Your mama make you anything yet? You aren't gonna spit eggs at me again, are you?"

"No," she said with a laugh. "That was so funny. Mama made porridge, like in the story with the bears."

Ahhh. The cornmeal staple. As smartly as they dressed, it was nice to know they ate like regular people sometimes, and his daughter wouldn't be too good for him someday. "Maybe I'll have some of that. It's the breakfast of champions, you know."

"It's okay, I guess. Daddy says it makes you strong and healthy. You can eat mine too. Will you get sick again?"

"Oh, I suppose so, but I'll get better like I did this time. Just like if you get sick, you'll get better. That's called good genes, and you and I have the same good genes."

"And Mama and Daddy too?"

Woah. He'd almost slipped up, although she was still too young to make the connection that he'd just referred to her as his daughter. "And Mama and Daddy too, sweetheart. You got nothin' to worry about."

All through breakfast, Hale did his best to keep up with her chatter, loving every minute of it. He found himself having to remind her to eat so they wouldn't be late for school. All too quickly the hour was up and it was time to go. He felt like he hadn't had enough time yet.

"Go get your backpack, Baby Doll. Don't wanna be late for school."

"Okay, but oh! I have the pictures from the story, and Mama put them on my backpack so I wouldn't forget because I made them for you."

She ran off, and when she returned, she was wearing her backpack and carried a short stack of hand-drawn pictures. She eagerly offered him her works of art.

He held them like they were precious, feeling the pressure in his chest and tightness in his cheeks that meant he was holding in his emotions. He paged through them, admiring her work, recognizing in pencil and crayon the stories she had been telling him over the last couple weeks.

"Boy, Eddie. These sure are pretty. I'm gonna hang them in my new place, and I'm gonna look at them every day and think of you. I hope you draw me lots more too, because I don't have anything on the walls. I miss my view, and you know what? With these hanging up, I won't miss it so much anymore."

He hugged her deeply, holding her an extra moment. Who cared if they were late for school?

Finally releasing her, he split the pictures into two small stacks and folded them carefully. It was a shame to fold them, really, but there was nothing to do but pocket them in his leather jacket for the ride home. In one pocket, though, he felt a little resistance. Did he leave something he'd forgotten about?

Pulling it out, he was surprised to find a condom wrapper. No—not just a wrapper. The condom was inside. Along with the condom package was a small separate piece of paper. He didn't recognize the handwriting. It certainly wasn't his own. It said simply: *Look here*.

Look where? He checked his pockets for more but found nothing, so he examined the condom wrapper. On it was printed a picture of a lighthouse logo with the stamp, *Lighthouse Condoms, Milwaukee, WI*.

Hale's heart quickened. Look for what? He'd only been looking for one thing. In fact, the last couple weeks had been consumed with it, his emotions ruled by it. The excitement was a balloon expanding in his chest.

The Night Visitor.

But how? And what the hell? His mind wanted to deny it. It wasn't logical. But someone had put this in his pocket. It didn't come from him. What else could it refer to?

"Are you getting sick again?" Eddie looked up at him with frightened eyes.

"No, no, darlin'. I was just thinking about those pictures and keeping 'em safe in my pockets. I was thinkin' about where I was gonna hang each one." He smiled down at her. "C'mon, let's get you to school. Don't want to be late!"

Moments ago he had been dreading the sadness of saying good-bye. Now, as much as he loved her, he couldn't get to school fast enough.

He almost didn't dare hope, but regardless, mere minutes from now, he planned to be on his bike riding fast to Milwaukee.

ON THE road with the cool air whipping past, Hale racked his brain. There were only two ways that paper had made its way into his pocket.

The first was Wilma. She had time the other night to slip the paper into his jacket pocket. Hale's eyes had been closed; he wouldn't have seen her do it. He'd never mentioned anything about trying to find someone though—unless she was the "friend" who had broken Benz's fingers. It was possible someone could have paid her to transfer the note—or just asked her. Maybe she knew more than she let on. She had definitely known Hale was thinking about someone else. She also made it her business to know things. She had known who he was, known his name, and come to think of it, Hale had never even told her which apartment was his.

The second way had taken some figuring. He remembered a guy running into him the night he had ridden his bike. He could barely remember any details about the stranger, though. Hale hadn't seen his face, and he'd been too pissed off to commit much to memory. Something could have been slipped into his pocket at that time. Maybe Benz's inquiry had actually paid off. Maybe whoever it was had found a way to get Hale the information without ever involving Benz.

Benz might be able to shed more light on the situation, but Hale wasn't going to tell him yet. Something weird was going on, and while Hale hoped he was on the right track, this might not be about the Night Visitor at all. But then, what was it?

A trap? That was unlikely. A quick web search on his phone informed him the condom company was legit, which he knew from his own personal experience with the brand. He had the location of the business. It seemed ridiculous that someone who wanted to get the jump on him for whatever reason would send him to a condom company.

He motored past the seemingly abandoned air defense systems that surrounded the city of Chicago. Still operational but certainly out of use, the structures reminded him of a boneyard. In contrast to his surroundings, Hale felt alive. Hopeful. For most of the remaining ninety minutes it took him to make the trip, he continued to hope. He hoped this was what he thought it was. He hoped this was the lead he had been looking for. He hoped this led him to the kid. And once he met him, he hoped… for what, exactly? The fantasies he'd been harboring were unrealistic, to say the least. He'd have to let those go. But he could make sure the guy was okay and get information about what was going on. He could satisfy his own curiosity, perhaps make an ally. Even adjusting his expectations, he found plenty to hope for.

Hale wasn't naïve enough to think he was just going to show up and spot the Night Visitor. This might take time. Since he didn't feel much like doing a stakeout of the place in broad daylight, he figured the best way to get information would be to make himself a part of things. He was going to ask for a job. If that didn't pan out, well… he'd think of something.

When he finally arrived at his destination, the nerves set in. Funny—he didn't get this nervous before a fight.

Lighthouse Condoms was located in a warehouse district south of the high-rises of downtown Milwaukee. It wasn't the only manufacturing industry around. A number of them were in this area, all of them looking somewhat similar. Glancing to the skies, Hale saw several machines angling through different trajectories, at different altitudes. This area was patrolled by both MPD and private drones, making a stakeout nearly impossible.

Hale didn't see a business sign, but GPS said the location was correct. The building in front of him was made of Cream City brick, darkened with age to an almost black color. It was four stories, boxy and rectangular. The windows on the bottom floor had been filled in, indicating most of the business was located on the second floor and above. On one end of the building was an open garage. He angled his bike in that direction.

He saw no one. It was close to eleven o'clock, so it made sense that everyone would be inside working. He parked his bike to the side of the garage. At places like this, the entrances weren't exactly well marked, and Hale saw no sign of a welcome mat. He decided to take the door nearest the garage, waving to the camera he saw stationed above the entrance. Nothing wrong with being friendly and making a good first impression. As he reached for the door, he heard a click. It opened. So someone was watching the camera, then.

Walking in, he was surrounded by shelving and storage bins in a relatively high, open space. He saw no sign of people. At the end of the room was a freight elevator likely connected to the garage, as well as a stairway. Hale took the stairs.

Arriving at what must have been the third floor, Hale found himself in a typical office area. Anything but typical was the gorgeous tan-kissed woman with big brown eyes staring daggers into him. She stood as though she expected him. Hale put on his warmest smile. This was, after all, a job interview.

"Hi. Name's Hale. I've come to inquire about a job." His voice gave no hint of his nerves.

The woman eyed him skeptically. He extended his hand, but she stood with her arms crossed and made no attempt to shake it. He withdrew it, keeping a smile on his face. This was not the effect he usually had on women—except for Jess. He had no doubt her crossed arms put her in reach of a gun.

"Who sent you?" the woman asked after a pause. She tucked her short dark hair behind an ear as she lifted her chin, extending her height into something more formidable. She was dressed casually, but the way her clothes fit, she obviously knew she was gorgeous. She stood tall with her chest out, looking him directly in his eyes. It was a challenge.

"No one sent me. I'm an honest man looking for work. I'm relocating from Chicago."

"Why would you come here from Chicago?"

"I'm trying to save money. I have a daughter I need to support."

He hadn't intended to play the daughter card. Hell, he hadn't planned what he was gonna say at all. Apparently, though, he said the right thing, because she relaxed and nodded.

"As far as I know we aren't hiring, but I'll let you talk to the boss. Wait here a minute."

She disappeared through a doorway at the far end of the room. Hale spent the next moments looking around, trying to get a read on the place and looking for anything to give him an advantage or an in with these people. He was scouting it like an Arena. Unfortunately, aside from the desk where he saw a laptop and some invoices and notes with numbers, the room was pretty bare. Numbers weren't really his strongpoint either.

After a couple minutes, the woman returned with the man who must be the boss. He struck Hale as being very average. He was a black man, a little shorter than Hale and overweight, past middle age with only a trace of gray in his beard. Hale was pleased to see the boss was dressed very casually, as Hale wasn't exactly dressed to impress in his leather jacket and jeans. The boss man wore a completely neutral expression, and as he walked forward, Hale extended his hand.

"Gin tells me you've come looking for work," the man said, shaking his hand.

"Yes, sir. My name's Hale."

"Ray. I run this place."

"I appreciate you taking the time to talk to me."

"Ginny says you have a daughter?"

"Yes, sir, that's right."

"And is that your bike outside?"

"Yes, sir, it is."

"Nice bike."

"Thanks. After my little girl, she's my greatest joy."

"We have a certain fondness for Harleys in this city."

"Do you ride?"

"From time to time, though I don't have one of my own."

If this was the job interview, he wasn't doing so badly.

The man studied him for a while without speaking. "Can you drive a truck?" he asked after the pause.

"I can drive most anything. Driving is what I like to do best." Actually he'd never driven a truck before, but how hard could it be? He hoped his answer wasn't so vague as to make that obvious. Maybe he should have outright lied.

Ray paused again. Hale sensed he was coming to a decision and had the sudden urge to cross his fingers.

The man nodded. "Okay. This is what I can offer you. We have one driver already, but he's been laid up for a bit. You can fill in for him when he's not able to work. I can also offer you part-time routes of your own in one of our smaller vehicles. It won't be full-time work, at least not to start. But if this works out and something else opens up, you're welcome to stay on."

Hale smiled, relieved. "Thank you, sir. That sounds fine."

"Don't call me sir, call me Ray. Is part-time work gonna be enough for you with a little girl?" Ray raised his eyebrow at him, and Hale suddenly got nervous. Was this a trick question? A test to see if he was lying? He decided to go with as much truth as possible.

"My girl, she lives with my wife's family. So…." Hale became silent, unsure of what to say.

Ray nodded, seeming to respect that Hale was uncomfortable. "So you're married?"

"No," Hale said. "She's passed away some time ago now."

The woman, Gin, who had been watching him this whole time, nodded at that. Hale felt like he had passed the test.

"Come back tomorrow around seven in the morning. I'll have you train with our driver for a couple weeks. That'll be solid work. After that I'll train you in other positions too. Between filling in here and there, I suppose we'll be able to get you near close to full-time work. The pay won't be great to start, but after a couple months, it'll be a livable wage."

"I appreciate that, sir… I mean, Ray. Thanks. Thanks a lot." Hale shook his hand again enthusiastically, giving Ray a genuine smile.

"Ma'am," he said, nodding to the woman and extending his hand again toward her. "I appreciate the opportunity."

She eyed his hand before extending her own. That was more like it. Her handshake was stronger than Ray's. "You can call me Gin," she said. "I'll talk to the other driver, and we'll see you tomorrow morning."

Hale didn't miss her gaze leaving his eyes to travel down his body. She was checking him out, sure enough. He smiled knowingly at her. He would take any advantage he could get. "See you tomorrow," he agreed, before turning and leaving.

The smile stayed plastered on his face all the way back to Chicago. He didn't even attempt to hold his fantasies in check.

This had to be it. Hale couldn't fucking wait for tomorrow.

Chapter 18

Justin stopped pacing and leaned against the truck. He looked up the empty road. Where was this guy? True, it wasn't even seven yet. He needed to stop being negative. Think of the positive. Yes, he could use the extra help catching up with the deliveries. Yes, he wouldn't have to feel guilty if he ever found himself unable to work for a while—not that he would ever lose a Fray again. Yes, Gin had said she got a good vibe from the guy, and she was a pretty damn good judge of character. Yes to all of this, but still….

Mr. Mays had told him to look for a friend, and wasn't it convenient this opportunity should suddenly arise after that conversation? Was the universe trying to tell him something? If so, then maybe the universe would be kind enough to also tell him what the hell he was supposed to talk about while he was trapped in the truck with this guy ticking off the miles for the next two weeks. He'd tried to come up with a list of conversation topics since last night, but he had nothing to talk about.

He trained. He fought. He worked. That's it. He couldn't exactly talk about the fighting, and therefore couldn't exactly talk about training. That left work. He drove a truck, and the guy already knew that. Oh—and he watched cartoons with his little brother, but that wasn't exactly a topic of great interest to anyone over thirteen. He had his family, but he really didn't care to talk about them. That was personal.

They could talk about their respective ideas about why the world was the way it was, what had happened to the ground, but that was like talking about the weather. He could bring up completely random facts gleaned from Internet self-education or talk about things he read. All in all he had a solid twenty minutes of conversation. Or approximately one-two hundred fortieth of the time he needed to fill. He'd done the math.

He had a sneaking suspicion he'd end up talking about all of the girls he'd fucked. That's what guys liked to talk about, right? And what was he supposed to say? Yeah, my sister brings her girlfriends over for me to have sex with because they know I'm a safe lay. He was sure he screwed more women than most men, and yet when he racked his brain to single out one who was particularly memorable, nothing came to mind. They were all just fine. It was a way to get off, to think about something else for a short time. Nothing meaningful had ever come of it. Justin wasn't interested, didn't have room for it in his life.

Still, it was something. He could look forward to two weeks of talking about his sexual conquests. What a strange word—conquests. If anything, they were more like agreeable business arrangements. Or—Justin smiled to himself—maybe he was the trophy. He had a good body, so he was a catch, at least from the neck down. Plus he liked to be on the bottom with the woman riding him. It was less work, and the whole point was to relax a bit, wasn't it? So how many of those women had gone on to talk about him like he was the object of their conquest? It would certainly make for a better story from that perspective.

Then he heard it—the sound of an engine. Gin said the guy drove a Harley, and sure enough, there he was in the distance. Justin straightened, then changed his mind and relaxed against the truck again. Better to look casual—but had the guy seen him posing?

As the helmeted rider neared, Justin got a better look. For a Harley the bike was relatively streamlined and not as loud as he expected. It was all black and not decked out with anything to make it flashy. The man riding it looked just as sleek in black jeans, black jacket, and a black-visored helmet. He pulled to a stop outside the garage, about twenty feet from where Justin was leaning on the truck, and cut the engine.

Justin counted off a few seconds, but the man didn't move, seeming to watch him. All right, then. Justin could play friendly, make the first move. Besides, he wanted to get this over with.

He stood up and walked over to the black-clad stranger. "How's it goin'? I'm Justin," he said, trying to sound confident as he said his name. Extending his hand, he noticed brown curls poking out of the back of the helmet. The man got off the bike and removed the headgear. His hair was loose and wavy, and the man ran a hand through the dark sandy locks before turning to look at Justin.

Justin found himself staring into blue-gray eyes the color of denim. Suddenly he was lost. He recognized those eyes. He had made a point of studying those eyes, magnifying them in videos so he would see the humanity there. He had looked into those eyes not two weeks ago in the dimness of a candlelit church. He was looking into the eyes of Black Jim.

And Justin froze. He couldn't think, couldn't breathe.

The other man paused as well, his pupils dilating. He knew. The man recognized Justin; there was no doubt.

Time passed. The world spun. But Justin could only stand still.

"It really is you," the man said at last. Justin merely nodded in response. There was no use in denying it. To Justin the man before him was clearly Black Jim, but different. Softer. Even in black leather, with scruff hiding very faint bruising, the man didn't hold the terror Black Jim instilled. Of course, that didn't mean Justin wasn't still scared shitless.

"I can't believe it," the man said. God, those eyes were penetrating. Instinctually, Justin wanted to shy away from that gaze, but he didn't. He was being studied and automatically tensed, his muscles readying. He knew that look. The man was looking at him like prey. The tip of the man's tongue played across his lips before disappearing. Justin couldn't look away.

Abruptly the man's expression relaxed. "I'm Hale," the man said. "I've been looking for you… Justin, you said?" Justin nodded. How did this guy not want to kick his ass? Justin realized his own hand had been hanging in the air since his introduction ages ago.

The other man looked down at Justin's hand, finally breaking the gaze. The spell lifted. Justin relaxed, his muscles loosening—though he still felt like an idiot with his hand out. How funny he had only felt this man's fists in the throes of violence, and now he was going to shake his hand. Hale's grip was firm. He was confident enough not to try to prove anything with a handshake, but the power in those fingers could bring a man to his knees. Justin's body warmed as he remembered.

"God, it's good to know your name," Hale said. Justin felt his own hand lingering on Hale's. He felt the callouses under Hale's fingers and noticed the hair on the side of Hale's hand. He was *actually touching* Black Jim in a genuine way that didn't involve pain.

Justin felt another squeeze on his hand. "Justin, say something." Hale made no move to let his hand go. They were standing with their hands still clasped. Suddenly, and almost instantly, Justin was hard.

Hale was looking at him, expectation turning into worry. Jesus, what to say? He couldn't just stand here holding the man's hand. His head wasn't working. He was no good with words. Fuck it all.

Justin tugged on the hand in front of him, pulling Hale toward him. Justin noticed a look of surprise as he released the man's hand and grabbed him into a hug, careful not to press his erection against him. It only took Hale a second to relax and return the hug.

Justin exhaled, putting more weight on Hale. This was going to be okay. This expressed what he was feeling better than any words could. The fear, the nervousness, the awe and admiration, the desire… and the sadness.

"I'm sorry about the glove," Justin said, holding to Hale tightly.

AND JUST like that, all those fantasies Hale had tried to put aside on the ride over in an effort to convince himself they couldn't be real came roaring back with a vengeance, and they all went straight to his dick. Hale would have to test these waters. Watch for more signals. Maybe the kid would be up for more than Hale thought.

Or maybe it was just a hug.

Though Justin was taller, Hale couldn't help feeling like in some sense, Justin was indeed a kid. Make no mistake about it, Justin was all man, but Hale felt the protective surge he only experienced with a few select people in his life. He had the need to make Justin feel better.

"It's okay," Hale assured him, giving a brief squeeze. "No harm done. Really."

He liked the feeling of the kid in his arms, but he needed to let go before his jeans got uncomfortable. He patted Justin on the back twice before putting a couple steps' distance between them.

Hale didn't want to ever stop looking at him. No way could he have hit that face if Justin hadn't been wearing a mask. The man was beautiful. He had a strong jaw and cheekbones that were pronounced without being severe. His brown eyes, honey-colored skin, dark hair, and full lower lip gave him a striking look with an indeterminate ethnicity. In demeanor he seemed genuine, if not outright shy. The softness made him appear kind—and simply stunning.

Out of nowhere something clicked for Hale. "That girl upstairs who talked to me, that's your sister, isn't it? Gin? Was she the one…."

Justin's nervous look kept Hale from finishing the sentence, but he was sure the girl who looked so much like him was his sister, and from her tough-as-nails demeanor, he was almost certain that's who was at the church with Justin. But it was probably best not to speak openly at Justin's place of work—their place of work. That's why the kid looked nervous. "Can we go someplace to talk? In the truck?"

Justin looked around with a frown on his face, searching. "No, not the truck," he said. "It might not be safe. Bugged."

Bugged? Really? Hale raised his eyebrows, but the kid didn't explain any further. "I suppose we'll have to drive somewhere," Justin said instead.

Good enough. Hale nodded, the relief and excitement giving rise to an extra wide smile. He glanced down, feeling almost bashful, and ran a hand through his hair. "God, there's a million questions I want to ask you," he admitted.

Looking up, he saw Justin smile for the first time. Not wide, but enough. A crooked half smile, and it was damn cute on him. "I can't believe you don't want to kick my ass," Justin said.

Not kick it, no. Hale cleared his throat. "Unless you got a place in mind, there's a rest stop just south of the city off 94. The building isn't there anymore, but they still have the turnoff with a woods nearby."

"I know the spot. Truckers use it to rest up, grab a couple hours. Go ahead and pull your bike into the garage, and we can go."

Justin turned to get in the truck, and Hale let his gaze linger on him as he walked away. Justin was wearing blue jeans and a gray hoodie, but the hoodie didn't go down far enough to cover his ass. Hale watched Justin step up into the truck, the slightly loose jeans stretching taut over the firm muscles of his backside. With an audible sigh, he moved his bike into the garage. No harm in looking, he told himself as he joined Justin in the truck.

"If it's all right with you," Justin said, "I'm going to hold off on the training part for a bit. We're gonna skip past the first couple of stops, but we'll pick them up on the way back."

"Yeah, of course."

"I just, um…." Justin looked around nervously. His cheeks were flushed, as though he were embarrassed. Hale found it endearing, the way he was getting flustered.

"It's cool," Hale said. "You just drive, and I'll pay attention to what you're doing. I learn best by watching anyway."

Justin looked relieved, and Hale smiled at him. He could say the smile was meant to reassure the kid, but in actuality, Hale was grinning because he'd given himself an excuse to keep his eyes on Justin for the next forty minutes solid.

"Truth be told," Hale continued, "I've never driven a truck before. I've driven just about everything else, including farm machinery, but never a truck."

"Farm machinery?" Justin asked as they pulled out of the drive.

"Yeah. I grew up in a small community. We took care of our own. Completely self-sufficient for the most part. Can't say it was much of a life. Land wasn't great for crops on the ground."

"You grew right on the ground?"

"Yeah. We were pretty old-fashioned. It was one of those weird religious things. You know, 'God hath wrought judgment upon the land' bullshit. Cleansing the soul would cleanse the earth. I don't have to tell you that didn't work out so well."

"Wow," Justin said. "That's… heavy."

Hale examined him for any sign of what he might be thinking, any sign of judgment. If anything, though, he read concern in the creases of Justin's forehead.

"Yeah," Hale said. "It was heavy."

"I'm sorry," Justin said. "I don't mean to make you talk about all this—"

"No. You aren't making me talk about anything. I'm the one who offered. If anything, I'm sorry for making you listen."

"You don't have to be sorry," Justin said, glancing briefly at Hale. He was blushing again. "I don't mind at all."

"Was that an invitation? You better be careful. I might end up giving you my whole life story."

"I'm okay with that."

"Good," Hale said. He was getting a real positive vibe from Justin, and that had him excited in more ways than one. Why couldn't he stop smiling? Good thing the kid wasn't looking at him or he'd think Hale was crazy. "I'd like to know more about you too," Hale offered.

"Oh." The downturn in Justin's voice indicated he was a little uncomfortable with that. Hale loved how easy this kid was for him to read.

"What's wrong?"

"Nothing, really. It's just… I'm not very good at talking about myself."

"But you're not afraid to?" Hale challenged.

"Um… no!" Justin said, half laughing but sounding offended.

"Just not a talker, eh? That's fine. Mind if I ask questions, then?"

"Go right ahead."

"Got a girlfriend?"

"What?" Now Justin was for sure blushing, and being very careful to keep his eyes glued to the road. Gripping the steering wheel none too lightly too. Hale couldn't help but laugh out loud. Part of him enjoyed making the kid uncomfortable. Maybe that was the fighter in him, always looking for an advantage.

"Don't worry," Hale offered. He didn't want the conversation to go south. He'd back off. "You don't have to answer. I can be a little pushy sometimes."

But damn he wanted to know the answer.

They drove in silence for a while, Hale watching him, noticing his long legs as he worked the clutch and gas, the bulge of his bicep when he made the small motion to shift gears.

"No," Justin said, as though several minutes hadn't passed. "I don't have a girlfriend. Do you?"

"No," Hale said, schooling his inner excitement. He wasn't sure he wanted to go on with this next part, but he supposed he should. Justin actually seemed easy to talk to, it was fun to make him blush, and the more Hale talked about himself, the more likely Justin was to reciprocate. So, Hale pushed on. "I was married for a while, though. My wife died in childbirth six years ago. I have a little daughter, Eddie."

"I'm sorry," Justin said. His look of concern was touching before his expression changed to one of shock. "I mean, sorry about your wife… not your daughter," he added hastily.

Hale laughed again, trying to set him at ease. "I knew what you meant. It's okay."

"Where do you… er… how do you take care of her? Must be hard… without your wife," Justin stuttered, clearly uncomfortable. Hale needed to find a way to take this conversation back to lighter territory.

"Actually she's never lived with me. After my wife died, I was in no condition to take care of a baby. I kind of went off the deep end, you know?" Hale felt a little guilty for the half-truth, because he went off the deep end a long time before Eddie came around, but he was trying to keep it light. "She lives with my wife's sister and her husband in Chicago.

That's where I live too. We lived in the same rise for a couple years until a few weeks ago. I miss her a lot, but she's better off with them."

"She must miss her dad a lot."

Hale shrugged. "She misses me, yeah."

Justin took his eyes off the road for a moment to look at Hale. For the first time since he'd gotten in the car, Hale turned away to look out the window.

"She doesn't know, does she? That you're her father…."

Had he been that transparent? Hale looked back at Justin, raising an eyebrow. "No, she doesn't."

"I'm sorry. I don't mean to get too personal."

"Hey, I told you I'd tell you my life's story."

"Yeah, but you were just being nice."

"You think I'm a nice guy, huh?" Hale smiled at this. "Funny thing, Justin. After fifteen minutes you know more about me than almost anyone else in this world. What is it about you?"

"Ah… the awkward silence? People tend to want to fill it. I've had girls tell me their life story."

Hale felt a twinge of jealousy. He'd said girls, plural. "Is that the secret? Good-lookin' guy like you, I'm not surprised." Hale anxiously watched how Justin would receive the compliment. "You must get tired of having your ear talked off."

Justin gave that quirky half smile Hale had seen earlier. If the mood had been heavy, that slight raise in the side of Justin's mouth seemed to lift it. "There's a big difference between them and you, though."

"Beyond the obvious, I'm guessing. What's the difference?"

"I'm actually interested in what you have to say." For the first time, Hale got a nice look at Justin's teeth as he got a full-on face-changing smile. Such a handsome smile. Hale's heart fluttered. He didn't know what else to call it, and he wasn't sure if it was the words Justin said or that gorgeous smile that did it.

God, he was a sap. Whose heart fucking fluttered, anyway?

JUSTIN GRIPPED the wheel. He must have been doing a lot of that, because his hands were sweaty. Gross. He needed to keep his hero worship under control. Because that's what this had to be—hero worship.

Glancing at Hale, he had to remind himself to keep his mind—as well as his physical reactions—in check. And his eyes on the road.

What he was feeling was not okay. When it had been all fantasy, that was one thing. But now that Black Jim had stepped off that bike and entered the realm of flesh and bone, he needed to stop looking at Hale like some forbidden food on a plate he was trying to ignore. No, actually food on a plate would be okay, because he didn't want to have sex with food on a plate.

This was so wrong. He side-eyed Hale, who appeared to be watching Justin handle the rig. He didn't dare meet those eyes. That man—so not food. No, Hale was all man.

Justin was familiar with Hale's body. They had gotten up close and personal, after all. But seeing him without the greasepaint was… distracting. Hale was so handsome—in a very rough, almost dirty kind of way.

It wasn't fair, because even with his eyes strictly on the road in the diesel-scented air of the cab, Justin could smell him. And he smelled good. Justin caught the aroma of something leather and rustic, like Hale had been infused with the fresh fall air.

Okay, he needed to stop.

But he couldn't. How do you control your thoughts? Especially when fucking *Black Jim* was sitting only a few feet away from you. It was beyond words. That would account for Justin's very awkward attempts and failures at conversation. He liked to let his fists do the talking. Maybe that's why his hands were sweaty—he couldn't hit anything. Black Jim's opinion of him was likely changing from decent fighter to flustered fool.

Maybe he could put aside the notion of the flustered fool in Hale's mind. He had to keep it all business. He'd need to stop looking at those blue eyes that practically took the place of the overcast sky. He'd need to stop marveling at the brown curls that hung low on his neck, and how he finally knew what color that hair was. He'd have to stop thinking about how he'd like to run his hands through it, or touch the dark scruff along the side of Hale's face. What would it feel like?

Reflexively, Justin put on his blinker to turn into the rest stop. And holy shit. That was quick. Where had the time gone? Actually, come to think of it, they hadn't talked for the last bit of the trip. God, he hadn't even noticed. What had Hale been doing, just watching him the whole time? Now that Justin didn't have to concentrate on driving any longer, he wouldn't have an excuse to keep quiet. He'd have to fucking talk. He made an effort to swallow, his mouth suddenly dry.

He parked not far from the one other truck in the lot, a driver probably sleeping from a late night on the road. He cut the engine and took a quick sip of water from the bottle on the console. His swallow was uncommonly loud. He set the bottle back down, looking at it. He wanted more, but he already had to pee. He *could not* take a leak with Black Jim nearby. No way. Hell, he couldn't even look at him. He heard Hale open the passenger door, and Justin took one last breath. *Here goes.*

Exiting the truck, he discreetly wiped his hands on his hoodie, and then made sure things were locked down. He met Hale in front of the truck but kept his eyes on their surroundings, examining the area. Clouds were filling the sky, blocking the sun, but the world seemed hyperalive. It wasn't the peak of fall color yet, but the leaves were changing. Perhaps because of the recent lack of rain, many had already fallen, and a breeze carried them rustling across the lot.

Hale gestured toward the woods, and wordlessly they began walking away from the truck. Pavement crunched underfoot, turned to gravel by time and kept clear of vegetation by the trucks. They passed the remnants of the rest stop building that had long since been burned out by truckers who wanted to keep it free of passing vagrants so they could use the turnoff.

They walked to the tree line where they could talk in private. Not private, exactly, because Justin heard the buzzing of a drone approaching. Out there it was probably a federal patrol model. Weaponized. Both he and Hale instinctively quickened their pace, though there was nothing abnormal about truckers walking into the woods. Nature called and all that—a fact Justin would personally attest to at the moment—though two men together might seem odd. Thankfully the drone was perhaps a quarter mile away and didn't look to fly directly overhead.

Justin let Hale take the lead, walking two steps behind him. That way it didn't seem odd that they weren't talking. Hopefully, anyway.

Entering the roadside forest, Justin put his hands in his pockets and kept his eyes to the ground. The vegetation was somewhat sparse, but the trees were fairly thick. Many plants had completely died out over the last generations, due to either ground contamination or climate change. This summer the area had been under water. It had been unusually wet early in the season, making the highway impassable and forcing Justin to drive some rather inconvenient detours. In the last couple months, however, it had been completely dry, and decaying leaves carpeted the forest floor, broken by patches of green where the heartier plants grew. Fallen trees, perhaps dying breeds, crossed their path frequently. Sporadic dry leaves crunched underfoot.

The stifled forest growth made him think of Griz. The old man always said the ground contamination and the viruses were one and the same. The epidemics that killed all the people killed the ground. People shit it out, bled it out, coughed it out. Every living thing was infected with the same poison, trying to heal. Someone, somewhere, had to know the truth, but there was no distinguishing the truth from the misinformation, from all the theories and conspiracies plastered all over the Internet, spewing from the mouths of feuding government officials or sloganed by competing food and drug corporations. Where did you go to find the truth?

Not that it even mattered. Justin kicked at a lonely chestnut. Food mattered. Survival mattered. Gin and Charlie and Griz mattered. People took precedence over truth. Griz would agree with that. God, if only Griz could see him now—doing exactly what the man wanted. Making a friend. Hopefully. Ugh. Justin wiped his hands inside his pockets, then brought them out in the cool air. He cracked his knuckles and flexed his fingers, the sound loud even with their tramping gait. It almost seemed like finding the truth to the Thinning would be easier than the prospect of what he was about to do—or try to do, anyway. This didn't even seem real. Fucking *Black Jim*.

They kept walking, Hale leading like he knew where he was going. Once well out of sight of the road, he looked around as if searching for something but didn't slow his pace. Instead, Hale altered his direction and walked over to a tree that was larger than most. Justin watched as Hale sat down, leaning his back against the tree.

Hale patted the leaf-covered ground next to him. "Have a seat. This seems like more of a sit-down conversation."

Okay. Justin wiped his hands again on the inside of his pockets as he sat down. The tree wasn't so large that they had any space between them, and they bumped shoulders. Oh God.

Justin pulled his knees up and leaned forward, giving Hale some space. Except they were touching at the hip, producing a sensation like electricity at his midsection. So much for not getting distracted.

"How did you find me?" Justin began before his mind could wander. He stared straight ahead over his knees, looking into the forest. Bunches of small spindly ferns poked up through the leaf litter.

Behind him he sensed Hale stretching out, extending his legs and putting his hands behind his head. Great. Now if Justin leaned back he'd be leaning right into Hale's arm.

"I don't know, exactly," Hale said. "My handler had been looking for you, but he'd reached a dead end. Then somehow someone slipped me a note, said where to find you. I don't know who did it. Benz might—that's my handler—but I haven't talked to him yet. I wasn't sure this was about you, not until this morning."

"I saw him following us, the night at the church."

"Yeah," Hale admitted. "I wanted to make sure you were okay."

Really? So that's why. "Even after the glove? Why?"

"Why don't you tell me about the glove first? Answer for an answer."

Perfect. Answering questions Justin could handle. "Scarecrow—he told me they wanted me to use it—the Shadow Masters or whoever. He said… he said they wanted me to cut your face."

Hale was silent. Only seconds, but it was too long, so Justin added, "I never planned on using it like that, but I didn't see a way out, not completely. So I slugged you low. Weapons weren't something I ever signed up for, but now…." He supposed he couldn't get into his current predicament with Scarecrow, how he couldn't afford to lose anymore, how he'd have to do whatever it took. Fucking Scarecrow. "My handler said it was because you wouldn't lose. No one would bet against you."

"So you even went against the Shadow Masters, as you call them?"

Jesus. Justin hadn't thought about it in those terms before. "Yeah, I guess. I didn't really think it through." Thank God he'd given a hell of a fight, or who knows what might have happened to him for so blatant a—

Justin felt a tap on his shoulder. He looked behind him to where Hale was leaning against the tree, and met the man's eyes. They were serious and soulful. "Thanks, Justin. My career—hell, my life as I know it—it would be gone if not for you. You might think no one noticed, but I did. So thanks."

So he *had* noticed. Holy shit—Black Jim had just given him props—had *thanked* him. Justin couldn't hold back a smile. And what was that feeling that was coming along with it? A newfound sense of bravado. "You're welcome," Justin said. "You know, I would have kicked your ass if I hadn't had to go easy on you."

He almost wanted to take it back, but then Hale opened his mouth and laughed, his eyes crinkling at the sides. As young as he looked, he was older than Justin. "I'm not sure about that, but you definitely wouldn't be looking at this beautiful mug here," Hale said, gesturing to his face. It sure was a beautiful mug.

"Who are *they*?" Justin asked quickly. "The people behind Shadow Fray?" He resumed his forward gaze after asking the question so as not to stare. Somewhere overhead a chattering squirrel filled the brief silence.

"The Shadow Masters? I don't know," Hale said. "I have an idea. My handler, Benz, he's my brother-in-law—"

"The one taking care of your daughter?"

"Yes. He's a former... I don't really know what to call it. Muscle? Hitman? Anyway, he used to work for some people. He still does, but not in the same capacity. They're people who run a lot of different... investments. Any way you can think of to make money, they have their hands in it. Gambling and drugs for sure. Politics maybe. He works at the Excalibur in Chicago. I don't know, and I don't think he knows, who these people actually are. Certainly we don't know names. I don't even know if Shadow Fray is all one big organization or if it's representative of competing factions, a way for different gaming houses to make money." Justin nodded. What Hale was saying made sense. Anyone making their best guess would have said the same, and it was what the media speculated after the Mutual Conglomerate Arena. Organized crime basically.

Hale took a big breath before continuing. "All I really know is they asked Benz to get involved, find someone to fight. At the time I was ready to put a bullet in my own head. I was young enough, scrappy, and needed something to live for. My death wish was an asset at first. I was a fucking beast. Gradually I started taking care of myself. The game became important. So did my family. In a way, Benz saved my life."

"He sounds like a nice guy," Justin said, trying to be supportive. "I wouldn't have thought.... I mean, the guy is built like a tank."

"He's a good guy to have your back. But what about you? How did you get into it?"

Justin wasn't sure how all of his pieces fit together. He'd learned too much in the last few weeks. "I think it's because I have a kind of… benefactor. He's been a friend of my family for as long as I can remember. He always kept an eye on us. He said—well, I think he might have been one of the people you talked about having investments. He might have even used that word. When I was young, he had me training, all different fighting styles. I never stuck with one for too long. Wrestling, jujitsu, MMA—some of the trainers seemed just off the street. Our rise has a little gym—a weight room, really, but I'd train there or at a couple different places nearby, a month or two at a time, from before I started school all the way until I was sixteen."

Justin paused. He didn't want to go into this next part. Good thing he wasn't in a position to look Hale in the eye. But how much should he say? Hale had been pretty open and honest, so he should probably return the favor. Maybe this was what Griz had been talking about, that friendship wasn't easy. Justin took a breath and continued.

"When I was sixteen, my mom died, and my benefactor left town. It was just me and my sister and our two-year-old brother. We dropped out of school. I tried to find work but couldn't. Gin was the only one who could, and it wasn't enough. I stayed home with Charlie during the day, and at night sometimes she…." He was unable to find the words to finish the sentence. But he did want to keep going. He suddenly had the urge to power on, to get it all out, like he was vomiting words. He'd never told this to anyone.

"We owned our condo, but we still had to survive. It wasn't easy. Some guys she'd bring back to our place, but we couldn't do that all the time, and I couldn't leave Charlie alone. No matter what, though, I always had her back. She can take care of herself, but if a guy stepped out of line, I was there. It wasn't often, but it wasn't rare either." He was rambling, could feel his temperature rising as his hands fisted at his side. The words kept coming. "That's how I got my knuckles bloody. That's how I really learned to fight. Unless you want to put someone down permanently, you have to learn how to hit hard and hit fast, so they won't get up until after you're gone, and they'd never think to fucking come near you again."

Justin flinched when he felt a hand on his shoulder. It was just Hale, but he had to suppress his first instinct to turn and stick the guy in the face. He sensed Hale tense up, as if he knew what Justin was thinking. Stupid emotions. The guy was just trying to be nice, and at least he wasn't saying anything. Might as well keep talking and be done with it. Justin took a couple deep breaths and relaxed into the touch, even as he kept his eyes forward.

"When Charlie started school, Gin and I could both work at Lighthouse, and that helped. We've had a few lean years for sure, but we get by. My first handler, Joe—I think he was a pusher. He came up to me after I beat down some druggie Groundlings on the street. It wasn't a big fight or anything. The circumstances were sketchy, but when he pitched me fighting in an actual Arena for Shadow Fray, I thought, why not? I can take care of myself. Turns out he was legit. After I lost my first Fray, I didn't know if I'd hear from him again, but eventually I got another offer. Did better. After Joe died, I needed a new handler. Luckily I had the info on my next Fray already, thought I'd try to hook up with that handler. And that's it." Minus a few painful details about Joe in order to protect his sister, but for the most part, Justin was more honest than he'd ever been before—with anyone. He had to admit, it felt good. Freeing. He wanted to pat himself on the back. But nah, because Hale still had that hand on his shoulder.

Justin leaned back against the tree. Hale put his arm around him.

Oh God. Don't overthink it. Maybe this is just how guys act. Slow down, heart. This is just normal guy stuff.

From the arm not around Justin's shoulder, Hale extended a closed fist to him. It took Justin a second, but then he got it and gave Hale a fist bump. See, normal guy stuff. "What was that for?" he asked.

"Sounds like we both have been through stuff. Just felt right. Seems like you're a good guy and I'm happy to know you. That's all."

Hale sounded so sincere, Justin wanted to turn and look at him. But no, their faces would be way too close. The silence grew, and he felt the need to fill it. "Next question is yours."

Justin wanted to kick himself. It wasn't Hale's question. It was his. His brain wasn't working right.

"Will you train with me?" Hale's question didn't immediately sink in.

"What?" In Justin's excitement, he forgot to be embarrassed by the closeness and turned to look at Hale.

"Will you train with me?" Hale wasn't smiling, not exactly. He looked—excited?

Maybe Justin was projecting, because oh hell yes, he'd train with Black Jim. But he didn't want to sound overeager. Be smooth. "Well, yeah, but… what do you mean by training, I guess?" Oh God. His cheeks began to burn.

"We fight. Not all out. Well, maybe all out, if you want. After talking with you, though, I think if we're going to stay in this game, then we need to come up with new strategies. Disarming an opponent, for instance. And it would really help to have a training partner."

As amazing as that sounded, Scarecrow's recent warning still made Justin cautious. It would be breaking the rules. "Are you sure it's safe? I mean, the weight room at my rise isn't appropriate for sparring between two grown men. Do you have a place?"

"Why not right here?"

"Now?"

"No, not now. But we can start tomorrow. Just a couple hours in the morning. We can park the truck and it shouldn't be noticed, as long as it's not the only one. If I meet you at six, we can be here before sunrise. It'll give us plenty of time to train and get back to work."

Justin looked up. The leaves would soon be off the trees, and they wouldn't have much cover. "What about the drones? I don't want to be paranoid, but—"

"No, I get it. We do need to be careful. Let me take care of that."

How? That didn't make much sense, but training in the woods for one day wouldn't exactly be suspicious even if they were seen. Would it? Or was he throwing caution to the wind in order to fight Black Jim again? Even sitting still, Justin began to sweat—but it wasn't nervous sweat this time. He was excited. A lot. For more reasons than he cared to analyze.

"Tomorrow," Justin said. "Sure. We can take it from there, I guess." Hale smiled for real this time. Despite small laugh lines, the smile made him look like a kid, brightening those blue eyes.

Suddenly they were too close. Justin sprang up, dusting off his jeans. "How old are you, anyway?" he asked.

"Thirty-six. You?"

"Twenty-three."

"Shit, I feel old. Help me up, would you?" Hale extended his hand and Justin grabbed it, lifting him to his feet. He noticed how dirt and leaves clung to the seat of Hale's black jeans, and he had the urge to help him brush off.

"We should get back to work, I suppose," Justin said.

Hale nodded. "Just one more thing, before we get back in the truck and I can't ask you anymore, and then I swear while we drive you can ask me anything non-Fray. But I want to know about your handler. Scarecrow. Tell me about him."

Justin found himself unable to meet Hale's eyes. His hands automatically clenched. "I'd rather not."

"Benz told me, vaguely, about what happened after I left the church. That's partly why I had him follow you. I had the sense you might be in trouble. Are you?"

Justin didn't want to talk about Gin and Scarecrow, but maybe he could skirt around that. He nodded. "Until very recently I thought I would kill Scarecrow myself."

"And now?"

Justin clenched his teeth. Fuck it. He was all in. "He fucked my sister. I want to kill him, but a friend advised me not to."

Hale's eyes widened. "Shit. I'd say that's trouble."

"The guy's a murderer and all-around asshole. I cringe every time I have to talk to him. I hate him." Justin nearly spat the words.

Hale took a step toward him. "Then I need you on my team. I don't know how yet, but I promise you—Benz is a great guy. The best. I know he'd take you on. I guarantee it."

"You don't have to do that." The offer was too good to be true. Impossible. And this was Justin's mess, his responsibility. He didn't need to be rescued. Why did everyone think he was so weak? He could seriously punch Hale—though that was more the lingering anger that came with thinking about Scarecrow. Christ, he needed a damn sedative today. "Thanks, but I can handle it. I can take care of myself."

Hale must have sensed his feelings, because he put his hands up in a calming gesture. "Of course you can. It's not about that. I think you're fucking fierce. That's why it would be good for us to look out for each other. It's for me as much as you. Besides, you nearly beat me. I'm sure I could do it again, but if you're on my team, I won't have to." Hale was baiting him. The smirk said as much, but Justin decided to ignore it. In all honesty it would solve everything and bring him closer to Black Jim. Too good to be true or perfect solution? Maybe only time would tell, but it was worth a shot.

"You'd do that? After the glove and everything?"

"Stop with the glove. You *saved* me. Why are you feeling guilty about it? Yes, I'd do that. And more than that. I owe you, Justin. Think of it that way, and let me make it up to you. First I'll help you get out from under Scarecrow. That's the main priority. You don't have to be alone in this anymore."

Justin looked up. He was so weightless, he could probably float away into the cloudy sky. Somewhere nearby, he heard the buzzing of another drone. He'd still have to keep his feet on the ground. Be cautious. Wary.

"How are we going to do it?" Justin asked.

"I don't know yet. Let me talk to Benz. But we'll get rid of Scarecrow any way we have to."

Hale looked concerned. Serious. God, if anyone were to have his back, who better in the world than Black Jim? This man had exploded into his life like a bomb, and all the junk Justin had been carrying around with him was blown clear. He was free.

"Thanks," Justin said. The word was inadequate, but hopefully Hale understood.

Justin looked in his eyes for what seemed like the hundredth time, if a hundred wasn't nearly enough. And then Hale's words made Justin smile. "I can't tell you how good it feels not to be alone anymore," he said. The drone got louder, and Hale motioned that they should head to the truck. "Time to go?"

Justin nodded and walked with him, close by his side.

Chapter 19

HALE YAWNED, stretching as he stepped onto the broken pavement outside the rest stop. This time three other trucks were parked in the lot—the same ones that were here when he'd left just over an hour ago. God he was tired. If he hadn't already been up for four hours, he might even be nervous. He'd put a lot of work into this plan, stopping both on the way home last night and on the way in this morning.

Okay, maybe he was still a little nervous.

Couldn't beat the predawn view, though. He watched Justin walk around the truck, double-checking to make sure the trailer was locked. His friend was wearing the same gray hoodie as yesterday, but instead of jeans, he wore a pair of gray sweatpants that, while loose, draped his butt perfectly.

Hale had opted for a similar outfit but in his typical black color. When Justin was done with the inspection, Hale started walking toward the woods. Justin fell into step next to him, close to his side. Justin seemed to be warming to him, though it kinda sucked that Hale would have to lead the way—he'd love to be looking from behind.

"You talk to Benz last night?" Justin asked as they entered the shadowed area of the forest. There was just barely enough light to see, and Justin stepped a little closer to him.

"Yeah, for a long time. Like I said, he's more than willing to take you on." Which was true, but Hale wasn't going to mention how nervous it made Benz. "We haven't worked out the problem of how. It'll happen, though. Don't worry."

It was rare for Brawlers to change handlers. As far as Hale knew, it happened only when the handler met an untimely end. The Brawler could try to hook up with a handler at the next Arena or wait to see if the bosses sent a new one. There was no clear-cut system and no guarantee. Justin's popularity would work in his favor, but even if they paid Scarecrow off, it wouldn't be easy to get Justin over to Benz. Something like that had never been done before.

"What about the note? What did he say about how you found me?"

"He said I'm an idiot for not telling him first. And he's right. I am an idiot—a throw-caution-to-the-wind kind of guy. Hindsight is twenty-twenty, so why bother trying to think about stuff until after it's happened? Live, then learn, that's my motto."

"That's a lot of sayings."

The kid could be little snarky after all. Hale liked that. He flashed Justin a grin. "Yeah, you and Benz are gonna get along fine. Meeting you is working out really well as far as I'm concerned, so he can call me an idiot, but I can't imagine a better outcome than this right here." Hale gestured between them and turned the wry grin into his most winning smile. The kind of smile he would use to get things. Justin returned his smile with half of one of his own, his teeth lighting up the dark.

So damn handsome. Okay, Hale had to admit it at this point. He was trying to seduce the guy. And it felt good—it felt right. Justin needed to be seduced. He was giving Hale all of these subtle hints—the way he let himself be touched, the way he had leaned into his arm yesterday, the way he was blushing right now—not to mention the energy they shared when they fought. Hale knew something was there; he just needed to find a way to unlock it. To help the kid over his hang-ups.

This was somewhat new for Hale as well, but he was happy to find he didn't have any hang-ups. As a kid he'd been into guys. That didn't go over so well on a religious compound. After he was discovered goofing around with boys—kid's stuff, really—he'd been circumcised. As a reminder to live a pure life, they'd permanently scarred his dick.

Since then, every time he'd fucked someone, he liked to think of his dick as his middle finger. *Screw you, Mom and Dad. I'm going to put my cut cock wherever I damn well please, be it man, woman, or Uni.*

And fuck you too, God, while I'm at it.

Janie was the last cisgender woman he'd slept with. After his wife, sleeping with other women didn't seem right. To try it again would remind him too much of her. Or maybe he simply wasn't interested in going that direction right now. What did it matter?

Before and since he'd slept with plenty of Unis, as well as intersex or transgender prostitutes, Wilma being the most recent. He'd never been with a man like Justin, though. He'd never had the opportunity. Relationships between cisgender men weren't spoken about openly, while the other relationships, particularly with Unis, were considered a necessity of the times.

Hale was really just an opportunistic son of a bitch. He preferred prostitutes, and males weren't offered at the places he frequented. Giving pleasure to someone else wasn't a priority when you were a paying customer. Now, though, he couldn't stop thinking about turning Justin's body into a playground. Justin's expressions and half smiles were always so guarded. What would his face look like if Hale were able to give him real pleasure?

He began to tent his sweatpants. Good thing it was dark, but he needed to slow his roll. Honestly he wasn't doing all of this simply to get into Justin's pants. He didn't want to hurt the kid or force him to do anything he didn't want to. But he *really* wanted Justin to want to. As long as his motives were pure, he supposed he could press on.

He'd even settle for motives that were 90 percent pure. Actually, more like 50 percent was okay. Half and half was very reasonable. And 50 percent higher than his motives usually were. So that was good.

"So what did Benz say about who's behind this? Who gave you the note?" Justin asked. Hale straightened. That's right—they'd been talking about Benz. God, it was easy to get distracted by Justin.

"Oh, that. He honestly didn't know. He thought the most likely candidate was his friend, but that's because she was the only known candidate. It could also be someone within the system acting covertly for their own interests. He said we'd probably never find out. He's not going to investigate. He said it would be 'foolhardy.' That's his fancy way of saying dumb."

Justin seemed to agree. "So we just move on, then?"

"Pretty much. We take what we're given and look the other way." At those words, Hale pulled to a stop. They were here.

It was a bit brighter in the open area before them. Even though it was cool out, Hale was sweating slightly. Here goes nothing. "And here we are," he said, gesturing to the clearing in front of them.

"You've done some work here. When did you do that?" Justin asked, looking surprised and impressed. Hale smiled widely.

"Last night and early this morning. This area had smaller stuff growing. It was easy to cut down. I moved a few fallen logs, cleared out the space a little. And then over here—come look."

He led Justin to an area adjacent to the clearing, near a fallen log.

"Check this out," Hale said. This was the part he was proudest of and the part that had taken him the longest. He bent down and lifted. It looked like he was lifting part of the forest floor into the air. Even in the dawn's light, his work was holding up.

He had used the log as well as a natural dip in the terrain to hollow out a small area. He'd created a sort of crevasse. Over the crevasse, he'd placed a piece of supported canvas. On top of the canvas he'd fixed leaves, twigs, and all other manner of debris. It now acted as a hidden trap door. Hunters would call it a blind. The whole thing was large enough for two people to lay down, completely hidden from sight.

"Wow," Justin exclaimed. "I didn't even see that."

"I'm good, yeah? Made plenty when I was a kid. So I figure we just have to be aware of our surroundings. We can hear the drones coming. When we do, we hide out for a couple minutes so we aren't caught fighting out in the open. With the cover of the trees, we should have enough warning. We saw two yesterday and neither of them flew directly overhead. This should be safe enough. What do you think?"

"I think it'll work," said Justin, sounding impressed. "At least for now. Maybe we can find another place or two so we can switch it up, a warehouse or something, but I think this is a good start."

"Awesome. I'm glad you approve." Hale put the canvas back into place on the forest floor where it blended in seamlessly. "Now, are you ready to start?"

"Of course," Justin said, smiling more than halfway and taking his hands out of his pockets. "What did you have in mind?"

"Some basic disarming techniques. I had Benz talk me through a few and did a little research myself. I can't practice with him because he has a broken hand—"

"Really? How'd that happen?"

"He needs better friends."

"Aren't you his friend?"

"More like his brother, but he could still do better than me. Probably best for you to keep that in mind too." There—Hale had given Justin fair warning, relieving himself of all due responsibility for anything that might happen from this point forward.

"I'll take my chances," Justin said, looking into Hale's eyes, his expression starting to shift into the steely look of a challenge.

And Hale was getting aroused. It was difficult to hide a semistiff cock in sweatpants. At this rate he was going to have to employ a technique he hadn't needed since he was a kid and think about his schoolteacher back on the farm. She was a real dick-shrinker. Maybe then he'd be able to keep his mind on more immediate goals. Like weapons. And fighting.

"We have to assume the time is coming when we'll face a handheld weapon," Hale said, rolling his shoulders and stretching his neck to warm up. All the stuff to keep the focus above the waist. "Handlers are going to be checking knuckles and gloves for anything hidden, based on what's already happened. Benz thinks the natural progression is going to be to hide stuff around the Arena beforehand."

Justin nodded. "Can we practice some of the holds you used on me, like when you took off the glove? I was going easy on you until it came off, but I was still impressed."

Hale found himself smiling, from the compliment and the challenge. "Holds. Yeah, of course. Let me show you this, and afterwards we can do whatever you want." Cling to each other and roll around on the forest floor? Maybe they should skip knife practice....

No—need to focus. God, he was distracted. Although, he could try to turn the tables and distract Justin. Nothing wrong with harmless fun, right? He couldn't help a smile, and bent down quickly to hide it, eyes on the forest floor. He searched the ground and then picked up a rather small but thick piece of wood as a stand-in for a blade. He flipped it to Justin, who had to think fast to catch it. "Here. Hold my wood," said Hale, no longer trying to hide the smirk.

While he didn't typically go for innuendos that could be matched by a twelve-year-old, it certainly had the desired effect, as Justin's expression lost its challenge in favor of blushing embarrassment. Hale laughed. "Kid, you're too easy to take off your game. And you think *you* went easy on *me* that night?" Hale stepped into Justin's space, looking into those scared brown eyes.

Suddenly he felt the poke of wood under his chin and was forced to look up—sharply—at Justin. He'd gotten sucked into those eyes and hadn't been looking down at all. Whoops.

"Do a man a favor," Justin said, eyes flashing. "Don't call a *man* a *kid*, especially when you're throwing your wood in his face. It's weird."

Hale felt the color draining from his face. Ouch. But okay—fair enough.

Justin backed away, holding the stick in front of him like it was a blade. "Now, what game are we playing here?" The man-boy in front of him smiled as though he had the upper hand. Which, Hale had to admit, he kind of did. "You try to grab my wood before I can poke you with it?"

Hale lunged forward, extending both of his hands. In one fluid motion that looked like a clap, he blocked the inside of Justin's wrist with one open palm, and with the other open palm hit the back of Justin's knuckles where he was gripping the stick. The piece of wood went sailing ten feet through the air before landing on the forest floor.

Justin gaped at Hale.

"You lose," said Hale, mustering all the bravado he had into those two little words.

"How'd you do that?"

"Quickly."

Justin scowled at him. Hale retrieved their "blade" and put it back into Justin's hand. "Keep that pointed at me, and I'll slow it down for you," said Hale. He showed Justin how blocking the inside of the wrist held the arm stationary. As Hale's other hand forced Justin's grip to curl inward, his fingers had no choice but to begin to open.

"You can't keep a closed fist when your wrist is forced inward," Hale explained. "Your fingers naturally start to extend, and your grip is lost. The knife comes flying out."

Justin nodded. "I'm impressed. I've disarmed guys before but never like that and never that easily. Can we try it again?"

Hale and Justin practiced, each taking turns. They held their makeshift blade at different heights so they could get used to adjusting their angle of attack. If the knife was held high, you had to attack from below. If it was held low, you had to come down from above. The most difficult was when the knife was held right in the middle of the body, and it was a toss-up whether you'd go at it from above or below. It took Hale some trial and error to figure out what worked the smoothest.

He lost track of time. Erotic thoughts were pushed aside—more or less. He wasn't used to this level of intensity and focus. Breathing deeply, he enjoyed the moment of self-awareness. He was calm. At peace. He flashed his smile at the kid. "Hey, Justin?"

"Yeah?" Justin looked rather grounded himself. His smile was open and unguarded.

"If I call you kid again, you can smack me upside the head."

Justin laughed. "Good to know, but I'll take it easy on you, at least at first. I know it's hard in your old age to develop new patterns of behavior."

"Bastard!" Hale grabbed him and put him in a playful headlock, but really it was more of a half hug. He couldn't explain this sense of closeness he was feeling, but he loved it. Justin's ass grazed his crotch as they wrestled playfully. Hale's body crackled with electricity, all of his senses becoming hyperaware. Pinpricks played across his skin. He became cognizant of their hard breathing and the different cadence between Justin's breaths and his own. Above them a single bird chirped. He could feel splashes of brightening sunlight on his skin, and the colors around him were vibrant and alive.

The moment was shattered by a sound. He heard a buzzing in the distance. He froze.

"Drone," he said, grabbing Justin's hand. He felt slightly panicked, which didn't make any sense since they weren't in any immediate danger. Maybe it had just been a surprise, spoiling whatever had been about to happen. Which was what, exactly?

He led Justin to the blind and lifted up the canvas, ushering him in. Hale got in as well, crouching down and extending his body to lie down while he lowered the lid over them. Bits of leaves and dirt fell into his face, and he shut his eyes. He pressed air out of pursed lips to get rid of any dirt that had fallen near his mouth and reached up to brush off his face. Apparently, Justin had the same idea, because they bumped arms. He opened his eyes.

He and Justin were face-to-face, lying on their sides without much room in the small space to maneuver. Hale's heart thumped so loudly he expected to hear it in the moment of silence that followed, like the world was on pause.

The kid—Justin—looked a little afraid in the dim light. Likely Hale looked the same, because his insides felt like mush. A little more carefully, he reached up and brushed off his face, and then reached over and did the same for Justin. "Close your eyes," he said. "There's some right by your eye."

Hale let his hand linger on Justin's face, his thumb rubbing against Justin's cheek.

Justin opened his eyes and looked at him. Hale saw desire, no mistaking it. But he also saw fear.

Hale looked down to Justin's mouth and noticed how full his lower lip was. He noticed a small speck of dirt and moved to stroke it away with his thumb.

Old gnarled schoolteacher. Old gnarled schoolteacher. What was her name again? Oh, fuck it.

This was the moment. Justin's breath was hot on his cheek. With it came a pleasant spicy scent like clove, and the lingering heat of sweat. They were so close they were breathing the same air.

Hale's desire was as palpable as the blood pulsing through his veins. He leaned in closer, staring at that lip. The anticipation was killing him. He licked his own lips, moistening them, opening them slightly, inching closer. Slowly.

Justin looked down, lowering his chin. Blocking him. Shit. So he wasn't ready yet. Not for kissing anyway.

Overhead the buzzing of the drone got louder.

Justin may not be ready for kissing, but the tent in his pants definitely said he was feeling the same thing Hale was feeling. Hale wanted to reach down and free him for a closer look, but he brought his hand down to Justin's shoulder instead. "Are you okay?" Hale asked.

"Yeah, I'm okay. Just… embarrassed."

Embarrassed and very turned on. Hale slid his body a little lower, so the tip of his erection rubbed against Justin's through their sweatpants. "No need to be embarrassed," he said. "As you can see, it's a natural shared reaction."

Hale gyrated his hips very gently, maintaining the smallest amount of contact, rubbing up and down ever so slowly, cock tip to cock tip. If this felt anywhere near as good to Justin as it did to Hale, the guy wouldn't be long in taking the bait.

"Is it? Is it… natural?" Justin asked, his voice trembling, uncertain.

"It feels natural," Hale said. He tried to study Justin's lowered face but couldn't see him clearly. "It feels good," he added.

Justin nodded, still looking down, but Hale heard his breath hitch as he returned the motion of cock head on cock head in miniscule increments, almost imperceptibly.

Fuck, Hale wanted this so bad. He could feel the wetness beginning to seep through his sweatpants, the glide between them indicating Justin's pants were getting wet as well. But something was wrong. He could sense the discomfort in Justin, see the tight muscles in his body indicating the stress. He saw the internal conflict, saw that Justin's body was saying yes, but his head was saying no.

"Dammit," Hale said out loud. "I can't do this to you."

"What?" Justin said, looking up, clearly caught off guard.

"I said I'm stopping."

He could hear the drone growing quieter as it went off into the distance, and he stood up, lifting the blind and letting in the bright sunlight. Too bright.

Hale was shaking with nervous energy. He was used to taking what he wanted, and he wanted nothing more than Justin. Right now.

He extended a hand down to help Justin up, and thankfully the kid took it. Their erections were painfully obvious.

"I can tell you got stuff going through your head," Hale told him. "The way I grew up, I have an idea what that feels like, and I don't want to do that to you. I know what guilt feels like. And you know what? If I didn't have enough other stuff in my life to feel guilty about, I might feel guilty about what almost happened just now. But I don't feel guilty, not about that. I feel plenty guilty about my wife, my daughter, all the crazy shit I put people through. You don't know the half of it." Hale realized he sounded angry and tried to reel it in, but his emotions were all over the place. "I know enough about guilt to know there's nothing here between us to feel guilty about. I guess I need you to know that too, before we go any further."

Fuck, why was he so pissed? He just cockblocked his own self, so who was he mad at?

"We should probably get back to work," Hale said, already walking away.

He didn't wait for Justin to follow.

JUSTIN DIDN'T like the feeling of not being able to talk openly in his own house. Everything was so screwed up. He was so paranoid. Who might be listening? Who might be watching?

He was swimming in a stormy sea, with all the ups and downs. Just when he felt able to take a breath, he'd be shoved back under. One minute happy and excited and the next freaking out.

He braced himself on the railing of the balcony outside their unit. He had a clear view in three directions: east over the endless lake, south to rises lined up like dominoes to the downtown center, and west over the city flats. The sun was setting, lending a golden hue to the scene. From up here he was able to look out and imagine how things must have been. At one point people looking out on this same view led carefree, frivolous lives. Justin didn't like to look back on the past, but tonight he envied those people.

Gin stroked his back. "It must be bad," she said. "I can count on one hand the times where you've said you need to talk."

"I don't even know if I can talk or should. I'm constantly afraid now."

"We're outside. We'll talk quietly. I'm sure it's fine." She moved in closer next to him, putting one hand on the railing but keeping her other hand on his back. It was like she was making their own little enclosed bubble within the six square feet of private balcony outside their fourteenth-floor apartment.

"It's Hale," Justin said softly. "The guy who started training with me yesterday."

Gin's brow creased, confusion evident on her face. "What about him?"

"He's Black Jim."

Gin wasn't often at a loss for words, but her shocked expression was apparently all she could offer him.

"Oh my God," she said at last. "Are we in trouble?"

"No," Justin said. "He's actually really… nice. Sort of."

"How did he find us? And why?"

"He was looking for us. Remember the car that followed us, with his handler? He said he wanted to make sure I was okay."

"But how did he find us? I thought that stuff was supposed to be secret."

"It is, but he's definitely more connected to people than we are. Someone slipped him a note, but he doesn't know who. It's pretty sketchy."

"Someone who knows your identity?"

"Yeah. I guess so."

"That's scary. I can see why you've been acting like such a freak the last couple days. Why didn't you tell me right away?"

"I just found out yesterday."

"But you waited until now. Why? What's happened?"

"We started training today—fighting, I mean. We're going to be training partners. We practice in this wooded area where we won't be seen, before we do our deliveries."

"Jesus Christ, Justin, can you skip to the important part already? I'm waiting for the bomb to drop, wondering what could be bigger than what you've already said. I don't have the patience, so what is it?"

This was the blessing and the curse of having a twin. She knew him too well, and he'd just have to come out with it. Why was he so scared about this? This was Gin. She'd never....

He didn't want to finish the thought, so he blurted it out: "I'm finding myself strangely attracted to him."

She looked at him with an expression of pure shock. He turned away, looking down over the balcony. He felt like his stomach dropped and fell fourteen stories to the ground below. No, not fourteen. Thirteen stories. They called it the fourteenth floor, gave it the number fourteen, but they still lived on thirteen. Calling it something different than what it actually was didn't change the reality. It just hid it. Kept you from thinking about it. Except for when you did.

"Oh. God," she said at last. "I can't believe you."

Shit. Not good. His arms were shaky against the railing. Fear or nerves maybe, but he was also getting angry. Defensive. This wasn't right. "What the hell, Gin? I don't need your permission."

"No shit, Justin. You've been jerking off to this guy for years. I can't believe you had me scared half to death over something so obvious."

"What? How—"

"I'm not stupid. When you jerk off, you're in the next room. And I know about that greasy cloth you come and grab beforehand too."

Justin exhaled sharply. He came slowly back to an equilibrium, the relief almost superseding the embarrassment. Almost.

She stroked his back again, and when he glanced at her, she was smiling. "You're really torn up about this, aren't you? It's okay. Everybody does it; they just don't talk about it. You think I haven't been with girls before?"

"No, I *know* you have but... it's different with guys, isn't it?"

"Why? You have an itch, scratch it. Who knows, maybe you'll get it out of your system."

"You think?"

"I'd tell you not to go blabbing to the whole world about it, but this is you we're talking about. You'd never tell anyone. You can certainly talk to me about it. And say something to Charlie, or he's going to be pissed at us for having this little powwow out here without him. I can feel him brooding through the wall as we speak."

"Yeah, okay. I guess I was just worried about what you'd think."

"Justin, you're so serious. It's like you didn't get to grow up. You're like forty years old inside. This is stuff kids go through when they're twelve or sixteen or even twenty-three. Let yourself go through it. You'll come out okay."

"You think I'll grow out of it?"

"Well, it's not like I'll swear off girls, but to some extent, yes, I do. At least you'll be able to move on, you know? Get your head back on straight."

"Okay." Justin nodded. "I can do this." If he kept saying it, perhaps he could convince himself.

"What about Hale?" Gin asked. "Getting sweaty and rolling around might be a pretty good way into his pants. Is he going to be open to it?"

"Oh, that won't be an issue."

"There you go. See. It's probably natural for guys in your profession. You beat each other up, and then you beat each other off. Makes perfect sense."

"I don't want to kiss him or anything." He clutched the rail on the balcony. Why had he said that?

Gin shrugged. "Let me know how things go. So he's nice?"

"Yeah, mostly."

"I suppose this means he's off-limits to me, though. Too bad. He's pretty hot."

"Gin—" The warning was in Justin's tone of voice.

"You know it's happened before. I had a girl or two I sent your way. Keep it in mind, maybe return the favor."

She was probably just messing with him, so Justin laughed softly.

Beneath the laugh, though, something was gnawing at his gut. Things with Hale weren't quite as casual as he'd made them seem, or as

Gin believed. He was hiding the truth, at least partly. What would happen if anyone knew how he really felt?

How did he feel, anyway?

"Oh, by the way," Gin said, "Griz wanted to talk to you. Did he text you?"

"No. I'm not sure I'm up for it tonight. I'll try and go see him tomorrow."

Justin still had to chat with Charlie, and he'd already done more than enough talking for one day.

Chapter 20

HALE WAS learning that Justin was fairly inscrutable, but it seemed doubly so right now in the dim morning light under the deep shadows of the forest. The kid sighed again—for the third time since meeting him that morning. Christ, the sun wasn't even up yet. It was too early for this shit. Something was bothering him, and Hale could guess what it was.

Truthfully he wasn't upset with Justin. Not really, anyway.

Sure, Hale wasn't thrilled with the way things had ended in the woods, but he blamed himself. He needed to be less of an asshole and back off a bit. What was he hoping for anyway? Chances were Justin wasn't gay. He might be down for a one-off—someday—but he probably wasn't going to be interested in much more than that.

It wasn't worth it.

He needed to be happy with Justin's friendship, because after spending two full days with him, he didn't want to jeopardize that. The silence in the truck yesterday had been stifling.

Hale caught his own sigh before it escaped. At least yesterday would be enough to feed his fantasies for some time. Years even. He couldn't think about it now or he'd get hard.

He'd just keep to himself how sexy he found Justin's gray sweats. Looking at him from behind, he could practically see what his ass would look like, the generous muscles parted so cleanly down the middle where the seam of his sweatpants fell. He'd also begun to associate the image of Justin with a hoodie. He filled it out so well with his broad swimmer's chest, but beyond that it was the perfect accessory for him—something he could hide behind, hands in the pockets and the hood up if he wished. It fit his personality—strong yet distant, imposing yet shy. With a severe case of blue balls last night, all he'd had to do was picture Justin in that hoodie with the zipper wide open and his bare chest underneath it. Hale would love to rub his hands over that chest beneath the soft cotton and tease those dark nipples while the cold metal zipper lightly scraped against his hands and arms.

Hale had never had a fetish before, but he could suddenly understand the appeal.

When he heard Justin sigh yet again, Hale let out a sigh of his own. He'd been hoping they could just move on, that things would be okay between them, but clearly that wasn't the case.

"What's on your mind?" Hale asked, his tone gentle.

"Nothing. Why?"

Typical macho response. "When someone is as quiet as you, a sigh sounds like thunder. You've done it four times now."

"You've been counting?"

"Not on purpose. It's like when you hear gunfire out your window, you can't help but count the shots. So what's up? If this is about yesterday—"

"Oh, no. It's not that." He must have read Hale's skeptical look, because he made an effort to explain. "Honestly. It's just that…." Justin shook his head.

"It's okay. You don't have to talk about it if you don't want to. I only wanted to make sure everything between us was okay."

"Yeah, we're cool." Hale could've sighed with relief, but he could do without any more sighing. "I'm just wary talking about my family. It doesn't come easy to me. Especially with Charlie. He's my little brother, and he's got a disability. I'm really protective."

"I can relate, at least partly. I had sisters, but I bet we were nowhere near as close as you and Charlie." Especially considering he walked away from them. Abandoned them.

"Charlie's mad at me right now. Normally I'd be walking him to school in the morning, but since you and I are training, Gin's had to do it. I think he misses our time together. He's pretty particular about his routines. He and I had a little chat last night, but he's still kind of pissed."

There was no mistaking the sadness in Justin's voice. But what should Hale say? What do you say to another guy when it comes to emotional stuff? With Eddie he'd hug her and kiss her and tell her everything was going to be all right. The idea of doing that to Justin was very appealing but probably wouldn't go over well. So…. "That really sucks." It sounded lame, even to his own ears.

Justin kept his eyes to the ground. "Yeah. He'll get over it eventually, I think."

"Maybe you can bring him with sometime," offered Hale. "Maybe he'd be okay if he saw what you were doing."

"Yeah?" asked Justin, his eyes lifting. "You'd be okay with that?"

"Of course. Maybe sometime you can meet my daughter too." The idea felt right, but maybe it wasn't wise, involving Eddie in something that might be dangerous. Jess would have something to say about it, of course. But the more Hale thought about bringing their families together, the more he wanted it to happen—someday.

"I'll talk to Charlie," Justin said, the tone of his voice completely changed. "I bet he'd love to come watch." Hale felt like giving himself a pat on the back. He'd cheered Justin up, so that sexy smile on Justin's face was his doing.

As they arrived in their clearing, the day was a bit brighter than it had been only ten minutes before.

"It's your show today," Hale said to Justin. "I've never disarmed men in a real situation, not like you." Justin had mentioned his actual experiences protecting Gin, and while Hale was curious about those, he also understood the importance of keeping some things buried. Every fighter had them—secrets like embers beneath the ground that you'd only dig up for a fight, when you needed the burn. Instinctually he knew not to ask, so he listened.

"First thing is to realize you're going to get cut," Justin began. "Whatever the weapon, it's best to assume they'll be successful using it. That way, when you see the blood, you can keep fighting. Freaking out will just put you at more of a disadvantage."

Hale pictured Justin's half-naked body. He hadn't ever noticed any scars, and he'd looked at him pretty thoroughly in all the videos. Had Justin been cut before? Too personal? "Cheery thought," he said instead of asking.

"It's really not so grim. Whoever has the weapon, remember, that's all they have. They have one blade, one gun. You have two hands, two feet—your whole body can work for you. They have only the one point of attack. As such, you have the advantage."

Hale nodded. "Makes sense."

"Next thing you want to do is create space. They can't cut you if they can't reach you."

Picking up a stick to function as their blade for the day, Justin took Hale through some moves. One involved rotating your body while at the same time delivering a direct punch upward to the opponent's hand, which could send a weapon flying. Another clever tactic involved attacking the opponent's groin first, before adding the rotating punch to disarm. In each case it was important to spin away so if the attempt was not successful, distance was maintained.

As they went through the motions, practicing and changing positions, Hale was struck by how similar the movements were to a dance. He wasn't much of a dancer, but if you threw in weapons and blood splatters, he figured he might not be so bad. Or maybe he just needed a partner like Justin.

Shortly they got into the serious stuff that involved more muscle than raw technique, and quite a bit more body contact. Justin showed him how to rush an opponent, deliver an opening attack, and continue in, grabbing the forearm and twisting it to break the wrist. It was far more dangerous but much more effective at disabling the attacker.

Hale relished the first several times Justin ran into him, and he into Justin.

After what seemed like the fiftieth time, he was ready to call uncle.

"Maybe we should wrap it up for today?" Hale said between heavy breaths. "It's getting kind of late." He actually had no idea how much time had passed, but he didn't want to admit he was getting worn out.

Justin wasn't breathing as heavily, but along the sides of his head his hair was slicked back with sweat. He glanced around the sky; Hale guessed he was judging to see where the sun was.

"Just a little bit longer?" Justin asked. "I'm really starting to get into it."

Hale put his hands on his knees and glared at Justin. "Not that I'm getting tired or anything, because I'm not, but if I get too many more bruises on the right side of my body from you slamming into me, I'm not going to be able to move tomorrow." Not to mention this wasn't the kind of body contact that gave him incentive to keep going. Perhaps if they were working on submission holds, he'd be more inclined to stick it out.

Even so, the look of disappointment on Justin's face had Hale questioning his decision. "How 'bout this?" Hale offered finally. "Let's sit down for a few minutes. If I'm not numb and turning purple, we can practice a bit longer. I could hydrate a bit anyway."

Hale walked over to a tree and picked up a water bottle he'd brought along. "Sit with me?" he asked, lowering himself to the ground. He took a drink and then extended the water to Justin.

Justin didn't hesitate. He came and took the bottle from Hale before turning to sit. He groaned very audibly as he sat down and held his side.

"See!" Hale said. "I knew you couldn't be invincible. This shit hurts, man. We gotta take it easy, you know? Don't want to overdo it before the next Fray. Any word yet on your next one?"

"No." Justin settled next to Hale, shoulder to shoulder—much closer than they had started off yesterday. Friendly-like. "No word yet. You think it'll come soon?"

"Probably," Hale said. "Typically every four to six weeks when the demand is high and people want to see you. Sometimes they'll crunch it up to make it interesting, sort of like they did for you last time. They probably want to give you a rest. Me too. That last Fray was killer. So epic. We earned a little break."

"Epic? Really?" Justin was naturally flushed from the workout, so Hale couldn't tell if he was blushing.

"Really," Hale assured him, patting his knee. Friendly-like, right? Hopefully he wasn't going too far.

To his utter shock, Justin reached down and put his hand on Hale's. Justin's fingers curled down for a firmer grip. And there their two hands lay. Together. On Justin's knee.

Hale's heart was thundering. Warm from the workout, his skin grew even hotter.

"Can I tell you something?" Justin asked.

"Of course." He gave Justin's knee a squeeze. God, those legs. He wanted to move his hand up to touch those deliciously thick quads.

"I'm sore as hell. The only reason I didn't want to leave is… well, I was waiting for a drone to come by, but there haven't been any today. I thought if we stayed a little longer…."

Hale felt his eyes widen. He tried to look Justin in the eyes, but Justin was looking down at their hands. Was Justin really saying what Hale hoped he was saying?

He tentatively stroked Justin's knee with his thumb. He moved his hand a little higher to cradle the inside of Justin's leg. Was this a dream? If so, Justin was enjoying it too, because he leaned back against the tree and closed his eyes.

Hale moved his hand up Justin's thigh. The cotton under his hand was slightly damp but very soft. Justin breathed out deeply—it was a sigh, but completely different than those Hale had heard earlier.

Justin's hand moved to Hale's leg and mirrored Hale's motions, stroking up the inside of his thigh. Within the span of five seconds, Hale was hard. He leaned into Justin so they were temple to temple. He could feel the dampness of Justin's hair and smell the clean sweat evaporating from his body.

This was really going to happen.

"Justin?" Hale asked softly. Justin opened his eyes and turned to look at him, his expression uncertain. Hale looked up into the sky, smiling. "I think I hear a drone."

Justin laughed. It was the only sound around. Even the birds were silent.

Hale took Justin's hand and stood up, pulling Justin to his feet. They were both moving a little gingerly, sore and very hard. "You think we should go into the blind?" asked Hale, unable to control his wide, eager smile.

"Yeah, we probably should." So Justin was playing along. His smile was nervous, but his eyes shone with excitement, and that hard-on proved it, didn't it?

Hale's dick seemed to lead the way, pointing like a divining rod to where he would finally get lucky, complete with the twitch. Hell, he'd be happy to throw Justin down on the forest floor and take him in the broad daylight. Still, the dimness of the blind was comforting. He didn't want to scare Justin off, so Hale was more than happy to do this his way.

He carefully raised and then lowered the lid of the blind to keep from getting showered with dirt. His heartbeat stuttered as he wondered how things would start. But much like yesterday, he and Justin were cock to cock, lying on their sides, facing each other.

It was Justin who said, "Maybe we can continue where we left off?" He was gyrating his hips, brushing the tip of his cock against Hale's through their sweatpants.

Hale inhaled sharply, audibly, and put his hand on Justin's bicep. "God, you're a tease. And it feels so damn good." Hale looked into Justin's eyes, a little darker brown in the dim light but shining and playful. He moved his hand up to Justin's face and felt the soft, bristled texture of his cheek. It looked so smooth in the half-light, he marveled at the slight roughness of the touch. Reveled in it. Justin was right—he wasn't a kid at all. He was all man.

Hale glanced down to Justin's bottom lip, then ran his thumb across it. He wanted to feel those lips. He leaned his head in closer for a kiss….

But suddenly Justin lowered his chin, showing Hale the top of his head. Hale tried not to be disappointed, and instead inhaled the scent of Justin's hair—sweat and leaves and dirt. Unexpectedly, Justin grabbed him, his fist circling Hale's cock firmly through the cotton pants. Hale groaned and pulled him in closer, thoughts of the kiss almost forgotten—postponed, Hale assured himself. Just postponed.

If he couldn't have Justin's mouth, he wanted his cock. Hale moved his hand down Justin's body, letting it linger on his hip before ducking it under the band of his sweatpants. He slid his hand down to cup Justin's balls. He could feel a dampness, along with sparse hair. Hale found himself unable to play at any type of seduction. He wanted Justin badly, wanted to feel him. He slid his hand up over Justin's naked cock.

Justin paused in his orchestrations, his breath hitching. Hale marveled at the thickness of Justin's cock. He was more than a handful, and Hale could tell as he grabbed him that he was uncut. He slid his hand up, bringing the skin up on the head, before letting it fall back down. He fingered the tip briefly, running his thumb over the sensitive triangle on the underside as Justin inhaled sharply again.

Hale loved this. He loved to see Justin emote and take pleasure. He only wished he could see his face, that he wasn't looking downward. If he couldn't look at his face, though, he would look at that fat cock. Bringing his hand up, he grabbed Justin's waistband and shoved it down. Justin had to help a little within the confines of the blind. Hale watched as Justin's dick rose up to rest against the black hair below his navel. The cock was thick and gorgeous, the head rising up completely from the surrounding foreskin.

"God, you're beautiful," Hale said, placing his hand around it again. Justin didn't speak but made small sounds, vocalizations with his breathing, almost like a hum. Sounds of pleasure. It was music to Hale's ears.

Justin used his own hands to pull his sweats down a little farther, and then reached over to grab Hale's pants. Hale lifted his hips, his erection springing free as Justin pulled down the material, the cool air adding to the freedom he felt.

He had a moment of self-conscious thought as Justin examined him. Slowly, Justin reached his hand down and slid it along Hale's naked length. "If I'm beautiful," Justin said, "then you're fuckin' gorgeous." Hale's cock flexed involuntarily at the compliment, a bead of precome appearing at the tip.

Hale looked down at their cocks—Hale's longer but Justin's thicker, and both straight as rods. He wanted to burn that image in his mind. He'd never seen anything so hot in his life.

They each used one hand and began working in tandem, somewhat awkwardly at first. Reaching across each other's arms wasn't exactly the most convenient, but it worked. Beautifully, in its own way.

Justin stroked him roughly, his grip strong, his skin toughened from frequent use of his hands. Hale had never experienced anything like it. Nothing compared to this.

It was hard to concentrate, and he didn't give much thought to technique as he worked Justin's cock. Justin was slicker than Hale, the fact that he was uncut aiding in the smoothness of Hale's motions. Hale made sure to run his finger along the underside of the head to give Justin the experience of the roughness he was so enjoying, and heard him hum again.

Sweet music. Hale loved it. Needed more. He hated religion, but still the ingrained thought came, unbidden. *Please God, let this happen again.*

His and Justin's movements became more frantic, their hips shifting deeper to push into each other's hands.

Hale spoke softly, words like whispers. "Justin, God, you feel so good." Either Justin's hand on his cock or his hand on Justin's cock? Both, really. No need to explain.

"Look at me, please," Hale found himself almost begging. *Please, look up at me.*

Justin raised his head, eyes fierce. That one look was enough to let Hale know Justin was here with him. Hale leaned his forehead against Justin's. They were very close, breathing the same air. It wasn't a kiss, but it was enough.

Justin tensed against him. "Let me see you come," Hale breathed, his words so very close to Justin's mouth.

Justin's hand stopped moving on Hale's cock, and Hale could sense the orgasm beginning. Justin didn't speak or scream, but the sound he made was nonetheless unrestrained, even if it was quiet. Hale watched as come surged from Justin's cock, hitting the dried leaves between them. He gripped Justin's dick harder, continuing his motions with a single downward stroke for each spurt that came from him.

Justin buried his face in Hale's neck, and Hale felt the warm, wet breath against his skin. Damn, that was sexy.

Justin's hand found its way to Hale's cock again, his strokes determined. Hale was starting to feel a little pain at the head of his cock from the rough play. He was gonna be a little chafed. He could spit, or use Justin's come to lubricate himself—but no, he liked it like this. He loved the feeling of Justin's rough hands on him, liked the slight burn on his skin.

As though a switch had flipped, Hale was coming. He grabbed Justin's bicep and gave a couple pronounced thrusts of his hips into Justin's hand.

"Fuck," he said, feeling the come coursing up. It shot out over Justin's hand, landing on Justin's forearm and spurting into the leaves where Justin had spent himself moments before. Hale buried his head into Justin's hair, his mouth open, teeth bared as his body continued to spasm and spend.

Gradually the intense sensations left his body to be replaced by his heavy breathing and rapid heartbeat. "Fuck," he said again.

"You say the most romantic things."

Hale laughed. "Did you just crack a joke?"

"I don't do jokes," Justin said, but his smile was wide.

"But God, what you do to me." Hale embraced him. It wasn't cuddling exactly, but it would do… until next time.

Justin returned the embrace, and Hale had the urge to say something. He wanted Justin to know what he was feeling. But what was he feeling, exactly? Whatever it was, it was hella strong. Hale loved having Justin pressed against him, their spent cocks touching, Hale's still sensitive.

Before he could formulate any words, Justin spoke. "I suppose we should get back to work."

Hale sighed. "Yeah. I suppose we should." Talk about romantic.

He wanted to stay here, holding Justin and being held. Soon, Hale promised himself. After all, he wasn't one to give up without a fight.

Chapter 21

LOOKING AT Hale, Justin saw the sun through the driver's-side window as it inched lower toward the horizon. It lit Hale from behind, giving his features a soft glow, a golden hue to his brown hair. Justin almost wished for more time in the truck. Turns out talking wasn't so bad, even after the line they'd crossed this morning. In fact, it was kind of like… a date? Not exactly like an old movie, but that's what it felt like. An old movie, where people talk fast and everything that comes out of someone's mouth is the perfect thing to say.

Hale was easy to talk with, and things in the truck today were so much better than yesterday and the day before. No awkwardness at all. Justin was finding it pretty easy to explain about the truck, the routes, and the business end of things.

"See those double-tire skids?" Justin asked, sitting in the passenger seat. "You pass them on the freeway all the time. Ever consider why a huge semi would have to put on the brakes so hard?"

"I've seen it happen," replied Hale with a smile. He'd been driving since the rest stop, and Justin had to admit, he was impressed with Hale's comfort behind the wheel. "Those are what's left after the air brakes fail. The emergency brakes kick in, the wheels lock up, and you have to steer her off the road. Scary thing to see when you're behind one on a bike."

"I'll bet it would be. Scary thing when you're behind the wheel of the truck too."

"Thankfully I have pretty good reflexes. Wanna stop back at the rest area? I can give you a demonstration."

Justin felt his face getting hot remembering their morning tryst, and he couldn't help the smile. "You tryin' to get a rise out of me?"

"In more ways than one. Is it working?"

"In more ways than one," he agreed, visibly adjusting himself to put his hardening dick in an "up" position to avoid tenting out in his sweats. Talk about a semi.

He looked over to see Hale staring at him intently. "Eyes on the road," he taunted Hale. "That was a test. You're failing miserably."

Hale looked back to the road. Rather reluctantly, it appeared. "Can't help it," Hale said more softly. "You make me want to do things to you that I ain't never done before."

The heat spread through Justin's body. He was probably still blushing too, but so what? He was okay with that. He just had to envision their talk like a fight. If Hale got him to blush, that was like a hit. Justin had to figure out a way to counter. He smiled a silent chuckle. Adjusting his cock was a very effective counter.

The rest stop was only ten minutes ahead, but since it wasn't quite evening, Justin figured their truck would be a little more conspicuous, especially if it was parked there twice in the same day. But still, to do it just one day wouldn't hurt.

God, was he actually considering this? Twice in the same day? Yes, he was. What had happened to him? This morning had been a revelation, and the more Justin thought about it, the more he wanted to do it again—and then some.

"It's still pretty early," Justin said. "We have a couple stops to make coming back into the city, but fifteen minutes to stretch our legs wouldn't hurt."

Hale's mouth fell open. "You're serious?" he asked, excitement plain on his face.

"I think I am," Justin said. "Unless, of course, you don't want to...."

"Fuck that!" Hale said. He leaned over, and Justin could barely hear his next words. "Can't stop thinkin' about it. Want your hands on me again so bad."

"Eyes on the road," Justin reminded him, laughing. Truth was, he couldn't stop thinking about it either. And not in a bad way—in a very good way. He still had reservations, but his dick was taking precedence over the voices in his head. Still, they'd have to keep the innuendos to a minimum. There better be some way to secure the truck, because when it came to Hale, Justin wasn't sure he could hold himself in check. Not anymore.

Thinking back to the morning, Justin kept returning to the sound of come hitting dry leaves. That first release. Had his eyes been closed, and that's why that sound reverberated in his mind? Something that would seem inconsequential had him hardening at the memory. That sound was like a thunderbolt, electricity striking to his core. It was going to be a very long autumn if every time he heard leaves rustling his mind was going to take him back to that spot—back to their first time.

So, yes. Justin did want a second time today. And many more times after that.

So what, if the thought was also a little scary? It actually felt freeing to answer questions that had been weighing on him. Was he ever really into girls? He had always tried to deny a part of himself. He never thought it should be any other way—every guy was like that. They had urges that were part of the environment, urges that were the result of the world being so screwed up. It was okay to have those urges, but you shut them away. He compartmentalized them into one of those damn little boxes in his head.

Because you fought it. You didn't let the world beat you.

What did it mean that he kept thinking about kissing Hale, feeling his scruffy face under his hands as their lips and tongues met? Was he bent?

People had been gay before. Who's to say that if Justin hadn't lived a hundred years ago, he wouldn't have been gay? Maybe the world hadn't made him bent. Maybe he was how he was supposed to be. But how did you know?

Those thoughts were for a later time. He wasn't afraid of thinking them. He liked to live in his own head, liked to think. He didn't know what it would mean if his suspicions were true, didn't know if that would make things any easier. He still had to live in this world, even if it wasn't what made him.

He could fight the world, though. As long as he didn't have to fight himself or the people who mattered to him.

Of those, the only one he could control was himself. Everything else was a little scary. More than a little scary. But he wouldn't beat himself up.

Or he would try not to anyway.

He could talk to Griz about it too. Griz had been around a long time, and he had said something the other day. What was it? Something about Justin making friends. "It didn't need to be a woman." Justin hadn't considered it at the time, but maybe Griz was more perceptive than Justin thought.

Griz had wanted to talk with him too, Gin had said. He'd make a point to go to him tonight. It wasn't Saturday, but he'd send the old guy a text and see if he was up for a chat later.

He reached into his hoodie pocket to pull out his phone and then remembered he'd put it in the glove box this morning before they trained. He reached in, grabbed it, and saw he had five missed calls in the last hour.

And three texts from Gin.

Where are you?

Need you home.

Now.

Justin's heart dropped. "Oh no."

"What's wrong?" Hale asked, more than concerned. Panicked. Justin's own panic must be contagious.

"I don't know," Justin said. "Bunch of missed calls."

He dialed Gin. She picked up on the first ring.

"Justin?"

"Gin. What's wrong?"

"You need to come home."

"What's wrong?"

"It's Griz. Justin, I'm sorry… he's… dead."

Justin closed his eyes for a moment. He had the sensation of sinking, the grief trying to overwhelm him like a wave, but he held it at bay. It was okay. They had known this was going to happen. It's not like he hadn't been prepared for it. He needed to be present, to help, to get himself home.

"Justin?"

"Yeah. I'm here, it's just…. How's Charlie?" It was easier to focus on someone else.

"We're doing okay, I guess. Just need you home."

"I'll be there in thirty minutes."

"Justin?"

"Yeah?"

"They don't think it was an accident—I mean, it wasn't natural."

"I don't understand." Now the wave was on him, overwhelming him.

"The nurse was gone, and Devin—he says that how it happened, it doesn't seem right."

"Oh God, no…." Justin buried his head in his hands. He thought back to the red-haired man he'd seen leaving Griz's place. Thought about how once it hadn't been safe for Griz to be here. But the old guy had come back. Come home. For Justin.

"There's a lot we don't know yet," Gin said after the next moments of silence.

"Don't say any more. I'll be home soon. I love you guys."

"Love you too."

Justin closed his eyes and took deep, steadying breaths.

"Justin, man, what's wrong?" That's right, Hale was in the car with him. God, good thing Hale was driving.

"My friend—my benefactor I told you about—he's dead." He said it flatly, without emotion.

"Damn. I'm so sorry. If there's anything…." Hale paused. "I'll get you home. Don't worry about the job tomorrow. I'm sure I can handle it." Hale reached his hand over. Their seats were not close, but Justin grabbed the proffered hand. Hale gripped it, holding it firmly, before releasing it. Justin felt the absence of the hand keenly.

Maybe it was better not to hold or be held at all. Maybe an ending like Griz's would be inevitable for the people Justin was close to. The more people in his life, the more people he would have to protect. Justin hadn't protected Griz.

For the remainder of the ride, his mind replayed the same idea, like a song on repeat—he was the reason Griz was dead.

JUSTIN USUALLY welcomed the silence of home. The quiet was comforting and easy, a refuge from obligation. But not today. Oppressive silence greeted him when he stepped through the doorway. Charlie sat between Devin and Gin, and all three of them were on the sectional, not talking. They'd been looking down, to the side, off into space, not seeing, but when he came in, they turned to him. Stood up. Looked at him. Time seemed momentarily frozen, the absence of sound heavy with loss. A vacuum.

Then Charlie moved, almost running to him. Justin crouched down, embracing the boy and picking him up. At ten years old, Charlie should not be so easy to pick up, should not welcome it like a smaller child. But Justin was going to let Charlie be who Charlie wanted to be.

Gin followed close behind, and Justin embraced the both of them. "How are you doing?" Gin asked him.

"I'm doing okay." For now. The uncomfortable quiet spread even to his emotions. He hadn't cried, but he was finding memories from his youth poking at the edges of his brain, wanting to come out of the little boxes he put them in, wanting to get out. "How are you guys?"

Charlie nodded to him with those wide baby-blue eyes. He didn't look sad or scared, though this would be his first real experience with death. His eyes did express worry for Justin. That was Charlie's role though—the caretaker. Like when he'd made Justin little ice presents after the last Fray. Like when he'd helped Griz with his shoes. Griz….

As she moved away, Gin tried to smile, probably for his benefit. Her eyes were sad but dry. She seemed more concerned for Justin than anything else. "We're okay. We just wanted you home."

Justin set Charlie down and turned toward Devin. In a moment of awkwardness, he was uncertain of what to do or what to say. Devin was a little unfamiliar for a hug, but a handshake was terribly inadequate. That's what people did at times like this, give a hug, right? Justin opened his arms and embraced the tall man, patting him on the back. He couldn't help but take in the spicy scent of aftershave and notice that under the suit, Devin was built well for someone of his age. His embrace was strong. Why was Justin noticing these things now?

"I'm so sorry about your grandfather," he said to Devin, releasing him.

"I'm sorry too. He was probably more a grandfather to you than he was to me. I didn't know him until Denver. But I will miss him. He was a great man."

Justin nodded. "I can't think of a better way to describe him."

It was plain Devin had been crying. He looked heartbroken, but other emotions were boiling under the surface. He was restless, a tic in his fingers, eyes that looked everywhere. His jaw was clenched.

"Can you tell me what happened?" Justin asked.

"Not exactly," said Devin. "We'll probably never know for sure. But I can't ignore the signs. The nurse disappeared. I have people looking for him, but I don't expect to find him."

"Can you trust the nurse?"

Devin shrugged. "It was a new one. The old one never came back. I don't think the nurse is the biggest of our worries."

Justin thought again of the man with red hair and nodded.

Devin continued. "The pillows were placed strangely. As if someone had used one to…." He swallowed and looked away. "It looked like he was propped up when they were done. It didn't look natural."

"Would he have been conscious?"

"It looked like it was peaceful. No signs to show otherwise. Maybe he was asleep, or even drugged, but…."

But probably not. Griz was old and weak. He couldn't fight—or maybe he didn't even try.

A tear slid down Devin's cheek, and Justin watched him wipe it away. "But again, it's not like we're going to do an autopsy. I don't need one to tell me what happened. It's not like the cops would do anything. I have to decide if this is something I want to pursue or if this is bigger than me." Devin ran his hand over the short hair on his head, then turned to look at Justin. When he continued, his voice was rough. Defeated. "In all honesty this is bigger than me. I don't think Griz would want us to look into this. It's eating me up inside, but that's really what it comes down to."

Justin nodded. "You're right." Griz wouldn't want them looking into it. Justin certainly didn't want Devin looking into it. He didn't want another person dead because of him. If anyone did something about it, it would be Justin—alone—and he had no idea where to even begin.

"I feel like this is my fault," Justin offered.

In response all the man did was shake his head, rather sternly. What did that gesture mean? Guilt settled like a weight on Justin's shoulders.

"I need to go, make some arrangements," Devin said. "I'll let you know about the service. I think it's in our best interest to have it as soon as possible." He put a steady hand on Justin's shoulder and attempted a smile. "Don't be strangers. I don't know if I'll be sticking around here much longer, but until then, I expect it'll be awful lonely up there."

Justin nodded numbly. Devin hugged Gin and Charlie before leaving.

Awful lonely. Yeah. Justin understood loneliness. His own circle of friends got a lot smaller without Griz.

Shadow Fray. Hale. Griz. All of this was too much coincidence. Justin meets Hale, Griz dies. It was naïve to think there wasn't a connection. They'd broken the rules. This was a warning. To ignore it could be more deadly than it already was. Who would be next?

He needed to stay away from Hale.

Things suddenly looked very lonely indeed.

THE CARE Bears was unable to hold Justin's interest. It had been a sweet gesture from Charlie, the choice of cartoon like a message. Charlie liked to work like that, and the boy was extra snuggly before falling asleep on the couch in the crook of Justin's arm.

But Justin found strangely little comfort in the proximity tonight. Why? He still hadn't cried. What was wrong with him? If only emotions could be as plain as the silly representations in the cartoon. But his tears wouldn't come. His feelings had no label. His mind was unable to stick to one thought for very long, constantly veering off and then circling around to where he'd been before.

And always there was Hale. It seemed inappropriate to think of him under these circumstances. Maybe it was because no matter how hard he tried, Justin couldn't separate Hale from Griz's death. They had to be connected.

He would bet his dominant punching hand that the old man orchestrated the situation with Hale. It had to be Griz. Hale said he'd gotten a note that told him where to look for Justin. Griz had also encouraged Justin to have a friend. Hell, he'd all but said Justin would never make it alone. The old man hadn't long left, and it would be just like him to make sure he, Gin, and Charlie had someone to look out for them when he was gone.

Something in Justin's gut told him that was the deathblow. Griz had said he'd influenced things, but he was never allowed to interfere. Maybe meeting Hale outside an Arena was considered interference, and Griz paid the price.

Only one choice, then. Justin had to back off from Hale before someone else got hurt. He'd have to ask Hale to leave him alone, to give up the job. Could he do that?

Yes. He'd do anything to survive, to keep his family safe.

Counterargument. What if Griz really did die so he and Hale could meet? If Justin backed down, threw it all away, then Griz would have died for nothing. Griz's death had to mean something. Justin thought back to their last meeting. Had he promised Griz he would try to make friends? He couldn't remember. Already his memories of the man were slipping away.

No. He couldn't give up Hale, not completely. They'd have to spend time apart. They definitely couldn't work together. They couldn't train together. And they couldn't be more than friends. He'd keep his promise to Mr. Mays, even if he hadn't really made one. He'd keep his end of the bargain, but he'd do it in the safest way possible.

Hale wasn't going to like it, but Justin would have to convince him somehow. It felt like a resolution, but he'd already changed his mind so many times. He didn't know what to do.

The cartoon ended. Charlie was breathing softly. Gin too had fallen asleep on the other end of the sectional. Very carefully, Justin extricated himself. Charlie stirred and took a deep breath but didn't wake.

If only Justin could sleep so soundly. But maybe there was a way to decide all of this, a way to finally make a choice.

He stood, waiting for blood to return to his tingling arm before he moved. No—his feet worked just fine. He clenched and unclenched his fingers in a willful act of avoidance. He was delaying the inevitable. He had been all evening.

When he turned on the burner phone from Scarecrow, he was going to have a message. The idea made him cringe, like a punch you could see coming but couldn't stop. A text message would confirm everything he had been thinking, that someone in Shadow Fray—the Shadow Masters—had orchestrated this whole deadly affair. It would be one more coincidence where there were already too many.

But maybe it would be good to have confirmation. At least then he would know where he stood—that he was right and not just paranoid. So get it over with.

He retreated to the guest room. He was surprised by his steady hand as he pulled out the phone and switched it on.

No. No, he didn't want to know he was right. Better to be paranoid. Better to at least be able to hope. Maybe things could continue like they were, and he and Hale had a chance for something. Things this morning had felt so right, and not just the sex part—when they were fighting, it was like they were in their own world. When they talked, time flew by.

He took a deep, steadying inhale, waiting for the screen to synch. *Please, God.* Even though he wasn't in the habit of praying, he definitely believed in God. He didn't ask for much, but a sign right now would be nice. Like in a movie from the Old World.

The message would be the sign. If there was a message, he'd back off. He and Hale would separate. Perhaps eventually, Justin could be distant friends with a man in another city.

The phone beeped as it came to life. Found a signal.

If there was no message from Scarecrow, Justin was going to up the ante and kiss Hale. After all, he was finally coming to terms with his feelings. He was stupid for not taking the chance, for not doing it already. He'd been afraid, but now he wouldn't chicken out. He'd give things a chance. It was a bargain. A bargain with God.

Shit, he should be counting to sixty. How much time had passed? Twenty seconds? He wasn't supposed to leave it on for more than a minute.

He counted to twenty. Nothing. He'd give it to the count of forty to be safe and then shut it off.

He got to thirty. Thirty-two.

The phone beeped a death knell as the text came through.

10/24. C U Saturday.

Justin turned the phone off.

Chapter 22

IT WAS too good to be true. Hale's relief could only be measured in comparison to the amount of time he'd spent hoping this was what he'd see when he pulled into work—this exact image. Justin was leaning against the back of the truck, waiting for him.

Hale hadn't expected to see him today—merely hoped. He had come early like usual, well before sunrise, telling himself he needed the extra time to do the job alone. Lies. He'd come hoping to see this. In the purple predawn, he got a thrill from Justin's shadowed image—back against the rig, one foot propped behind him, arms crossed.

He pulled his bike into the garage as Justin watched him. Something was off. But of course something was off—Justin's friend just died. Hale had the urge to jump off his Harley, run to him, and hold him.

As Hale walked to him, Justin didn't move. The posture that had seemed rugged and sexy now appeared closed off. Justin was trying to shut him out. That was fine. Expected, under the circumstances.

Hale put a hand on Justin's shoulder. He needed to touch him.

"How are you doing?" he asked gently. Up close, Hale could see Justin looked exhausted, his eyes heavy like he hadn't slept much.

"I've been better," Justin breathed out. Screw this. Hale grabbed him and brought him in for a hug. Justin stiffened but then softened, encircling Hale with his arms. Hale urged Justin's head down for more closeness. Justin sighed, relaxed completely, and buried his head on Hale's shoulder.

Hale just held him.

He could feel the occasional tremor, heard a small sniff letting him know Justin was crying. Not hard, but crying nonetheless.

And he was honored. After only a couple days, he knew how closed off Justin could be. Crying on another man's shoulder wasn't in Justin's repertoire. Hale held him a little tighter, flexing his muscles to let Justin know he was strong enough to hold him, that this was okay.

Everything will be okay. That's what he'd tell Eddie if she started crying, what he wanted to say to Justin now. But Justin wasn't a child, and as much as Hale wanted to make it okay, he couldn't. He said the only thing he could. "I got you, and I'm not letting go. You won't be alone in this."

Justin sniffled against his shoulder. "God, you're making this so difficult."

Making what difficult? Hale sensed Justin was getting ready to pull away and flexed his arms again, holding him even tighter. Nope, he wasn't letting go. No way. Justin put more of his weight on him then, the tremors becoming more pronounced though the tears were mostly silent.

It took a moment for Hale to think of something he really wanted to say. As he began, he knew his own voice would sound rough. "You know, when my wife died, I cried for months. I didn't even cry for the right reasons. But you, you have reason to cry. Use me. I'm here for you. Maybe if I wouldn't have been crying alone, I wouldn't have cried so long. I could have saved myself so much grief and trouble. So let me do this for you. Let me be here for you."

He held Justin for a while, and finally his friend calmed down a bit, breathing easier. When Justin pulled away for the third time, Hale let him go but stayed close.

Justin wiped the moisture from his face with an open palm. "Why do you have to make things so hard?"

Hale took a moment to adjust himself in his jeans. "I know it's entirely inappropriate in this situation, but it can't be helped. You have that effect on me."

Justin actually cracked a smile, letting loose a small burst of air that may have been half a laugh. "Yeah, well, feeling's mutual," he said, taking a second to give his own jeans a yank at the zipper. The smile faded to nothing. "But that's not what I meant."

Hale wanted to growl. He had a bad feeling in the pit of his stomach. He'd done his best to play off the signs, but now it was obvious something was up. But best not to jump to conclusions. He'd hear the kid out. And yes, dammit—if Justin tried to pull some childish shit now, he was "the kid."

Justin glanced around nervously. "Do you have time for a walk?"

"Of course," Hale said. "I don't know why I came so early. I guess… it was a slim chance, but I was really hoping to see you." Justin looked like Hale had punched him.

No. Fucking. Way. If this started going in the wrong direction, Hale wouldn't take it. He'd grab the dumb boy and tie him up if he had to. Take him in the right direction. To his bed. In Chicago. Until he saw reason.

They began walking away from the warehouse. Getting jumped was the least of Hale's worries right now, but it didn't seem safe to wander in the dark out here. Justin was a bit aimless, so Hale walked toward the cover of an adjacent factory. Even now he was protecting the kid. Seemed like Justin mostly needed protecting from himself.

Frowning, Justin looked like he was having a difficult time beginning whatever he had to say. Outwardly, Hale forced patience, but inside he was having a hard time keeping down the panic. He clenched his fists and rubbed his thumbs against the knuckles of his index finger. This really did look bad.

Several minutes passed. They neared the next building, and Justin still wasn't talking. Dammit. Hale couldn't take this anymore.

It was time he beat Justin to the punch.

"This is far enough," he told Justin and grabbed his hand. Justin looked shocked but let himself be pulled to the building's wall where Hale dragged him down. "Whatever you're afraid of, we should be okay here, at least for a while. But before you say anything, I want to let you know, I'm not going anywhere. I'll jump through whatever hoops you need me to jump through like a trained mutt, at least for a while. But if you even think of cutting me loose, I swear to God I will park myself outside your door and howl at the moon until you let me in. I mean that literally. I know where you live now."

"What? How?"

"I followed you after work, dumbass. Having me parked outside your place is not going to be very discreet."

"Hale!" Justin was getting angry. Good. Justin tried to pull his hand away, but Hale wouldn't let it go.

"Hale, I can't—"

Hale covered Justin's mouth with his free hand to keep him from finishing the sentence. He pushed into him and forced him back onto the gravel, which couldn't be too comfortable. Especially not when Hale lay out on top of him. "Don't say another word, Justin. Don't screw this up. I know you feel something for me. I know it. I know you're scared. So whatever is going through your mind, you're going to tell me. You're going to tell me everything. And then I'm going to help you fix it. Enough of this no-talking shit." Hale's blood was boiling. The instinct to attack, to force, to take, turned into a threat: "I beat you once, and I can do it again."

Justin kneed him in the balls. "Get the fuck off me!"

All the air left Hale's body. He rolled to the side, cupping himself, as though that would somehow quell the pain.

Justin bellowed. "How do you even know what I was going to say? You overbearing asshole!" Justin swiped his hand on the gravel, showering Hale with stones. It actually felt good in comparison with the nauseating pain emanating from between his legs up into his gut.

"Tell me I'm wrong," Hale croaked. "Please tell me I'm wrong, and I'll do anything to make it up to you."

He glanced up at Justin, who was on the ground but sitting up, a frown on his face.

Justin exhaled deeply. "I can't tell you you're wrong, because you weren't. But now… I just don't know."

Ouch. But wait. "Weren't, past tense?" he asked Justin. "You changed your mind, you mean." Hale put on his most pitiful face. It wasn't difficult. He also kept his hands on his balls even though the rough edges were coming off his pain. Yeah, he was milking it.

"You're a tenacious, stubborn bastard, you know that?" Justin asked, glaring down at him.

"Yup."

"I'm sorry I kneed you in the balls. That was pretty low." Justin scooted over to Hale and helped him sit up.

"That's okay. I'm a tenacious, stubborn bastard, and I deserved it." Hale groaned and decided to use his advantage. He plopped his head down in Justin's lap.

Justin snorted. "You just don't stop."

"Never will," Hale agreed. *So say the words, Justin. Tell me you'll stay.* But the plea never left Hale's lips. He'd made his point. Still, his heart felt a little bit broken, like it needed a Band-Aid or something. The kid had been trying to bolt on him. Leave him.

That hurt.

Justin put a hand on Hale's forehead, the glare turning into more of a gaze as he looked down at Hale. His fingers absently began running through Hale's hair. Justin's other hand fell on Hale's chest. And suddenly, Hale was okay. He wasn't feeling pain. Justin's hands felt amazing. Getting kneed in the balls was almost worth it.

"You win. I'll tell you everything." Justin's eyes were dark as he turned them from Hale's face to gaze off into the distance. "I was trying to protect you, but it's clear to me now you'd just end up killing yourself with your own brand of crazy, because you won't fucking give up." Hale brought his hands up and placed them over Justin's hand on his chest. Even when they were getting each other off in the forest, things hadn't been this intimate.

"Talk," Hale demanded softly.

Justin took a breath and began. He spoke quickly, as though the words were escaping his mouth and running for freedom. "My friend Griz, I'm pretty sure he was killed because he's been helping me in Shadow Fray. I'm pretty sure he's the one who got us together with that note, and if he wasn't, it's too much of a coincidence that you and I met, and practically the next day he died. His death was no accident, and I've seen shady characters around him before. He had to leave Milwaukee a long time ago. Coming back here was a risk for him, a risk he undertook mainly for me. So something is up. I don't want anyone else to die, because if they do it'll be my fault. Also I got a new Fray last night."

Hale's mind was swirling. "But… wait. Jesus Christ. Slow down. I feel like you said fifty things in the span of fifteen seconds." Done on purpose, no doubt. Why was Justin being so damned aggravating?

"See?" Justin said, lifting his hands up in a shrug to the sky, now barely beginning to lighten. "I'm never talking again. It doesn't work."

Oh, if that didn't piss Hale off. He sat up, swiveled around behind Justin, and put his arms around him. He forced calm. "I take it back," Hale said. "I'll take any talking I can get. You did good. Just let me think a second."

Justin was tense in his arms, but in a few moments, he started to relax. Hale was seeing a pattern here. The kid was like a scared animal that needed petting. Justin's voice was more conciliatory when he spoke again. "Maybe I'm pushing you away. Maybe I'm trying to piss you off," he admitted.

"Well, it's not working," Hale lied. Justin leaned back into him, and the lie became a little bit smaller. He kissed Justin on the temple near his hair. There—take that. A kiss as a weapon.

Justin breathed deeply in his arms. "At least it's all out now," he said.

"Give me some time to think about this," Hale offered after a pause. "Let me talk to Benz, see what he has to say. But this isn't your fault. You didn't kill your friend, Justin."

"But what do we do? What if we aren't supposed to be together?"

"You mean, what if certain people don't want us to be together?" Hale paused. What would they do? He didn't have an answer, not yet. "I don't know, but I do know this. You and I fight—that's what we do. We fight. And not just in the Fray. We fight for what's important."

Hale felt Justin nod against his shoulder. "Okay," Justin said, seeming to come to agreement. "We fight."

One more battle won, then. At least for now, but there were more to come. Hale held Justin tightly and he didn't let go. Not for a long time.

HALE WATCHED Eddie sleeping. She was twitching in that restless sleep kids sometimes have when they first nod off. Cute. If only he could sit and watch her sleep longer, but he had things to discuss with Benz. Setting the reading tablet next to the bed, he slid his arm out from under her. Trickier than an escape from a hold in a Fray, but she didn't stir.

Benz was waiting for him in the living room. Thankfully, Jess had made herself scarce after a late dinner. They were alone.

Benz took up two-thirds of the couch, sprawled out in a way that was both relaxed and imposing. Hale had the sudden urge to laugh, maybe because things looked so bleak. He'd been unable to come up with any solutions on his own. He had nothing except information to bring to this conversation.

"Why do I have a bad feeling about this?" Benz asked as Hale sat down. Hale angled toward him, taking up as little space as possible and sitting forward with his arms on his knees.

"Because you're either smart or psychic, and psychic is really the only option with you."

"Funny guy. What's up?"

"Seems Justin's friend who died was involved with Shadow Fray in some way. Justin thinks his friend was the one who got the note in my pocket, and someone killed him for it."

Benz appeared to mull it over for a moment. "Interesting theory. What do *you* think?"

"I never heard of the guy, so I have no clue," Hale answered. "But it sounds plausible."

"Who's his friend?"

"Gristopher Mays."

"Never heard of him."

"Who's your friend? Could she have done it?"

"Killed him?" Benz asked, confused.

"No. Given me the note."

Benz shrugged. "I'd say it's more likely this Mays guy. But why would he do that?"

"Because I'm smart and you're nice," Hale answered glibly.

Benz didn't respond. His facial expression didn't change.

So much for levity. "I'm guessing," Hale began slowly, "it's because he wanted Justin out from under this Scarecrow guy, and like I said, I'm a smart fighter and you're a nice handler. See? I wasn't joking."

Benz rolled his eyes, which struck Hale as comical considering he was a giant in a suit. "Seems rather roundabout, like a lot of trouble to go through for a handler," Benz said.

"Maybe, but consider what happened to Scarecrow's last Brawler."

Benz grunted. "True enough."

"So here's the thing. What if Justin is right and this was some kind of warning? What if this happened because we're breaking the rules?"

"Breaking the rules is an understatement for what you're doing."

"I'm not denying that. It's got me so paranoid I searched the condom truck from top to bottom. I didn't find any bugs, but it's a big truck."

"Bugs I can help you with. I'll get you a device from the club. Light blinks real fast by a mic and gets real bright near a camera. Should give you some peace of mind."

"It would. And Justin too." Hale took a deep breath and studied Benz's face. "What do I do about Justin?"

Benz leaned forward, steepling his hands. Hale waited quietly.

"I think," Benz said, "you need to be careful. But I also think they can't touch you—or him—at least not right now. After the numbers on that last Fray, you're more popular than ever, worth too much. You can't keep working that truck job, though. If you're right about this killing being a message, then that job is rubbing the killer's face in it. Quit the job and it'll look like you're backing off."

Hale raised an eyebrow at Benz. "Just quit the job? That's it?"

Benz looked confused. "What do you mean?"

"I mean you're not going to tell me to stay away from him?"

Benz cracked a smile at Hale. "No, I'm not going to tell you that. I can't say I'm not worried, but I'm not blind. I can see this guy means something to you."

"You're right." Hale hadn't planned this moment, hadn't even thought about it much, but now that it presented itself, he decided to get it out. "But I gotta be honest—the kind of relationship I'm looking for with him—he's not just a friend and training partner." Hale paused, gathering himself. He wasn't scared exactly, but he was surprised by how difficult this was. Better to get it done with—and quickly. He shifted his gaze to the side, not looking Benz in the eyes, unwilling to pause or be dissuaded by what he might see there. "He's more than a friend. I was ridiculous today. With all this shit going on, the kid was gonna back off. I felt like he was gonna rip my heart out. But I convinced him to stay with me, at least for now. I wanna be with him. Need to be with him." That was plain enough, right? He turned his eyes back to Benz.

"Like I said, Hale. I'm not blind." Benz's calmness was hard to read. Had he not understood?

"And you're okay with it? With me… kind of bent?" He went with the slur, just throwing it all out there.

Benz paused dramatically, his mouth dropping open. His expression was no longer difficult to read, his words angrily slow and precise. "Fuck you for even asking." Wow. Benz didn't cuss.

"Sorry, but… most people would have a problem with it. I didn't think you would, just making sure I guess."

"I'm not most people," Benz said, gentling his expression. The big man sighed, sitting up straight. "For the record, I've killed men. It doesn't sit well with me. It was wrong. Seeing my brother happy? It's the opposite of everything that's wrong. Screw everyone else and what they might say. I got your back on this."

"What about Jess?"

Benz laughed. "Man, now I know you got it bad if you want to bring her into this. I love her for a reason. She'll be fine with this. Edna too. We take care of our own."

"You serious?" Hale asked. "You think she'll be fine with this? I was married to her little sister. I wasn't the best husband. And you think she'll be okay with me moving on for the first time since Janie died… with a man?"

Benz laughed again. "Well, when you put it like that—"

"I'm glad you find this so amusing."

"A lot more amusing than your sad attempts at humor, yes. Don't worry. When it gets down to it, we're family. You let us raise your daughter as our own. That holds more weight to your character than anything else you've ever done. If Jess is a little angry with you at first, well, that's normal, isn't it?"

"You're right. That is her normal."

"I'll talk to her about it. You'll see."

Hale shook his head skeptically. "If you say so."

"Seriously? With everything else you have going on, you're worried about what Jess thinks?"

"Dude, I'm kinda scared of your wife."

Benz laughed again. For such a big guy, you'd expect he'd have a big laugh, but it was surprisingly normal. Maybe the constriction of his suits kept him from bellowing out. Hale couldn't help but smile himself.

"I'm glad you got my back, Benz."

"Always, brother." They bumped fists, but then Benz brought him in for a hug. Damn, but Hale was lucky to have him. It was almost cute the way the big guy liked his hugs. And Hale had to admit, he liked them too.

Releasing Benz, the seriousness of the situation set in.

"What about Justin?" Hale asked. "We gotta get him over to our team. If this friend of his was murdered…." Hale shook his head. How did you justify something you knew in your gut? "I feel like it's more important than ever."

Benz nodded, brow furrowed. "I wish I knew how."

"You don't have any contact with the bosses—the Shadow Masters?"

"Communication is strictly one way, and even if I could, I'm not sure it would be wise. Best to let things die down a little."

"So what do we do?"

"I don't have any bright ideas yet. We watch the situation closely. If we have to get drastic, we can, but no need to jump the gun. We watch and wait, and maybe an opportunity presents itself."

"That's the best you got?" Hale asked. He didn't want to wait on this, consequences be damned.

Benz read his tone well. "Waiting sucks, I know, but we need more info. Let's just see how things go at his next Fray."

"That's in two weeks."

"Just two weeks," said Benz, trying to sound comforting, "then we reevaluate."

So that was it, then. Hale steadied himself with a deep breath before moving on. "I take it no word on our next Fray?"

"None." Hale figured as much, but it was only a matter of time.

In that moment, Hale solidified a thought and turned it into a promise. He would find a way to be at Justin's next Fray, wherever the Arena might be. Benz would be pissed, but Hale had two weeks to tell him. It was dangerous and stupid, but he had to be there—for many reasons. Not the least of which was the fact that Hale was far more concerned about Justin's next Shadow Fray than he was his own.

Chapter 23

THE TRAIN wasn't moving fast enough. Justin looked out the window, trying to still his thoughts, but he didn't like being a passenger. He'd much rather be in the driver's seat.

Saturday was a day to spend time with Griz. But not this Saturday. He was on a train to meet with someone he hated. Someone who had slit a man's throat and fucked his sister. And Griz was dead.

The passing landscape outside his window didn't register. He needed to fill his thoughts with something more positive before he went insane. Like Hale. If only he were with Hale instead of on this train. The thought lined up the two extremes in his life: Hale and Scarecrow. Hero and villain. If he hated Scarecrow, then he… what? Loved Hale?

No. As much of a connection as he felt to the man, it was far too early for that. He'd only known Hale for four days. Of course, he'd lusted after Black Jim for years. Surely that was swaying his emotions now.

Thinking back to yesterday, it was crazy how Hale had known Justin was going to break things off. How the hell had he done that? And how had he changed Justin's mind so quickly? All without Justin saying a word.

A person who knew his thoughts without his having to say a word. It put a smile on his face but also made him nervous enough to break out in an instant sweat.

In a way he was trapped. He had no doubt that pulling away from Hale would cause the other man to come after him all the more fervently. Hale wouldn't back down from a fight. Justin got that message loud and clear in their tussle yesterday. The alternative was to give in and let Hale get close to him. In either case, Hale won.

Justin was pinned down. He wasn't sure he liked that at all. At the same time, he kind of loved it.

So confusing.

For a fraction of a second, he thought he could talk to Mr. Mays about it. Then he remembered.

He would *never* have the chance to talk to Mr. Mays about it. The funeral was tomorrow. How was it possible to have his heart feel open for the first time and yet broken at the same time?

Despite the many conflicting thoughts, on one point he was certain: the last thing he wanted to do was give time and energy to Scarecrow. He had too much other crap going on right now that he should be focused on. As the train pulled into the Racine stop, it became a resolution. He wouldn't let Scarecrow get to him. He was going to disengage emotionally from this meeting. Just get the info, get out, and be on the next train back. That was the plan.

He found Scarecrow in their usual meeting spot, looking out the window as if he expected Justin to come from the roadside direction. As Justin walked up on him, he was pleased to see Scarecrow's eyes widen in alarm as he turned around. He definitely gave the old man a start. He couldn't keep the smirk off his face, even though Scarecrow was scowling.

"It's not wise to sneak up on a guy," Scarecrow snapped. He kept his hands in his coat pockets. He was probably packing. Coward. He certainly did look jumpy.

"Sorry," Justin said, even though he wasn't sorry at all. "Took the train."

Scarecrow didn't respond. He seemed to be scanning the station, maybe to see if anyone had followed Justin. Did Scarecrow know about what had happened with Griz?

Justin looked at him more closely. His eyes were bloodshot, but he didn't look high. Maybe hungover? Usually his handler was running the show, trying to use intimidation to act in control. Today he was oddly silent. His red-rimmed eyes looked at Justin but also past him and to the sides.

"So…." Justin began, offering the other man an opening. Scarecrow didn't bite. Fine. He'd stick to the plan. "Tell me about the Arena so I can get out of here."

With another glance around the station, his handler reached into his coat pocket and pulled out a thick envelope. "Take this first," he said. "It's more money."

Justin reached for it, then paused. This made no sense. "You paid me at our last meeting."

"Not enough," Scarecrow said, shoving the envelope into Justin's hand. "Ah, numbers have been going up, so I'm giving you more. Double."

What was this? Something didn't feel right, but Justin wasn't going to turn it down. For all he knew, Scarecrow had been cheating him anyway.

"Where's your sister?" asked Scarecrow.

"Not here." Justin wanted to ask why he wanted to know. Why the hell would she be here, especially after Scarecrow's warning? But he was going to keep this as simple as possible. Short answers. Keep the anger down.

Scarecrow ran a shaky hand through his thinning hair. Maybe he really was high. After another endless hesitation, he reached into his pocket and produced a small slip of paper along with a photo. Justin didn't look at it, just took it and transferred the info to his hoodie.

"This one's at a nuclear power plant south of here across the state line. The power plant ain't in operation anymore, hasn't been for a hundred years. I gave you a GPS photo so you can see the layout. It looks maintained, probably for safety reasons, but it doesn't run."

"Power plant sounds big," Justin said. "How will I know where to go?"

"You're home team, kid. It's not actually inside the building. It's outside, in a fenced-in area. It'll be a cage match. There'll be some transistors but nothing loose. I'll clean it up, make sure there's no rusty metal to break off. I'll meet you at the main entrance exactly forty-five minutes before show time, which is 11:39 p.m. on 10/24. It's on the slip. If you're earlier, you'll sustain a financial penalty."

That was interesting. Justin had never been the home team before. He'd have to put some thought into his image. He'd be the one waiting before the camera this time, not the one walking in. Hale could help him out with that.

But shit—his last Fray with Hale. The glove. With everything going on, he hadn't even considered whether they'd give him a weapon. That must be why Scarecrow was acting so strange. Justin's stomach turned sour.

How had he not been worried about a weapon, especially with this new arrangement involving Scarecrow and Gin? "They want me to cheat," Justin concluded. "What is it this time? Another glove or something new?"

"No," Scarecrow said, "nothing. There's nothing." That was a relief. Or was it? Did that mean his opponent would have something?

"What about the other guy?"

Scarecrow shrugged. "We wouldn't know, would we?" Justin crossed his arms, anger rising at the glib response. Scarecrow appeared to take notice and softened a bit. "Look, stuff has been popping up in Frays lately, it's true, but it's not all sanctioned, and they're cracking down. You bring a blade of your own, word is you're out for good. I expect many of these guys we've seen bring weaponry are going to disappear, like permanently. Word will get around fast. We're not in charge. *They* are. The Shadow Masters. And they don't want you out yet, kid. You'll be fine."

Justin wasn't buying it. "I bet that's what Black Jim thought before I came after him with that fucking glove," he blistered. He was close to his breaking point. "Just... don't get lazy. Don't take it for granted. And make sure you do your fucking job."

Scarecrow nodded. "You sure your sister's not here?"

Did Scarecrow think he was lying? This was bullshit. He turned his back on Scarecrow and walked away. He had a funeral tomorrow. He didn't have any more time for this man.

He felt a tug on his arm and whirled around, hand fisted and ready to strike.

Scarecrow jumped back and held up a hand in alarm but didn't let go of Justin. "Easy, easy. Just one more thing. Tell your sister... our deal is off. For you too. I should never have done that. I'm sorry."

"What if I lose?" Justin asked. Not that he was planning on it.

"It's okay if you lose," Scarecrow said. "I'm not gonna be like that anymore."

Justin shrugged his arm out of Scarecrow's grasp. Why the change of heart? Maybe he should be relieved, but looking at this pathetic guy in front of him, he still wanted to beat his face in. It didn't change anything.

Justin turned again and walked away.

Chapter 24

Justin couldn't sit still in the pew. Normally this church was a comforting place, almost austere compared to the grandeur of the Basilica. He'd been to St. Hedwig's many times before, sitting between Charlie and Gin just as he was now. Hell, this is where Charlie went to school. But this time was different. He had the urge not just to leave but to run out the door. The only funeral he'd ever been to was nothing like this.

When his mother had passed after a violent and sudden illness, the gathering had been much smaller. His mother had been well-liked, but those she cared for professionally were sick or elderly and tended to die. Those she'd cared for in other ways wouldn't have gone to her funeral. Justin remembered Griz being present; everyone else had disappeared after that day.

This funeral was completely different. Looking at all of the people around him, Justin questioned how many of them had even known Griz. Not many.

Funerals were usually small affairs, if they were even held. But not for Uppers. The sight of the pageantry had Justin grinding his teeth. When someone important died, it was a rare chance to come out and be seen, a chance for the community of Uppers to gather in the same place. It only happened during funerals and weddings, and funerals were much more common. It was also the only time the Uppers didn't clamor for the balcony, because there were so many of them. At these occasions you sat in the front where you'd be seen.

None of these people had visited Griz when he was sick. Not one.

Justin pulled at the sleeve on his borrowed suit. Devin was tall but slimmer than Justin, and the jacket was too tight. It was hard to breath. He needed to be done with this charade and take off the fucking mask. Ginny put a hand on his knee, and Justin realized he'd been bouncing it nervously. She moved her hand from his knee to his hand and grasped it firmly. Justin took a deep, steadying breath. He looked at her, a silent thank-you.

Gin appeared much more comfortable in this environment. She was naturally beautiful, but today she would put any Upper to shame. She wore a form-fitting black dress with a confidence that gave the impression of power. She had on small diamond earrings that had belonged to their mother, and her mother before that, along with a bracelet Justin hadn't seen before. Her hair was slicked back a little more than usual, putting her neck and face on display. The diamonds sparkled amidst the black of her dress and hair and stood out against her honey-toned skin. So simple and yet more beautiful than any of the gaudier displays of money surrounding them.

Charlie seemed to be doing fine. He was clearly distracted and looking around as much as possible without drawing attention to himself. From time to time, he'd turn his head all the way around to look up to the balcony, where Sister Tim was busy playing the organ. While it probably wasn't appropriate, Justin let him look. He didn't care what impression they made on these people, and if it comforted Charlie to look up and see her, who was Justin to deny him that? She, at least, had been very kind and comforting to them before the service.

Devin sat stoically next to Charlie. The man was still a bit of a mystery to Justin, but some of his family had come in from Denver on a train, arriving that morning. Ray was there, sitting on the other side of Gin. All together they took up one pew in the church, second from the front.

The front pew was reserved for the very elite, in this case, the mayor and her entourage. Justin had never seen her in person before. His eyes were drawn to her, even though he was seeing her from behind. She reminded him of an older version of an actress from the Old World, the mother in *The Parent Trap* from the 1960s. There was nothing maternal about the woman in front of him, though. She looked fierce and pinched, her red hair tied back in the tightest bun he'd ever seen. He noticed it was streaked with gray. She didn't hide it. She sat so straight and still, it was like she was made of porcelain. The unbreakable kind.

Had Griz known the mayor? A man like Griz had to have many contacts, if not friends, but who were they? Had Justin really known the man well at all? He couldn't help feeling like he should have learned more, talked to him more, asked him more questions.

Of course, it wasn't like Griz let him get a word in edgewise, was it? Justin smiled at the thought. Griz had seen him for the quiet boy he was and accepted him. That's why Griz had given him the gift of music.

Justin blinked away any wetness coming to his eyes. He certainly wouldn't cry here. No one else was. It wasn't appropriate to cry at funerals.

Ginny squeezed his hand, and he realized he'd been bouncing his knee again.

After what seemed like an interminably long time, the funeral was over. The service hadn't really been about Griz at all. It was just a bunch of Bible passages and talk of all the things he'd seen and lived through, a testament to how the world had changed in his lifetime. The sickness, the coastal flooding, the poisoned ground. There was no one thing that changed the world. It was all the little things adding up. He supposed for Griz, it was a lot of little things that ended up killing him—but it was Justin who finally brought him down, even if Hale said otherwise.

Justin's legs were itching to run from the church, but he forced himself to walk down the long center aisle. Being in the second pew allowed him to be one of the first outside, thank God. He breathed in the fresh air as though he'd been starving for oxygen. Their group walked down the steps to stand near the road, which was closed to traffic to accommodate all the people.

Justin hadn't had much of a chance to meet Devin's family yet, beyond introductions. They were Griz's family too. Did that make them his family as well? As they gathered in a group, he relied on Gin to start the conversation. That was her job in their relationship and one she excelled at.

Surprisingly, though, it was Devin who spoke, and in hushed tones. "You guys don't have to stick around for this, unless you want to. We'll have a private ceremony tonight, away from all these people. Griz would have hated this." Devin's previously stoic façade broke into anger. This Justin understood. Whoever had killed Griz was probably here, or at least the person who orchestrated it—

"And this must be Griz's family," the mayor said from behind their little group, pronouncing family in three syllables and drawing out the word like it had gotten stuck in her teeth. Justin hadn't been paying attention—he should have seen her approaching, should have been more aware of his surroundings.

Immediately, Devin's face turned to stone, his expression gone.

"Mayor Cram." Devin's head nod looked more like a small bow. "Such an honor to have you come to my grandfather's funeral. He'd be very pleased."

She smiled without showing her teeth. The mayor wasn't dressed as extravagantly as many of the other guests. She wore a navy suit with simple jewelry, her accessories a lot like Gin's. He supposed you didn't need much jewelry when you wore an entourage. She was flanked on both sides, and Justin had the eerie impression of being outnumbered.

"Such a shame more family couldn't be here," the mayor said. "For someone who lived as long as he did, I assumed there'd be more of you." She surveyed them all, pausing on him, Gin, and Charlie. Why? Because their skin tone wasn't the same? She especially gave Charlie a long look, him being the palest of them all.

Justin nearly laughed to see Charlie scowling back at her. The mayor clearly wasn't used to such a reaction, but in one swift second, she schooled her expression into an icy smile.

Justin's near laugh died just as swiftly when the mayor turned her gaze to him. He saw her eyes narrow, a brief intensity lighting them before the smile again took precedence on her face. "I believed he might have more friends in attendance. I understand he was very outgoing—and yet it's only you." Justin's blood turned cold. He'd seen that look on fighters before in an Arena. Instinct wouldn't let him look away, and while the mayor's eyes were hazel, they seemed to burn with an amber fire.

The mayor moved her gaze back to Devin. "Shall we walk down to the lake? I assume that's where you'll be disposing of the ashes."

Devin blanched. "We won't be disposing of his ashes."

"Turning him into a keepsake? That's a shame. The last funeral here, we all walked down to the lake. It was quite a sight, all these fine people dressed up in their best. It was like a parade. Such a worthy send-off." Again she fixed her eyes on Justin. Her voice took on an almost flirtatious quality, her look appraising. "I'd much enjoy the opportunity to talk with some of you. Are you sure you won't change your mind?" Justin felt a chill. Did she expect him to answer?

"Quite sure," Devin said dryly, coming to his rescue. "Griz hated the water." The lie was perhaps a little too quick to be passable.

"Hmmm. How odd he would move back here in that case. Perhaps he should have stayed in Denver. I assume you'll be going home to Denver yourself after all this is over?"

"I haven't decided yet."

"I see," the mayor said. "Well, enjoy your stay for as long as it lasts."

She eyed all of them one more time. "I suppose there is no point in sticking around if things here are wrapping up. This has been a pleasure. Thank you all." With one last smile, she turned and began walking away. Justin felt like he'd been dismissed, even though she was the one leaving.

It was deathly silent.

"Good-bye!" Gin shouted loudly and far too enthusiastically.

The mayor turned and stared. Justin glanced nervously to the side to see Gin waving and smiling brightly. The difference between Gin and the mayor was Gin showed her teeth when she smiled.

After pausing with a confused look, the mayor turned her back on them and walked toward a large black SUV parked nearby at the side of the church, where the road was open.

"Girl, you are crazy," Ray said as he sidled up to Gin.

Gin was saying something back to Ray, but Justin didn't hear what it was. As the mayor got into the car, Justin noticed the driver.

From a distance, Justin could see that the driver was a familiar man with red hair. Just like the mayor's.

HALE KNEW how to be quiet. It had been a long time since he'd had to creep stealthily through a dark forest. Never mind this was more of an overgrown park. He still had the skills.

Being quiet had sometimes meant the difference between eating and starving on the compound where he'd grown up. He wasn't the best shot, so in order for him to be successful, he'd had to get close to his prey.

The body control he'd learned as a fighter had only enhanced his abilities since then.

So he believed, anyway, yet he nearly smiled in the dark. Yeah, he was full of himself. In addition to his ninja-like qualities, he could sew, fix farm machinery, and castrate dogs. He was a man of many hidden talents.

Right now, though, he was just a man hidden.

The moon was only a sliver over the water, the people he was watching mere shadows. He carefully avoided stepping on any branches. The sound could either be carried away or muffled by the shifting breeze. This lakefront area was overgrown with sparse trees and long weeds cut with footpaths. Hale sat down with his back to the trunk of a tree. His black clothes and dirty face would hide him well in the newly fallen dusk. Though he wasn't exactly hidden, anyone passing by who did notice him would take him for a druggie Groundling sleeping one off. It was far less suspicious and more effective to hide in plain sight, and now he was free to openly observe the scene on the shore.

Even from thirty yards away, it was easy for Hale to tell which man on the seawall was Justin. Those broad swimmer's shoulders were made starker with the suit Justin was wearing. In the darkness, the triangle shape of his body was easy to recognize, and the smooth lines did not betray the sadness Justin must be feeling inside.

But Hale wasn't here to be lusty. He wanted to make sure his boy was okay. He didn't want to get off on the stalking thing. He couldn't help it, though. Apparently he liked watching. He liked it a lot.

He curbed his thoughts by driving his skull back into the rough bark of the tree. Justin was going through hell. Without the suit would those broad shoulders be slumping? If only Hale could do something besides watch.

He hadn't even come to Milwaukee with the intention to watch Justin, not exactly. He'd come to drive around and scout out buildings that might make for good training locations. They couldn't keep using the woods. Hale was going to quit the job after Monday, or whenever Justin decided to come back to work. He wanted Justin to take whatever time he needed, yet seeing him at work tomorrow would be really nice, if unlikely. Hopefully the kid would make it through this without trying to run away again.

Hale couldn't be blamed if he'd happened to ride by the church where the funeral was being held; plenty of other curiosity seekers had been about. Too many, in fact, so he'd circled around Justin's building to catch a glimpse of him returning home. After that he'd decided to walk by the lake to take a break from riding and stretch his legs. That he could see the windows of the fourteenth-floor condo where Justin lived was pure coincidence. Come nightfall he'd been expecting to return home, but he had spotted the solemn gathering heading out from the building toward the lake.

That he was watching now was hardly intentional at all.

An MPD drone passed by directly overhead, and he could tell it made the group uncomfortable by their glances upward and their shifting feet, but no one made a move to hide. Hale could see Gin move in closer to Justin, her shapely figure easily discernable. Holding Justin's hand was a child who looked to be the same size as Eddie. Surely that was Charlie, a fact that became more obvious as Justin pulled the kid in close. Hale's heart broke a little. Even in silhouette he could see the outline of pain. And to see another man holding a kid—at any other time, it would be a huge turn-on. But not now.

Hale couldn't hear anything being said. Somber tones would not carry far. He saw the tallest of their group sweep his arm out over the lake, and saw a swirling shadow fall to the water and expand as it was carried by the wind. Ashes.

After the ashes dissipated, the man also took whatever container had been holding the cremains and flung it out into the waves to be claimed by Lake Michigan.

A few brief minutes elapsed, and the party stepped away from the water's edge to head back into the building. Their track would take them on a path only about fifteen yards away. It would be difficult but not impossible for Hale to be spotted. Truthfully part of him hoped Justin would turn and look his way. Even if Justin didn't acknowledge him, he would know Hale cared enough to show up, creepy stalker that he was.

The group numbered ten in all. Hale also recognized Ray. No one spoke. As they passed by, all eyes appeared to be on the ground. No one was looking his way. Hale focused on Justin. He looked handsome in the suit, even if it was a tad long in the sleeve and tight in the shoulders. His body posture indicated that he must feel very overwhelmed. Not beat down but stressed. Sad.

Hale wanted him to turn and look. If he could see into those eyes, perhaps he could share some of the pain. His compulsion to help, to ease the hurt, was so powerful it had him clenching his fists.

But there was nothing he could do.

Justin didn't look up—but the child holding his hand did. Hale's heart skipped a beat as Charlie stuttered in his stride. He found himself unable to look away as the child gazed at him. The boy smiled and raised his hand, waving quickly before continuing along.

Hale was frozen at first. But then a smile formed on his lips. He raised his own hand and waved back, even though Charlie was no longer looking.

Hale sat and pondered his next move. He could wait a little bit and call Justin. They were nervous about saying too much on the phone, or at least Justin was, so Hale didn't expect a conversation to last long. It could be Justin was being paranoid, but the situation being what it was, Hale figured it was better to play it safe. Maybe just a quick text or call to say Justin was on his mind. Even if he didn't answer, he'd get the idea. If he did answer and Hale happened to be in the neighborhood scouting locations, could be he'd want to get together—

Suddenly, in the deepening darkness, Hale saw a shadow drop from a tree about thirty yards opposite him. His first thought was the guy was an amateur—who wouldn't look suspicious coming out of a tree?

His second thought was a panicked one: Justin wasn't paranoid after all. The figure moved toward him on the path. Hale was about to get a much closer look at whoever had been watching Justin. He tried to lean farther back against the bark of the tree and froze.

At about fifteen yards, the figure appeared male. Hale had the urge to jump the guy and beat him into talking. But then what? Kill him? No thanks. Acting on impulse would be foolhardy, to use a Benz word. No physical violence, at least not tonight.

Instead he tried to study the man. He was Hale's height, looking just shy of six feet. Black clothes, dark hair. At five yards, Hale stopped breathing and tried to discern any distinguishing features, but it was difficult in the darkness. He finally settled on the guy's brow. He had a fairly pronounced forehead with bushy brows, a smallish nose. He was stocky and muscular but moved haphazardly like a thug, not carefully like an athlete. Hard to tell his age, but he looked to be in his prime. In the small amount of light available, Hale noticed the glint of a ring on the guy's hand—a wedding ring.

As the man passed, Hale squinted to hide the whites of his eyeballs. Then the guy was past him. Hale breathed quietly and listened to hear the direction the man was going.

He could follow, but if he were caught, it could mean more trouble for Justin.

On the other hand, it might give them some idea of who was watching them. If they found out who, they could figure out why. Also, wasn't it better to know your enemy?

Hale paused a beat and then, swiftly and silently, got up to follow.

Chapter 25

IT WASN'T like Hale to be late.

Justin paced the garage nervously. He'd resolved to ask Hale to give up the job. Scarecrow's odd behavior and the strained meeting with the mayor had Justin jumping at shadows. Too much was happening. He wouldn't cut Hale off, but they'd have to cool it for a while, even though it was the last thing Justin wanted. He hoped Hale would understand. He could always claim he needed time to grieve. Hale couldn't deny him that. But where was he?

Finally, Justin heard the bike. He exhaled deeply. If he needed any more justification about what he had to say to Hale, his nervousness over ten minutes of tardiness sealed it. He couldn't go on like this.

He watched Hale pull up. For a moment, Justin forgot his fright. The man was a stud on a bike, Black Jim on wheels. Justin decided he would have to start a fantasy that involved Hale not taking off his bike helmet. Or was that just an excuse to avoid kissing him? Not that he was going to avoid it anymore.

Hale removed his helmet and hefted a duffle out of his saddlebags. He looked at Justin fiercely. The look had an intensity behind it that was more than lust. It was his fighter's gaze but turned possessive and protective. Justin's pulse quickened.

Hale went to the truck first and deposited his bag inside.

"Uh… how's it going?" Justin asked. Honestly he expected a little more comfort, considering the weekend he'd had.

After slamming the door to the truck, Hale walked right over to Justin. He got very close, pressed his body in. Now this was more like it—though still confusing. No matter. Justin liked the closeness, craved the gentle press of their bodies. Hale extended himself up, as if he were going to kiss him. Justin steadied himself. He wasn't going to wimp out on this. He closed his eyes.

But then he felt the tickle of Hale's lips on his ear. His breath was warm, his words like velvet. "Sorry I'm late. I got you this." Justin opened his eyes in time to see Hale slip something out of his pocket and into Justin's. A phone. "Keep it with you at all times. It's the only way to be sure it won't be tampered with."

Justin expected Hale to pull away, but he didn't. He put his arm around Justin and leaned in closer. Justin could feel the prick of scruff against his face as Hale's jaw moved with his soft words. "We need to be safe, so I have to quit after today, but there's no way I'm losing you. I got something from Benz and checked the truck. It's clean. There were no bugs. We can talk safely there."

Justin nodded. He wanted Hale to keep talking. He was developing a whole new appreciation for conversation, at least when it was whispered in his ear. Close. "We'll stop in our woods, one last time. I hope you brought your workout clothes."

Justin nodded again. Hale leaned in closer, embracing him fully, pressing his body in tight. His mouth remained by Justin's ear, and Justin felt the soft tickle of tongue, or maybe his ear was just damp with Hale's breath. It sent a shiver through him.

"It's good to see you, Justin."

Justin didn't realize his eyes were closed again until he felt the cold absence of Hale's body and opened them. The man was smiling at him from a few feet away, his blue eyes gleaming.

"Ready to go?" Hale asked loudly.

Justin licked his lips, nodded. He had to tell his heart to slow, his feet to move. Hale was going to have to drive this one.

JUSTIN WAS handling this better than Hale expected. No sign of a freak-out yet. "Which building did he go in?" Justin asked as they walked through the forest shadows toward their clearing.

"1505. About five rises down from yours. He didn't come back out. There's no view of your place from that building, so I'd assume he lives there or knows someone who does. At any rate, it's a start. Chances are, if we try, we can find him again."

"Are you sure you'll recognize him?"

"Pretty sure," said Hale.

On top of what Justin had told him about the mayor, it seemed as though they had a couple leads. Now if only they knew what to do about it.

"So what do we do now?" Justin asked, seeming to read Hale's mind.

"Benz says we lie low for a little bit. Wait and see. I don't like waiting very much, but—"

"No," Justin said. "I mean, what do *we* do now?" Oh. Hale was flattered Justin was at least asking him this time. He had a whole seduction planned, and it had started back at the garage. It looked like Justin was going to be more willing than Hale had predicted. If that didn't make his heart beat just a little faster.

"We go to ground. That's why I got the phones."

"So we don't see each other for a while."

It looked like Justin didn't like that idea very much. Maybe Hale should have played hard to get, rather than running toward Justin any chance he got. Dry leaves crinkled underfoot. It hadn't rained in months.

"How about every few days, for the time being?" Hale asked, grabbing Justin's hand as they walked. He might be pushing his luck, but he couldn't resist. Justin's hand was hot in the chill air, but he seemed okay with the hand-holding. Possibly—he wasn't exactly looking up, but Hale wasn't letting go. "I'll scout around for safer locations. If you have any suggestions, let me know. I have a couple ideas. I need a little time, but I'm on it."

Justin looked up and studied him, before nodding. "I'm going to trust you," he said. He gripped Hale's hand a little more tightly. Hale's heart soared. "Besides," Justin said with a smile as they arrived in the clearing, "your idea here was a pretty good one. I'll miss this place."

"Me too," said Hale, melancholy tainting his feelings for a second. He chased the feeling away with the delight of holding Justin's hand. God, how was holding someone's hand so intimate? This simplest gesture felt so right. He was holding another man's hand, their fingers wrapped together, interlocking like pieces in a puzzle.

Justin got a mischievous look in his eye. It wasn't a look Hale had seen on him before, but he liked how it turned Justin's brown eyes from puppy dog to devil. Hot. "You know," Justin began, "since it's our last time here, I was thinking… maybe we could sweeten the deal a little bit."

"Oh?" Hale's voice was a little high, and he was forced to swallow. "I mean… what did you have in mind?"

"A bet."

"A bet?" What was up with his voice? It was like he was going through puberty again.

Justin smiled widely and took Hale's other hand, stepping closer. So close Hale had to look up at him slightly. He could feel Justin's breath, his lips inches away.

"I have a feeling you've wanted something from me," Justin said, his tone teasing, his lips so close. "If you win, you can have it."

"Uh…." Why wasn't Hale's mind working properly?

"Unless, of course, you don't want to…."

Justin shrugged and made as if to turn away, but Hale kept hold of his hands and pulled him closer, his crotch touching Justin's thigh so Justin could feel how much he wanted to.

"And if I lose?" Hale growled. There was no chance of that, of course, but he wanted to know what Justin wanted.

"When I win, I get to do what I want to you."

"What?"

Justin laughed. "That's the bet. The loser has to do what the winner wants… since it's our last day here and all." Justin smirked. "Besides, I think we both want the same thing. I just took a little longer to come around."

Justin pressed himself into Hale, his erection thick against Hale's hip.

Justin's mouth hovered centimeters from Hale's lips, barely grazing them as he asked softly, "Is it a deal?"

You bet your ass it is. "You're on."

Hale was practically salivating. The loser has to do what the winner wants? The boy better be careful what he bets, because Hale had a pretty good idea what Justin was thinking, and Hale's mind was a whole lot dirtier than that.

Chapter 26

Third Fray, Exhibition. Arena: State Line Rest Stop.

"I DON'T see either of us tapping out, so how are we gonna do this?" Justin asked. "You want to hit full-on?"

"Full power, sure, but you have a Fray coming up. No hits to the head, face, neck, spine… or groin." Hale's emphasis of the final two words gave Justin a pang of guilt. But just a little one. "Loser is the one put in a submission hold to a verbal count of three."

"You know that means we're going to end up rolling around on the ground, right?"

"You got a problem with that?" Hale challenged with a grin.

"Yeah, I do." He eyed Hale and then lifted his hoodie and T-shirt over his head, casting them off to the side. "I don't want to get my clothes dirty, but I'm fine now." His nipples hardened. Christ, it was cold out. But he had way too much pride to cover up again, and from the look he was getting from Hale, he figured the distraction would work to his advantage. It was how he was used to fighting in a Shadow Arena anyway.

Justin sauntered up to Hale, flexing his wrapped hands. "You wanna fight or just stare at me all day?" Justin wasn't very verbal in most of his matches, but he was finding the taunting and trash talk might come a little easier against Hale. He smiled.

Hale looked at him like he was going to make Justin pay and enjoy doing it.

Justin held up his fists for Hale to bump so they could get started. It looked like Hale was about to do just that, but he paused, an inch away from bumping in. "Oh… Justin? Just so we're clear…." Hale leaned forward a little, as though he were engaging in a conspiratorial whisper, but his next words were sharp and not a whisper at all.

"When I win, I'm not asking for a kiss—I'm taking your ass."

The moment of panic that immediately followed made Justin lose a second. He didn't feel the knock on his fists, although distantly he registered it happening. Hale immediately followed it with a knee to Justin's gut. A little bit behind, Justin was able to block, but not fully.

Emptying his mind, ignoring the pain, he reached down and grabbed Hale's descending knee. He lifted and pushed forward, dropping Hale to his back on the forest floor.

Justin was on top of him in no time flat. Hale tried to block, but Justin grabbed a wrist, leaving only one hand for Hale to guard with. Justin hooked punches into Hale's side and chest. One. Two. Three blows he landed, and he didn't hold back.

Hale tried to recover, but Justin had him down solid in a full mount. If this were a Fray, he'd start the ground and pound, and Hale would be finished.

This fight was potentially over too soon. For all Hale's bravado and trying to rattle Justin, Justin had him. But despite what Hale had said prior to the fight, Justin wasn't ready to be done yet. Even if it did end up costing him more than he bargained for.

He let Hale's wrist slip out of his hand and gave the man a little room to maneuver.

Hale scooted back, wrapping Justin's thigh with his legs and grabbing him around the head and shoulder. "Almost, kid," Hale panted. Hale used his grip to leverage Justin down, scooting out from under him even more. Both were now in crouches, and Justin found himself with his face bent near Hale's crotch.

Instead of trying to break the hold, Justin gave in suddenly. He buried his face in Hale's midsection. He could smell the laundered synthetic along with new sweat, could feel Hale's semihard cock under his chin. Justin ducked down a little farther and gave a playful nip to the top of Hale's shaft through the material.

Hale's grip relaxed as he gave a surprised cry. Justin used the opening to change his arm position and grab both of Hale's legs under the knees. He lifted, and unless Hale wanted to end up on his back again, he needed to stand up. As he did so, Justin slid his arms up Hale's body. He had no time to linger or play this time. He had to be on his guard. They were at a draw—back to standing.

Justin bounced back, eyeing Hale. From the bulge in Hale's sweats, it looked like he had his mind on more than sparring. Good. Time to take it up a notch.

"What made you think I was going to kiss you?" Justin taunted. "The thought never crossed my mind…." He cursed himself for not being more specific with the bet, because a kiss was indeed what he had been thinking. Oh well. No reason for Hale to know that. No reason Justin couldn't change his mind, anyway, and he just had. "Why don't you turn around for a second and give me a look at my prize before I knock your ass back to the ground again?"

Hale's eyes darkened. "You wanna fuck me? You're gonna have to fight better than that." Hale moved in slowly, circling Justin like a shark in an old movie.

Justin stepped in, circling in return. The distance between them fluctuated; they were swiping, playing, looking for an opening as they danced. They each jabbed for the chest and shoulders several times, but without the head as a potential target, it was easy to watch for and block. Justin's legs began to burn as he and Hale bobbed and swayed through the leaves.

Hale was crouching lower as they sparred, and Justin noted the strategy being used against him, wary. On Justin's next jab, Hale ducked and went for a hold on Justin's leg, but Justin cut back, Hale's fingers only grazing him.

"You have a gentle touch," Justin said, smirking.

"Just wait," Hale warned. "Later I'm—"

Justin took another jab at Hale's chest, going for the surprise hit. Hale dropped back and grabbed Justin's arm, pulling him forward. Shit. Hale was fast. With Justin off-balance, Hale was able to grab both of Justin's arms. Justin closed the distance, pushing his arms forward before Hale could get a good grip, forcing a clinch that looked like an embrace, body to body.

"Ha!" Justin laughed. "Thought you—" Justin lost his words as his back hit something, hard. Shit, he'd gotten turned around. The bark of the tree behind him cut into his back as Hale pushed against him.

"Maybe I'll take you against a tree, Justin. Make you like it rough. Force your body against it while you scream my name."

Justin pushed aside the image—and not because it was unpleasant. They ground against each other, jockeying for foot position. Damn, this was pretty hot. Justin felt the scruff of Hale's cheek against his bare shoulder. He was sweating freely now, which made it a little more difficult for Hale to grip him and try to take him down. The tree wasn't comfortable, but it was keeping him up.

Hale changed his tactic; instead of trying to get Justin on the ground, he pushed into him, crushing him against the tree so tightly Justin could barely breathe. Something had to give. Justin relaxed slightly in his grip and gyrated his hips. He was hard and rutted up against Hale while he tried to catch his breath. He could feel Hale's hardness pressed against him, Hale's face in Justin's shoulder.

Justin lowered his head and licked Hale's ear.

He hoped the distraction would be enough. Hale was tight against him, so Justin shifted one leg behind Hale's ankle. He pushed against Hale, and Hale stumbled backward over the hook.

It wasn't much of an opening. Unable to escape, Justin used the minimal space he created to spin around. Rather than get pushed forward into the tree again, he dropped onto all fours. Hale followed and had him from behind now, pushing on top of him to bring him to the ground, but at least Justin was free of the tree. He flexed his ass to see if Hale would fall for the distraction. Unfortunately, Justin found it a little distracting himself.

Hale's fingers slipped as he struggled to get a grip around Justin's sweaty midsection. He could use that.

Justin scooted backward and lifted his hips. It wasn't flirting, but hopefully Hale thought it was. In fact, it was a move he'd used at the church. Like then, Hale started to shift with gravity, sliding up Justin's body and falling forward. Hale fell to the ground head first as Justin stood yet was somehow able to get his feet under him. Justin stayed low and lunged for Hale's knees, grabbing him and driving him backward. Once again, Hale fell on his ass, but the guy was fast—he bounced up and backed away before Justin could get on him.

Back to draw.

Justin was breathing heavily, his words choppy yet precise. "Almost had you again. Is that what they mean when they say head over heels? Because you've fallen for me twice now."

Hale growled as Justin smiled.

Hale's right leg whipped out and caught Justin behind his thigh with an outside kick. Shit—he'd gotten complacent. He bounced back with a limp, his leg muscles stinging, trying to shake it off. Justin attempted to rebound and close in again while ignoring the pain. It was a mistake, because he didn't have full use of the bruised muscle yet. Hale saw the weakness and dashed forward. Justin blocked for a punch, but Hale drove in with his knee, catching Justin in the soft flesh right under his sternum.

Justin wanted to gag but breathed through it as he hopped backward, regaining his balance and, at least outwardly, his composure. Damn. How did this go from sexy to shitty so quickly?

"How you dealing with the pain?" Hale joked, perhaps giving Justin a moment to catch his breath.

"Just fine, thanks."

"Good, because this is nothing compared to what you'll get later. I hear the first time really hurts."

"Make a mental note for yourself, asshole."

"I'll make your ass—" Hale's breath left him in a wheeze as Justin threw out a hard right hook, pounding into Hale's breastbone. That would leave a mark.

Hale tried to block as Justin faked another right but came in with his stronger left hook, landing the hit on Hale's shoulder between bicep and triceps. Not as effective, but he'd take what he could get. If he bruised the muscle, it would take a little power off Hale's right arm attacks, not that Hale was punching much.

Hale bounded back to get out of range. A little distance and the dance continued.

Justin entered what he called the zone. Everything else fell away. It was just him and Hale. They began trading kicks, as with these rules it was harder to play a punching game, something Hale seemed to have figured out early on. Neither one was gaining the upper hand. If this kept up, it would come down to pure stamina.

The sweat ran into Justin's eyes. He was dirty and getting dirtier by the minute. Bits of leaves stuck to his body, and soil stained his skin. None of that mattered. All that mattered was beating Hale.

Both were wary of a takedown. Justin breathed out his frustration. This fight wasn't going anywhere, tending toward more kicking than anything else. Despite Justin's longer legs, Hale was fast enough to always get away. What should have been a direct kick would be a glancing blow. Hale would manage to sneak quick attacks, in and out like a striking snake. The open area of the forest clearing was working to Hale's advantage. Hale was moving a lot more than Justin, though. Eventually he would have to wear down. Get slow. Justin needed to stay in the game until then.

Twice Justin dove for Hale's legs, trying to take the fight to the ground, but each time Hale slipped out of his grasp, landing punches on Justin's back as he shifted away. It was like Hale was just toying with him.

Screw that. Justin would not be his plaything.

Justin made as if to go for Hale's legs again but this time bounded fully toward Hale, staying high. He caught Hale off guard, striking with his dominant left, a hook that smacked into Hale's chest. He felt Hale go a little soft and hooked again to the same spot.

Hale was struggling for breath, which made the takedown surprisingly easy. Fast, fast, fast—in the tussle of bodies, Justin wrapped his arms around Hale's neck and under his chin in a classic guillotine position. This was it. He had Hale right where he wanted him.

"One," Justin counted. Hale was squirming beneath him, trying to shift onto his side or back to break the hold. Justin was so slick with sweat that what should have been a sure thing suddenly became questionable.

"Two." Hale somehow twisted onto his back. Fuck. Justin tried to keep his grip around Hale's neck and as Hale twisted, Justin rolled with him.

Both on the ground now, Hale was on his back and Justin only partially on top of him, no longer in position to keep counting. Justin still had a grip on his neck, though. Hale shifted some more underneath him and planted a hand on Justin's thigh.

Justin felt Hale actually lifting him up, like in a bench press. Impossible. What the—somehow Hale flipped him, and Justin landed on his back on the ground.

Hale quickly swiveled and twisted, jumping on top of Justin and pushing him into the ground. How had he done that? He latched onto Justin's arm, bending it at a weird angle. Justin tried to escape, his heart beating like crazy, the panic a warning, a precursor to doom. He had to get out of this. Fast, fast, fast.

He rolled, risking injury to his arm. He wasn't going to lose this fight.

Hale seemed surprised by the move, paused for a second, but rolled with him. They flipped, spinning on the ground, turning again and again, but each time Hale's grip on Justin's arm tightened. When they stopped rolling, Justin was on the bottom, and Hale in even better position on top. Justin's face was pressed into Hale's stomach as the man drove him into the ground, his grip like a vise.

"One."

Now it was Justin's turn to squirm, but he couldn't roll anymore, couldn't move. His arm felt like it might snap.

"Two."

This was it. He was going to lose.

"Three."

Hale released him.

Justin lay on the ground.

Hale kneeled next to him, panting.

On his back, Justin could see the blue sky overhead, clouds drifting lazily in the bright morning light.

He'd had him. He'd had Hale. Had him twice. How had he lost? Again?

Justin sat up. Looked at Hale. Glared at him.

Hale gave him a mischievous smile. Justin wanted to punch it.

"Fuck!" Justin screamed to the forest. He picked up some debris from the ground and flung it.

A bet was a bet, but he didn't have to like losing, and he didn't have to like what was coming next.

He got to his feet, noticing the surprised look on Hale's face. He stomped to where he'd discarded his shirt and hoodie. He grabbed his things and without looking at Hale, said, "I'll meet you at the truck. You can claim your prize. But I'm not fucking kissing you."

Justin walked fast. He was exhausted, but his rage had him wanting to run. Where were these emotions coming from? He liked Hale. A deal was a deal. So what was his problem?

Maybe he was being a sore loser. Maybe it was the endorphins from the fight. Maybe it was all the shit that had happened in the last week. Maybe this was all happening too fast.

But a deal was a deal. Justin wasn't afraid of a little pain. So what was he afraid of?

And then it hit him. He was afraid. The anger was just a mask. He was terrified.

He was terrified of a kiss, and now he was going to have sex. God, he needed to man up. He wanted this, right?

All these stupid fucking emotions. But what was about to happen didn't need to mean anything. They were attracted to each other. When people were hot for each other, they had sex. This was the natural progression of things. Everything was happening the way it was supposed to. He had nothing to be afraid of.

Just have fun with it. You want this. So why was he practically running away?

As the truck came into view, Justin slowed down. He took a few deep breaths.

He could do this. He just needed to calm down.

Arriving at the truck, he tried the door handle and then remembered Hale had the keys. Dammit. Now he'd have to wait for him and look him in the eyes and try to explain his behavior. He really didn't feel like talking.

"Hey!" Hale shouted, seemingly enraged as he grabbed Justin's wrist and spun him around.

"What the f—" But Justin didn't have time to say the word or even finish the thought.

Hale shoved him backward against the door of the truck, the step cutting into the back of Justin's knees. Gravity tried to bring him down, but the cab held him up, along with Hale's strong hands that were grabbing him under his arms along his ribs, pinning him in place.

"You don't have to kiss me, but I sure as hell am kissing you."

Suddenly, Hale's lips were on his, Hale's tongue pushing deeply into his mouth.

Even in his anger, Justin welcomed it.

Justin pushed his face forward, forcing his own tongue into Hale's mouth, their teeth knocking together.

He dropped his shirt and hoodie, grabbing on to Hale as if for dear life. No more thinking. Only feeling. And Hale's mouth felt so good.

The kiss was awkward with power, like a bulldozer on an anthill. Hale bit Justin's bottom lip and sucked on it. Gasping with the novelty and pleasure, Justin let his head go backward into the metal of the cab, opening his neck. So be it. He exhaled his anger, his next breath a gasp of desire.

Hale seemed to hear it, becoming bolder. Hale's teeth slid from Justin's lip to his chin, biting it, his tongue flicking out, teasing the sandpaper texture. Christ, it felt so good. Hale used his tongue, gliding it along Justin's neck over the sweat-slick skin. Sweat from the fight, or from this new heat that was building in him?

He couldn't maintain this half-back position with his knees bent, so he pushed Hale away, his hands on Hale's shoulders. He stood to his full height as Hale continued to trace down his neck, using his tongue and teeth on Justin's collarbone.

Justin gasped again, thoughts jumbled. He'd been wrong to deny this experience. He wanted Hale like he'd never wanted anyone before. How could he let Hale know? How could he reciprocate?

"Let me kiss you, Hale." In the place of fear and anger was a need, a request, for tenderness.

Justin tilted Hale's head up and looked into his eyes. He saw all the contradictions hidden there. They were dark eyes but lit with a gleaming brightness. They were sad eyes—the eyes of a lonely man. But he also looked back at Justin with joy and a hint of childlike playfulness. They were the eyes of hunger—a hunger partially satisfied and a new, bottomless hunger opening up. They were eyes of violence hidden now by a lovely gentleness. Blue had never been so beautiful.

Justin grabbed Hale's face and lifted it to his own, using his grip to hold Hale in place so Justin could control the kiss, lips and tongue turning it from something desperate and primal into something more sensual. Hale physically relaxed in his hands. Their tongues moved more slowly, softly. He slid his hands down to Hale's waist. The distance between them closed, Hale pressed completely against him.

It felt so damn good—this delicateness in their embrace, in their tongues sliding together, their lips moving close. Even the sounds were now soft—sounds of breathing, sighs of want and satiation.

Justin craved this softness. He loved the sensual feeling of Hale's tongue in his mouth, and he allowed himself to think of Hale inside him elsewhere. Would it feel as good as this did?

Without his knowing it, he had moved his grip to Hale's taut ass. As the kiss continued, Hale countered, his hands sliding along Justin's hips, above his sweats to the skin on his lower back. Hale's hands were slick and smooth with Justin's sweat. He reached down under Justin's pants to seize his ass and pull him closer.

Justin liked Hale's hands on his ass.

Their erections pressed together. Justin being taller, Hale's hard dick ended right under Justin's crown. The protruding ridge was rubbing up against that very sensitive triangle beneath the head, the most sensitive spot.

"Yes," Justin breathed. His voice was shaky and soft and barely his own. He had wanted this for a long time, wanted it badly, but had let too many thoughts get in the way.

But he was ready now.

At some point their kiss had stopped, and Justin's forehead was against Hale's. In the sudden quiet, Justin could feel his heart beat, hard and fast. He could feel Hale's heart too, a distant thud behind his own. Hale's head turned up, Justin's turned down—they were breathing heavily, lips nearly touching. Justin couldn't be close enough, wanted to crawl inside Hale's skin.

Hale moved one hand up to the back of Justin's head and ran it through his hair. "Justin," he said. "I have wanted this… for so… long." It took him three breaths to get out all of the words.

"You've only known me for a week," Justin countered, smiling.

"Then I must want you real bad, because it feels like I've been waiting forever."

"Me too." He could feel himself shaking, could feel Hale shaking too, perhaps from the strain of their fight. Perhaps from something else. "I'm sorry I ran away."

Hale kissed him again softly on the lips. "I'd chase you anywhere. Won't let you get away. Right now, I want to take you into the cab."

"Why do you think I let you win?"

THEY BOTH laughed, adding a little levity to the situation. Hale had the urge to call him on the obvious lie, but instead he took Justin's hand in his. "Come," he said and pulled him toward the cab. He opened the door and ushered Justin in.

Hale's hand shook on the cab door as he hoisted himself up and in. His stomach seemed to drop through the floor to the pavement below. He was nervous. What the hell was going on?

Justin moved to sit on the sleeper in the back, while Hale went up front. He pulled out his phone and stuck it in the console. Within a few seconds, music filled the cab, loud enough to cover any noises they might make.

Hale hurriedly grabbed a bottle of water from the glove box. When did he get so parched? He began to move to the back but had a second thought and reached to grab another bottle for Justin. He sat down on the small bed next to him and handed him the water.

"Thanks," Justin said.

They both took long pulls before tossing the nearly empty bottles aside. They sat for a moment, and Hale felt the extreme awkwardness of the situation. Was he sixteen? He should take charge. Justin was certainly waiting for that. Where was all his strength? His bravado? Should he tell Justin he was nervous too?

Justin reached to a storage space under the bed, retrieved a condom and lube, and set it on the bed between them. Justin turned his eyes to Hale, and Hale saw how young he suddenly looked. Hale needed him, needed to take care of him and make him feel good.

His nerves didn't disappear, but he looked at those lips and had to kiss them again. He and Justin leaned together—not touching with their hands, just their mouths. The kiss went on, not gentle and not hard. Determined.

For long minutes.

"I love kissing you, Justin," Hale finally said. "It's something we're going to have to do more often." Justin quirked a half smile—was it in trepidation or agreement? Regardless, Hale felt his bravado returning. He wanted this man and wanted him badly.

"Stand up," Hale said. The cab was tight, but Justin could stand, barely. Even so, he instinctively ducked his head.

"Take your pants off," Hale said. "You're beautiful, and I want to see this." He was cautiously speaking in low tones, and it gave his voice a rumbling sensuality, a deepness he felt in his chest.

Justin quirked an eyebrow at him but hooked his thumbs in the front of his pants and slowly began sliding them down. Hale saw the deepening dark hair as he lowered the waistband, and saw half of his hard cock. Justin stood like that for a moment, smiling. Finally he placed his hands at his sides and pushed down, letting the pants fall to the floor.

Hale was familiar with Justin's cock. He'd certainly thought enough about it since the last time he saw it. But now it was on display, thick and erect, the head completely free of the foreskin. It was at his face level, and Hale wondered briefly what it would be like to slide it into his mouth. For now he just wanted to look.

He reached over and grabbed Justin's ass, pulling him closer.

"Hale! Careful, I should have taken my shoes off first."

Hale chuckled and steadied him as he wobbled closer. "God, you're beautiful," he said again. He needed to touch it. To feel it in his hand. He grabbed Justin's cock around the base. Sliding his hand up and down, he watched the head disappear and reappear under the skin.

"I love your cock," Hale said. He wanted to lick the bead of moisture that appeared at the tip. "You're so thick. I'm glad I won."

Justin smiled, seeming to revel in the attention he was getting. "Yeah, but you're bigger," he replied, losing a little bit of the big smile.

He must be nervous. "I'll be as gentle as possible," Hale said. "No promises, because this… you… could make me lose control." Hale looked up at him, continuing to stroke. Justin's smile returned. "Besides, you and I, we can take a beating, right?"

Gah. That hadn't come out right and probably was not comforting at all, but this couldn't be all snowflakes and puppy dogs. He released Justin. "Turn around," he said. "I've never had a back view."

Justin obliged, turning carefully with his pants at his ankles. God, what an ass. It was large. Strong. Powerful. Hale couldn't wait to sink himself in deep. He reached out to grab it on both sides, spreading the cheeks in anticipation, catching a quick glimpse of what he wanted to see. Then he gentled his touch, tracing down the curves with his fingertips, feeling the small hairs that got a little thicker as they disappeared between his legs. He touched not the skin, but the hair, gliding along the soft surface. Justin shivered.

Driven by a sudden urge, he leaned in and bit Justin hard in the middle of his cheek. Justin cried out, sounding surprised rather than pained. Hale released his teeth and kissed the spot, admiring the mark he left. "Sorry," he said softly against Justin's asscheek. "I can't help myself."

He kissed it gently again, inhaling against Justin's hip. They had really worked up a sweat. They were both somewhat filthy, but Justin had that clean-sweat smell about him, along with autumn and clove.

Hale lowered his head and ran his tongue up the cheek, stopping at his waistline to kiss him again, and then running his tongue toward the middle. His chin fit in the cleft of Justin's ass, and Hale kissed his lower back. He lingered, teasing with the tip of his tongue to get a hint of the saltiness. He made that hungry sound that wasn't quite a growl, but the human male equivalent of one.

He pushed Justin indelicately to the bed beside him, noticing again his look of surprise, but Hale smiled at him and saw the spark in Justin's eye that let Hale know he was enjoying this. A lot.

Good, because the kid had given him a fright. He thought he had pushed too hard, lost him. Again.

Hale got down on his hands and knees in front of Justin, which was hard to do with the seat behind him. He undid Justin's laces and pulled off his shoes and socks, before removing Justin's sweats and casting them aside. With Justin's bare feet in his lap, Hale firmly caressed the soles and wandered up to those gorgeous bulging calves. He bent to kiss the side of Justin's knee and saw his ab muscles tense up as a shiver went through him.

God, to see that reaction. He was making this up as he went along. Aside from Janie he'd paid for most of his sexual partners, and seduction and readiness wasn't part of the game. He better not screw this up and scare Justin away again. He needed to make Justin like it.

"Now it's your turn to watch me," Hale said, and Justin's eyes widened, his pupils dilated. He stood and peeled off his shirt, dropping it on the floor.

Hale moved for his pants. "Wait!" Justin insisted. "Stop right there." He looked at Hale's chest in the span of a breath and said, "Come closer." Hale complied. He'd comply with anything Justin wanted, bet or no.

Justin reached up to run his fingers in the hair along Hale's chest, his nipples, his abs. "This…." Justin's voice faltered. His touch was almost reverent, and it sent shivers through Hale's body, muscles tensing involuntarily.

Hale smiled and raised his eyebrows, encouraging Justin silently to continue.

"If you only knew…." Justin laughed a little. "If you only knew how many times I paused and replayed a few seconds of video, just to see this."

Hale laughed in return, genuinely amused. "I loved to watch you too," he admitted. How could two people be drawn to each other as they were, watching each other, wanting each other, and then have this? Their meeting had to be serendipitous. He was certain they were supposed to be right here, right now, in this moment together.

Justin's hands felt incredible on Hale as they continued to massage his torso and chest, grazing through his hair. "You trim?" Justin asked.

"A little." Mostly so a fighter couldn't grab it through his shirt, but if Justin liked it….

"I thought so. I really like it. It's manly." The compliment had his dick twitching.

Justin reached up to grab Hale's nipples. He leaned from the bed to put one in his mouth and run it between his teeth.

"Goddamn," Hale sighed. Justin bit harder. Hale bit his lip and withstood it for as long as he could before hissing with the pain. Justin immediately let go and kissed him there before settling back on the bed. Turnabout was fair play. Hale made his growling sound again.

He lifted Justin's chin and kissed him again. Quick and forceful, but not violent as their initial kiss outside had been.

He took a step back. "May I continue?" he asked, seeking permission.

Justin nodded readily. Hale noticed a long string of precome dripping from Justin's hardened dick. Justin reached down to grab his own cock, but Hale stopped him.

"Don't touch, not yet," he insisted.

"I'm getting kind of messy down here."

"I like to see it. Lets me know you're enjoying the show. You are enjoying it, right?"

Justin looked at him hungrily. "Keep going," he demanded, placing his hands on the bed and leaning back.

Hale almost went for the pants but smiled instead as he remembered his shoes should be first. He pulled them off quickly, along with his socks, putting one hand on Justin's shoulder to steady himself. "No fair. I'd be getting a better show if you did the pants first," Justin said as Hale leaned over him, his groin inches from Justin's face.

"Patience, my lad."

"Fuck patience. Just get your fucking pants off."

Hale stood, dropping his pants quickly and stepping out of them, only his tight boxer-briefs left on his body, his cock poking above them.

"Let me," Justin said. Hale stepped forward. Justin slowly lowered the briefs to the floor, and Hale stepped out of them. Fully nude, he reveled in Justin's dark gaze.

Justin made a little spinning motion with his hand, and Hale turned slowly, letting him look. He clenched and unclenched his ass as he did so. He heard Justin hum with satisfaction.

God, he really liked being watched. Maybe he always had, he'd just never applied it to his sex life before. Maybe love life would be a better term. Heat came to his face.

Hale completed his turn, his length straining as Justin looked on. Justin seemed to sense that it excited him. He placed his hands on Hale's thighs and looked directly at his cock. Hale flexed and bobbed his cock a little, almost involuntarily. He was getting more turned on from a gaze than he ever had before from a touch.

Justin ran his hands up the inside of Hale's thighs. It tickled, and Hale breathed in sharply, his cock bobbing again. Justin's hands kept going, running in the hair between his legs and grabbing his balls, kneading them. "Yes," Hale said quietly. Hale suddenly had a vision of dipping his cock down and driving it into Justin's mouth. As Justin studied him up close, was he thinking the same thing?

Finally, Justin grabbed Hale's cock firmly, running his thumb in the soft triangle under the head, lubing it up with the bead of liquid that must have been there. That was the spot. It lit up all of Hale's body from the tips of his toes to the top of his head. He moaned softly.

Hale wondered if Justin would ask about him being circumcised. Did he like what he saw?

Justin looked up at him, now seeming very serious. He turned back to Hale's cock and spit directly on the head, then on his hands, before rubbing up and down the length. Hale rocked his hips. Justin's hands were strong, not gentle, and they felt better than any hands Hale had ever had on his cock. Why was that? He had never been so turned on in all his life. For a moment he considered letting Justin jack him off, releasing him from his bet.

But Hale really wanted this. He wanted to be inside Justin. Justin, who was both strong and gentle, a man with a soft voice who loved a few select people fiercely. Could Hale be one of those people? This hot, hot man who gave him a feeling deep inside his chest like he had been punched.

Hale stopped Justin, sliding Justin's hands gently into his own.

"I want you, Justin." How could Hale communicate what he was feeling? That it was Justin, not just the sex he wanted. "Justin…." Couldn't do it. No words.

"Lay down with me?" he asked instead.

Chapter 27

Justin was glad the sleeper was so small, because it meant he and Hale were pressed together. He couldn't get close enough, even when they were touching, hands and tongues roaming restlessly.

Despite all the sensations, there was no doubt where the most powerful feelings were emanating from—at least the physical ones. He rutted against Hale's thigh, giving out a pleasurable moan when Hale clasped his cock. To be touched like that was at once satisfying and confounding, seeming at first to quench but then stoke, the need burning within him. It was never enough.

"God, I can't get enough of you," Justin said, breaking their kiss.

"Are you ready to try?" Hale asked, his blue eyes glinting.

"Um… yes." *Kind of.*

"Um?"

"Well, a bet's a bet, right?"

"Yeah, but Justin—"

"It's fine. I'm willing to try. One of us has to be the first to do it. I'm the one with the bigger balls, apparently, so I'll go first."

With that, Hale slid his hand down the length of Justin's cock to grab his sac and tug gently on it. It produced a pleasurable sensation in the pit of his stomach, a dull ache causing him to groan softly.

Hale's hand slid lower down the bed to where the lube and condoms lay. In the short pause as Hale began to prepare, Justin took note of the music playing in the cab. He didn't recognize it. Did Hale like music as much as he did? There was still so much he didn't know about the man, stuff Hale didn't know about him.

"What's the music?" Hale's slick hand covered Justin's cock. "I know a lot of music but… fuck… not this one."

"It's Old World. Kings of Leon. 'Closer.'"

"I like it. Sounds like you."

"Like me?"

"Like the music I would have picked for you, I guess. Gruff. Strong. Fuck. Your hand feels so good." Justin shifted from his side onto his back to give Hale better access. Hale was looking down at him, his blue eyes intense and hungry.

"Spread your legs for me, Justin."

Justin complied as much as possible in the limited space as Hale applied more lube to his hand. Justin's breath quickened. Was it nerves or anticipation?

Then both of Hale's hands were on him, one on his cock, one working his balls. Justin could feel the lube dripping down his perineum, mingling with the sweat that had him already slick.

Gradually one, then two of Hale's fingers followed the drip, massaging the area under his balls, and then dipping even lower. Hale's rough fingers had Justin breathing into the touch, pressing back against the fingers, almost squirming.

Looking down, Justin saw Hale's cock, which was long and hard. It bobbed with Hale's ministrations, precome visible on the tip. Hale was clearly more than excited attending to Justin down there.

The man had a very nice cock. Impressive. Almost scarily so. The tip was smooth. Rounded. Soft. Justin hoped that would help in what was about to happen.

Justin's breath caught as Hale's fingers grazed his hole.

"Relax," Hale urged tenderly. His fingers grazed again, a little harder this time. Justin couldn't help but lift his hips into the touch. He watched as Hale looked up his body admiringly. "I love watching you," Hale said. "I love watching your reactions. You're so fucking beautiful I can't stand it. I could come just from stroking you and seeing you twitch."

Hale's hand left Justin's cock, moving up to caress his abs. With what Hale's other hand was still doing, Justin couldn't help but keep flexing his abs, his breaths becoming erratic. Hale's excitement quelled any embarrassment Justin had about being touched so intimately.

One of Hale's fingers slowly circled Justin's hole.

"Relax now," Hale said.

Justin smiled. "I am. I've done this part before."

"Oh yeah?" Was that a look of dismay that crossed Hale's face?

"What?" Justin said. "You've never had a girl put a finger in your ass before?"

"No. Can't say that I have." Hale frowned a little bit, breaching Justin with the pad of his finger, pressing against him.

"Shit," Justin said. "Feels good. I mean, what you're doing now feels good. Not having a girl stick her finger in your ass. I mean… that feels good too, just not as good as what you're doing right now. Fuck… I'll shut up." Certainly blushing, he looked away.

Hale laughed. "No, you can tell me. I want to know. It's important to know."

"One finger feels good," Justin said. He looked back at Hale. "It seems like you've done this before."

"I'm good at improvising," Hale said, grinning. "Just like when I fight."

Hale's finger pushed in a little farther, circling right inside Justin's hole.

"God, yes," Justin said.

"More?" Hale asked.

"A little bit." Hale pushed in deeper until Justin inhaled sharply, just when it started to feel a little uncomfortable.

"Stay there a little bit."

"You want two fingers?"

"I don't really like two fingers. It hurts."

Hale looked at him skeptically. "Well, I'm not sure how this is going to work if you don't let me open you up. I'm no expert, but…."

"Fingers are too pointy, too bony," Justin said as Hale kept one finger inside of him and circled with a second, pushing, teasing. "God, yes. That feels good. I'm hoping your dick is a little softer than fingers, even if it is bigger. Let's just try it that way first."

"As you wish," said Hale, leaning forward to kiss Justin. As their lips met, Hale's finger pushed in, breaching him deeply. His ass clenched around the finger. Justin felt mostly pleasure, only a slight discomfort. Hale's mouth on his own kept him from making any exclamations, Hale's tongue distracting him as the finger worked in and out in a circular motion, pushing against the inner walls.

Justin gasped as Hale's finger curled upward in a hook, hitting his prostate.

"You like that?" asked Hale, moving the tip of his finger back and forth. Justin's cock bobbed and flexed with every small stroke, precome leaking and dripping down his shaft. It was like Hale had found a string that ran from Justin's cock and balls right to Hale's finger, and he was pulling on it, turning Justin into his puppet, his plaything.

Justin groaned. "Yeah… I like it." Hale moved his hand from Justin's stomach back to his cock and began stroking him.

Justin bucked between Hale's finger and his hand, hips pushing down and back up again in a maddening seesaw of pleasure. Justin lost track of time. The sensations, Hale's kiss, and the music fused together, working on him like a drug.

At last, Hale paused and shifted. "Do you think you're ready?" he asked.

"Sure," Justin said. No knowing until you try, anyway. He breathed deeply, trying to relax. "Just work a little more lube in first." Hale complied and began stroking himself as well, his cock rigid and clearly wanting. "Jesus, you're so hard," Justin exclaimed quietly. Truly it looked almost painful, in a beautiful sort of way.

"I can't wait to get inside you," Hale said, his hand leaving Justin. He opened and applied the condom, slicking himself up with a generous amount of lube. The cot was getting pretty messy with the stuff. Oh well.

"What will be most comfortable for you?" Hale asked.

"I want to see you," Justin said. "I want to look at your face. I want to see you as you enter me, watch you when you come."

"Fuck, yes."

Hale positioned himself between Justin's legs, looking down at him, eyes raking Justin's body. His hands glided along Justin's stomach, over his cock, and along the inside of his thighs. Justin loved this attention, almost couldn't believe it. This was his fantasy. The man looking at him, touching him—this was Black Jim. But now he was even more than Black Jim, and this was better than any fantasy. Hale lifted Justin's legs, hooking them up on his shoulders. He kissed the inside of Justin's knee, and….

"Jesus!" Justin said, shivering.

"Sensitive there?"

"I guess so. No one's ever done that before. Just you." Justin could barely catch his breath. Hale smiled and kissed him again, softly. It sent little tremors through Justin's body, a slight tickle spreading through him. More than that, though, the gesture was so tender, Justin felt himself opening up to Hale, in more ways than one.

Hale stroked his long cock a few more times and then dipped it down, teasing the head across Justin's entrance.

"Damn, that feels good," Hale murmured, closing his eyes.

"Yeah, it does." Justin breathed in deeply, feeling ready. Very ready.

Hale pushed forward gently, and Justin winced as his ass resisted. He tried to relax, used his own hands to spread himself a little wider. "Slow…." he prompted.

Hale looked down, leaning forward slightly.

Damn. It hurt. How was this going to work if it was already hurting and Hale hadn't gotten inside him yet?

Justin forced himself to relax further, and this time moved his own hips downward.

At last he felt himself open somewhat, the tip of Hale's cock entering him.

He winced again. It burned. Hale leaned forward a little bit more.

Justin gritted his teeth. "Stop there for a second. Just work it for a minute."

"I'm not really even in."

"Don't be so impatient."

Hale frowned, shaking his head. "This is never going to work."

"It's got to work. Just use your dick like you used your finger for a while."

Hale gazed at him intently, his eyes determined. He withdrew and Justin felt him circling his hole with the head of his cock. Pushing forward, then withdrawing, circling, and pushing gently again.

"Just like that," Justin said. That felt good. Why couldn't the whole thing feel like that? As the pleasurable sensations continued, Justin began to meet Hale's forward pushes with pushes of his own. He began sweating as his hips moved, bearing down.

And then he felt the breach again, this time easier, as Hale slipped in.

"Fuck yeah. Open up for me, baby." Hale's voice was like an aphrodisiac.

Justin bore down, and Hale penetrated an inch or two before Justin felt resistance again… with quite a few inches to go.

Justin placed his hands on Hale's thighs to keep him from going deeper. "Just wait a second," he said.

Hale growled. "You're killing me here, Justin."

"Yeah, just wait until you're where I am." He could feel a burning as Hale's cock pressed against what felt like an inner wall.

Hale grabbed Justin's cock and began stroking it. "Oh yeah," Justin said. "Keep doing that." As his hips began moving again with the motion of Hale's hand, he pushed himself down. Hale tentatively pushed back.

No fuckin' joke. It hurt. It felt like he was trying to stretch a tiny rubber band over something too large, and it was about to snap. He focused on the pleasurable sensations on his cock and continued to bear down.

"Justin, open your eyes." He hadn't realized he'd closed them. "Look at me," Hale said. "I love that you're doing this for me. You feel so good. So tight."

Hale used his free hand to drip more lube at the breach and also drizzled some on Justin's cock as Hale continued to work it with his hand.

Justin looked into Hale's eyes. "Kiss me," he said to Hale.

As Hale leaned forward for the kiss, Justin shifted into him, moving him deeper. As their lips met and Hale's tongue entered his mouth, his cock slid in.

Justin continued to feel the burning and pinching, but as Hale went in deeper, a pleasurable fullness spread inside him. Hale kissed him hungrily. Justin put his arms around Hale's neck, hooked his legs around Hale's back, and pulled him in.

Hale continued to push forward. How much of him was left to go? The fullness gradually turned into a slight ache in the pit of his stomach as Hale sunk in deeper. Totally committed now, Justin drove his heels into Hale's ass, urging him to continue the rest of the way in.

"Fuck," Hale cried, pushing in to the hilt. Justin's head rocked back, and he pulled Hale's body to him tightly. That feeling he had of wanting to get closer to Hale, of not being able to get close enough, was finally and fully satiated.

"You okay?" asked Hale.

"It feels strange. But it's good too."

"I want to move inside you."

Justin nodded, and Hale placed his hands on either side of Justin's head, holding him. Justin felt the weight of him, smelled the musk of forest and sweat as Hale began to move his hips. The sight of this man on top of him, with his hard body and hairy chest, had Justin forgetting about the pain. His heart and mind and so much of his body wanted to welcome him in.

"Just breathe through it," Hale urged him, before kissing him deeply. Justin used their closeness to rub his cock against Hale's stomach. Despite the discomfort of the invasion, the more movement he allowed, the more stimulation his cock would have against Hale's skin. He began to return Hale's slow movements, urging him on.

"That's it, baby. Let me in," Hale said as he quickened his pace. Still slow but now rhythmic, moving in and out but staying deep, not withdrawing too much.

Justin ran his fingers through Hale's hair, grabbing it in his fists. He had the urge to give Hale a little pain too. Justin yanked Hale's head back and ran his teeth along Hale's neck, biting him, feeling possessive just as he was being possessed.

"Jesus, yes," Hale cried. Hale buried his face against Justin's shoulder, his movements picking up speed.

"Oh God, Hale." He could hear Hale's heavy breathing at his ear, knew the combination of his own pleasure and pain was bringing Hale ecstasy. The thought spurred him on, the pain becoming a need. "Harder," he urged.

Justin could feel it building inside him, his body rising to orgasm already. This time was different, though. It seemed to be starting from deeper within. "Harder, please."

Justin was breathing heavily, wordless sounds accompanying the breaths. He had never felt so full or so close to anyone before.

Hale lifted his head to look Justin in the eyes. His face was strained with effort… or was it overcome with emotion? His eyes glistened in the light of the cab, sweat streamed down his face.

Justin rocked up into him, his cock pushing against Hale's stomach, leaving trails of precome and lube in Hale's treasure trail, which was now slicked tightly to his skin.

"Fuck, Hale, I'm gonna come."

Hale smiled. "Do it. Come for me. I want you to come with me inside you."

Justin clutched Hale's hair more tightly as Hale grinned and continued to pump his hips.

Justin curled up against him, searching for friction as the maddening crush built, his cock swelling, turning into an organ of uncontrollable sensation.

"Oh, fuck," he whimpered as Hale continued to take him, faster now, his hole totally open to him, the distant pain a fiery brand heating his whole cock to the point of combustion.

The build was unbelievable. Justin's body was screaming for release and yet kept taking him higher, higher than he had ever been before.

Hale pushed Justin down into the thin mattress, thrusting deep and using his body weight to finally give Justin the friction that sent him over the edge.

Justin's breath hitched as the first spurt exploded from his cock, slicking their stomachs where they were pressed together. Hale lifted up, freeing Justin's cock as another spurt rocketed up, hitting Justin's neck and chest.

"Nice—" Hale crooned dryly, continuing to thrust his hips, Justin's muscles contracting, abs clenching, forcing out his release, each time the semen hitting a little lower on his body.

Finally he was spent, the smell of his own come sharp in the air.

Justin watched as the sight of his orgasm drove Hale into a frenzy. Hale continued to fuck him greedily, faster than before, withdrawing farther before slamming into him. The man looked like a fucking god.

While Justin's eyes drank their fill, his sensations began to normalize. His breath hitched, the pain returning dully with each thrust but growing sharper. He tried not to grimace but couldn't manage to school his face. The harder, deeper thrusts felt like they were splitting him in two, hitting his stomach from the inside.

Damn, Hale was big. Justin could do this. He could hang on a little bit longer. Just a little bit longer….

HALE WAS close. So close. But looking down, he could see Justin's grim expression.

A few more thrusts and he would be there. He wanted to go faster, harder.

He gave in to those desires. Just a few more seconds.

Justin's pained grunts cut to him, and Hale collapsed on top of him. Fuck.

Fuck. Fuck. Fuck.

"I'm sorry," Justin breathed as Hale's cock throbbed inside of him.

"It's okay," Hale managed, though it definitely felt like it was *not* okay. "Are you all right?"

"I was," Justin said, "up until I came. I think next time we need to make sure you come first, and I'll be all right."

"Next time?" Hale said, raising an eyebrow at him. Hell, if Justin agreed to do this again, Hale could live without finishing.

Justin laughed, his cheeks flushed. Hale kissed his swollen lips. He looked freshly fucked, and if Hale didn't feel a sense of pride at that.

Hale carefully withdrew, watching Justin clench his jaw, feeling the muscles around him as they aided in the escape.

Hale peeled off the condom and began stroking himself, kneeling in front of Justin. Justin's thick cock lay against his belly, his come smeared on his body. Looking down, Hale saw he had some in his own chest hair as well.

"I think I'm not such a great bottom," Justin said, gazing up at Hale, his eyes focusing on Hale's hand and cock.

"Shush. It'll take a little bit more practice is all. I thought it was fantastic."

"I like watching you like this. You're so fucking hot. Every inch," Justin said, his brown eyes transfixed.

Hale was getting off on being watched too.

He used his free hand and grabbed Justin's cock. He needed to touch it, feel the swollen yet soft texture of it, and run his fingers along the dripping head. Justin's body drove him wild.

He wanted to tell Justin to use his mouth, swallow his cock and get him off. God, just the thought of it had his dick pulsing in his hand. "Turn over for me," Hale said, running with a new idea.

Justin looked a little unsure, so Hale said, "Don't worry. I'm not gonna go for more, even though I want to. I can tell you've had enough for today."

Justin rolled over, but before he could settle back down into the mattress, Hale grabbed him around the chest and lifted him up so that Justin was kneeling in front of him. He released his cock and moved his hand to Justin's stomach, pushing Justin's body back into him as his slick cock slid up and down the top of Justin's ass. He thrust his hips up again and again, holding Justin like a vise. He inhaled in Justin's hair, moved his mouth to the side of Justin's head, and bit the bottom of his ear. He was reminded of cats mating, how one dominated the other and grabbed on from behind. The feeling of closeness was overwhelming. He never wanted to let go.

"Justin...." Hale breathed.

"Come on my ass, Hale. Mark me."

"Fuck yes," Hale said too loudly. He pushed Justin down into the mattress, pulling back on Justin's hips to bring his ass up. He ran his hand along his length, his swollen glans spreading Justin's cheeks, filling in the gap. He ran the head of his dick down lower as he stroked the base of his shaft. He got a look at Justin's hole, puckered and red from the fucking. He brought his cockhead down lower, rubbing it over the creases of Justin's entrance.

Damn, that was hot. Hale could feel himself getting close again. God, how he wanted to push in. Maybe just a little....

Justin flexed his ass for Hale, pushing back a bit as Hale's head rode the entrance.

"I'm close, Justin. God, I wanna fuck you so bad."

Hale didn't take Justin's silence for consent, but Justin had said that first outer area was comfortable. Maybe just the tip.

Hale's breathing became more labored. He stroked himself harder, the tip of his cock pressing a little more into Justin's hole. Justin clenched and then opened up slightly for him.

The tip of Hale's cock slid in, just barely. It was like the sweetest taste, the most tantalizing teaser of more to come. God, how he'd like to shoot his load right now, right into Justin's ass. All he'd have to do was leave his dick right there, and Justin would be his. Hale could mark him as his own.

"Fuck, Justin!" Hale had to fight back against thrusting forward and skewering Justin the way he wanted to. He continued to stroke his length and watch as Justin clenched and unclenched for him, could feel that tightness against the tip of his cock as he rocked back and forth ever so slightly.

The need became so intense, the denial driving him crazy and finally pushing him over the edge. With a cry, Hale pulled out, stroking his full length as he shot across Justin's back. As he continued to come, he dipped his cock back down between Justin's spread ass, watching the come mark that golden skin. Fuck, yeah. Now that was a beautiful sight.

Hale continued to stroke but now more slowly as aftershocks swept his body. He milked the last drops from his cock, slapping them out against Justin's ass.

Spent, he collapsed by Justin's side, pulling him close. The sweat and come on their bodies intermingled as they spooned.

"That was amazing," said Hale, for lack of anything better to say.

"Yeah, it kinda was."

"Just kinda?" Hale said, nonplussed.

"Mmm, yeah. But I expect it will be even better when you bottom."

Chapter 28

WHEN THE truck finally pulled into the garage, it was dark. With their early-morning activities, work had taken a lot longer to finish up. Justin had texted Gin and Charlie, and no doubt they'd be expecting an explanation when he got home. He wasn't looking forward to that.

Things in the truck had been a little quiet. Justin felt the darkness of the twilight like an impending sadness.

He felt like he was about to say good-bye.

Hale had been quiet as well, which made it worse. It took some effort for Justin not to read into it. After all, Hale had been right there with him when they… what? Had sex? Made love? Even if things hadn't finished in the way Hale hoped, it had still been pretty… special. A fun time, yeah, but also more intimate than that. Justin shivered with the thought of Hale's kiss on his knee. His ass throbbed faintly, rousing the memory of Hale inside him. God, they had almost done it bareback—technically had, a little bit. Had that been a mistake?

The warehouse was quiet. It looked as though everyone had left. As Justin got out of the truck and walked around, Hale moved to meet him. They were alone. Justin felt alone.

Hale grabbed Justin's hand as they came together behind the truck, reaching up with his free hand and pulling the garage door down. Enclosed in darkness, Justin couldn't see Hale's face. He couldn't see anything.

Then Hale's strong arms closed around him. Justin leaned into him. Hale nuzzled his cheek, the scruff catching Justin's own lighter growth. In the darkness, Hale's lips moved along Justin's jaw and found his mouth.

The kiss was soft at first, but quickly turned desperate. It ended with both of them face-to-face, breathing heavily. Hale's thumb stroked Justin's jaw tenderly, his other hand angling Justin's head down from behind.

Justin didn't want to lose this. "I feel like I'm saying good-bye," he said, his voice soft.

"No, not good-bye," Hale insisted. "I'll meet you here on Thursday after work. I gotta pick up my paycheck, right? We'll do something. I'll have found somewhere by then. I promise."

Justin nodded into Hale, but he needed more than Hale's words. A lot more. Justin spun him, pushing Hale up against the garage door and kissing him urgently. Hale relaxed, turning soft in his arms. Justin wanted this moment to last, but of course it wouldn't.

"God, I love it when you take control," Hale said after several minutes had lessened the intensity of the kiss. "More than any words you could say, it lets me know that you...."

"That I what?"

Hale laughed a little. "I don't know. Wishful thinking, maybe, but I like it."

"Don't mistake my silence for something it's not," Justin urged. What had Hale been about to say? "I'm sorry if things were a little weird in the truck, but I can't shake this bad feeling I have. I don't know where it's coming from."

"I do," said Hale. "Your friend died. We have people watching us. Your handler's an asshole. You and I are not supposed to be together, and yet here we are. It puts a lot on a man's mind."

"Yeah." Hale really did seem to get him.

"I've been thinking about it too, almost nonstop," Hale said. Hale's lips brushed Justin's as he talked. Though Justin couldn't see him, the closeness of their conversation was more comforting than any look could be. "Even though we haven't solved anything yet, we are far better off than we ever were before. You know why?"

"Why?"

"Because now we have each other. I don't have all the answers yet, but I promise you—the first thing I'm going to do is find a way to take you from your handler."

Hale pulled down on Justin's head, and now it was Hale who kissed him, invading Justin's mouth with his tongue. Hale flipped Justin around, pushing him against the wall, leaning into him. Their cocks, hard yet again, pressed between their bodies. The sadness from before abated swiftly, replaced by desire and a sense of safety. More than that, a sense of hope.

Hale growled into his mouth, the sound greedy and forceful before he pulled away.

"I swear it, Justin. That man's gone, and soon. Because from now on, you belong to me."

Hale stepped away as Justin tried to catch his breath. The garage door began to rise, letting in the natural light of the night outside. Hale walked his bike over to Justin and got on but didn't put on his helmet.

He leaned in for a kiss and Justin met him eagerly, but this time the kiss was soft and tender. Hale pulled away all too soon.

In the darkness, Justin could see Hale's intense eyes, the look on his face that was desire mixed with sadness, the clench of Hale's jaw that told Justin he was biting back words. Justin's heart hammered. Hale wanted to say something….

Instead, Hale kissed him one last time before putting on his helmet.

"Thursday." He started the bike.

"Thursday," agreed Justin. Then Hale was gone, riding out of the garage and into the night. The sound of the motor gradually died, only to be replaced by the rapid beating of Justin's heart.

I think I love you too, he thought.

End, Opening Round
Round Two Will Begin after a Short Timeout

Bradley Lloyd is a Chicago-born author who studied Creative Writing at the University of Wisconsin-Milwaukee. He was raised in a conservative religious household but became aware of his sexuality at a very young age—about the same age he learned of his ancestry to Hans Christian Andersen. Inspired by this knowledge, writing became an outlet that helped him cope with inner conflicts and bullying.

Of course, he was no angel and occasionally used his storytelling powers for evil. He once convinced the neighborhood children that gnomes had been real before all being turned into lawn ornaments.

Later, these experiences lead him to work with middle-school students. Now a teacher in the inner city, he shares his love of writing with a captive audience of kids, who are thrilled with true(ish) tales of their haunted school building.

Interestingly, his favorite UFC fighter and former world champion was a student at his school, and when Brad is not reading or writing, you might find him hosting the next UFC pay-per-view event party. His dreams of becoming an ultimate fighter are realized vicariously through his stories and video games.

Brad is happily married to a wonderful husband. Their tenth anniversary was also the day same-sex marriage became legal, and they were couple number seven at the courthouse.

You can read more of Brad's (free) tales on his website BradleyLloyd. com, check him out on Medium, follow IMBradleyLloyd on Facebook and Twitter, or e-mail him directly at IMBradleyLloyd@BradleyLloyd.com

COUNTERMIND
ADRIAN
RANDALL

In a postprivacy future, secrets are illegal and all communication is supervised. Telepaths are registered and recruited by a government with no qualms about invading the minds of its citizens. Fugitive psychics are hunted by the Bureau of Counterpsychic Affairs, or Countermind.

Alan Izaki is one such fugitive, as well as a hacker, grifter, and thief.

Countermind agent Jack Smith is hunting him through the twisted underbelly of Hong Kong.

But Alan possesses a secret so dangerous and profound it will not only shake Smith's loyalties, but the foundations of their society.

And Alan isn't the only one on the run. Rogue psychic Arissa binti Noor escapes Countermind, in search of brilliant game designer Feng Huang. She hopes that together, they can destroy the government's intrusive Senex monitoring system.

Their goals seem at odds, and their lives are destined to collide. When they do, three very different people must question their alliances and their future, because everything is about to change.

www.dsppublications.com

desert world

ALLEGIANCES

LYN GALA

Desert World: Book One

Livre once offered Planetary Alliance miners and workers a small fortune if they helped terraform the mineral rich planet. People flocked to the world, but then a civil war cut the desert planet off from all resources. Half-terraformed and clinging to the edge of existence, Livre devolved into a world where death was accepted as part of life, water resources were scarce and constantly dwindling, and neighbors tried to help each other hold off the inevitable as the desert fought to take back the few terraformed spaces.

Temar Gazer claims to be the victim of water theft. His claims could be a simple misdirection intended to help him escape a term of labor after his criminal prank caused irreparable damage to a watering system. However as the only member of the council arguing against a short-term slavery sentence for Temar, Shan Polli can't escape the fear that something darker is happening. The more he investigates Temar's story, the more he finds that his world is not as free of politics or danger as he had assumed. Together, Shan and Temar must get to the bottom of the conspiracy before time runs out for the entire planet.

www.dsppublications.com

HEARTS
OF
DARKNESS

ANDREA SPEED

Kaede Hiyashi is sick and tired of living in the shadow of his father, supervillain Doctor Terror. Brilliant but crazy, Doctor Terror sends his son to Corwyn, California, for reasons Kaede can't imagine. Sent to accompany and protect him is Ash, a genetically modified supersoldier raised and trained by an infamous death cult.

Corwyn is lousy with superheroes, led by the obnoxious Dark Justice. Kaede finds himself dancing around Dark Justice as he digs into his father's mysterious business and teaches his socially awkward—but physically lethal—bodyguard to acclimate to "normal" life. Can these two wacky supervillains figure out what Doctor Terror wants them to do, solve the riddle of the villain known as Black Hand, and keep Dark Justice from raining on their bloody parade? The course of love—and world domination—never did run smooth.

www.dsppublications.com

DEADWORLD
This Is How It Ends
NICK WILGUS

Deadworld: Book One

High school juniors Billy Gunn and Rory Wilder return from a weekend camping trip to find a mysterious plague has wiped out their small town of Port Moss, Mississippi. The question of why is only the beginning—especially when the dead refuse to stay dead.

Figuring out what happened is job one for Billy and Rory. But complications quickly set in. Not only do the dead rise, but a freak storm threatens torrential downpours as winter looms. And enormous ships appear in the sky, bringing with them alien visitors with technology never seen before.

Left without electricity and modern conveniences, Billy and Rory must figure out a way to navigate horrific zombies, advanced alien life forms, and apocalyptic storms, as well as deal with their growing love for each other in a world gone mad.

www.dsppublications.com

www.ingramcontent.com/pod-product-compliance
Lightning Source LLC
Chambersburg PA
CBHW070431120726
47910CB00003B/730